I0835170

Ashes of Immortality

Black Wings of Death

Ashes of Immortality

Black Wings of Death

THE GUARDIANS LIGHT SERIES
BOOK 6

Kasey Hill

Azoth Khem Publishing
Huntsville, AL
May 2026

AZOTH KHEM

ISBN: 978-1-952880-38-4
First Edition 2026

Azoth Khem Publishing
29931 Copperpenny Drive NW
Harvest, AL 35749
www.azothkhem.com

Ordering Information:
Quantity sales and exclusive discounts are available on quantity purchases by corporations, associations, and others. For details, contact the publisher at the address above. For orders by U.S. trade bookstores and wholesalers, please contact Azoth Khem Publishing: Tel: (256) 221-5498 or visit www.azothkhem.com

Printed in the United States of America

Check out these other series by Kasey Hill

The Guardians of Light Series
Firefly of Immortality
The Shining Ones
Firefly: The Half-Blood Angel
The Valley of the Shadow of Death: Nephilim Rising

Dark Woods Series
Devil's Claw

The Whispering Spirits Series
The Haunting at Foxwood Village
Dark Coven

Coming Soon to The Guardians of Light Series
Firefly of Immortality II
Ashes of Immortality: Black Wings of Death
Ashes of Immortality: Crowned by Ash and Flame
Ashes of Immortality: The Shadowed Verse
Ashes of Immortality: Anniel Unveiled
Alpha and Omega
Firefly of the Apocalypse

Coming Soon to The Guardians of Light Series Universe

The Guardians of Light: Revelations of Raziel Series
Bloodlines: Into the Shadows

For my Luxina, the starchild

Note to Readers/Trigger Warning Page

You have been with me for five books, and I couldn't tell you how much I appreciate you following my series! However, this series has moved from the Young Adult category to the New Adult category because my characters are no longer coming of age. With this shift comes new content. Young Adult has strict content restrictions. Some of you read Firefly of Immortality before I went back and edited it again, removing certain plot elements. Sophie's/Anniel's abuse, which she sustained while "locked away in the tower," as well as the kidnapping by Michael in book one, was much heavier than the page now reads. I did not shy away from the heavier and darker content you will see in this new installment of the series. Black Wings of Death opens that doorway back up. With that said, it is my duty to alert you to the content and provide the necessary trigger warnings so you can choose whether to proceed with the series. Your mental health matters!

Trigger Warnings

Forced Consent: For most of the series, you see this, but it's not as prominent in the earlier books as it is in this book and any installments moving forward. Bodily autonomy was always a manipulative tool Alpha played with, but this book pushes it deeper from psychological manipulation and back into sexual abuse and physical abuse as well.

Sex: Sex has always been implied with fade to black or very minimal explanation in the prior books. This book, though not extremely spicy, has mild to moderate heat. A majority of the plot takes place in the Lust Terrace of Purgatory. There wasn't a way to deliver the plot without also delivering sexual content on the page.

There are scenes of **MMF** as well as **dubious consent** during the intimate scenes.

Sexual Abuse: Mentioned but not elaborated.

Torture
Abuse
Betrayal
Kidnapping
Imprisonment
Emotional Abuse
Abuse of Power
Trauma
PTSD
Suicide Ideation
Graphic Violence
Graphic Depictions of Hell
Forced Cheating
Manipulation
Manipulation through Intimacy
Religious Implications of the Afterlife

The plot set in Purgatory includes an MMF scene. While it suggests it is "sinful" in nature and would be a proponent to land you in hell in the afterlife, this is not my personal opinion. This series is tailored to mythological lore in both Gnosticism and Christianity/Judaism. Whatever opinions the characters hold about those situations are based solely on mythology and fiction and do not reflect how I view the LGBTQ+ community. I spoke with several members of the community to ask whether the specific narrative presented would seem offensive before moving on with the plot elements. I believe in the freedom to love whoever you want, and another person's bodily autonomy is not my business.

Ashes of Immortality

Black Wings of Death

PROLOGUE: DAMIAN

WHY DO I have to be so stupid? Why am I all of a sudden so damn insecure around Luxina? All of the abuse Alpha put me through weakened me instead of strengthening me. Around her, I didn't have my feet on the ground. I had no stability. I free floated. It was amazing and nerve-wracking all at once. I wanted to give her everything, and at the same time, I was afraid of the world being jerked out from beneath my feet. She was easy to get along with, easy for me to love her, but why was I so jaded when it came to accepting her love for me?

Honestly, though, how could she love me so much, as hideous as I look? Scars littered my body. I was a monster on the outside, and the way I looked matched how people viewed me. People only ever wanted me for my power, so how could I truly believe she wanted me out of love? Who could love someone who was a monster toward others and looked the part as well? There was some truth behind what Alpha had said through her. She didn't need me here because she wanted me. She required me to be away from Alpha so I wouldn't be his weapon of mass destruction. I know that. Everyone knows that. It was the only reason most people wanted me away from Alpha. They didn't want him to be able to use me against them, and he indeed used me like a puppet. I answered his every beckon call and did so much shit to others in his name. The amount of torture I subjected to people who disobeyed Alpha or fell out of rank was gruesome and grotesque. I also knew what would happen to me if I did not abide by his orders. Was Luxina any different than him? She had said it herself. She needed me this. She needed me that. She can't just all of a sudden *want* me, can she?

Being wanted, as opposed to being needed, was two very distinct actions. I have always been needed. Needed physically. Needed sexually. Needed in ways that would make your stomach turn when I carried out the request. I am not Alpha's monster, but he made sure everyone saw me as a monster and would never want me. Even the dark fey that helped me in Nightmares and Shadows had said it. I have a face only a mother would love. Granted, I hadn't always looked this hideous, but this has been the only face Luxina has ever seen. She didn't see me prior to the abuse. It started slow, just here and there. Alpha would backhand me if I did something wrong. I would wipe the blood from my mouth and apologize shamefully for disappointing him. It escalated little by little from backhands across the face to being hit with objects. Once, he threw his chalice of wine at me because I grabbed the wrong profile of grape, and it knocked me out for a bit. When I woke up, he told me to clean up the mess and sent me to my room.

The beatings intensified to him using his powers on me every so often. There was one time when I was in charge of cleaning out the horses' stalls, and one of them got loose. I had to chase it down and force it back in. When he was told by one of the chain gang members, he tossed a lightning bolt at me. I was scorched for days, unable to heal the burns. Asmodeus rubbed salve all over the burns whenever he got a chance to sneak into my room. Asmodeus did a lot for me whenever I would feel that sting of Alpha's wrath. He'd sneak me something to eat whenever Alpha ordered me confined without food or water. He made sure I stayed alive, and I'm not sure why. I never understood why he took a liking to me. I watched how he carried on with the other Forsaken and even the demons, and it made absolutely zero sense that he would care for me as much as he did. The only other person aside from him who looked out for me was Mammon. He would give me warnings or a heads-up whenever the chain gang was ordered to my room for punishment. There were a few times he left me weapons behind so I could fight back, but I'm pretty sure Alpha figured out what he was doing because the hidden weapons stopped.

If Luxina really knew what all I had been through, she wouldn't want me. She wouldn't love me. I was damaged goods, broken on the inside, wounded both outward and inward. Unless broken people are her project to fix, and that's what she was truly attracted to. I know without a doubt that if she knew the dark secrets I kept within myself, what really happened behind those locked doors when no one else was around, she would be disgusted with me. There were times I just wanted to die when they left me naked on the floor of my room. They used my body much the same as Alpha used me as his weapon. And when I fought back, it was a more intense of an experience. If she knew what they really did to me, would she really love me? Or would she look at me with pity, like trying to help and fix a wounded dog? No one can ever know what Alpha allowed them to do to me… if he really knew what it was. He never witnessed the torture or abuse, so it could have just been them taking liberties with me. Or he knew, and that's why he slowly became disgusted with me, and every single little infraction I made, he lashed out at me because he found me disgusting. If he didn't know, would he have stopped it? Or would he have not cared either way? And if he didn't care, others wouldn't have cared either and would probably find me just as revolting as I find myself.

"Take it easy, Damian. We're training, not really fighting," Praeziel yelled, ducking from my sword.

I snapped from my thoughts, nodding apologetically.

"My head's not in it right now," I replied as I sheathed my sword.

"It's ok. Training for the day is over anyway," Praeziel offered sympathetically, removing his armor and putting it away in his bag. "How is Luxina?"

"Awake," I sighed.

"Why are you out here with us and not in there with her?" Praeziel chided.

I didn't answer as I shoved my weapons back into my bag.

"You let him get to you, didn't you?" Praeziel asked.

"Who?" I asked, pulling my shirt back on.

"Alpha. When he had control over her, he said something that got to you, didn't he? About her?" Praeziel continued.

"Maybe. So what?" I huffed.

"Whatever it was, don't believe it. Don't let it sink in. You go back in there to her and forget everything. Don't break the bond you two have," Praeziel reassured.

"I'm not... breaking the bond. I just have some things to work through. It has nothing to do with her. It's all me," I replied.

"Well, don't let her think otherwise. She's more vulnerable now than when she was before. She has the dark half of her soul back. It can consume her more easily than most because she's never experienced it before," Praeziel warned.

"Yeah," I replied. "I hadn't thought of that."

I dropped my bag on the porch of Starfire's cabin and walked through the doorway. Luxina stood before one of her portals. Where was she going? Was Starfire sending her somewhere? Why hadn't she told me anything about it?

"Luxina?"

Luxina glanced back at me with determination in her eyes. I looked past her to where she was going. On the other side of the portal doorway was a darkened room. As I stared more closely, I saw chains on the wall, and a flickering light bulb lit the room every so often, but quickly cast it back into darkness. I knew that room. I knew that place.

"No!" I shouted as I began to sprint over to her to tackle her to the floor.

"I love you, Damian," she said, and then she stepped through the portal faster than I could get to her side. It closed behind her as I tried to jump through at the last minute. I thudded to the floor.

"No, no, no, no, no, no!" I shouted over and over, pounding my fist onto the floor.

I rolled from all fours to a sitting position, cupping my head with my hands. What was she thinking? What am I going to do? I had to get to her. Alpha would… Fear tore through my body. I *had* to get to her. I had to get to her before Alpha got his hands on her. Anxiety ran through my veins, and I felt weak and nauseous momentarily. There was no telling what he would allow to happen to her… like what happened to me there. I wasn't there to guard the door as I had before. I only ever allowed them in when they were giving her injections. They weren't going to touch her as they did me. I absolutely refused to allow that to happen to her and Xavier. But now, she was there alone. She was vulnerable, and she had no one to protect her from those fiends Alpha let run amok. I needed a plan, and I needed one fast.

Starfire calmly walked to the center of the floor, and all of my emotions bubbled to the surface. "Why didn't you tell me she would do this?" I seethed, jumping up to my feet in anger.

"Because I didn't know how this day would have gone. There were two possibilities. The first one was that when she woke up and told you how much she loved you, you would welcome it with open arms. The second possibility is what happened. You put up a wall," Starfire replied, clasping her hands together in front of her.

"Why did she go? How does this have anything to do with…"

It sank in. Luxina wouldn't just risk going to Alpha unless she had a plan. Her reasons for going had to be simple enough, but at the same time, they had to mean something more than just going for revenge or blood. She was going for one specific reason. She was going to kill Alpha, or at least try to. She wanted to right every wrong ever committed against me. This would be her proof.

"Do you see now why, Damian?" Starfire asked, kneeling in front of me.

I looked up at Starfire with tears welling, forcing them back down. "To prove how much she loves me," I choked out.

"So, you know you can't stop her. She's going to do this or die trying, but you won't be able to stop what she is doing," Starfire offered, brushing my hair with her hand to soothe me.

"Then, we will both die together," I avowed through gritted teeth, jumping to my feet and heading for the door. "I'm not letting her do this alone."

"You'll never find them, Damian…"

CHAPTER ONE: LUXINA

OBVIOUSLY, THINGS DIDN'T go as planned when I stepped through the portal back to Chernobyl to confront Alpha. As it closed behind me, I was startled by the voice in the dark.

"Luxina, you came back after all!"

I spun around to the voice to see Alpha sitting in a chair behind me in the dark. He wasn't afraid and was quite composed with his leg crossed over the other.

"Hello, Alpha."

"What is she doing here?" another voice shrieked.

I turned around to see my mother walking through the door and closing it behind her. She looked just as awful as Damian had looked when he found us after escaping Alpha. Her face was gaunt, with dark circles under her eyes. She looked as if she had been in a fight recently, as fresh marks adorned her face and arms.

"Ah, Sophie. My favorite little angel. Your job is done. I no longer need you. You brought me exactly what I needed. Little Luxina here."

The realization settled in when he said the words. I had fallen for the trap he set. He knew that every single thing he said to Damian would get under his skin. The constant abuse he was put through at Alpha's hands had worked his mind in ways no one could comprehend. I thought I was being defiant by trying to show him how much I cared. But instead, we played right into Alpha's hands by me coming here. He wanted me to defend Damian. He was always five steps ahead of us and knew every single move we intended to take. And now, instead of coming here to kill him, I knew he planned to take me instead.

"You used me to get my daughter?" Sophie asked, confused. "I thought you needed me."

I had no idea how long Alpha had been using my mother, but it was evident that for a really long time, she had been Alpha's favorite. Her expression painted a very blatant picture of betrayal and heartbreak.

"No, Sophie. I no longer need you. It's time for you to go back to sleep and Anniel to come forth," Alpha declared.

Anniel? I thought to myself. Before I could say or think anything, the door behind my mother opened, and in walked my dad, just as Alpha grabbed me and snapped his fingers to disappear.

"Daddy!" I shouted, and then we were gone.

Alpha let go of my arm, pushing me as he did so, and I hit the ground in front of a throne that sat in a beautifully ornate room. Gold trimmed the walls, and the ceiling was open to the view of the sky. But it wasn't just any sky. It was the galaxy, deep space as far as the eye could see. Stars, nebulae, planets, whatever existed in the open fields of space, I could now see. Memories flashed through my head, and I knew exactly where I was thanks to Xavier. Alpha had brought me to the Summit, a place I had longed to witness and experience for many years. This was Alpha's throne room, although when Xavier had been here, Lilith occupied the throne. I slowly got up to my feet, hesitant that he would knock me back down to the ground.

"I'm not going to hurt you," Alpha cooed as he sat down on his throne, leaned into its backing, and crossed his legs. "No one here is going to hurt you either. I'm sure Damian has told you so many stories about how awful I am and how I am a monster who mistreated him. But I have to beg to differ. That boy was a handful, and I could barely keep him in line."

"I almost died last time I was with you," I hissed, glaring at him in a defensive stance. My eyes darted around the room to see who "no one here" meant, landing on a sole angel standing guard at the far wall.

"And that was my mistake," he replied earnestly. "I was trying to bend you to my will, and I apologize."

"Apology not accepted," I sneered. I had to come up with a plan quickly and escape, but I knew time wasn't on my side. Plus, there was no telling how many angels stood waiting for Alpha's orders to seize and capture when commanded if I did run. I didn't even know where I could run to. As if Xavier was answering me silently, pictures of the halls appeared, and it was like I was running through them all the way to the entrance to the garden. *If I can make it to the garden, the seelies will protect me. They are our allies now.*

He smiled. "I didn't expect you to accept the apology. You're too much like your father to simply believe words. You need action as proof."

I inspected his face, eyeing him closely. "You look different than last time I saw you," I stated, squinting at him. "Younger."

His smile turned into a smirk, and then he explained. "Whenever I am fed new power, or if I withdraw the power I have used to create things, I grow younger. We aged with every single use of our powers. Being a god didn't come with instructions. So it's still a learning curve. Had we known using our powers would rapidly change our bodies, we would have been more mindful of what we created."

"What do you want with me?" I prodded, walking the floor in front of the throne and admiring the room. Even while in danger, the beauty of this place lulled me into a sense of awe. Memories did this place absolutely no justice. The colors here were so much more vibrant than on Earth. It was like a pure light spectrum here. Angels could see the full light spectrum, unlike humans, but even this looked more radiant than what I was accustomed to.

Alpha watched me, bemused. "I have someone I want you to meet," he replied casually. "Adam?" he called out, not once taking his eyes off of me.

From one of the passageways, I heard footsteps approaching. I turned to see who was emerging from the shadows, and my breath caught in my throat. "Xavier?" I whispered.

It can't be Xavier. Xavier was me, and he was in me. There's no way Alpha has him. And why did he call him Adam? The boy walked closer to me, and as the lights from the sky above splashed across his face, it was, without a doubt, the face and body of Xavier who stood before me.

"Hello, Luxina," he said politely. "My name is Adam." He held out his hand for me to shake.

I took his hand cautiously and gave it a small shake. "You look just like Xavier," I murmured, my eyes tracing every inch of his face.

"It was a rather unfair and cruel joke the universe played on you three," Alpha chimed in. "Having to absorb Xavier as you did isn't something anyone should have to endure. When I learned about the prophecy, I knew I had to right the wrong being committed. So I created Adam just for you in Xavier's image."

My eyes snapped from my mesmerized state of gawking at Adam, and I glared at Alpha. "That doesn't make him Xavier," I protested heatedly. "He may look like him, but he is not Xavier."

"But what if he could be?" Alpha asked, leaning forward in his throne. "What if Xavier could come back?"

I shook my head. "Xavier was the missing piece of my soul that I needed to be whole. He can't come back."

"You survived once, split apart. The fracture you initially had healed, so he is his own separate person inside of you. It didn't affect your powers without that portion of your soul. It didn't affect you as a person," Alpha retorted. "Xavier can once again exist if you wish him to. He doesn't have to be shoved down deep inside of you for you to feel whole."

"If that were the case, I wouldn't have needed to absorb him back," I refuted.

"I am the all-powerful god," Alpha replied, raising his hands to the sky. "I can do anything, including bringing Xavier back. He could exist again in Adam's body. Besides, was the prophecy actually real? How do you know it wasn't something made up just so you would be down a person when it came time to fight off the apocalypse? How do you know the apocalypse is even going to be real? I don't plan on destroying the universe. But this way, you can have Xavier back, and the world won't end because of it."

"But Adam has his own conscience. It would be just like me with him shoved into the shadows," I explained, glancing over at Adam, who didn't seem to mind the idea. "He wouldn't be Xavier at all."

Alpha pinched the bridge of his nose in frustration. "Just say yes!" he demanded, pounding the arm of his throne with his fist.

I retreated a bit from him, glancing between him and Adam. "No," I stated. "You can't have half of my soul."

Alpha ran his hands across his face and through his hair, then composed himself in his seat. "Well, until you agree, I guess we will just have to lock you up until you change your mind," Alpha hissed, narrowing his eyes at me with a wicked smirk to follow. "Belphegor!" he called.

There was shuffling of feet, and he emerged from the same passageway Adam had come out of.

"Yes, my liege?" he replied, kneeling at the throne in front of Alpha.

"Take her to Purgatory," Alpha muttered with a flick of his wrist. "Have Uriel lock it up behind you."

"You're not serious, are you?" I snorted, glancing between the three of their faces. "There's no such thing," I laughed. "Purgatory is made up."

"Is it?" Alpha asked, cocking an eyebrow, amused.

I glanced around nervously at everyone. No one seemed to refute the idea of Purgatory. Belphegor walked toward me and grabbed me, and I fought him with every ounce of strength I could muster.

"Get your hands off of me!" I screamed. I punched and kicked just as Damian had taught me.

"She's a feisty one," Belphegor laughed as he struggled to keep his grip on me while my elbow caught him in the eye.

"Do you need help?" Alpha muttered. "She's one little girl."

"I got her," Belphegor replied, wrapping his hand in my hair and giving it a hard yank. "Off we go, princess," he sneered as he walked me away.

"Does she really need to go to Purgatory?" I heard Adam ask as we left the throne room.

"Yes," Alpha replied lowly.

Belphegor walked me down winding corridors until we finally arrived near a door where a woman, whom I could only assume was Uriel, stood. The door glowed an ominous red color. She pivoted in front of the door, holding a key, and slipped it into the keyhole. The door slowly opened, and Belphegor pushed me through it, kicked me to the ground, and walked back out of the door, leaving me alone in the dark as the door slammed shut behind him. I ran as fast as I could to the door, but I heard the click as it was locked just as I reached for the handle. I twisted it, but I was too late. I was trapped in here now. I huddled in the corner of the space I was left. It was total darkness that surrounded me. I couldn't see anything. However, I could hear the sounds of this place echoing off the walls, which frightened me to the core. There was moaning and groaning as well as snarls and snaps. Whatever creatures Alpha had created and put here were most likely ravenous beasts he hadn't fed in a long time. The other sounds must be the souls of the humans he trapped here for their sins.

I wasn't alone for very long when a searing pain shot through my body. It crawled along my skin, and I doubled over on my side on the ground. I screamed and heaved, clawing at my chest as it tore through every inch of me, flames licking the ground around me. I had no control over my powers and couldn't recall the fire back to my core at all. I felt like steam was being trapped in the furthest reaches of my body, building into combustion, and at any minute, I would burst and splatter everywhere. And just as quickly as the thought crossed my mind, I exploded in one large fireball, and then everything felt empty.

The darkness that surrounded me didn't compare to the void I floated in. Everything began to rush through my mind. The big bang of the cosmos sprang life into the vast void. I saw the moment that creation began, all the way through to Alpha being created. It was both a mesmerizing and an intense experience. Did I die? Is this what death is like for us? I heard a faint voice and recognized it as my dad's.

Daddy?

Luxina! he gasped.

What's going on? What's happening? I pleaded.

We are ascending, he explained. *Your mother took her elixir.*

Where are you? Damian demanded.

I don't know. Some place Alpha created, I whimpered. *There's nothing but darkness where I am. I thought I was dying. I exploded.*

We all did that, sweetie, he said. *We will find you. I promise.*

Hurry, Daddy! There are monsters here. I am pretty sure they are the ones from the vision that Alpha plans to use against us. I can hear them, I whimpered.

We will be there as soon as we learn where you are, Anniel replied.

Mom? I asked.

The darkness of wherever I had been faded, and I sat up from the spot where I was left. My skin now glowed, and my eyes must have adjusted to the darkness because I could see around me. I felt different but didn't understand why. I had created a crater and sat in the bottom of it, staring up at the deep walls formed from the explosion. I sighed and began to climb to the top of the massive hole, slipping and sliding on the loosened dirt. When I was nearly at the threshold, a hand shot out for me to grab.

"Take my hand, and I will pull you out," Adam called, leaning over the hole.

I smacked his hand away and finished climbing out on my own. "I don't need your help," I snapped.

"Fair enough," he replied, taking a step back.

I stood up from the edge of the cliff and dusted myself off. "Why are you here?" I demanded, patting myself down and brushing off dirt.

"I didn't want you to be left alone in here," he answered, sitting down on a boulder.

"Where exactly is here?" I huffed. "Alpha said Purgatory, but everyone knows Purgatory doesn't exist. It was just a made-up poem by a person who had too much time on his hands."

"Father created Purgatory because the mortals dreamt it up," Adam replied, rubbing the back of his head nervously. "You're on the seventh terrace."

"What's the seventh terrace?" I questioned, crossing my arms and staring at him.

"The sin of Lust," he answered, glancing around to avoid eye contact. "Since you seduced Damian's obedience away from Father, he thought it was fitting to place you here."

"I didn't seduce Damian," I snapped, glowering at him. "I showed him real love, something Alpha never showed him."

"Father doesn't show love to those who are disobedient," Adam retorted, his once kind face now twisted into a jealous anger. "Damian never listened to anything he was told to do."

"I see Alpha has you wrapped around his little finger," I mused, smirking at him. "You probably bend over backward to please him, don't you?" I cocked my eyebrow, toying with him.

"I do everything Father tells me to do," he replied earnestly.

"Why do you call him Father?" I asked, scrunching my face in disgust. "He is a terrible parent."

"Because he is my father," he answered, standing up from the boulder. "Just like you call your father, what was it? Oh, *Daddy*."

I glared at him and started to walk away.

"Where are you going?" he demanded.

"I am finding my way out of here," I replied, not slowing my pace.

"There's no way out," he urged. "One way leads to the abyss, and the other leads to the other six terraces, and there are monsters and demons on every level."

"I will fight my way out then," I called out over my shoulder.

He ran up to me and grabbed me by my wrist, stopping me. "No!" he ordered. "It's too dangerous!"

I wrenched my arm from his grasp. "You don't tell me what to do!" I shouted, standing my ground, ready to fight him. "I can fight my way out!" I insisted as I began walking again.

Again, he grabbed me by my wrist and pulled me back to him. I lost my footing and stumbled into his chest. He breathed slowly as I stared up into his eyes. He peered back at me, and it was like stepping into the past with Xavier. For a moment, my heart fluttered, but I quickly pushed the feeling down. *He is NOT Xavier!*

"You can't fight those things without help," he stated calmly and quietly. "There are too many of them."

He felt so familiar to me, even though I didn't even know who he was. He felt like Damian, looked like Xavier. It was so alluring to be near him. I shook the feeling off and took a step back.

"Help me escape then," I whispered, staring intently into his eyes.

He ran his hand through his hair as he glanced around nervously. "I can't," he replied.

"Why not?" I demanded, stomping my foot.

"Father would punish me for acting out of line," he answered, putting his finger to his lip for me to be quiet.

When the time comes, I will help you escape, he thought. *There are listening ears in here.*

I huffed. "Fine." I trudged back to the crater in the ground. "What am I supposed to do until then?" I asked.

"Just wait," he replied with a shrug.

I studied his face. His looking like Xavier really threw me for a loop. He didn't seem all too threatening. But I knew as Alpha's little lap dog, he couldn't exactly be trusted too much. Those who were loyal to Alpha were venomous snakes waiting to strike you where you least expected it. As devoted as he was to Alpha, there was no way I would believe a single thing he told me. Deep down, I knew I would have to take him out along with Alpha if I ever truly wanted to escape this place. So, for now, I had to bide my time and pretend as best as I could that I believed him. I had to convince him that I liked him, or else who knows what he would do to me in the name of Alpha.

"Will you wait with me?" I pleaded.

"I can't stay," he replied. "But I will be back when I can to check in on you and make sure you're ok."

He started to leave when I stopped him. "Wait!" He turned around to look at me. "Do you want what Alpha wants with Xavier?" I asked. "Do you want his soul? You are your own person, you know. You don't need a piece of me to be someone."

He stood quietly for a moment before he answered. "I will do what Father asks me to do."

And with that, he turned around, waved his hand, and walked through the portal he brought up. It closed behind him, leaving me alone once again. I sat there thinking about the whole interaction with him. He was obedient to Alpha even if he didn't agree with what Alpha wanted to do. He was nothing like Damian. It took mind control and torture for him to do what Alpha wanted, and if he didn't, then Alpha would punish him even more for it. Is Adam afraid that what happened to Damian would happen to him as well? Does he walk on eggshells to be the perfect son? I couldn't help but feel resentment from him in regard to Damian, as if he were to blame for all of Adam's problems. I slumped down against the stone wall beside the crater, feeling defeated. For a brief moment, I thought about how protective and demanding Adam had been with me. Was that really him, or was that the part of him trying to imitate Damian? The feelings I had when I touched him, I didn't like at all. It felt just like when I would touch Xavier or Damian, a moth drawn to the light. It was almost as if he had a part of Damian in him, but that was impossible. Damian wasn't split in half like I was, and Alpha created Adam recently, or so he said. But nothing explained why he felt so much like... my other half or like home, even though he wasn't either. So why was I so innately drawn to Adam?

Don't fall for it, Xavier whispered to me.

Well, hello there, I mused while relief washed over me. *Don't fall for what?*

Whatever it is that Alpha and that Adam have planned, Xavier answered. *I don't like Adam trying to get close to you and being all Damianish. It's ick.*

Damianish? I asked, confused.

"Oh, look, Luxina is in danger. I'd better save her or die trying because I truly love her, even though she has no clue how I feel until I tell her. But I will kill anyone who tries to hurt her." Does that ring a bell? he asked.

He is not Damianish, I replied, rolling my eyes.

How can you not see the plan here? Xavier demanded. *Alpha wants to put me into Adam's body so Adam can become a Shining One like us.*

And you think Adam is going to try to sweep me off my feet and help Alpha to do that? I snorted. *I see you have a lot of faith in me.*

I felt what you felt, remember? Xavier said. *Something is off about Adam. He shouldn't have that effect on you like that. So don't fall for any of his bullshit until we figure out everything. Like how he was created in the first place. Alpha had to have done something special in order for you to have the same inexplicable draw to Adam as you do us.*

Stop already! I was growing angry. *I love Damian. It's the whole reason I am stuck here in this place. It's my punishment for showing him love. Nothing is going to change that. Not even whatever Adam is. He's not going to get to me, and he's not going to change my mind.*

We will see, Xavier retorted and went quiet.

Xavier?

Nothing. Once again, I was utterly alone without anyone to talk to. Story of my life…

***

I'm not sure how long I was left alone before Adam came back again. Whatever monsters and demons hid in the shadows in here stayed in the shadows. I hadn't been bothered once, and it was either because Alpha was waiting me out, or they were sizing me up to eat. Either way, it had been eventless. There were times I tried to leave, even though Adam had warned me not to, but it seemed like no matter which way I went, it was an endless walk, and I always ended up back where I began. It was a futile effort trying to escape, just like he said, except no one attempted to stop me. I even attempted to use my powers to raise a portal, but I wasn't able to. Somehow, Alpha was able to block anyone's abilities there except for Adam's. It made absolutely no sense. There wasn't a single moment I could think of that I couldn't use my powers, other than when items with unicorn hair were used. But as a god, those things shouldn't work on me anymore.

"Hello, Luxina," Adam said, breaking the silence as he stepped through a portal.

I stood up from my seat against the cave wall and walked over to him. "Adam!" I breathed more excitedly than I should have been. "You're back!"

"Excited to see me, are we?" he mused with a devilish grin.

"There's absolutely nothing to do here or anyone to talk to, so yes. I am excited to see you," I retorted, rolling my eyes. Maybe if I sweet-talked him enough, he would help me escape. It was a long shot, but I had no other recourse, so I might as well try.

He casually strolled toward me and then circled me as he looked over every inch of my body. I didn't know why, but all of a sudden, I felt very insecure, as if he was scrutinizing every aspect of my being. He stopped in front of me and peered down at me with tantalizing eyes.

"What?" I asked self-consciously.

"Nothing," he murmured. "You're perfect. Not a scratch on you."

"Nothing has tried to bother me down here yet," I replied.

"They will soon," he remarked with a grimace. "Father issued orders to start your harrowing."

"What's a harrowing?" I prodded nervously.

"He plans to torment you," he replied casually. "Unless you agree to what he wants to do."

"Well, I am not agreeing," I snapped. "And if that's the case, it won't be his first harrowing of me. He did the same thing when he gave me all of those injections last time he kidnapped me. I don't break."

A smirk tugged at the corners of Adam's mouth. "I know," he mumbled.

"Why are you here, Adam?" I asked, growing impatient.

"I paid Damian a visit," he taunted, pacing around me once more. "He's looking good for someone who was beaten within inches of his life and left to be ugly and unlovable. Not a scar on his body. I'm beginning to think that was all lies."

"What did you do to Damian?" I implored, grabbing his arm.

He stepped closer to me, and I could feel the magnetic pull I had with Damian become stronger. I let go of his arm and just stared at him.

"I haven't done anything to him… yet," he answered. "Just testing the field."

"Yet?" I asked. "What do you mean yet?"

"Father and I have discussed it. When Father gives me the signal for the kill order, I will be sent to dispatch him," he responded nonchalantly and waggled his fingers. "No more Damian."

My heart thudded, and panic tore through my body. "You can't do that!" I pleaded. I needed to get out of here. I needed to warn Damian about Adam.

"Not right now, I can't," he sighed. "But soon I can. He has some new power that manifested, and he can slow down time. Once I am able to acquire that power of his, it will be match for match against him."

"I don't understand," I replied, shaking my head. "How do you have any of his powers to begin with?"

"You haven't figured out how I was created yet, have you?" he inquired with a smug grin.

"No, I haven't," I answered impatiently.

"Father created me from Damian's blood," he stated with a smirk. "I am essentially Damian, but look like Xavier. Two of your weaknesses."

I swallowed the lump forming in my throat. Alpha was indeed ten steps ahead of everyone. This explains why I can't help but gravitate toward Adam. Alpha made sure I wouldn't be able to resist Adam's advances. Nausea rose to the back of my throat, and I swallowed it down. This was a new low even for Alpha.

"I see it has clicked for you," he mused with a smirk. "Now you understand why every time we touch, you feel that magnetic field circle around us."

"I love Damian," I insisted, breathing heavily.

"No," he replied coolly. "Your twin flame bond makes you love him. You don't love him for him. It's just the bond. So in the end, you will love me too."

Everything Xavier had warned me about now started to make sense. Alpha wants me to love Adam, so he made Adam to be like Damian. He thinks the reason I love Damian so much is because of the twin-flame bond. I didn't even know we had the bond until we were told about the prophecy and how I was split in two.

I shook my head, angered at how little my feelings were understood by nearly everyone when it came to Damian. "I love Damian for more than just his bond to me," I sneered. "I loved him before I even knew him as a person. Then, getting to know him made me love him even more. I won't love you the same way."

"Maybe," he rebuttaled. "Or maybe not. Your mother faced the same dilemma over and over throughout the millennia. Being faced with different angels every incarnation, and your father having to battle for her heart. Guess who won each time? Not him."

"No one ever won until the end. She was murdered every single eighteenth birthday because she refused to give in to the other angels. He won the last time," I spat. "And if you mean the affair she had with Lucifer while locked in the tower, I am not my mother."

"I can feel your desire, Luxina," he cooed, stepping closer to me. The same storm rolled behind his eyes that had unraveled me with Damian. "I know that every word that leaves my lips sends goosebumps down your spine." He ran his finger along my arm, and shivers erupted. My knees buckled. I could remember his hands and how they had made my heart flutter, but this time it was more intense. My soul cried out in divine perfidy. "I know every time I touch you, you get a little feeling that grows in your stomach." His hand wrapped around my waist. Every heartbeat that thudded in my chest felt like betrayal. His hands were like roses and thorns, as every tremble they caused felt like blades shredding the thread binding me to Damian. He leaned in closer and whispered in my ear. "I know he hasn't touched you, and that ache radiates into your core." He exhaled, tingling the hairs in my ear, teasing my neck with goosebumps, and I couldn't help but lean into it. I wanted this… or did I? His scent was intoxicating, and embers awoke in my soul while my body ached for Damian. Adam wasn't the one who fought for me, cried with me, or bled for me, but he was what I wanted in that very moment, going against every hushed whisper saying he wasn't Damian. How could he wrap his fingers through my soul? I could feel them etching and burning his fingerprints deep within me as if he were claiming me.

Luxina! Xavier shouted, breaking me out of the trance I had become wrapped up in. I pulled away from Adam, too ashamed to even look him in the face.

"I see dear old brother interrupted," he sighed. "Father will fix that for us soon." He waved his hand, and a portal appeared. "I'll be back." He stepped through the portal, and it vanished. I hit the ground, shaking and in tears.

Xavier, what am I supposed to do? I asked in between sobs.

I don't know, but we need to come up with something quick, he replied. *We can't fight that pull at all. I even tried to stop you and couldn't.*

Damian, I need you, I cried.

CHAPTER TWO: DAMIAN

STARFIRE WAS RIGHT. I had left immediately from Lightshade and made my way to Alpha's lair at Chernobyl. By the time I got there, everyone had packed up and left. All that was left behind were remnants of the experiments Alpha had been conducting. Bodies lay dead, rotting in the cells they had been held in as prisoners. The Forsaken were scattered throughout the entire building from whatever fight had taken place. This place had long since been abandoned, even though there were fresh remnants of those who had been turned to ashes. The smell still lingered in the air from whatever came through. *Why would Alpha have sat around waiting in here? Had he been controlling her still, somehow, someway? None of it made sense.*

When I arrived back at Lightshade, I wasn't in the mood to talk to anybody. I was the reason that Luxina did what she did. I had let Alpha get into my head. He had a funny way of doing that. Even though he no longer had access to control me the way he had done for all of these years, he was still able to manipulate me the same way he always had. I was not prepared for the next set of events that took place as I walked back through the door of Starfire's cottage. Seeing Sophie there, but learning her real name was Anniel, wasn't even the astounding reveal of a lifetime. Learning that Incaendiel was my real father was the ultimate bombshell for our little family. Alpha and Lilith, and their little games, were master chess players. They both were always ten steps ahead of us, even when we thought we were gaining a solid foothold in the game.

Everything came quickly and in a blur all at once, and I hardly had time to think or even breathe. As soon as Anniel took her potion to deactivate the enchantment placed on us, we became our true selves. Starfire didn't tell us that we all would explode and turn into gods. It never crossed my mind that we were also enchanted since Anniel and Incaendiel were, and it transferred to us while we were a part of them. It made sense now, even though Starfire never explained anything at all, and we had to figure it out on our own most of the time. She was about as bad as Alpha and Lilith with her half-truths and "It's not my place to tell you. You have to figure it out on your own" bullshit.

We all learned valuable lessons in Lightshade. We learned that the protective barrier that we thought kept Alpha out was a lie. Anyone could come and go as they pleased. We learned that Alpha created Adam in the spitting image of Xavier. I'm still pretty pissed about that, too. That wound is still fresh, and Alpha knew that. Alpha has a plan for Adam and Luxina, but nobody is sure what it is. Since Alpha controls the reality of his universe, he can manipulate everything in it, including the visions both Gabriel and Starfire had. Starfire can no longer see what Alpha has planned. Just the thought of Alpha using Adam the same way he tried to use me when it came to

Luxina and Xavier makes me want to boil him alive. I'm still stuck in his game even though I escaped it. Of course, he would strike at me this way. I showed him my weakness. He was playing poker, and when he saw my hand, he knew exactly how to hit me where it hurts the most. Luxina was the one single thing I cared about most in this world now, and he was trying everything he could to take that away from me.

When Adam showed up, Incaendiel didn't even let me know it was him. I can only guess it was because he knew I would try to kill him. He guessed right. Had he not given Adam the upper hand and "given him a chance to see our side," everything that spiraled out of control wouldn't have gone that way. Adam wasn't on his radar like he was mine. I knew how dangerous he could be. I witnessed Alpha and his little projects. I knew what he put into me and what he drew out of me. It was my blood that ran through his body. He was created from me. I know how dangerous I am, and he showed us what he could do. It took me years to perfect my abilities, but Adam only needed a year of intense training, according to Lilith. Who knows when he was truly created? Who knows what all of mine he would inherit? That scared the hell out of me, especially if he also gained access to my power over time.

There are certain things he hasn't attained yet. I just acquired them myself. Hell, we just learned about who we are. Talk about a revelation. We were the first ever gods of the cosmos. They called us the Guardians of Light, and Alpha destroyed what was left of our universe to build his. He slew my grandparents, and when they knew he would return for the rest of us, Anniel and Incaendiel, or should I say Is'hari and Vahr-Zul, absorbed us into them to protect us. Alpha had no idea we existed. He just took what he wanted, and when he later found out about us through the thought manipulation of Anniel and Incaendiel, he and Lilith orchestrated a grand plan. The game of *Where's the Garden of Eden* sprang to life. Disgusting honestly. What they put Anniel and Incaendiel through for millennia is one of the harshest things anyone could survive. And why? One: Because he couldn't control Incaendiel. Two: he needed them to procreate so Luxina and I would be born, and he could snatch us up.

I'm not sure how long he worked at Anniel, but she had become his weapon, his protective guard dog. Their fated love was torn into shreds by Alpha and Lilith. They repressed all of Incaendiel and Sophie's memories from their past lives. They put them into sleep mode to hide important information from them. They completely warped everyone's reality and bent it to their will. He even manipulated the top-ranking angels to do his dirty work for him. To know Alpha planned to use Anniel in the end was a surprise since she wasn't in the visions he gave everyone. It was probably his master plan all along. Besides the showdown with Adam, which we know is coming, Incaendiel will have to fight Anniel in the end unless she can find a way to meld her psyche as he did, if that changes anything at all. Incaendiel becoming one with his psyche was intense. For a brief moment, I really thought he was going to kill me so he could destroy Lilith. He came so close… Alpha doesn't even compare to the amount of fear I felt when I saw him emerge from the smoke and ashes. His body glowed with this natural, fiery haze, and his eyes were like balls of gaseous fire. He was massive in body build, taller and more buff than both Metatron and Lucifer. His voice sounded like a deep, growling microphone. All of the angels now feared him and walked on eggshells around him. The Vahr-Zul part of him could control his powers at ease, but the broken part of Incaendiel that had grown for millennia without Lilith waking him for more training was also still present. The very broken part of him that Alpha and Lilith toyed with to make him feel less than worthy and a problem. Everyone remembered his inability to control himself, and with the powers he has now, they all fear he will lash out and smite them by accident.

"Distracted?" Samyaza asked, breaking me from my thoughts as we stood in Starfire's library.

"Sorry," I murmured as I ran my hand through my hair. "It's just been…"

"I get it," Samyaza offered with a smile.

He held the Watcher's Eye up in the light as he inspected it.

"How does that thing work?" I asked, staring at it to see if I could see anything.

"To mortals, it works a lot like a hag stone," he replied.

I scrunched my face. "What's a hag stone?"

He chuckled and shook his head. "Alpha didn't teach you anything except to fight, am I right?"

I shrugged my shoulders. "I was just a weapon to him. He didn't even really teach me to fight. Asmodeus trained me, mostly."

"Didn't you travel through the Nightmares and Shadows realm in the Otherworld? I mean, surely one of the fey has told you what a hag stone is," he commented as he handed the Watcher's Eye over to me.

"No one tells me anything," I mumbled, turning the relic over in my hand. "Besides, they only tell you the answers to what you ask."

"A hag stone is a rock that has a natural worn hole in the middle of it, usually from being in contact with running water directly pouring onto it. It allows the wielder to see through any glamours fey have cast to walk among the mortals, showing the wielder the fey's true self," Samyaza answered. "Usually, a mortal can hold this up," he began, emphasizing the relic in the air, "and they can see angels or Watchers. The difference being, it's more like a looking glass than it is a hag stone. Same principle, just different power."

"And angels nor Watchers have never used it themselves?" I asked as I perused the spines of the books on the shelf in front of me.

"We haven't really ever needed to before," Samyaza responded. "There was never a need."

"Well, let's give it a try," I offered with a shrug.

"That's what I have been trying to do," Samyaza huffed. "I have tried direct light, shadow, sheer will, pretty much everything I can think of to try and get it to work."

"What about fire?" I asked. "Holding it over firelight might work."

I held out my hand, and he gave me the relic. I walked over to the fireplace in the room and stirred the embers around that still had some life left to them. I held it to the small glow of the flames, and as the amethyst heated from the radiating warmth, it was as if glass were forming at the center of the piece.

"It's working!" I exclaimed, and he rushed over to my side. "Now what?" I asked, looking at him.

"Think of what we need to know. Think of the Watchers to find them and then think of Lailah to find her," he answered.

I nodded and returned my attention back to the stone in my pocket, focusing on finding the Watchers Alpha had taken prisoner. The amethyst began to show me things within the small translucent circle. I could see the Watchers, bound at the hands and feet, just sitting or lying on the ground.

"But *where* are they?" Samyaza asked.

As I thought the words, the scene in the middle began to pan away from them into the darkness surrounding them. Something shot out in front of the eye quickly, as if trying to elude being seen.

"What was that?" I mumbled as we watched.

A deafening howl split the room, and I nearly dropped the amethyst from the startle as I grabbed my ears.

"What is *that*?" I demanded.

Samyaza had his ears covered as well, and the sound filled the room, becoming louder and louder.

"It's the screams of torment!" he exclaimed. "They're in Tartarus."

"How do we make the sound stop?" I urged as I pressed harder on my ears.

"Think of Lailah!" he yelled.

As soon as her name crossed my mind, the screams stopped. We both removed our hands from our ears, and I held the crystal back over the fire. When the scene developed in its center, Lailah sat in the middle of the ground in an ample, vacant, dark space. She was surrounded by a few of the Forsaken that belonged to Alpha's crew.

"That's Aker," I said, pointing at one of them.

"Is that Berberos?" Samyaza asked, squinting his eyes to see better.

"Looks like it. I can't tell who the others are from this angle," I answered.

"Well, let's see where they are," Samyaza prodded.

I nodded, and the scene began to move just as it had with Tartarus. It was very similar in style to the last place, and I was just about to remark that it must be Tartarus still when I saw a creature moving in the shadows.

"Is that a—"

"Three-headed dog," Samyaza finished. "They're in Sheol. That's Hades' favorite hellhound, Cerberus."

"Alright, well, let's go tell the others," I remarked, tossing the stone up in the air and catching it in my hand.

Samyaza and I made our way outside to look for the group. We came around the corner of Starfire's cottage when I noticed them huddled in the back. We walked over to them, and you could feel the tension in the air. I looked around at them, stopping at Incaendiel's face. He looked angry and aggravated.

"What's going on?" I asked.

No one seemed to want to answer. Finally, Asmodeus spoke up. "Strategizing," he grunted and then stalked off from behind the cottage toward the training arena. Incaendiel started to walk off after him when Samael stopped him.

"Let him go cool off," he said and patted his shoulder.

I wondered what had been said to piss Asmodeus off. He wasn't one to get angry over nothing, so something must have been said or done to make him mad. These days, it wasn't hard at all for Incaendiel to piss people off, though, so he must have said something that struck a nerve.

Incaendiel nodded, then turned his attention to Samyaza. "Did you find her?" he inquired, changing the subject.

"We did," Samyaza replied, grimacing.

"Well, where is she?" he asked, waiting for him to answer.

"She's in Sheol," I responded. "She's being guarded there by Aker, Beberos, and a few others."

"We were also able to locate the other Watchers as well," Samyaza chimed in. "They are in Tartarus."

"Seems easy enough," Incaendiel replied. "Should be a cakewalk."

Samyaza and I exchanged glances. A cakewalk indeed.

"What?" he asked, looking between us.

"Alpha has a whole slew of those creatures and more in Tartarus," Samyaza replied. "We would have to fight our way in to get to them."

"What about Sheol?" he asked. "Anything there?"

I shook my head. "None that we could see, but you know Alpha. What we could see was just who Alpha has guarding Lailah, but as I said, I was only able to see a handful of them. Plus, there are the human souls there as well. So we have to be careful using our powers, or we will destroy the souls before they recycle to the Giving Tree."

"I don't see the problem," he replied. "We can take a handful of Forsaken and angels."

I shook my head. "It won't be that simple. Sheol has its own monsters from the various voids of the cosmos," I replied. "Like Cerberus, Hydra, and all."

"I forgot about them," Incaendiel replied, chewing on his nail, deep in thought. "We go to Sheol first and bring Lailah back, and then on to Tartarus to release the Watchers."

"We still need to free Luxina from Purgatory as well," I piped up. No one ever remembers that we still have to save her. Adam had warned us we needed to do it quickly because she was in danger, and if I was right, he was the one putting her in danger.

"We will be better in more numbers going into Purgatory," he replied. "There's no telling what Alpha has stashed in there to keep us from getting to her. I can guarantee you it will be worse than Sheol or Tartarus."

"We will need to bring offerings to Charon so he will let us through the river," Azazel added.

"That, and you need to make peace with Hades, or he won't let you through either," Azrael remarked, walking up to us. "He is still Lord of the Underworld. We need his permission to go through."

We all groaned.

"What?" she asked, looking around at us.

"Hades is so pompous," Samael replied, rolling his eyes.

"I don't even know why Alpha agreed to let him continue to be the Lord over the dead," Metatron agreed.

"Alpha didn't agree to anything," Azrael laughed. "Alpha has no control over the death deities, just like he has no control over the reaper angels or Maveth. *All* souls in the cosmos go through him and the other death deities as we carry them there."

"It doesn't make him more likable," Michael chimed in, scrunching his face in disgust.

"He thinks that he is better than everyone else," Azazel added.

"Well, whether you personally like him or not, he is the only way in, even if you pay Charon the token to take the river," Azrael chirped.

"Well, then, it's settled," Incaendiel interrupted. "We make peace with Hades. Samael, gather the tokens from Starfire for Charon. I know she has them somewhere among her relics."

Samael nodded and walked around the building to go inside.

"How many of us are going?" I asked.

"You're staying here with Samyaza," he replied.

"But—" I began to protest.

He put his hand up. "It's not because you need protection or because I think you won't be safe. Lightshade needs protection in case Adam comes back."

"I thought I wasn't allowed to fight him," I quipped, raising an eyebrow.

"Why not let Damian come with us, and you stay behind to protect Lightshade?" Raphael offered. "You handled Adam without breaking a sweat and without hurting him."

Incaendiel stood thinking it over. "Fine. I will stay behind. Take Asmodeus with you," he urged, looking at me. "And you mind Samael as well. He is first in command."

I nodded and ran off to find Asmodeus, grinning from ear to ear. Incaendiel never lets me do anything since he thinks I will get hurt, and it's annoying. I spent my whole life living with Alpha and was in danger at every waking minute, but as soon as he learned he was my real father, he became this overbearing, overprotective helicopter parent. I was trained to be at the forefront of every fight. He had to let loose of the reins at some point. I haven't even really been keen on the idea of calling him dad. The only times I have called him dad have been to snap his focus back to reality. It seems like the only option there is when he sinks in too deep. He couldn't honestly expect me just to change and be all mushy-gushy father-son stars in my eyes toward him just because the truth had been revealed. I still had to grow up without him as my father and with tyrannical Alpha as my guardian. It takes time to come to terms with revelations like that, and I wasn't ready to be someone's son. I wasn't ready for anything, honestly. I took care of myself mostly with help from Asmodeus here and there, and even he couldn't stop everything that happened to me. Does Incaendiel really think he could do any better at protecting me?

As I checked arena to arena, I found Asmodeus with Praeziel talking off to the side. I hurried over to them, catching the last bit Asmodeus had to say about Incaendiel.

"He thinks he can tell him what he can and can't do, but even Alpha didn't have that hold over him. He always bucked at him," Asmodeus said.

"Incaendiel is trying to do what he thinks is best for us all," Praeziel remarked with a shrug. "This is all new to him. Damian as his son is new to him. He is just trying to protect him like he protected Luxina all of those years. Before he even learned he was his son, he was trying to protect him and guide him. Cut him some slack."

"And look where that got him," Asmodeus huffed. "He never trained Luxina, leaving her defenseless, and Alpha took her. He is setting him up for failure by not letting him handle Adam the way he needs to be handled. Damian doesn't need to be leashed. He needs to be set free to do as he pleases. He was leashed long enough with Alpha."

At least I wasn't the only one who felt like Incaendiel was hovering too much, but for some reason, it made me angry hearing Asmodeus talk about him.

"He's just doing what he thinks is safe for us all," I chimed in as I walked up to them. "I don't like it any more than you do, but he is hard-headed, and when he comes to a decision, he is bull-headed. But he also has the weight of the cosmos on his shoulders. We don't need to bog him down with petty stuff."

Asmodeus fell quiet with a glare on his face. "What's the plan?" he asked, changing the subject.

"We are going to Sheol to get Lailah," I replied.

Asmodeus furrowed his brows. "We?" he reiterated.

I grinned mischievously. "Yep, we," I answered. "You ready?"

"Boy, am I ever," he breathed, rubbing his hands together excitedly. "I am getting cabin fever here."

"Let's go find Samael," I replied. "He should be at Starfire's cottage."

Asmodeus and I headed over to the cottage. Samael came out of the door, headed back around the cottage, and held the coins Starfire had given him for Charon. "Are we ready?" he asked, looking around at everyone.

"Yep," I replied, walking up with Asmodeus at my side to join everyone.

Keep him safe, Incaendiel projected to Asmodeus, and he gave a nod.

You have my word, Brother, Asmodeus replied in his head.

I can hear you both! I interrupted, rolling my eyes.

"Alright, let's go," Samael replied, with Metatron, Azazel, Michael, Raphael, and Asmodeus falling in behind him as he walked off. I headed up the tail end of the line.

"Is Starfire portalling you in?" Incaendiel shouted after us like a worried mother.

Samael gave him a thumbs up without turning around, and we continued around the cottage. Starfire stood in front of the porch with a portal already open.

"Good luck, everyone!" she exclaimed.

We all nodded and entered it one by one. I gave one last look behind me, hoping to see Incaendiel before I stepped through, but he still lingered behind the cottage. I don't know why, but he gave me a sense of encouragement, and it made me feel safe knowing he had my back. I liked it when he trusted me enough to do things without him. I turned around, took a deep breath, and stepped through the portal.

Damian, I need you.

Luxina?

CHAPTER THREE: LUXINA

IT WASN'T LONG after Adam left that he returned, unusually cheerful. "Told you I would be back soon," he beamed as he walked from the portal and over to me. "I had to go pay your little daddy a visit."

"What did you do to my father?" I demanded, jumping to my feet.

"Nothing personally. You see, I have failed the last two attempts I have made at battling him. And since he was planning on storming Tartarus to release the captured Watchers, Alpha thought it would be fitting just to portal Tartarus to Lightshade. Cool, huh?" he gushed.

A tear slipped from my eye as I thought of all the poor warlocks in Lightshade who were now in danger. Reikal being one of the top ones.

As if reading my mind, he stated, "Oh, yes. The death count is going to be phenomenal there. Do you know how many monsters have been locked away in Tartarus? There are *soooo* many!"

More tears began to betray my eyes. How could Adam be so ruthless? Everyone expects it from Alpha, but if Damian could remain the kind-hearted person he is, why couldn't Adam? I know Alpha made Damian do things that were horrible, but he always regretted them later. Even if at first he relished being Alpha's number one soldier, he knew he had to fake it to make it. Adam… he thrives in the chaos Alpha creates.

"There, there," he soothed mockingly. "I am sure your daddy will be fine. Now, Damian, on the other hand, is in Sheol rescuing poor Lailah. He is in for a real treat."

He reached out and wiped away my tears. I felt helpless and hopeless. He lifted my chin so my eyes would meet his. *I am sure they will really be fine,* he thought to me. *But I am sorry for this next part.* Something hard hit the back of my head, and everything went dark. When I came to, I was strapped down to a table. I tried to break free from the straps, but they seemed to tighten the more I struggled. My head ached from whatever Adam used to knock me out, and my vision was hazy.

"There she is!" Alpha cheered in glee. "Welcome back, Luxina."

I looked around the room, and it warped and shuddered as dizziness took over. My eyes landed on Alpha, and I tried to focus, but his face looked like a funhouse mirror. Beside him stood Adam, his face solemn, warping the same way.

"Where am I?" I asked, still trying to free myself. I pushed with all of my might to bring forth my powers, but they were still blocked.

"Still in Purgatory, I am afraid," Alpha replied. "Those pesky little powers are suppressed here until you're purified. But until then, they are indisposed."

"Why am I tied to this table?" I asked weakly, moving my head from side to side to peer around the room.

"Why, we are going to extract little Xavier, of course," he answered.

My eyes went wide. "What?!" I demanded.

"Can't have him getting in the middle of you and Adam again," Alpha beamed with a wink. "And I won't lie to you. This is going to be extremely painful. Quite possibly end with your death as well."

"I thought you said it wouldn't kill her?" Adam inquired, alarmed, quickly moving closer to the table.

"I said it might not kill her," Alpha retorted. "If you don't want to be quiet and watch, then go somewhere else."

Adam's lips tightened, and he glanced from Alpha, then at me, and finally stalked off from the room we were in.

"At least he is obedient," Alpha mused. "Couldn't get Damian to listen like that."

"Maybe if you didn't beat him half to death all the time, he would have listened to you," I spat. "You treated him like a dog and expected him to cower to you."

"No, see," Alpha began, pointing at me. "Damian listened to me just fine until he learned about *you*. I don't know what it is about the women in your lineage, but apparently, it makes men hate their fathers. Maybe it's all the rushing sex hormones. Who knows. Because until *you*, Damian listened to every little thing I told him."

"You don't think that won't happen with Adam?" I sneered, lifting my head from the table and grinning at him. "I mean, it runs in my lineage to seduce and sway. Or at least that's what you've told Adam I did with Damian. It also runs through Damian's blood to think for himself."

"Adam doesn't love you, dear girl," Alpha laughed as he prepared a metal table with instruments beside him. "Damian loved you. Adam is just doing what I tell him to do. He doesn't have real feelings for you. He has no soul. Don't you understand that? Your soul is what loves, not your heart. It's just the twin flame bond in Damian's blood, and he knows it. He understands that. Adam, much like your mother, is my little lap dog. And when I say bark, he barks. When I say bite, he bites. And when I say kill, he kills."

"You're not a father," I laughed in his face. "You're just power hungry. You don't have a single bone in your body that screams nurturing. It's why you hate my father. He knows how to be one."

Alpha let out a bellowing laugh. "You really think that's why I supposedly, I will say supposedly, hate your father?" he asked. "Oh, my dear child. No." He leaned in closer to my face. "It's much deeper than that. You see, I created your mother and your father with Lilith. I knew the entire time they were gods, and we were enchanting them so they wouldn't be more powerful than us. We also couldn't let all of the angels think we chose favorites, or else it would have been anarchy. When the time was right, and it was our turn to retire and let them reign, we would remove the enchantment. I loved your father. Still do in fact. He's my son."

"But?" I asked.

"Your parents were from the very first universe to ever pop into existence, and I killed their parents and stole their souls. Your father remembered it all and *hated* me for it. We had to put up a barrier in his mind so he wouldn't remember, but that anger and contentment and resentment bubbled to the top all of the time," Alpha explained. "My own son hated me because I took him and saved him from a dying universe where he would have dissipated into nothing had he stayed. The ungratefulness of it all. The audacity he had to place all that blame on me when I was just trying to be a good father."

"What?" I asked in shock, processing everything he said.

"That's right, little firefly. You are Valiyren, primordial goddess and the fifth to exist in the cosmos," he answered, picking up this syringe-type instrument. "Now, do hold still, little one. This is going to hurt."

He plunged the needle into my chest cavity, and I howled in pain.

Xavier, I thought. *Get Damian.*

Everything went dark.

***

The room was spinning when I opened my eyes. Adam stood at the foot of the table while Alpha pilfered around the room.

"It should have worked!" Alpha yelled. "I have used it on many a god to steal their powers without killing them."

Adam's eyes met mine, full of pity and guilt. "What else is there to use?" he asked, keeping Alpha distracted from me. "Since you're siphoning a soul instead of powers, maybe that's why it failed."

"I am not sure," Alpha huffed, banging his hands on the counter at the wall. "For now, take her back to the cave and begin the harrowing. Quickly, before she wakes up, I don't know how long I can keep her powers under."

Adam moved from the foot of the table to the side of the table and carefully unlatched the straps from my wrists and hoisted me up into his arms. He looked down at me, and his face was serene and caring. If I didn't know any better, I would say he truly did have feelings for me.

"And Adam," Alpha began.

"Yes, sir?" he asked, turning to face him.

"Remember what we talked about," Alpha stated, his eyes saying more than he did.

Adam nodded. "Yes, sir."

Alpha waved his hand, and a portal appeared. Adam walked me through it, and it closed behind us. He laid me gently down on the ground and sat down beside me, pulling me so my head could rest in his lap. I went to open my mouth to speak, but he shushed me.

"Don't try to talk," he spoke softly. "Xavier is still inside you, but Alpha did a lot of damage to your chest trying to extract him. You're going to need to heal for a few days before you can speak or move."

A tear slipped down my cheek as fear began to settle in. If I couldn't move or speak, how was I going to defend myself during the harrowing?

"I will keep you safe," Adam murmured, stroking my hair. "No one will hurt you while I am here at your side. I swear. After seeing what he was doing to you..." He paused and cleared his throat. "It won't happen again. I won't let it."

Even though they said Alpha failed, I still felt like Xavier was missing. I didn't feel whole like I had before Alpha began. *Xavier? Are you there?* Nothing but silence echoed my silent question. The exhaustion overtook me from the procedure Alpha had commenced, and I drifted off to sleep in Adam's lap, with him stroking my hair.

***

I awoke to the sound of monstrous howls and metal clanking. I pried my eyes open to see Adam sword fighting with beings that looked human but were hideously disfigured, with black eyes. They were most likely the lower demons created by the Forsaken when they had grown bored with killing seelies. As he fought with his sword with one hand, he used his other hand to shoot ice daggers through the air, taking down beast after beast that Alpha had created.

I felt something at my foot and looked down to see this huge slug-like creature opening its mouth and slowly devouring me, starting with my shoes. Every kick I made against the creature and every sound that slipped out sent searing pains through my chest. I tried to wiggle away, but with each little movement I made, the thing slurped more of my body into its mouth like a limp noodle. I heard a whoosh in the air and a splat sound, then looked down where the creature had been. Adam had cut it in half with his sword. He stood in front of me and encased me in some sort of shiny blue shield before unleashing a deafening howl, followed by shards of ice. The ground froze beneath everything and encased them with ice to the point where they couldn't move, so that the ice shards would take them out one by one.

When the tempest was over, and the snowy ice cleared the air, bodies lay strung out as far as the eye could see. He went to my feet and finished pulling the creature off my legs, then tossed it to the side before collapsing to the ground at my feet.

"See," he began, breathing heavily. "I told you I would keep you safe."

Is this what Alpha calls a harrowing? I thought to him.

He nodded. "This is just the beginning, too. There will be more coming."

How did you encase me in that shield? I asked, trying to scoot closer to him, ignoring the pain radiating in my chest. He grabbed me under my arms and pulled me over to him, resting my head once again in his lap. "I guess Damian hasn't figured that power out yet, then, right?" he asked, running his fingers through my hair.

I shook my head. *Alpha never focused on his powers; instead, he mainly focused on turning him into a fighting machine. I guess he was too afraid of showing him what he could do in case he rebelled.*

Adam stared at me blankly. "Why *did* he rebel?" he asked.

He didn't, I explained. *He did every single thing he asked of him, including kidnapping me. Alpha rewarded him with punishment, torture, and starvation. He even tossed him into an arena and sent all of these monsters,* motioning with my eyes around the room, *plus even more after him, after he defeated the first few he created for him. My dad pulled him out of the arena before they could kill him.*

"Why didn't he use his powers to vanquish them?" Adam inquired. "He is powerful enough to do that."

His powers, much like mine and the rest of my family, are rooted deeply in emotion. Without proper control, they spiral. He would have destroyed everyone sitting in the arena, including those who were on his side. Not to mention, we weren't at full capacity yet, either. We were still enchanted.

"So he cares for everyone around him at all times?" he remarked, confused.

I nodded. *He is a selfless person. He had many chances to escape from Alpha, but refused to do so just so Xavier and I would stay safe. When he learned Alpha had my dad, he wouldn't run unless he could be freed as well. Even Starfire went there to rescue him, and he declined.*

"And it's that empathy that enraged Alpha?" he prodded.

I'm not sure, I mused. *I don't think Alpha has been a happy person for a very long time. Since before the fall, I guess. When he learned that something he had created had become more powerful than he was, he became a completely different person, or so I assume. The way he mistreated all of his children during the fall, apathy like that just doesn't pop up for no reason. Is he nice to you?*

Adam was quiet for a moment. "You need more rest," he replied, changing the subject. "I will keep watch."

I smiled up at him. *Thank you.* As he stroked my hair, I was lulled into sleep once more. As my eyes closed, I could see the questions in his eyes, and I hoped I had at least made him question his loyalty to Alpha after everything he had witnessed and then heard.

***

I stirred to the sound of arguing.

"If you do another experiment on her, it will kill her!" Adam shouted, planting himself in front of me.

"Why do you care? Have you grown soft for her?" Belphegor snarled, trying to push him out of the way. "Becoming Damian's little mini me?"

Adam grabbed his arm, and it turned to ice. "You either leave and tell Father that she needs more time to heal from the last time, or I break it off and start working on other bits of your body." He stared Belphegor down, and he backed up.

"Have it your way," Belphegor spat, walking away. "When he locks you up like he did Damian, you will have no one but yourself to blame, just like that little bastard."

"Yeah, you just worry about you, how about that?" Adam sneered. He turned around to see that I was awake and frowned. "You weren't supposed to hear that," he remarked, glaring over his shoulder as Belphegor left through a portal.

"Not my first rodeo," I replied hoarsely. "How long have I been out?"

"A while," he answered. He came over and gently pulled my shirt down to inspect the wound left behind by Alpha's instrument. "It still looks pretty gnarly," he commented, putting my shirt back in place.

"Gnarly?" I asked, chuckling, then grimaced as the pain radiated.

"What's wrong with gnarly?" he asked earnestly.

"Have you been spying in on humans?" I inquired, smiling. "That is a human word."

"Oh," he replied, realizing why I was laughing. "No, I heard one of the Forsaken use it."

"Well, that explains it," I commented. "Have there been any more monsters?"

He shook his head and sat down beside me. "Nope. Just that idiot." He motioned with his thumb where Belphegor had been standing.

"Alpha will most likely punish you," I remarked. "This is how it started with Damian."

He waved the idea off. "Father loves me. He won't hurt me. He listens to me."

"That's what Damian thought as well," I warned. "And then one day, he was dragged into a dungeon, strung up to where his toes barely touched the floor, and then whipped with a specially made whip. Next, they beat him within an inch of his life. He had to be left hanging overnight so his fractured ribs wouldn't kill him. He was starved to the point he was skin and bones when he finally caught up to us before we made it to Lightshade. Your father is a monster to people he views as a threat or disobedient."

"Look, I understand that Damian was treated badly, whether his disobedience was the cause or not," Adam began. "But I am not Damian. Alpha isn't sitting around with a whip waiting to tan my hide for insubordination because I am truly and one hundred percent obedient and loyal to him."

"So, if he asks you to kill me, are you going to kill me?" I persisted, "You're a good little boy and do everything you are told, but sit here and act as if you care about me. Would you do it?"

"He would never ask me to do that," Adam replied, ignoring the question.

"Quit deflecting!" I ordered, glaring at him. "If he walked in right here and right now and told you to pick your sword up and kill me, what are you doing?"

"I'm not playing this stupid question game!" he retorted, anger painting his face.

"What are you doing?" I yelled.

"I'm killing you!" he blurted out and then immediately regretted. "I didn't mean that."

"Yes, you did." I sat there with a look of what I could only surmise as disgust and pity staring at him. "And that's the difference between you and Damian. Damian knows right from wrong. Damian would risk his own life to save mine. That is why I love him. I never have to fear him choosing himself over me, even if I don't want him to. He would still choose me over himself. He is selfless. You are selfish and serve only your own priorities and Alpha's. Damian looks after the well-being of everyone, the world, and the freaking cosmos. Alpha has so you warped in the head… *You* are the one who is pathetic, not

Damian," I stammered, pulling my knees to my chest. "You can go! I don't need you here."

"You need protection," he refuted. "The harrowing!"

"Yeah, protection from you," I shot back. "I'm no safer with you than without you, according to your own words. Now, please leave."

He stood up and dusted off his pants. "I'm sorry," he offered before opening a portal and leaving me behind as I asked.

CHAPTER FOUR: DAMIAN

WE SLOWLY MADE our way out of the portal with Samael leading the way. We trekked down a mountainside covered in lush green foliage, strange flowers, and trees that seemed to touch the sky because they were so tall. The river Acheron flowed crystal clear alongside the mountain. As we walked, we looked for any sign of Charon's boat. According to Starfire, Charon used the river Acheron in the mortal world to ferry people to the outer lands and cross over to the river of Styx. As we walked, I was steadily distracted from where I heard Luxina's voice calling out to me for help. I knew for a fact it was her voice, even though it was believed we couldn't communicate through thoughts this far apart. She needed me, and instead of planning her rescue first, everyone and everything else was being prioritized. I hated it. Every bone in my body screamed for me to just abandon this mission and go off to find her on my own. Slipping away unnoticed would be the hard part. There was no way I could break free from the leash Asmodeus kept me on. He acts like Incaendiel has me pent up when really, Asmodeus has always done the same to me as well. Maybe I could talk him into ditching everyone and going with me…

"Damian!" Asmodeus called out, breaking me from my thoughts.

"Huh?" I asked, trotting to catch up. I had fallen behind everyone, lost in my thoughts, and he looked pissed about it. There goes my chance of suckering him into my plan.

"Where's your head at?" he asked as I caught up and walked beside him. "It's not like you to get distracted on a mission."

"When we stepped through the portal," I began, and stopped.

"What?" he prodded.

"I heard Luxina call out to me in my head," I replied, stepping over some jutting rocks.

"I thought Incaendiel didn't think you could talk to one another still?" Asmodeus asked, maneuvering through the terrain almost as if he had been here before.

"Maybe he was wrong?" I answered with a shrug. "I know what I heard." I was quiet for a moment and decided what the hell. "Asmodeus?" I asked.

"Yeah, buddy?" he replied, watching his footing.

"If I asked you to, would you leave the group with me to go do a separate recon mission?" It was worth a shot to ask.

"You know Incaendiel would have both of our heads if Samael told him we ditched everyone here," he replied with a laugh. "I know you can kick my ass, but I am more afraid of him than you. Why? Where do you want to go? Do you just want to get out of here and shoot the shit or something?"

I shook my head. "Never mind. It doesn't matter."

He stopped in his tracks and reached over, placing his hand on my shoulder. "You can tell me," he urged. I was about to answer when Samael interrupted our conversation.

"There's Charon's boat," Samael called out, turning around and facing the group. "Everyone have their coins?"

"Maybe some other time," I mumbled as I fished my coin out of my bag and held it up as everyone else did. Samael nodded and turned back around. We approached Charon's boat as he sat sunbathing in his black cloak.

"I didn't expect to see Alpha's boys around here," Charon mused, sitting up in his chair. "I don't do favors for Alpha, so you can all leave."

"We aren't Alpha's *boys,*" Azazel sneered in disgust.

"I don't care what you think you are. Boy, girl, angel, demon. You're all the same when you work for that monster," he retorted, narrowing his eyes at her.

"We aren't his minions," I said, stepping to the front of the line. "We are his inevitable destruction. Will you please ferry us to Sheol?"

"Well, well," Charon replied sarcastically with a bow. "If it isn't Alpha's little soldier boy stepping forward."

"I'm not his soldier," I seethed, clenching my jaw. "I bow to no one."

"I've seen your handiwork, kid," Charon muttered. "You're Alpha's little attack dog."

I gritted my teeth. "That was before. I am no longer his sock puppet."

"Prove it," Charon challenged, standing up in his boat.

The more he talked, the angrier I became. I had so much pent-up rage when it came to people calling me Alpha's property. I clawed my way out of the hell he put me in, and I would be damned if people insinuated that I cared about him. A twig snapped as Metatron shifted his weight, and it sounded like the crack of a whip. I felt my powers leap forward before I could even control them. Everything around us turned to ice, even though I didn't mean for it to happen. Charon took a step back from me. "Caelvryn?" he stammered.

"Damian is fine," I remarked as I drew the ice back into me, casting a glance over at Samael, who shook his head in disapproval.

He looked around at all of us, sitting down and cowering in his seat. "What do you guys want?"

"Safe passage into Sheol so we can rescue Lailah," Samael replied. "It's funny you mention you don't work with Alpha's minions, and yet several of his Forsaken are guarding her in there."

"Well, tokens talk," he said, shaking his satchel of coins.

Samael held his up. "And we brought payment."

"Put them in the satchel and climb onboard," he huffed. "This will get you into Sheol, and you can pass through Erebus with ease."

"Funny how those tokens only talk when you want them to," Michael sneered as he dropped his coin in the bag. Charon glanced around nervously as we all did as instructed and placed our coins in his bag, and, one by one, climbed onto the boat. I was the last one on and placed my coin in his bag while staring him down. He eyed me suspiciously as I sat down beside Asmodeus. He kicked the boat off the shore and began using his punting pole to move it along the river, guiding it in the direction it needed to go. The crystal-clear water soon began to grow greener and then darker as we passed from the mortal realm into the outer lands. Afterward, we came across the guardians who made sure no one passed unchecked. However, they didn't stop Charon, and we continued on without an issue.

"That's what the coins are for," Charon replied as if he knew what I was thinking. "Otherwise, they don't let you pass into the outer lands and only let you leave when it's for a good cause."

I nodded in understanding and returned my attention to the scenery. Two other rivers sat off to the left of us. One shone like gold under the sun while the other was a dark as Nightmares and Shadows realm.

"The golden river leads to the Garden of Eden," Charon began as if giving a tour. "The black river is the river of Styx. That one leads us into and around Sheol."

He maneuvered his boat around to go down the middle of the stream, and the temperature of the air dropped dramatically. The atmosphere felt charged and heavy, like a lightning storm would strike at any moment. The smell of sulfur and decay wafted through the air, and we all pinched our noses closed. The water looked as black as the darkest voids with a looming mist rising from the surface. Inky black tendrils of smoke poofed into the air and then disappeared, leaving behind thick, oily bubbles. A slight blue and green glow marred the surface like a tantalizing serenity. Faces appeared in the water and quickly sank back under. The sounds of moaning echoed across the waters, followed by faint wails and whispers.

"Those are the lost souls who didn't have the coin to cross," Charon explained.

"Are they forever stuck in the river?" I asked, peering over the side of the ferry.

"If someone pays their token, then no," he replied. "They *have* to have a token."

I gazed into the waters, and my face began to distort, replaced by the face of Alpha that appeared on the surface. I quickly sat upright, afraid to peer into the murky depths again. What the fuck?

"It plays games with your head," Charon remarked. "It will show you things just to get you to touch the water, and then it poisons you."

The river led us deep inside the mountain, where it flowed a bit faster. The sun slowly disappeared from view, and there wasn't any light to guide our way. Charon struck a match and lit a lantern that hung from his punting pole. The light was enough to illuminate our surroundings, but only so far. We could barely make out that we were traveling down a dark tunnel.

"The water gets a bit rushed for a while as we cross over to the river Cocytus, so make sure you hold on. If you fall in the water, there is no saving you," he warned as the boat hit its first rapids.

The boat jerked and jostled as we moved rapidly down the dark, tunneled river. We all gripped the sides of the boat or held onto someone else who had a good hold onto the sides, so we didn't fall out. The boat hit one of the rapids and leapt into the air, crashing back down into the water. I nearly toppled out into the water as Asmodeus snatched my shirt and jerked me back into my seat. The boat began to spiral downward faster and faster, hitting more of the rapids that sent us into the air. The boat bounced off the walls as the river grew narrower. Red and purple hues streaked the turbulent water as sobs and laments drifted in the air. Grief gripped me deeply in my chest, and I felt like falling into the water to wash it away. Every single traumatic feeling I ever felt flowed through my core, drowning me in sorrow. The beatings. The starving. Feeling unsafe at all times. The unspeakable things they did to me in the dark. It all came crashing forward, and the air was sucked from my lungs as I doubled over in anxiety. I felt like I was back in the Nightmares and Shadows realm in the Otherworld, where all of those unseelies were committing suicide. I could easily just fall over the side of the boat, and all my problems would be solved. Everyone's problems would be solved. No one would have to worry if Damian went off the rails again. No one would have to baby me like the blubbering idiot I was. I could finally be at peace, and nothing that happened to me would matter anymore.

When the river leveled out flat again, the rapids ceased, and we were back on calm waters. The water looked pale and shimmery, as if the moon were casting a glow on its surface. It was utterly silent, almost numbing. Every despairing feeling I had felt melted away as fast as they had come on. The water was so peaceful and serene that it didn't even lap against the boat as we crossed it. Up ahead, there was a boat dock. Charon maneuvered the boat over toward it and docked.

"We have reached the river Lethe, and this is the end of the line for me," he said as he motioned for us to get out of the boat. "If you follow that passage over to your right, it will lead you to

Hades. Have fun haggling with him. He's been a real jerk lately."

"Thank you, Charon," I replied as I got out of the boat.

"Save the cosmos, kid, and I will thank you," he remarked, pushing the boat off from the dark and continuing on down the river until he was nowhere to be seen.

"Alright, game plan," Samael began as we gathered around him. "No one piss off Hades. Kiss his ass. Make him feel special. Refer to him as Lord of the Underworld." He looked at me. "And don't scare him off."

I rolled my eyes and shook my head. "I'm not a standoffish person."

"Have you met you?" Raphael chimed in with a chuckle. "You make every person mad, and then you get mad and lash out. Sounds familiar, too. Kind of like, I don't know, your dad."

I scowled and grunted. "I am nothing like Incaendiel." Everyone grew quiet, and I could only assume it was because I called him by his name.

"You know, it's ok to call him Dad," Azazel offered softly. "It might be weird, but he could use the pick me up from time to time. Alpha has put him through the wringer over and over. He doesn't need a mini tyrant running around making him feel like he's doing anything wrong. Especially when that something is being a father."

"We had a shitty father," Michael added. "I know he doesn't want to be anything like Alpha, so an encouraging word every now and then would work. Its new territory for him just as it is for you. Being lied to all this time about you is nerve-wracking. He would have burned the world down looking for you had he known you were his, and Alpha took you. Just like how he did when Luxina was taken. He didn't even know Alpha had you at all until you showed up with Lucifer and snatched Luxina. He found out about Xavier at the same time as well."

"Whatever," I groaned. "Can you all get off my back about this and focus on the mission?"

Samael pursed his lips and sighed. "Alright, let's get moving." Samael led us into the dark passageway. Every few spaces, buried in the wall, was a torch to light the walkway, but very dimly. As we walked, the only sounds we heard were our feet on the stone ground beneath us. It was eerily quiet and unsettling until a low growl cut through the silence of our walk, and we stopped in our tracks. We waited, listening to see if we could hear it again.

"What was that?" Samael whispered, studying the darkness ahead.

Another crackling growl emitted from the dark, and they all drew out their swords.

"I thought Hades was down this way. Not monsters," Michael whispered harshly.

"There's one monster that guards the gates," I answered quietly, squinting through the darkness to try and see any type of shapes lounging in it. "And we can't kill it, or we piss off Hades."

"What monster?" Asmodeus mumbled, readying his sword.

"Cerberus," I replied. As soon as I spoke his name, the monstrous three-headed dog broke through the dark, careening toward us. I pushed forth from the group and stood at the front, waiting for him to get close enough to tackle him to the ground. I was the strongest out of all of them, so I was the only one who could take him down without hurting him or getting hurt myself, or at least I hoped.

"Damian!" Asmodeus shouted, but it was too late.

I launched myself at Cerberus, grabbing hold of his fur below his neck. He snapped and snarled at me, each head trying to take a bite out of me. As I tried to pull him down to the ground, he lifted me from the floor as he shook his heads, trying to break my grip on him. I pulled my feet up, his teeth barely missing my feet just as I thrust myself upward and landed on the nape of his necks. I grabbed hold of his fur and jumped, bringing him to the ground below. I pushed his body against the wall and yelled, "Go!" to everyone. They rushed around us and stopped on the other side.

"Don't stop!" I ordered, struggling to keep the beast in check. "Get to Hades!"

“We can’t leave you!” Asmodeus refuted, stepping forward with his sword.

“Leave me!” I ordered, my eyes flashing power. “You can’t hurt his hellhound!”

Samael grabbed hold of Asmodeus’s arm and dragged him down the corridor. “Come on, everyone!” he shouted, and they all disappeared into the dark.

I lost my grip on Cerberus’s neck, and he smacked me into the adjacent wall. I thudded hard against the stone and slipped to the ground. He scrambled to his feet and walked over to me, saliva dripping from his bared fangs on all three heads. He put his snout right against my body as he growled and sniffed at me. I picked my hand up, and he snapped, pushing his one snout into my body as a warning.

“Who’s a good boy?” I purred to him, slowly raising my hand to scratch under his chin. He growled again but didn’t move. “Who’s a good boy?” I reiterated, baby talking to him. I scratched under his chin as he let out another lowly snarl before licking my face with his gigantic tongue. “That’s right. You’s a good hellhound, aren’t you?” I cooed, rubbing my hand across the fur on the top of his head and petting it.

Soon, all three heads were licking me as I scratched under each of their chins while calling them a good boy. His tail wagged, and he trotted back off into the dark from wherever he had initially sprang from. I was completely covered in gooey slobber, and no matter how much I tried to slosh it off, it stuck to me like glue. Once he was gone from sight, I began making my way to Hades' throne room to meet up with the others. When I walked in, they were surrounded by a fleet of nymphs all holding spears, pointing at them.

"And there's the final asset of Alpha's," Hades announced, standing from his throne. "Where is my dog?" he demanded, and the ground began to quake around us.

"He's fine," I replied, slopping off the saliva still running down my arms. "He scampered back off to his guard post."

"I don't believe you," Hades seethed, walking toward me. "Cerberus doesn't allow anyone passage unless I have declared we are having company."

I pursed my lips, then lifted my fingers to my mouth and whistled for him. He came bounding down the passageway and slid to a stop behind me. One of his tongues long licked me from the bottom of my back to the top of my head, once more drenching me in his sticky saliva. He walked beside me and sat down, all three heads panting.

"Feel better now?" I asked Hades while petting Cerberus's side.

"Impossible," Hades muttered with a scowl. "He obeys no one except—"

"Other gods?" I asked, interrupting him.

Hades' nose flared in contempt. "You are no god! You little half-breed angel!"

My eyes flashed their power at Hades, and I slowly walked toward him. "I am not a half-breed angel. I am one of the oldest gods in existence, and you *will* respect me as such."

"Caelvryn," he uttered as he slowly dropped to his knees with his hands raised. "Forgive me, my lord," he pleaded, placing his forehead to the ground. "If you're here, that must mean…"

"Yes, we are all here, and we are righting the wrongs of this universe," I answered in a voice I was unfamiliar with. I sounded the same way Incaendiel did when he used his god voice. "Justice shall be served against Alpha for his crimes against the cosmos."

"Divine justice?" Hades asked, looking up from the ground at me. "Vahr-Zul is here as well? Is'hari? Valiyren?"

"Yes," I answered. "And we seek an angel held captive in one of your pits."

Hades scrambled to his feet. "Lailah? Right?" he asked nervously.

I nodded. "Where is she?" I demanded.

"She is in the Fields of Punishment," a woman dressed in black stated, walking up to us. She was flanked by another woman and a man.

"Who are you all?" Michael asked, swatting the spear still thrust in his face.

"We haven't had the pleasure of meeting," she replied. "Guards, lower your weapons. That is no way to greet the Guardians of Light."

The guards all lowered their weapons and stepped back from the group.

"I am Ereshkigal," she said with a bow. "This is Hecate," she informed, pointing to the other woman dressed in black with an owl on her shoulder. "And this is Pabilsag," she informed, pointing to the man who was a dark shade of blue, holding a bow and arrow.

"Nergal is fine," he replied, raising his hand.

"I have waited *millennia* to finally meet you," Ereshkigal purred as she walked around.

"Why? I'm not that special," I muttered, shrugging my shoulders.

She giggled. "In due time, Caelvryn," she replied. "You will understand in due time."

I stared at her, confused, and was about to ask her what she meant when Samael interjected into the conversation, stepping forward. "Love how you two are getting acquainted, but we have a mission to complete. Remember, Damian," he urged, wide-eyed before turning his attention to Ereshkigal. "How do we get to the Fields of Punishment?" Samael inquired.

"Right now, you are in Erebus," Ereshkigal explained. "You have to walk to the ends of this realm and then follow the black road that splits off."

"But we warn you, it is not an easy walk," Hecate added, glancing between us all. "And I am afraid that once you pass the throne room here, your powers will no longer work," she said, looking at me.

"Why?" I asked as I walked over to her.

"This place exists outside of space and time," she explained. "It has its own pocket of magic set apart from the rest of the cosmos. Since time does not exist here, its existence predates the creation of gods and power. It is the land of the dead, and power doesn't radiate from those who are dead."

I nodded my head. "Understood." I turned to the group. "You all ready?"

They all nodded.

"Take that path," Ereshkigal stated, pointing to a road to the right that sat behind large, blackened gates.

"Thank you for your help," Raphael added as we began our trek from the Gates of Sheol.

"Oh, and Caelvryn?" Ereshkigal cooed. I turned around and continued walking backward to see what she wanted. "I will be seeing you again, hopefully soon. We have a lot to talk about, you and I." I turned back around, mulling over what she meant. Why would I be seeing her again? I don't plan on coming back here for any reason. Lailah is the only reason I am here now. What does she mean by that?

Samael nudged me as we walked, breaking me from my thoughts. "I thought I told you to stay cool?" he asked. "What was that about with Hades?"

"It worked, didn't it?" I replied. He narrowed his eyes at me. "Sorry, it just happens. I can't control it," I relented.

"Well, you need to work on self-control then," he reprimanded.

We all walked in complete silence, taking in the bleak and gloomy scenery. It was like walking through the galaxies, except that all the stars were gone. An eternal twilight, an endless dusk, surrounded us, and the mist that clung to the air muffled all sounds, including those of the rivers that crisscrossed to our left and right. They were sluggish here as opposed to the ones we saw coming in, and just as dark as the sky above, reflecting back the empty void. Soft moans and wails slipped through the cracks in the mist, casting an eerie, dreadful, somberness over the surroundings. The ground was cold and damp while ash, black earth, and shadows painted the land.

Along the banks, the souls of the newly departed gathered, waiting for Charon to grant them passage. He gave a short wave to us as he counted coins, sometimes pushing souls away who had no payment. Those who did not have payment for the boat or those who didn't have proper funeral rites wandered aimlessly around as shades. Sometimes moaning or wailing. Some faded into the mists, never to be seen again. Suicides or accursed dwelled on the fringes in its shadowy grove, along with the restless souls who lingered due to grief, vengeance, or unfinished business. Their whispers drifted in the heavy air, falling upon the deaf ears of those who sat and judged their fate.

Three judges stood off to the side, sorting souls for their proper passage. The ordinary souls went to the Asphodel Meadows. It was neither a place of reward nor punishment, but for the average soul to wander stripped of their memories, ambitions, or identities, waiting to be recycled back to the giving tree. Elysium was for the virtuous and heroic souls. It was paradise for heroes, demigods, and those who were beloved by the gods. Unlike the rest of Sheol, Elysium was like the paradise described as heaven. It had rolling green meadows, golden light, and fragrant gardens in an eternal season of spring. It was such a shame that beauty was reserved only for souls who were deemed worthy to live out in the Elysium. All souls should have a place there, instead of careful selection of their life's achievements to gain them favor among the judges. The Fields of Punishment and Tartarus were reserved for those who were wicked or evil during their lifetime, and their deeds determined which they landed. Violent criminals or tyrants who were mortal landed in the Fields of Punishment, while those who rebelled on a cosmic level against the gods and were either divine or half-divine landed in Tartarus. Like, had Hercules committed a heinous act that went against cosmic order, they would have shackled him in Tartarus as opposed to allowing him into the Elysium.

We carried on past the judges and followed the road as instructed when winged creatures cut through the skies above us. Blood dripped from their claws as their shrieks filled the sky.

"Keres," I muttered.

They began to drop one by one from the sky, grabbing at us with their claws. We all pulled out our swords and started swiping at them in the air. Raphael landed a blow on one of their taloned feet, cutting it clean off. It retreated, covering the area in its gushing blood. Another one dropped down from the air and ran its razor-sharp claw across Michael's forearm. He retaliated, slicing his sword through its wing. It dropped to the ground, and he walked over and cut its head off. More of them began to appear, making their way straight toward us. We would be here all day fighting them off if we stuck around any longer.

"There's the road!" Azazel yelled, pointing her sword toward the black cobblestone ahead.

We all made a run for it as the Keres continued their assault on us. Finally giving up the farther we ran down the cobblestone road, they turned their attention to some souls that had wandered off from the rivers and dove onto them, feasting endlessly as the souls howled in pain. As we ran down the path, the terrain grew rockier, and obsidian jutted from the path, tripping me as I ran. As I sat up and looked around, fire pits and sulfurous mists surrounded the road on either side. I could hear screams of agony, rage, and despair ahead of us down the winding trail. I climbed to my feet and caught up with the others just as they topped the crest of the route. A blasted wasteland sat on the other side with fiery chasms and rivers of boiling blood. Souls hung from cliffs while their bodies were being eaten away by the thunderous lightning that clashed against the bedrock. They screamed in torment as the electricity ran through them, scorching their skin and searing their insides.

The scorched plateau stretched on for miles under the starless sky as flames would burst from the clefts in the rock. The sound of chains rattled in the wind. Off to the side, souls writhed in ditches of both fire and frost, wailing and howling as their bodies burned and froze. More winged creatures hovered above the hellish wasteland, descending like hawks and tormenting the guilty souls, ripping them to shreds. The punishment here never ended.

"Furies," Samael hissed.

Damian! a voice shouted in my head.

Xavier? I asked in disbelief, momentarily distracted from my surroundings. It had been too long since I last heard his voice, and it was a breath of fresh air.

Luxina needs you! he urged. *I need you.*

How are you talking to me? Where are you? Why do you need me? I demanded.

I am in you, he replied. *Alpha is trying to separate me from Luxina, so I channeled into you.*

She needs you! I refuted. *Go back to her!*

If I go back, Alpha will extract me and put me inside Adam, he replied.

How is Luxina doing? What all has Alpha done to her? I demanded.

She's not doing well at all, he replied meekly. *Alpha is trying to break her with Adam. He has your twin flame bond with her, and it is so strong. You need to rescue her as soon as possible! Right now, he is harrowing her with monsters and demons while Adam is the knight in shining armor.*

What do you mean he has my bond? I seethed.

She is drawn to him like a magnet, and she cannot resist the pull, Xavier explained. *He is intoxicating, and even I cannot shake him whenever he is near. He's drawing her in like a moth to a flame, and the longer she is around him, the weaker she becomes to his temptations. She needs you!*

"Damian!" Asmodeus shouted, once again breaking me from my inner thoughts. "Get your head out of the clouds and back on the mission!"

I watched as everyone was being attacked by the Furies. Everything started spinning out of control as anxiety set in. He was doing it. He was doing exactly as I thought he would. He was using Adam to manipulate her. He was doing with Adam what he wanted to do with me, and Adam's bitch ass was falling right in line like the little stooge he was. Panic rose into my chest, and it started to get harder to breathe as I thought about Luxina, Adam, Alpha, where we were, and what was currently happening. I couldn't rein in my emotions and push them down deep any longer. I exploded in a howling rage. Everything around me slowed to a stop except for those in our group. Time stood still, and everything hovered in silence.

"I thought they said your power wouldn't work down here because of the space-time thing?" Raphael asked, looking around in amazement.

"I'm the god of time," I muttered. "Let's find Lailah and get the hell out of here. I have shit to do."

Everyone watched me as I pushed past them and hurriedly walked through the plateau. Off to the side was a cave, and it was the only place that matched what I saw through the Watcher's Eye, where they were holding Lailah. I marched over to it with the group hot on my trail. Inside, Aker and Berberos stood around Lailah. My freeze on time lifted, and they were startled at our sudden appearance, drawing their swords and pointing them at us.

"Well, if it isn't little Damian," Aker taunted. "We've been waiting for you." He looked over at Asmodeus. "And you, too. Traitor."

Lailah sat tied to a chair, unfazed by the whole ordeal.

"Just let her go, and you can walk out of here," I ordered, my patience already worn thin by everything.

Berberos laughed. "And what makes you think we would do that? You both have a bounty on your head, and we intend on collecting."

More Forsaken appeared behind them, foaming at the mouth for a chance to fight Asmodeus and me. I pulled my sword from its sheath and spun it around in my hand.

"Dealer's choice," I muttered.

I whipped the sword through the air, and it severed the heads of at least five of the Forsaken who stood behind Aker and Berberos before clattering to the ground. "Let's do this!" I shouted.

They all ran at us, and swords clanked against swords as they all fought. I dipped out and ran over to my sword, picking it up from the ground and bringing it up in the air just as Aker brought his down on me.

"It's going to be fun bringing Alpha your head," he sneered as he pelted me with sword strikes.

"I don't think you know this," I replied as my eyes began to glow. "But I'm not an angel anymore."

Icy flames erupted through my sword, and with each strike against his, it froze and chipped away at the blade until there was nothing left but the hilt. I pushed him against the wall of the cave and held my blade against his throat.

"You have two choices here," I muttered, the blade softly nicking his throat, leaving a trickle of blood cascading down his neck. "You can choose Alpha and die right here."

He struggled against my new strength. "What's the other option?" he asked, breathing heavily.

"Switch sides and join us," I replied.

"I would rather die!" he stammered, saliva dripping from his mouth.

"Fine. By. Me," I growled.

I released my hold on him, spun around while leveling my sword, and severed his head in one swift sweeping motion. I walked over to Lailah and untied her from the chair as the others finished off the last few remaining Forsaken. She stared up at me in horror and disgust.

"You *are* a monster," she spat, glaring at me.

"The monster who just released you from your prison," I snarled back.

I grabbed her arm to lift her from the chair, but she wrenched it away from me. "Don't touch me!" she ordered, staring daggers at me. I got close to her face and stared back as hatefully as I could muster.

"Lady, I don't have time for your bullshit," I hissed. I waved my hand, and a portal opened to Lightshade that I pointed to with my sword. "Now get your ass through the damn portal!"

CHAPTER FIVE: DAMIAN

WHEN WE EMERGED from the Sheol portal, it was a bloodbath in Lightshade. Nephilim and warlocks lay scattered across the ground, dead, and swarms of monsters from Tartarus were running rampant toward Incaendiel. He was luring them into the portal behind him.

"What the hell is going on!" I yelled as I tried to think of what to do.

Incaendiel stepped through the portal into Tartarus, and the opening filled with all of the monsters.

"Incaendiel, what are you doing?" I demanded, rushing toward the portal entrance.

"I have to use my power somewhere, and it can't be Lightshade!" he shouted back.

"Tartarus will cave in and either trap you forever or kill you!" I refuted as panic and grief tore through me once more.

"It's the only way!" he shot back.

"Don't do this!" I pleaded as he began to step through the portal entrance.

"Stand back!" he ordered, waiting for the last monster to surround him inside the portal.

He lifted his hand to snap his fingers to close the portal door.

"Dad! No!" I shouted as his fingers clicked against his palm.

The portal shut, and silence fell across the valley. The seconds ticked by like hours as I hit my knees and waited for him to come back, holding my breath. My heart thudded so hard against my sternum I thought it was going to explode. It felt like time had slowed, and the seconds ticked by in the most grueling and painstaking way. Then, I saw him appear off in the distance of the field where all the bodies lay. My grief and panic were quickly replaced by anger that rushed forth like a torrential storm, and I stood from my knees. I ran over to him and pushed him as hard as I could. Incaendiel stumbled back, and confusion spread across his face as I began to lay blow after blow against him with my fists, unleashing all the pent-up rage and wild emotions that swirled within me. The rage over Luxina. The rage over Alpha and Adam. The heartbreak. The panic. The grief. Everything bubbled to the surface, and I took it out on him.

"You could have been stuck forever!" I hollered. "Why would you do that?"

A blow caught him square in the jaw before he threw his arms around me and wrestled me to the ground.

"Let me go!" I yelled, kicking and screaming as my ice began to wrap up his arms. "Let me go! Let me go! Let me gooooo!" I didn't like to be touched. I didn't want to be touched. Every touch on my body felt like glass scraping my skin, sending me back to that dungeon where the chain gang used me like a drunken whore. My powers mounted, and I exploded in his arms. Everything went still as I froze time in its place while ice crept around the valley in perfect blue and white hues.

"You have to calm down!" he demanded, holding me as tightly as he could as I wiggled in his arms.

"You don't tell me what to do!" I cried, wrestling free from his arms as his heat melted the ice surrounding us. His arms were like suffocating pillows, and I gasped for every breath I sucked in as I struggled to free myself from him. I didn't even understand myself why I was so upset. I grappled with the idea of him being my father over and over. On one hand, at least it wasn't Lucifer, but on the other, I was still left to be raised by Alpha, and that pissed me off to no end. No one saved me. He didn't save me when I needed it the most, before they could…

"It was the only choice I had!" he defended. "I would have leveled Lightshade and killed everyone there!"

I stood to my feet and landed another punch to his jaw, leaving an icy bruise behind.

"Stop that!" he barked, his voice echoing and shattering the ice into crumbled shards.

Without even thinking, I raised my arms, and the shards rose in the air along with them. Tears streamed down my face in icy rivulets. He had chosen to abandon me to save everyone else. He had made a plan to go in there without knowing he would come back out okay. He left me as Luxina left me. Like my mother left me. Like Lilith left me in that cell where Alpha could do whatever he wanted to me. Where they could do whatever they wanted to me whenever they wanted. He left me like everyone always did. No one ever stayed.

"If you want to die so badly, why don't I just take you out right here and right now!" I cried, trying my best to be strong but feeling all too weak inside.

"I wasn't trying to die!" he explained as the shards all pointed toward him. "I was just trying to save everyone!"

"You're always trying to save everyone, no matter what the cost is to you!" I shot back, tears falling freely down my face. *No matter what the cost is to me.*

"Like father, like son!" he quipped.

"Stop calling me that!" I snarled and let the shards loose. *If I were your son, you wouldn't be so trigger-happy in getting yourself killed and leaving me behind for Alpha to take again.*

The shards each melted into puddles of water before they ever reached him, angering me even more.

"If you don't want me calling you that, then stop acting like it!" he retorted.

I couldn't take it anymore. Everything crashed down around me, and I hit the ground on my knees, heaving into my hands. "You're all I have," I cried. "If anything happens to you, there is no one left!" And it was true. Luxina was gone. I have never known Anniel as my mother. The only person I ever had was Alpha, and he was a sadistic bastard who got off on causing me pain. I was alone again in the world, and Incaendiel was my only lifeline, keeping me straight.

"No, Damian," he replied, walking over to him. "You have everyone. There's Asmodeus, who has been the only father—"

"That doesn't make him my father," I hissed, cutting me off. "I look up to him as a big brother, and I know he took care of me, but that doesn't make him my father. You are my father!"

I finally said it out loud. I finally admitted it to not just him but to myself. He was my father, and I had to let him in before it capsized me. He knelt before me and watched me intently as I rocked back and forth, my hands wrapped around my knees. He grabbed at me to pull me into his chest. I swatted his hands away and fought off his arms. He fought back until he had me pinned to him as I flailed my arms, hitting him in the back. I pounded my fists over and over until exhaustion swept across me. I stopped, and I let him hold me. I sank deep into his chest and heaved out my frustrations that I had let build and build. My freeze on time let loose, and everyone who was frozen still stood quietly as he rocked me back and forth, squeezing me as tightly as he could.

"I'm sorry," he whispered to me. "I had no idea…"

"Well, now you do," I cried, my voice cracking as I cried into his chest.

We sat there for what seemed like an eternity before I peeled myself from his arms. I looked up to see everyone watching us, and quickly swiped away the tears from my face. Incaendiel stood up and held out his hand to help me to my feet. I smacked it away and stood on my own. "Lailah is inside the cottage," I muttered and walked off.

My walk turned into a sprint, and I was running as fast as I could deep into the forest. Memories flashed through my head of when Luxina had taken off, and I had to run as quickly as I could to keep up with her. The thought of her made me push faster and harder. It was my fault that she was with Alpha. It was my fault that she was having to deal with him using Adam as a manipulation against her. She was being tortured. That was my fault. I could lose her love to Adam…

I cried out as I jumped in the air and let all of it out. My voice echoed through the trees, its power nearly toppling them with a sonic boom. I landed on my feet and slid to the ground, pounding it with my fist. I let out another deafening howl as the grief that had overtaken me on Charon's ferry bubbled to the surface again. Everything around me froze solid, and I beat my fists into the ice until they were bloody pulps. I ran my hands through my hair as the air started to grow light, and it became harder to breathe. I pounded my fists against the side of my head as I cried, slobber dripping from my open mouth and snot draining from my nose. I collapsed to the ground on my side, feeling empty and numb. I pushed my hands into the mounting snow piles, picked up the snow dust, and let it float in the wind. My breath left steam that clung to the air around me, even though it felt like icepicks in my lungs instead of air.

"Damian?"

I glanced up from the snow to see Asmodeus slowly inching his way over to me. Once he saw I was struggling to breathe, he ran over and scooped me up into his lap. He rubbed his hand against my breastbone.

"Breathe in," he instructed, and I did. "Breathe out." I exhaled.

He breathed with me, rocking me until my breathing came back to normal.

"What's going on?" he demanded as I shifted off his lap.

"Everything," I croaked as I wiped at the tears from my swollen eyes.

"Look, I didn't mean to yell at you earlier when we were on the mission," Asmodeus began, his eyes dropping to the ground in regret.

"It's nothing you did," I reassured him. "It's just everything. Luxina is in trouble, and I don't even know how to save her or even where Purgatory is located."

"How do you know Luxina is in trouble?" Asmodeus inquired seriously.

"Xavier told me," I answered, sniffling and wiping my nose.

"How did Xavier tell you?" he demanded, alarmed. "I thought he was part of Luxina now."

"He had to escape her and find me," I explained. "Alpha is trying to extract him to put him inside of Adam."

"So that assumption checked off with what he wanted with her," Asmodeus sneered.

"That's not all," I began and swallowed the lump forming at the back of my throat.

"What else is there?" he prodded.

"Adam does have my twin flame bond energy," I answered quietly. "Xavier said that neither Luxina nor he could resist it."

Asmodeus shook his head. "I don't believe it. Luxina loves you dearly. You don't have to worry about him winning over her heart." He jumped up from his seat, angry. "Why is Alpha such a sick and twisted father?" he demanded out loud. "He did this crap with Incaendiel and Anniel. Over and over. It was disgusting. And now, he plans to try and do it to you and her."

"I don't even know where to start to stop any of this," I stated, picking at a blade of grass.

"I do," Asmodeus offered with a shrug. "Chernobyl. We can leave now and check it out. See if Alpha left behind the location of Purgatory and all. See if he left anything behind."

"Really?" I asked, perking up a bit. "You would come with me?"

"Of course!" Asmodeus shouted with a laugh. "I'd follow you into battle anywhere, kid."

I nodded with a smile and stood up. I snapped my fingers like Incaendiel had, and a portal appeared in front of us. We could see the field outside of Chernobyl through the glassy door. We stepped through and immediately ran for the abandoned nuclear factory. We started room by room and went through everything Alpha had left behind for clues as to where he went next. I scoured through all of the rubble that was left behind from the Forsaken fighting against one another. They had all chosen a side, the leader they wanted to follow. Some chose Alpha, and some chose me. Once again, brother had been pitted against brother. I made my way to Alpha's office and slid the door open slowly. I glanced around on edge, expecting to be caught going into his office unattended. The room was a wreck. I picked through papers lying aimlessly on the floor, trying to find where Alpha could have gone, but I came up empty-handed. I walked to his desk and rummaged through the files that sat on top of the desk.

Anger brimmed to the surface, and I swiped everything off with my hands. A lamp and miscellaneous items hit the floor with a thud as I braced myself against the desk, fighting back the urge to smash everything in the room. *They should have been here! Why weren't they here?!* My eye caught a piece of paper sticking out from one of the drawers. I tried to open it, but it was locked. I grabbed hold of the drawer and yanked it hard, breaking the mechanism that kept it in place. It slid open, and my eyes landed on a gold mine of information.

Every single creature, beast, and experiment Alpha had created and conducted was in this drawer. I pulled out the heaping stacks of papers and plopped them on the desk. I grabbed the seat of the chair that he haplessly sat in while he worked from behind the desk and began to skim through all of his notes. Every single thing he had made was cataloged with what injection was given, what type of creature from which it was bred, everything. It had a list of their weaknesses, their strengths, and whatever special powers he had given them were also included.

I rummaged through a closet to the left of the desk and found a duffel bag. I quickly shoved all of the information I had acquired into the bag to take back with me to Lightshade. We would have the upper hand with this kind of knowledge. I looked in the drawer once more and found a few more things. There were the plans for the iron heart I had seen in a brief glance last time I was in here. I stuffed that in the bag along with all of the other files at the bottom of the drawer. As I lifted the last bit of paper, I noticed the bottom of the drawer had a false bottom to it. I carefully pried it up just in case it was a spring trap and stood back, awaiting some sort of climactic ambush as the last attempt from Alpha to stifle me.

Nothing happened. I leaned over the drawer and peered inside it to see what was so crucial that

Alpha had to hide it at the bottom of a locked drawer. There was a large box at the bottom. I picked the box up and turned it over in my hands. It didn't have a lock to open it with a key. It looked as if it had no lid seams either. *How do you even open it?* I shrugged, stuffed the box in the bag, and zipped it up. As I was about to walk out of the room, I noticed a map on the wall with different pinpoints marked with pushpins. They were all different colors and dispersed over the entire planet. I grabbed a pen from the floor and a piece of paper I had thrown from the desk, and began tracing the map, taking note of the longitude and latitude points where the pushpins were placed. After I had a rough copy of the chart, I flicked my fingers and set the trash on the floor on fire. No one would use this building ever again if I had any say in it.

The room roared to life as the fire quickly devoured the paper, and soon it raged, consuming everything in its path. I quickly snaked my way through the halls and out of the building as the fire chased after me. I sat in the meadow and watched my prison burn to the ground in earth-shattering explosions with glee. Whatever chemicals had been stored there by humans were flammable and merciless to the structure that held them captive.

"Were you able to find anything?" Asmodeus called out over the roaring flames.

"Everyone was right," I declared in defeat. "There's nothing really here. But I grabbed some stuff that might be useful. I also found a map that I made a copy of."

"We'll find her," Asmodeus consoled. "Together."

He extended his hand out to me and helped me to my feet. I grabbed the duffel bag of paperwork I had snagged from inside and tossed it over my shoulder. Asmodeus and I hadn't spoken much in the last couple of weeks since his arrival. I wasn't sure why, but it probably had to do with all of the changes. I had no clue if he feared me now or not because he kept his thoughts pretty quiet while around me. Going with him to Sheol was the first time we had been together longer than a few minutes. I really needed this adventure with him after my monumental meltdown in front of everyone. They might not have seen it all, but I am sure Incaendiel told them all about it when they prodded him about it.

"What's in the sack?" he asked, staring at it.

"A monster," I smirked.

He scowled, squinted his eyes, and furrowed his brows in annoyance as I chuckled.

"It's paperwork Alpha had hidden away in his desk drawer. He cataloged every single thing he ever created or experimented on with a long list of useful information we could use to defeat them," I replied, patting the bag in triumph.

"Yeah?" Asmodeus asked, surprised.

I nodded. "I also have the blueprint of that iron heart or whatever it is I had caught a glimpse of before. I bet that is what he put in that giant iron, whatever," I stammered.

"We'll give them a look over when we get back to Lightshade. We need to get a move on before the fire draws attention to this place while we are still here. There's no telling who Alpha has staking this place out. For all we know, he controls the mortals around here as well to guard the place," Asmodeus warned as he began to walk from Chernobyl.

"What's so bad about mortals?" I goaded.

"I am not allowed to harm them even in self-defense," Asmodeus replied. "We took an oath never to harm humans when we fell. I still stand by that oath."

"Oh, well, that would be problematic, then," I offered. "Let's get going."

We started trudging our way through the meadow. It was so similar to the one near Potter's Field that I found myself lost in thought, remembering the last time I had been there. It was when Luxina and Xavier became one to save me. She tried so hard to free me from Alpha, and I let him get inside my head, knowing very well that she loved me and wanted me. When she had touched my forehead, I felt every single emotion she had ever felt toward me. Every memory of me flowed through my mind. She had loved me without even knowing she loved me. And when I saw her crumpled on the ground, the field and tree on fire from her self-destructive emotions after absorbing Xavier, I felt helpless, hopeless. But I felt everything from her. I should never have let words replace what I had actually felt from her.

A strange noise snapped me from my thoughts as Asmodeus and I came to a halt walking through the towering wheatgrass. We both scoured the field as the wind blew, the wheatgrass bending back and forth in the slight breeze. We stood still and silent for a moment without seeing anything that matched whatever we had heard. We began our silent trudge, paying closer attention to our surroundings.

"Something doesn't feel right," Asmodeus whispered, taking each step carefully and methodically through the field.

"I completely agree," I mumbled, glancing to and fro.

There was nothing but this tall wheatgrass for acres. There weren't too many spots to exactly hide unless whatever tripped our senses was lying like guerrillas in the grass waiting to pounce. An almost electrical feeling filled the air along with a type of hum.

"I know that sound," I mumbled. "We need to leave now!"

We both sprinted to the edge of the wheatfield, where the towering silver birches swayed silently in the breeze as the hum grew louder. We crouched down in the brush as the flying beasts I had encountered in the arena circled the skies in the area.

"You're cloaked, right?" Asmodeus asked, grabbing his weapon and readying it.

"I don't even know how to cloak anymore. I am a god now, remember?" I hissed. "I think Alpha has been patrolling the area every so often to see if I would come and look for Luxina."

As the creatures approached, I saw Incaendiel in the air as well. He was using his powers to incinerate the creatures, but was also too close to the burning nuclear factory.

"Oh, shit," I mumbled as Incaendiel exploded in an atomic fireball, setting off a nuclear reaction in the area.

"Quick, behind me!" I ordered Asmodeus as the wave of energy pushed our way.

I didn't know exactly what I was doing, but I threw my hand up, and a translucent shield-type thing popped up in front of me as the fires reached us. The shield surrounded us on all sides as the fires burned around it, unable to penetrate the force field I had created. Once the fire had stopped rolling over us, I dropped my hand, and the bubble disappeared. Fire and smoke surrounded us as the trees burned. The fire slowly receded as Incaendiel withdrew his power, and a leveled wasteland was all that was left of the place. I looked around in the smoke-filled sky but couldn't see him. Asmodeus tapped my shoulder and pointed off into the field. Incaendiel walked slowly, looking around. When his eyes landed on us, he ran over as fast as he could and grabbed me to his chest.

"I thought I had killed you both," he breathed in relief.

"We are ok," I replied, pulling back from him.

"What are you doing here?" he asked, shaking his head and squinting his eyes at me. "This could have been a trap for you, like it was for Luxina."

"I had to come and find clues to find her," I answered.

Empathy settled across his brows as he understood my predicament. "Did you find anything?"

"I found a lot of stuff," I said, holding up the bag draped across me.

"Alright, well, let's get back to Lightshade then," he ordered with a snap of his fingers.

Instead of a portal opening, we were just immediately back in Lightshade.

"How did you do that?" I asked with a scowl. "Why can't I do that?"

"Practice," he smirked and then winked.

CHAPTER SIX: LUXINA

I STARTLED AWAKE as I felt eyes on me. I shot up from the ground where I had been sleeping to find Alpha peacefully gazing at me while sitting on a boulder.

"You look just like your mother," he cooed as he watched me. "Has anyone ever told you that?"

"Everyone tells me that," I muttered. "What do you want from me?"

He watched me as if amused by me. "When Lilith and I created your parents, we took on just one of them to train by themselves," he began. "I chose your mother because Incaendiel despised me, and we needed to train them while they were fully awake, both psyches at once. It took a lot for me to break her, but even in her obedient state, she still loved your father more than anything else. She often grappled with the dilemma I had placed her in. We spoke about it often."

"What does this have to do with me?" I asked, annoyed.

"Because apparently you have placed Adam in the same predicament Anniel finds herself in," Alpha mused. "He was very upset when he returned and finally asked me if I would ever order him to kill you."

"And what did you tell him?" I inquired, furrowing my brows at him.

"I didn't have an answer for him because I don't know," Alpha replied, standing up. "Technically, I have never given the order for your mother to kill your father. Her orders are to protect me at all costs from whoever tries to harm me. But if her orders were to kill him, then we wouldn't be here right now having this little chat."

He bent down in front of me, looking my face over. "I don't ever want to hurt my children, and by extension, that means you all as well."

"Then why does Damian have a kill order on his head?" I spat, glaring at him.

Alpha stood up and walked back over to the boulder. "I raised Damian. I loved Damian. And Damian betrayed me. It wasn't that he was disobedient like Adam believes," he began. "Damian chose your father over me. He had long chosen your father over me. I don't think he even realized it." He stopped for a moment. "Damian hates me just as much as your father does, if not more. I admit, I let the Forsaken have too much fun with his punishment when I should have stepped in and stopped it. It went too far, and that is my fault. I hit a point of no return with him, and I accept that." He turned around to face me. "But I did not issue a kill order on Damian. In fact, I have told Adam repeatedly that Damian is off limits unless it comes down to the final battle, and we can't reach a peaceful agreement with one another."

"How do you expect me to believe that?" I asked, shaking my head. "Adam said—"

"Adam lies!" Alpha growled. "Adam is power hungry. More so than myself. He wants Damian's abilities and doesn't care what the cost is to get them."

"So you've created a real monster," I stammered. "Another little brat who you can't control, but instead of him having a kind heart of gold like Damian, he is a cold, relentless killer. Besides, how do I know you're not the one lying, Mr. Grand reality manipulator?"

"Has he already gotten under your skin, Luxina?" Alpha pressed, holding his balled-up fist under his chin. "Are you falling for his act?"

"I'm not falling for anything," I retorted angrily. "I am simply looking at all the facts that have built up in your wake of destruction. You don't have the perfect track record."

He walked back over to me and leaned down. "Whatever you do, you must not give in to the temptations he presents. He is the grand deceiver, and you are his prey. Whatever he tells you isn't the truth."

"Why are you telling me all of this?" I demanded. "What's the point?"

"If he cannot get Xavier's power from you, or Damian's power, and claim it as his own, he will be coming after me," he replied with dead-set eyes. "And I have more power in me than most gods do. I have spent millennia siphoning it slowly from others. He will be an unstoppable force, one even you or anyone else can put an end to."

"And what do you want me to do about it?" I asked, cocking an eyebrow.

"I want you to kill him!" Alpha whispered harshly, staring intensely into my eyes. "Before, he kills us all!"

***

"How are we doing today?" Adam asked, portalling in while I sat still, thinking over what Alpha had told me.

"I thought I told you I didn't want you here," I grunted, rolling my eyes.

He held up a plate. "I brought a peace offering." He walked over to me and handed it over.

I gazed down at the treats on the plate. "Macaroons," I murmured. "They're my favorite. How did you know that?"

"Lucky guess," he replied with a shrug as he sat down. "Although, I don't know why they're your favorite. I tried one, and they're not all the hype."

"Hype?" I asked, munching on one of them. "Another human word. Belphegor again?"

He laughed. "Yeah, you caught me."

I set the plate down on the ground and stared intensely at him. "I need you to not lie to me," I began. "Whatever I ask, you tell me the truth."

"Last time we played this game, you got mad," he mumbled in reply.

"It's important," I reaffirmed. "I need to know."

"Ok," he relented. "Just don't make me leave again. I miss spending time with you."

I half-heartedly smiled at him. "Did Alpha give you a kill order on Damian?"

"When the time comes, and he asks me," he began.

"That's not what I asked," I said, interrupting him. "Has he told you that when the time comes, I am going to give you the nod for you to go ahead and kill him?"

"No, we do not have a preplanned kill order," he replied.

I breathed in deeply. "That's not what you told me before."

"Why are you acting so strange?" he demanded. He peered closely at me. "Father has been by to see you, hasn't he?" I didn't answer. "You must not listen to him. He lies!" he insisted.

"Let me read your thoughts freely," I requested. "Then we can see who is lying and who is not."

"No," he answered flatly.

"That makes you look guilty," I retorted, scrunching my face.

"I don't care. You can either take me at my word or believe others. No one will ever have access to my mind," he insisted, and grabbed my hand. "Please, believe me, Luxina. I would not lie to you."

His touch was my only weakness in this place. The electricity that ran through our hands pulled me in deeper than I wanted to go. I was drowning in his amber eyes, warm and familiar in all the wrong ways. Alpha's words echoed in my mind. *"You must not give in to him."* But even his words couldn't anchor me as I leaned in closely to Adam's face. Neither my body nor bond cared that it was Adam and not Damian who I hovered in front of me, our bodies barely grazing one another, the radiating energy like a memory from long ago. He reached out with his one hand and lightly touched my cheek, dragging his finger down my jaw and neck, sending prickling goosebumps down my spine, and I openly invited the touch. He grabbed me by the hips and pulled me into his lap. He lifted my arms around his neck as desire wrapped me in rippled confusion. I couldn't help but invite him in. His mouth found mine, like soft rose petals after a morning rain, stealing the breath from my lungs with each fevered movement. He pushed my arms from around his neck and pinned them to the stone wall behind me. With his free hand, he trailed his fingertips down my body. I gasped lightly as his presence overwhelmed me, and every moment close to him sent fire through my spine. His kiss deepened, and our souls sparked against one another as hot, useless tears slipped from my eyes. I rocked back and forth in his lap against his hand. Just as I was about to topple over the threshold, I heard his voice. The voice I have been desperate to hear.

Luxina, Damian uttered.

"Damian," I called out as I erupted in shivers, his voice breaking me from the trance, like shattered glass.

Adam pushed away from me. Anger boiled beneath the surface of his eyes. "He's always in the way," he muttered. He spun around and vanished through a portal. Once he was out of range of me, I regained my senses.

"Oh no." I ran my hands through my hair. "What have I done?" I cried, tears slipping out one by one. "Damian, I am so sorry," I heaved in sobs.

It's not your fault, he whispered to me. *Everything that happens is and will be my fault. Whatever happens, I forgive you.*

I spent the next several hours crying while Damian cooed to me how sorry he was and how much he loved me. I hoped that, with everything in me, Adam wouldn't return because I couldn't deal with him anymore. I don't know what spell he worked on me, but I couldn't fight any temptation about him, and I hated it. This was something more than just the twin flame bond. I had no thoughts of my own around him, and every action felt like I was compelled to do it instead of doing it willingly. Everything with Damian was willing. Everything with Adam felt completely and utterly wrong, forced even.

I fell asleep to Damian whispering to me. They had a plan to come and get me. I only hoped it would be as soon as he assured me, but considering I can't even leave this place, I doubt it will be easy for them to even get through the other six terraces of Purgatory or through the abyss.

***

I don't know how long I was asleep until I woke up to the sounds of snarling and growling. I scrambled to my feet, glancing around in the dark. My chest had healed enough for me to be able to maneuver around, but I was still left defenseless without my powers. I caught the gleam of a sword off near the boulder that Alpha had sat on and ran over to it, snatching it up from the ground. As soon as I picked it up, the first monster stepped forward. It looked like those rabid werewolves Alpha had created for Damian's arena. He had described them in enough detail that I could pick them out of a crowd of creatures. Its saliva sizzled as it hit the ground, moving each foot slowly as it advanced toward me. It dug its feet into the ground and launched at me. I jumped out of the way as it missed me and grabbed the fur on its side, pulling myself up on its back. I shoved the sword through the nape of its neck and severed its spinal column. It hit the ground dead.

I pulled the sword from its carcass, then barreled off its back and prepared for the next one.

Red eyes emerged in the dark as snarls and snaps echoed in the inky void. Screeches filled the air as a creature with wing-like feet began to hobble toward me quickly. I swung the sword and chopped its head off. With the scent of blood in the air, every beast that surrounded me howled and cried for food. I wished I had my dueling swords. I could use them much better than a long sword.

I slashed and hacked away at every single monster that came for me. Bodies piled up around me, and I was growing tired from the constant fight. I was caught off guard, and one of them knocked me down from behind. As I rolled over, it pinned me down to the ground, crushing me underneath it; my only defense was using the sword as a shield as it snapped at my face. I could hardly breathe from the weight of it pushing against my lungs. Before I knew it, the creature was lifted off me. As I drew in a ragged breath, I saw Adam fighting the beasts off like he had the first time.

One by one, he took them down with ease, hardly breaking a sweat when they were all killed. He walked over to me and reached his hand out for me to grab so he could help me up.

"Don't touch me!" I hissed as I retreated from his outstretched hand.

"What's your problem?" he protested. "I just helped save you!"

"I don't know what you do when you touch me or what special ability you have that no one knows about, but don't touch me anymore. I don't like it," I replied.

"You seemed to like it last time I was here," he spat, tossing the sword to the ground.

"I feel forced to do whatever you want to do every time you touch me!" I stammered. "Don't touch me again!"

"Fine," he said, holding his hands up in the air. "I won't touch you again."

"You didn't have to help me," I muttered, standing up from the ground. "I could have taken them all on. I had been taking them all on."

"You were being crushed by it!" he squealed. "It could have killed you!"

"I can take care of myself!" I hissed. "I don't need people to save me. I am *not* a damsel in distress."

"Well, without your powers, you pretty much are," he taunted, curling his lip up sarcastically.

"I was trained to fight on my own," I refuted. "I. Don't. Need. You!"

"It's not about need!" he yelled. "It's about want, and you can't deny that you want me. You want me every time I walk in this room."

"And when you leave, I am disgusted with myself!" I snapped. "I feel dirty. I feel wrong. It feels wrong. And it feels like it's forced on me without a choice."

He stepped closer to me, and my breathing kicked up. Just being in proximity to him made me ache. "Are you sure about that?" he whispered in my ear. "Because I am pretty sure I can feel your response to me just being close."

"And I don't want it!" I cried. "I don't want you!"

He glared at me. "It's because Damian is still in the picture, right?" he demanded. "Well, I can take care of that."

"What do you mean?" I asked, chasing after him. "What do you mean?"

"I will take him out of the equation," he answered callously. "And then you won't have any regrets, any shame, and you can fully accept the desire that blossoms for me whenever I walk in the room."

"Please don't hurt him," I pleaded, tears brimming in my eyes. "I'm sorry. I'm sorry. Please, just leave him alone."

Let him come for me! Damian demanded. *Don't you let him use me against you. I can take care of myself against that twit. Let him come!*

I don't want you getting hurt! I protested.

He is hurting you! And using you and doing... Damian stopped. *If I see him, I will kill him, Luxina. Let him come to me!*

I can't risk everyone in Lightshade being hurt again, I replied meekly.

If he touches you again, I swear my hand to the cosmos, I will hang his head on the wall.

"Stay with me?" I asked Adam sweetly. "And we can talk."

Luxina! Damian hissed.

"Talk about what?" Adam asked as he stepped closer to me.

"Anything that you want to talk about," I replied, smiling at him.

I won't let him hurt you, I said to Damian.

This is letting him hurt me, Damian retorted and disappeared.

Adam smiled. "Well then, I have a story to tell you."

I made sure to keep my distance and not let him touch me as we both sat down on the ground. "In the beginning," he began. "The first beings leapt to life from the dark void. Their names were Tul-Ama and Kharuun."

CHAPTER SEVEN: LUXINA

HIS THUMB RUBBED against my bottom lip, slightly tugging it as his other hand pulled me into his embrace. The pulsating energy in the air of Purgatory clung to my skin like electrical bursts of enticement. He peered deeply into my eyes, his amber eyes burning like a thousand suns while being cooled by the rushing waves of an ocean. Instead of shying away from his touch, I eagerly invited every moment of it. I pressed myself into him as our kiss deepened. I had never felt this need before, this want.

As his mouth moved from mine and down my neck, I fell into the moment. I bit my bottom lip as he picked me up. He ran his hands through my hair as I gazed at him. And just as quickly as it had begun, it came to a screeching halt when I woke up. I rose from my lying position, drenched in sweat and desire coursing through me. Sometimes the dreams were of Adam, sometimes they were of Damian. Other times, they are about them both at once, as if I was being forced to choose but absolutely couldn't settle on just one of them. And each time, my skin is on fire, not with just yearning but the longing driving so deep within me, I erupt in flames, unable to control anything about my person.

I sat there, breathing heavily, trying to quiet the jittery need for someone's touch. It had been days since Adam had been by, or at least it felt like days. There was no perception of time in this place. It's almost as if it moves quickly while simultaneously standing still. The air pressed down on me, making everything I felt even more intense. I felt like I was drowning in a pool of want and need. There were times I couldn't decipher whether the moment was a dream or if it was happening in real time. Everything had blurred together. The only thing consistent was the growing need blossoming in me.

"Luxina," Adam spoke as he stepped through a portal.

While fear still tickled the back of my brain, the heat blooming under my skin, sharp and immediate, chased it down into the farthest recesses of my head. The hairs on the inside of my ears perked up, and goosebumps rippled my body just from hearing him speak my name. I swallowed hard as I watched him walk to me, a smile tracing his lips, not quite reaching his eyes, and gazing at me with a bemused look. His chiseled face seemed to glow in the gloom and doom of the terrace, and I hated how easily my eyes trailed from his face down his shirtless chest. I had memorized every line, every ab, and every muscle, and could feel myself ready to break as my eyes landed on his belt buckle.

"Hello, Adam," I mumbled, my voice thinner than I meant it to be as I tried to refrain from eagerness, pressing my legs together.

My eyes snapped quickly back up to his as I fought with everything in me to calm myself in his presence. It was wrong, and I knew it, but I couldn't control any of the mounting feelings I had for him running through my chest and head. The heat thickened as he drew closer, pressing against my lungs. My body reacted before my mind could even ring the warning bells of danger, pulse skidding, and breath stuttering.

"Sorry, it's been a while since I came to visit," he offered as he walked closer to me. The static clung to me like wet clothes as his presence intensified the atmosphere. "I had some things I needed to take care of," he continued, and I watched beads of sweat form on his bare chest from the humid air that swallowed me.

I nodded. "That's ok," I breathed, swallowing again as my chest rose and fell rapidly.

I couldn't peel my eyes away from his body, so I bit my lip while wringing my hands together. I squirmed uncomfortably underneath his gaze.

He narrowed his eyes, watching me. "Are you ok?" he asked, inspecting me more closely.

I nodded and squeaked, "Yes." I knew my actions and my appearance had to present a completely different answer to him. In that moment, it felt like time was frozen as I slowly inhaled and exhaled, the sound echoing louder in my ears as I gazed at him.

"You seem… off," he insisted, scrunching his face. "Are you sure?"

I couldn't answer, even though I quietly screamed inside to run as far away from him as I could. The pressure in my chest was unbearable, like something inside of me was squalling in hopes of being let loose. I needed him too suddenly, too violently, and the realization terrified me and at the same time, beguiled me. I couldn't take it anymore. I launched myself from the ground, closing the distance between us as I barreled into his bare chest, reaching my hand around his head and pulling him in for a kiss. The moment my hands found him, the world narrowed. There was no room for thought, only the aching crave for sensation that shattered me deep within my pelvis. Heat. Friction. The dizzying relief of contact quelled the throbbing need that flushed my body. He was taken by surprise and pulled back a little, but I kept my grip on him, and he relented.

He pushed me against the cave wall as I dragged my fingers up and down his chest. This all felt inevitable, like the terrace itself had leaned in to watch. I was no longer choosing, and I didn't know if that made it better or worse. He pulled my head to the side and kissed my neck, quickly bringing my head back and running his mouth over mine. His touch frenzied me, and there was no control over it; it was so soft but rough at the same time. There wasn't a moral dilemma that broke me from the moment. There wasn't an earth-shattering revelation of a voice popping into my head. It was only me, primal and processing feelings I didn't quite understand. I hadn't needed another person within my personal space more than I did in this very moment. I needed to feel wanted. I wanted to feel consumed. Desire flooded me in waves that refused to crest, refused to break. Every moment only sharpened the hunger instead of easing it, my body demanding more even as something in me quietly recoiled. I grasped his hair in my hand while our mouths pressed harder and harder as the kiss became more frantic and intense. There was no hesitation, no guilt. It didn't exist at this point in my head. There were no thoughts of this being wrong. There weren't any thoughts of Damian. It was just Adam and me in the moment, and we tumbled into one another.

At first, it hurt, but as his body moved against mine, my hips met every single thrust with urgency. Soft explosions rippled my skin as it tingled under his hands. His nails dug into my hips as my nails left scratches down his back with soft moans and pants. Every breathless wave of pleasure left me wanting and needing more of him. I pulled his hips to me as I pushed harder against his body, crying out in blissful tears in his ear. He shuddered and groaned, collapsing on top of me, running his thumb across my lips before kissing them.

When we finally collapsed together, my skin still burned. We lay together on the floor, my body wrapped around his, both of us heavy breathing. I had thought that once everything had been said and done, the feelings I felt would go away. The ache inside me hadn't dulled, but instead, it had grown teeth. Desire pressed harder against me, and I felt like I was suffocating. *This should have been enough,* I thought distantly. But it wasn't. There wasn't any calming of my erupted flames. The pressure only intensified, flames licking higher beneath my skin, until the need blanketed me. The more I desired, the hotter and larger the flames grew across my skin. I needed more. It wasn't a want or a mere desire. I needed to feel it all again. I had to rid myself of the pressure this place had placed on my shoulders. And the only fathomable answer was to give in to the temptation it presented to me over and over, chance after chance. The terrace didn't want satisfaction. It wanted surrender.

"Your skin is beautiful when it glows with firelight," Adam murmured as he stroked my hair. The sound of his voice snapped something inside of me.

"Shut up," I demanded as I sat up and climbed over him, straddling his hips.

"What are you doing?" he asked, surprised.

I didn't answer. Instead, I bent down and kissed him again, starting everything all over again. The terrace welcomed me back without judgment. And again. And again. And again.

***

Adam stood up and began to put his clothes back on.

"Where are you going?" I asked more perplexed than I intended.

"I have to get back to Father," he replied as he buckled his belt. "I will be back again," he cooed with a wicked grin before kissing me.

"Please don't go," I implored. I crawled to him on my hands and knees. "Please."

"I will be back," he reassured before popping a portal up and leaving.

I was once again alone, and the itchy feeling of needing his touch crawled across my skin like spiders. I felt like at any moment I would burst, much like when we ascended when I was first taken. My skin began to burn like molten lava, desperate for some alleviation. Once again, I felt encased and blanketed by the pressure of the air as sweat began to bead and drip down my body. The rivulet trails seemed to touch me in all the erogenous places, leaving me shaking in need and want. The thought of escape was a distant echo as I wallowed on the ground, unable to soothe myself in the ways Adam relieved me. What if he doesn't come back? What if he left me here indefinitely this time as a steaming pile of lust? The thought of Adam not returning nearly toppled me over the edge in an anxious fury.

"Luxina?" his voice called out in the dark.

I snapped up from the ground as Damian emerged from the shadows. Indescribable emotions barreled through me as I clambered as quickly as I could to my feet and ran to his open arms. I threw myself into him as he wrapped his arms tightly around my body. I cried into his chest, which I hadn't noticed was bare until the wetness of my tears moistened my face. It was unusual for him not to have a shirt on, but at that moment, I didn't care. He pulled me away from his body and looked deeply into my eyes.

"I have missed you so much," he murmured as he dragged a thumb lightly across my bottom lip.

He leaned in and kissed me, and I welcomed the kiss as a range of emotions bubbled to the surface. Desire. Relief. Shame. Anxiety. Fear. More desire. His hands on my body cooled the licking flames edging me. Even though something tugged at the back of my mind that something was off, I pushed it aside quickly and wrapped my hands through his hair. His skin began to glow a luminescent blue that mingled with my fiery ambience as our kiss deepened between us. Everything in the world stopped. I felt complete. I felt the genuine desire I had for him emerge as his hands twisted around in my hair. Each kiss he planted on my lips was like salty waves from the ocean mixed with a heady musk. I pulled him tighter to my body as my flames erupted and burned wildly out of control. Nothing felt rushed or erratic like it had with Adam. It felt right. It felt good. It felt like everything I had wished it to feel like. It was perfect in every way possible. Instead of blistering kisses, it was cooling waters that enveloped me.

Finally, he was mine, and I was his, and we interlaced together in perfect balance. "I love you so much, Damian," I cooed in his ear. "I hope you know that and can feel that in this moment."

He ran his hand across my cheek and smiled. And we fell into one another again. Butterflies erupted in my chest as I let every urge I had ever had with him consume me. I touched his cheek and then his chest, which had always been off limits. The abuse Alpha had inflicted left him riddled with personal qualms, and being touched was one of them. Occasionally, I could graze his skin, but right now, he let me trace every part of him willingly and without faltering, with his trust in me not to hurt him. And I fell asleep peacefully in his arms, something I had not had in what seemed like forever. I was at home, in the arms that would burn the world down for me, and it was so serene.

CHAPTER EIGHT: DAMIAN

I LAY IN BED feeling the weight of exhaustion straddle every bone in my body. The only thing on my mind at that point in time was Luxina. I was angry at myself for putting her in the position she now found herself. It was only going to get worse for her, too. Alpha and his torments made me sick to my stomach. Adam was most likely violating her right now, and the thought of it made my skin crawl, and my stomach do flip-flops. I sat up in bed and began pacing my room. Even though I was tired, I had this manic energy that wouldn't go away. I put my boots on and headed out to the sparring arena. Maybe a couple rounds with someone would clear my head enough for me to sleep some. I walked around until I found someone waiting for a sparring partner. I couldn't see who it was until they turned around. It was Elisha, one of the Nephilim, who was a late joiner.

"Waiting for a partner?" I asked as I walked closer toward her.

"Yes!" she replied with a relieved laugh. "I thought I was going to wait forever for someone to choose to spar with me."

I laughed and picked up a sword. "Well, let's get to it then."

She nodded and picked up dueling swords, and soon, we were dancing around the arena just as I had done with Luxina when I started training her. Elisha didn't hold back, and it was sword against sword the entire time. It was refreshing compared to the others I had sparred with to train.

She had actual experience with this, unlike most of the newbies who strolled in here. She held up her hands in a time-out, and I stopped.

"You are whipping my ass," she laughed.

"You were hanging on pretty well," I replied with a smirk. "Better than some others. Who trained you?"

"Praeziel," she answered.

I nodded. "That makes a lot of sense."

"Who trained you?" she asked as we walked around.

"Alpha," I answered with a grimace.

"Oh!" she began, wide-eyed. "I didn't know that *that* was *you,*" she stammered as she blushed and tucked her hair behind her ear.

An unfamiliar feeling began to brew within me that I tried to shake off as I looked her up and down. The feeling grew in intensity, no matter how hard I tried to suppress it. Normally, it wasn't an issue for me to suppress desire, but as my eyes met hers, I couldn't help but want to run my hands all over her body. She was gorgeous, her clothes clinging in all the right spots. She caught me staring and cocked an eyebrow with a smirk.

"Want to go somewhere and…talk?" she asked, casually glancing over at me as she waited for an answer.

My mind was screaming at me to say no, but I was pulled to her, and I couldn't stop myself. "Sure," I replied.

She grabbed me by the hand and led me off to one of the cabins. Every single part of my body balked at me when I thought of turning back and going back to the arena instead of following her inside the cabin we stood in front of. Tiny pinpricks raced along my arms and chest, and goosebumps rippled along with them. As we walked inside, she quickly picked up her clothes off the floor. "This is where I am staying," she explained as she tossed the clothes in a chair.

I shut the door behind me, and she turned around to face me. An overwhelming need spread throughout me, and I walked over to her, placing my hand behind her head and pulling her face to mine. As soon as our lips touched, it was like a fire ignited inside of me, spreading quickly through my loins. My pants tightened below my belt as an erection rose, pressing against the zipper. I pressed harder against her mouth, running my tongue across hers as she openly invited every movement I made. She quickly pulled my shirt off and ran her hands down my neck and arms, following her fingers with her mouth. I didn't even flinch away as I usually did when someone touched me. Instead, I wrapped her hair in my hand and tugged her head to the side as I pressed my mouth against her skin and kissed her, lightly licking and sucking every spot my mouth stopped. Her mouth trailed my chest while her nails dug into my back. Flashes of Luxina's face broke through, and I pushed them aside as I stared into Elisha's eyes, her smile seductive and luring.

I pushed her down on the bed behind her and became frantic with every placement of my lips on her body, and I lost myself in the moment. We collided together in heaps of need, at times me on top and others her. Her body met mine in perfect rhythm and tempo. We finished together, and she breathed heavily as I lay down beside her. She propped up on one arm while she used her other hand to trace circles on my chest. I snatched her hand as I had done with Luxina so many times, and for a moment, she was frightened. I yanked her over to me and kissed her again, even more fevered than I initially had been. It felt like we were in that bed for hours. And everything repeated again and again and again. Realization finally hit me, and I abruptly stood up from the bed.

"What's wrong?" she asked as I quickly put my clothes back on. "Did I do something to upset you?"

"No," I replied. "It might sound cliché, but it's not you, it's me. I shouldn't be here."

Before she could protest, I ran from inside, slamming the door behind me. Every hair on my body stood at attention while goosebumps prickled every part of me. I still wanted more with her. I still needed more. Desire licked every part of my skin, and it burned with every single touch of her hands. I felt like I was going insane. Like I was still being touched, but I wasn't. I ran to a shower and stood under the cold water, hoping it would douse whatever was burning mildly inside. Instead, it intensified the feeling as the water ran across every nerve that screamed painfully for more. I quickly dried off and put my clothes on, hoping to make it back to my room.

"There you are," Asmodeus remarked as I popped around the corner of Starfire's cottage. "I have been looking for you. They want to go over what we found at Chernobyl."

"Can it wait?" I asked as I squirmed quietly. "I'm really tired."

"I just saw you sparring with Elisha," Asmodeus answered quizzically.

"Yeah, I was burning off some energy so I could sleep," I declared, trying not to look him in the eye.

"Damian, what's wrong?" he asked, a bit alarmed.

"Nothing," I mumbled. "I just need some sleep."

"There's something off about you," he prodded.

I met his eyes as he checked me over and saw the realization hit him.

"Let's go talk," he insisted, motioning to go inside Starfire's cottage.

I tried to look through the door and see who all was in there.

"They're not in there," he said as if reading my mind.

We headed inside and up the stairs to my room. He shut the door behind him as I sat on the bed with my hands in my lap. A constant pinching tore through my groin, almost like someone had their hand down my pants, twisting my manhood. At times, it was so intense that it felt like someone had punched me in the jewels.

"When did it start?" he asked.

"I don't know," I replied, shrugging my shoulders. "A few hours ago, I think. I don't know how long—" I stopped myself from answering.

"What?" he pushed, waiting for me to finish what I was saying.

"I don't know how long I was with Elisha for," I answered quietly, lowering my head in shame.

"Elisha?" he asked, dumbfounded. "The Nephilim you were sparring with?"

I nodded without making any contact.

"And you still want to... you know?" he asked, skirting the obvious statement.

"Yes," I hissed. "It won't go away!"

"You have been hit with the lust bug," he laughed.

"What do you mean?" I snapped, narrowing my eyes at him.

"Alpha used to have me go around to all of the humans and ignite lust in them," Asmodeus explained. "It was one of his sins, and it amused him when they couldn't control it."

"So you did this to me?" I demanded, standing up from the bed and then quickly bringing my hands in front of me.

He held his hands up defensively. "Easy there, killer. No, I did not," he replied.

"Then what the hell is going on?" I growled through gritted teeth. "I mean, I know I am a *growing boy,* but this is different. I can't stop it."

"Luxina is supposed to be in the Lust Terrace of Purgatory, right?" he asked, thinking to himself.

"Yes, to my understanding, that is where he put her as a punishment," I answered, pacing the floor as the ache grew intolerable.

"What if you are feeling everything she is feeling?" he wondered out loud. "What if that is what the Lust Terrace does. It just makes you frenzied with desire all the time."

"Maybe that's what Xavier was feeling when he said she couldn't stop herself as if she were being forced to do things," I mumbled, thinking to myself.

"If it's anything like what Alpha had me do with the humans, then I believe that is the answer," Asmodeus offered. "It's the only thing I can think of."

"I could still feel, you know, after I had finished," I said quietly. "What would that mean?"

"It means we need to get to Purgatory and get her the hell out of there," Asmodeus muttered in disgust. He opened the door and continued muttering. "First, your parents, and now you two. He is so twisted." He started down the stairs when he looked back. "Don't just stand there. Grab the bag and come on. They're waiting in the library."

"But," I started as I looked down and then back up at him, embarrassed.

"Put some jeans on," he offered. "It should help instead of those loose pants."

I glared at him and narrowed my eyes as he continued down the steps. I muttered obscenities under my breath as I quickly stripped out of the loose pants I had on and put on some jeans. They made it even more uncomfortable than it had been before. I could feel it pressing straight into the bottom of my pelvis. I snatched the bag I collected the papers in, along with the box from Alpha's lair, and grumbled as I headed downstairs. This was not how I had planned my day. All I wanted to do was spar and lose some energy so I could go to freaking bed. Now I am walking around with what feels like an armed stick of dynamite in my pants that won't go away. As I thought about Elisha and the time we spent together in her bed, the pain grew, and I groaned as I walked down the stairs, kicking my legs trying to shift myself inside the jeans.

I walked into the library, shutting the door behind me, and made my way over to the table. I tossed my bag up on it and began unzipping it.

"It's about time!" Metatron groaned. "We have been waiting here forever, it seems."

I scowled at him and focused my attention back on the bag.

"Geeze, what's his problem?" Metatron muttered to Michael.

"I don't have a problem!" I hissed, whipping my head around to stare him down.

"Damian, what's wrong?" Incaendiel asked, stepping over to me.

"Nothing!" I yelled. "I'm fine!" I shoved the papers into his arms. "Can I go now?"

"We need you here for this," he replied, eyeing me suspiciously.

Frustration ate away at me as the urgency radiated throughout my abdomen. Incaendiel laid his hand on my shoulder, and I pushed it off. "Don't touch me!" I begged, breathing heavily.

Asmodeus stepped over to Incaendiel and whispered in his ear. I watched as his eyes widened in disbelief. "You're sure?" he asked. "That can happen?"

"It's the only explanation," Asmodeus replied quietly.

Incaendiel pursed his lips tightly and looked at me. "Go," he ordered. "Just be back in like fifteen or something. We will start looking through it, and you can explain things when you get back."

I nodded and hurried to the door.

"What's going on?" Azazel asked with a chuckle. "He acts like Sam when..."

And then the room grew quiet. I shot her a dirty look before leaving the room. Whispers filled the room behind me, and I knew they were talking about me, which made my face grow red and hot. As I walked down the hall trying to make it back to my room, Azrael bumped into me.

"Hey, Damian," she cooed. "How you been?"

"Not right now, Azrael," I murmured as I tried to push past her.

She stepped in my way, determined to talk.

"I haven't seen you since, you know..." she trailed off. I knew what she meant. She hadn't seen me since the attack on Lightshade as she gathered souls from the field.

"I've been busy," I huffed, once again trying to move by her.

She blocked me again. "I've been wanting to talk with you," she continued.

"Have you seen Elisha?" I asked, quickly changing the subject.

"No, I haven't," she replied, raising her eyebrows.

I looked at her and really looked at her. She was petite, and her eyes shone a brilliant purplish blue. Her skin was creamy pale, and her hair was black as raven feathers. My breathing hitched as my eyes trailed her body, and my loins ached for another release. I watched her chest rise and fall with every breath she took, and I couldn't help but wonder what her breasts looked like underneath her clothes.

"Fuck it," I muttered as I opened the door next to us and pulled her into the room with me. I had to ooze the same desire that coursed through my body because as I pulled her face into mine and kissed her, she leaned into the kiss heavily, wanting and needing me as much as I needed her. My hands ran through her hair, and it felt like I was touching silk, which only pushed the ache deeper into my core. She leaned against the bookcase behind her as she tugged my shirt up over my head, and I immediately went back in with rushed lips. The fire between us grew in waves as my hands traced her face, and every trace of remorse or guilt I could muster left my body. She wrapped her legs around my waist as her hands and arms clung to my neck, clawing my skin in slow, deep movements. I licked and bit her neck as she moved her hips in sync with mine, grinding slow and hard. Her softs moans played with the hairs on my eardrums, sending waves of prickling shivers down my body as my movements came faster before reaching that moment of ecstasy. Her body shook, and her eyes were pools of desire as she unwrapped her legs from, and I set her down on her feet. Breathless, I stumbled over to the table beside me and sat down.

She stood there confused, but into it all at the same time, her chest rising and falling in heavy breaths, eyes wide and wild with fervor. And just when I thought I had defeated the devil, the feeling returned again, spreading across my body like icy hot tendrils. She stared at my erection, hungry and greedy, licking and biting her bottom lip. I ran back over to her, cupping her face in my hands as I kissed her again, picking her up and laying her down on the table while pushing the books off of it. Once again, heat built between us, and I ripped her shirt from her body, leaning down and kissing her chest and neck as I took her fast and hard. I picked her up from the table, pulling her as close as I could as I erupted in cooling waters. Her hands ran through my hair, gently tugging as my mouth caressed her lips. My knees buckled, and we both toppled to the floor. And like it had with Elisha, the realization of what I was doing snapped me from my trance-like state.

"Shit!" I muttered. "Shit shit shit!" I stammered.

"What?" she asked breathlessly.

"I'm sorry," I breathed as I put my shirt back on.

And then it dawned on her. "You feel exactly what Luxina feels trapped in Purgatory."

I nodded. She giggled with a wicked grin. "You are also radiating that energy to every person you touch."

"I guess," I answered. "I don't know how this works. I hate to do this, but I have to go. They're waiting for me in the library."

She flicked her wrist with a smile. "Go. We will talk later about this."

I rushed from the room and walked casually down the hall. I fixed my shirt and straightened my hair before I opened the door to the library. All eyes were on me as I walked in and closed the door behind me.

"What?" I asked, scrunching my face.

"These walls are thin," Asmodeus replied with a smirk.

My face grew hot with embarrassment as I looked around at everyone who sat quietly with their own looks of bemusement.

"Leave him alone," Incaendiel ordered, looking around at everyone in the room. His eyes landed sympathetically on mine. "We found these papers," he began, holding up a stack. "We thought you might know more about it than we do."

I straightened my stance and regained my composure. I took the stack of papers from him and began to browse through them. My eyes lifted from the papers and met his. He stared back at me intently as he held his crossed arms at his chest and his hand up to his chin.

"Is it—" he began.

"Yes," I answered before he finished.

"What?" Samael asked as he stood up from his seat.

"Not only is it a list of creatures he created, but it's also a device he made as well. Like a mutated angelic chariot that's alive but with gears and iron," I replied as I thumbed through the pages.

"There are also instructions hidden in the diagrams for this box I found with the papers."

Azazel started walking over to me when I held my hand. "Please, don't come over here."

She laughed. "You think you have any effect on me?" she asked as she ignored me.

As she walked toward me, her demeanor began to shift slightly, and she stopped. My eyes met hers, and I could see the embers glowing beneath them. She started to put one foot in front of the other and continued her walk over to me.

"Sam, stop her," I ordered as the ache began to grow once more.

Samael pulled her back, and whatever trance-like state she had been in seemed to break.

"What the hell," she breathed in a whisper.

"I don't know, but apparently I am dripping in lust," I sneered and returned my attention back to Incaendiel. "Are there any documents in there that explained Purgatory that I skipped over?"

"Actually, yes," Incaendiel replied as he pulled the papers out of my hands and thumbed through them. "It wasn't very much, but it matched the map that you drew out." He stopped and handed me the paper.

I scanned it over and walked over to the map he had hung on the wall. "You're right. It matches," I remarked as I looked from the numbers to the pinpoints.

Each number had a name, and that name was tied to the location on the map. I found the section for Purgatory and the seventh terrace. I pointed at the map. "There. That's where she is."

"Then let's go," Asmodeus declared, standing up.

I shook my head. "It's not that easy, according to the sheet. You have to go through the levels of hell, which there are nine of those. Then, you have to go through each level of Purgatory to get there. You can't just portal in either. His notes say he put up that defense. You can't leave each level of Purgatory either, without being cleansed of your sin. So we have to work through each level."

"What about a back door?" Michael asked. "Surely there's a way out, going all the way through. So why can't we start backward?"

"This says it used to be the Garden of Eden, but as a fail-safe, Alpha added another level in between the seventh terrace and the Garden in case anyone tried to cheat. It leads to the abyss," I explained, reading Alpha's muddled handwriting.

I was one of the few who knew how to read his writing. He often wrote in cryptic sentences, which is one of the reasons they couldn't make sense of any of the papers. A rippling wave crashed through me, and I gripped the top of the desk. I closed my eyes and breathed in deeply, trying to fight off the mounting urge. This time, it wasn't just my own lust. I could feel Luxina. I could feel everything that was currently happening to her.

"I need to go," I stammered as I ran from the room.

"Wait, we have to talk about the box!" Incaendiel called after me.

Every step up the stairs to my room was both enticing and painful. My skin burned, and the hairs on my body stood at attention. I yanked open my door, slamming it quickly behind me as the icy cold erupted through me, and once again, my skin was glowing its fiery blue ambience. Every emotion she felt, I felt. Every touch she felt, I felt. Every want, need, and desire that flowed through her flowed through me as well. I slid to the floor, breathless, and it started all over again. And again. And again. Tears fell freely from my eyes as I couldn't break the connection I had with her in that moment. I knew she was with Adam. I knew she was thinking of both of us. I knew everything in that moment. And I wondered if she had felt everything with me.

A knock on my door startled me from my thoughts. The moment had subsided, and I stood up to open it. Incaendiel stood on the other side.

"Can I come in?" he asked thoughtfully.

I nodded and opened the door wider. He walked in, and I shut the door behind him, then made my way over to my bed. I sat down quietly while staring at the floor.

"I'm not going to pretend to know what you're going through because I don't," he began as he leaned against the desk against the wall. "But if you need to talk about it, you can talk about it to me. What happened down there in front of everyone was uncalled for on their part, not yours. This is all new territory for us all, and they should not have made you feel embarrassed the way they did."

I remained quiet.

"With that said," he began again. "We can't have you running around here pulling," he cleared his throat, "girls into your oozing aura. So, you're going to need someone to be with you at all times so it doesn't happen anymore. Again, not your fault," he reassured me. "But it's not fair to anyone involved, yourself included. You're going to end up on an emotional rollercoaster that pitfalls into oblivion if we don't get this sorted soon."

"I can feel everything she does," I cried, my voice cracking. "I can't turn it off or stop it."

"So it's happening to her too?" he asked, concerned.

I shrugged my shoulders. "I don't know if it's just purely the terrace or not."

He gave a half-hearted smile. "If you're feeling the lust bug, trust me. It's the terrace."

"What if it turns real for her, though?" I asked, fighting the welling tears.

"Not going to happen," he declared.

"How do you know?" I pushed, looking up into his eyes.

"Because lust is not love," he reminded me. "Love runs deeper. Lust is only looking at the outside of someone, while love is peering through the windows to the soul. Desire is a basic bodily function. Love is earned. Do you still love her after Elisha or Azrael?"

"How did you—"

"Doesn't matter how I know who, what matters is the answer to the question," he firmly stated.

"Yes," I replied with a huff.

"Then that's the answer to your question," he assured. "Now, I know how hard it is for me to ask you this, but I need your head in the game. I completely understand the emotions, the anxiety, and all. But we need you, Damian. You're our key player."

I nodded and lowered my head shamefully.

"None of that," he ordered. "Nothing to be ashamed about."

I looked up at him and gave him a half smile. "Thanks, Dad," as he left the room, closing the door behind him.

"You don't really believe that bullshit, do you?" a voice hissed in the room.

I jumped up from my bed, alert, looking all around the room to see where it was coming from. "Who are you?" I demanded.

"Why, Brother. I'm saddened. You don't recognize my voice?" it continued.

I began tossing the room to see if someone was standing in there, cloaked, when the voice began to chortle.

"Oh, you poor thing. But tell me, honestly. Do you think he would tell you the truth, or just what you wanted to hear?" it taunted.

"Who the fuck are you?!" I screamed, kicking shit over in the room.

"Daddy would tell you anything to bring his precious Luxina home. Do you think he really gives a flying fuck about you? He hardly knows you. You're tainted goods. You're fucked up in the head. One minute you're sane and the next you're batshit fucking crazy."

I yanked the door of my room open to peer down the hall, and no one was there. I went to the room next to me and began tearing it apart, looking for whoever the voice belonged to.

"Do you really believe what he said to you? I mean, you and Luxina are currently living out the same hellish existence he and your mother experienced. And what did she do? She gave in to the first temptation she was presented with. Like mother, like daughter."

I grabbed my ears, trying to drown out the voice, rocking back and forth against the wall.

"Mmmmm, Luxina. She smells… intoxicating. Her heat is delectable. I've tasted it in my mouth as I swirled my tongue around her budding mound. I felt her from the inside as she rocked against me, sweat dripping off her body as waves of euphoria pounded through her over and over as she used my body as her fuck toy."

"Shut up!" I seethed, banging my fists against my ears.

"She called out my name as she ground against me. Tell me, Damian… do you think she would come for you? Do you have what it takes to make her moan and squirm? Or did you just give her pretty butterflies? Did she ever drip wet for you and beg you to take her?"

"Fuck you!" I screamed as I rammed my head into the wall.

I had to get his voice out of my head. I began to beat my head against the wall, harder and harder, dizzying myself.

"There's no way to get me out of your head, twinsie. Remember? We have the same blood. It just took some time for me to figure out the mind-to-mind communication. Have fun trying to sleep."

Another thud into the wall, and all I could hear was ringing in my ears. Hands were on me. He was here… Adam was here! I knew it. My vision was blurry, darkening, and lightening as the void of unconsciousness threatened to swallow me whole, and I fought with every ounce of power I could muster. I had to destroy him. I had to protect Luxina from the vile, repulsive cockroach he was.

"I will kill you, Adam," I panted, bringing my power forth.

Everything was black now, but I was still moving. All I could hear was the sound of my own heartbeat beating in perfect tandem with the ringing in my ears. I could feel the icy tendrils creep down my fingertips as the world came to a standstill.

"I will... kill... you," I mumbled as I began to lose hold of consciousness.

A laugh drifted quietly through my head as I slowly spiraled into silence.

***

"He almost killed Raphael!" a voice shouted as the inky abyss I floated in started to dissipate.

"I'm fine!" another hissed. "He was out of his mind! It wasn't on purpose! He was yelling Adam's name. I believe he thought Adam was attacking him."

"Which just makes him even more dangerous!" someone else bellowed. "He's been spiraling more and more lately. This was the last straw. He needs to be dealt with or locked up!"

"We are *not* locking him up!" another defended. "That's exactly what Alpha wants us to do!"

"He has the power to take us all out!" the first voice I had heard seethed.

"And so do I!"

I know that voice. I tried to stir. I tried to force my eyes open, but the darkness still held my eyes in vulnerability, so all I could do was listen.

"I'm sorry, Incaendiel. I would follow you to the ends of the earth, but his powers are too dangerous. He could kill us all in the blink of an eye." Samael. Figures. He's been breathing down my neck since meeting Charon.

"As long as you have been by my side, through all of my meltdowns, through all of me burning the world down around me, you would give up on him that quickly?" Incaendiel asked in disbelief.

"He's not you," Azazel replied heatedly. "He's fucked up in the head!"

"And so am I!" Incaendiel hollered, knocking something to the floor with a thud. "Aren't we all?" he demanded. "That was me not too long ago, and I heard you all! Just like he hears you all! How do you think that makes him feel? It makes us lose control even more because we have raging anxiety trying to please you all and prove we aren't going to blow the world up."

"We all don't hold a power like him," Samael defended.

"So, it's his power's fault, now, is it?" Incaendiel spat. "Always blame the power, blame the person, but never ask why the fuck they had the meltdown. Never ask what was going on in that moment. Same old, Sam!"

"Go to hell!" Samael yelled.

"I live in hell!" Incaendiel blustered. "We all fucking live in hell! And he had the worst of it! He not only has the trauma of what Alpha has done since he was a baby, but all the trauma before that, too! It lives in your muscle memory. And only Alpha knows exactly what happened to him when he was locked up being tortured. Have you ever noticed how he doesn't like to be touched, because

I sure as hell have. He has a lot of shit shoved down, and you all don't fucking help the matter."

"You either chain him, or we go," Samael insisted. "Him or us."

"Then fucking go!" Incaendiel spat. "Any of you who want him chained and have that ultimatum, go. I don't need you. I sure as hell don't want you around when all you think about is how monstrous we are. I'm sure Alpha will take you back with open arms. I will *not* chain him up as Alpha did. I will *not* treat him like he's disposable. He deserves better than that. He deserves to be shown people care about him for him and not because he's fucking useful in a fight. You all may think he is damaged goods, but he's *not to me.* He's my fucking son. I would rather let the world burn than for anything else bad to happen to him, and if that's what needs to happen, then so fucking be it."

The room went quiet.

"What are you doing?" Asmodeus asked calmly.

"I'm leaving with him," Incaendiel said as I felt his hands wrap around my body. "He's not safe here with the likes of all of you. You treat him like a weapon because he was trained as one, but he's more than a god damn weapon. And he's not damaged fucking goods, either. He was forced to grow up faster than us. He was forced into doing horrible things to survive. He was forced into exploding into a god. I will be damned if he is forced to live in a cage to make you all feel better about his presence. Instead of yelling at him and making him feel even worse about his lack of self-control, you all should be guiding him. You're fucking angels. It's in your job description to help the wayward soul."

The room erupted in shouting as everyone fought to voice their opinion. Hands began to grab at me, trying to pull me from his arms as if I were some prize that needed to be locked away.

"Don't fucking touch him!" Incaendiel used the god voice. I could just imagine what he looked like right now, most likely the way he did that day he unlocked all of his memories. I know I felt the heat radiating from his body. I could feel the footsteps leading us out of the room and the voices growing more quiet until it was dead silence.

"I'm… sorry," I croaked, a tear betraying my will.

"No," Incaendiel replied. "No, this needed to happen. I know who my family is now. Family doesn't lock you away when you need the most help."

"You shouldn't… have to choose," I mumbled, trying to raise my head but still lacking the strength.

"No, I shouldn't," he replied, readjusting me in his arms. "And they shouldn't have asked me to."

"It's ok to choose them... I know I am... a problem. I've been one... from the beginning. I'm dam—"

He stopped. "You're *not* damaged goods. *You* are the only reason I am still standing right here and not destroying the universe. Not them. I would choose you a thousand times over them."

"I don't want you to..." My head started spinning again.

"Well, that's too damn bad," he growled, carrying me through the dark like some hero. "The ones who deny help are the ones who need it the most."

"Adam... he... got in my... head somehow," I muttered. "I thought he was here." He continued walking with me in his arms. "Did I really almost kill Raphael?" I cried, and another tear rolled down my face.

"They're exaggerating what was going on when they found you and him," he replied. "Rafe explained that when he found you, you were barely holding onto consciousness while beating your head into a wall. You freaked out when he grabbed you to stop you, and his hands froze. He's fine."

"Where are we going?" I asked, trying to stay conscious but slowly losing the battle.

"Far away from the likes of them," he replied bluntly. "A place where you will be safe."

"Incaendiel!" a voice yelled. "Wait!"

"What do you want, Asmodeus?" Incaendiel demanded, not slowing his pace.

"To come with you," he pleaded. "I did not lie when I said I would follow you and Damian anywhere."

"No," I answered. "You're safer away from me."

"I am *not* afraid of you," Asmodeus hissed.

"You should be," I whispered before blacking out again.

Even though I drifted through the darkness, I could still hear Adam in my head.

"They're going to try and kill you, Brother," he warned. *"You can come with me and be with Luxina. Save Luxina, even. All you have to do is escape them all before you get locked away."*

"Incaendiel wouldn't lock me away," I protested. *"He wouldn't hurt me."*

"You're making him choose you over his brothers and sisters. Do you really think he's not just going to dump you in some dungeon under false pretenses of safety? No, Brother. He's going to leave you in the dark, chained and unable to escape, just like Alpha, because that's who he is. He is just another carbon copy of Alpha. And when he's not around, and you're all alone, they will slip in and do the same things that happened to you while you were with Alpha. But I can help you escape that fate. You can come with me! You can see Luxina. You can save her from Alpha."

"Damian! Don't listen to him!" Xavier hissed. *"Fight against his lies!"*

"Xavier, I have been looking for you. We have much to discuss," Adam mused. *"We can all be one, big happy family, Damian. You, Xavier, Luxina, and even me. Think about it. We don't need anyone else. We can just go create a new place to live with our shared powers. We don't need the drama of the old family. We just need the four of us, and together, we can live in safety and happiness for eternity. Just come with me…"*

CHAPTER NINE: LUXINA

IT WAS A DREAM. I know it had to be a dream. There was no way Damian was here with me right now. But alas, I could feel his arms wrapped around my waist as I lay here beside him. So many questions bubbled to the top, like the main one being, if he was here to save me, then why were we tangled up with one another instead of escaping? Was he now trapped here, too? Did he come here with a plan? Did Adam know he was here? Did he help him slip in? Does Alpha know? Oh, no. Alpha! Damian can't be here. Alpha will snatch him up and take him far away, where no one would be able to save him again. Damian isn't safe here. Why would he come here? To save me, of course, because I had to be stupid. I had to prove I loved him, so I fell into the hands of the person who abused him the most, just so he could win back his favorite toy. I wasn't going to let that happen, though. We would fight our way out of here if Alpha showed up. We would fight Adam if he turned out to be in on some plan to kidnap Damian and turn him over to Alpha. I would kill Adam for Damian. Damian didn't deserve to be at the hands of Alpha again. He didn't deserve to be tortured again or worse. Alpha would most likely kill him even though he swore he wished him no harm. I didn't know how much I could trust what he said was the truth and lies. All I knew was I couldn't trust either him or Adam. They were both equally evil.

Damian's hands began to move up my side, tracing patterns on my skin. My senses burned under his touch as he roamed my body, his hand gently slipping between my thighs.

"I see my present was delivered," Adam remarked, stepping through a portal before us.

I scrambled into a sitting position, placing myself between Adam and Damian. Adam raised his hands in defense.

"I'm not here to hurt either of you," he assured me.

"Then why are you here?" I demanded to know. "Why is he here?"

"He missed you," Adam replied with a grin. "So I got him here for you. Rather easy, really. After fucking with his head a bit, he was all too willing to escape from the rest of the group to come and save you himself, since they all turned on him."

I looked back at Damian, who sat up against the wall. "We can go somewhere new and make a new place for us to live," he assured. "We don't have to be caught up in the drama of the old family, the old way of life. We can be free from it all."

"But we have to stop—"

"Alpha would never find us again," Adam interrupted, squatting down. "Do you really think I want to be here with him? Do you think I enjoy the stone-cold shoulder he gives without a lick of compassion and empathy? I am not a monster. I want love just as much as anyone else."

"How do we get out of here then?" Damian asked, standing up.

"We give in to our carnal desires," Adam replied, standing and casually walking over to Damian. "Even the sinful ones. That's how we cleanse ourselves."

Adam reached out his hand and touched Damian's face, rubbing his thumb across his bottom lip. His hand slipped behind his head, and he drew him in, kissing him deeply as their tongues danced against one another. Damian wrapped an arm around Adam and pressed himself against Adam's body, unbuckling his pants and shoving his hand into them. My breath hitched, and I felt my heat rise as Adam did the same, and they stood there, embraced, stroking one another. Adam's mouth trailed from Damian's, nibbling down his body. Adam squatted before him, pulling his pants down and slowly tracing his tongue around the head of Damian's erection. A quiet part of me tugged at my sleeve to get my attention, to break me from the trance I was falling into, saying this is wrong. This isn't right. The sequence of events leading up to this moment made absolutely no sense, but the part of me that was completely wrapped up in the ever-growing pressure of the terrace ignored the tug as I watched. Every movement they made fascinated and intrigued me, pushing me to join in.

Damian's hands moved Adam's head up and down as he panted, and I watched, becoming more and more frenzied while doing so. Damian spun Adam around and ripped his pants down, rubbing spit on himself before pressing into Adam from behind. Adam's back arched as Damian ran his hands along his spine. Adam twisted, and Damian leaned down as their mouths met one another again. Adam motioned me over to stand before him, and I walked quickly over to him, stifling the inner scream growing deep within that this couldn't be real. That there was no way any of this would happen in reality. It had to be a dream. Adam leaned in, kissing me. I was no longer in control of any of my actions, and it felt like autopilot had taken over. I moved in a daze from him to Damian, and we kissed as he kept his movement steady with Adam. He switched from me back to kissing Adam as Adam's hand moved in between my thighs, and I gasped lightly, leaning into his hand that relieved the billowing fires kissing my thighs. I walked back to the front of Adam, and my mouth trailed from his neck down his chest and stomach, stopping at his pubic bone. I slipped him into my mouth, and he moaned. Reflexively, I reached down and touched myself, something I had never done before, but it felt right in the moment, expected.

"This is wrong," Xavier whispered in my head. *"You know deep down inside, this is not right. It's not real."*

"It's real," I assured him. *"I felt Damian's body myself. It's not an illusion. He's here, and I am giving in to all of the temptations."*

"Damian would never fuck Adam!" Xavier sneered.

"This place frees you of all of that," I protested. *"Here, Damian is free."*

And it was true. This place did free you of all the guilt, the shame, and the doubt. You could let go and do whatever you wanted here without punishment or judgment. It wanted you to do all the things I was experiencing and encouraged every single movement I had made while imprisoned here. It had freed me, freed my inhibitions. I had no constraints, and it lifted all restraints that would have normally held me back. Damian groaned as he dug his nails into Adam, finishing. Adam picked me up and pressed me against him, rubbing himself on me. It took very little friction for us to fall into one another's eruptions. Adam moved aside, and Damian stepped in front of me, picking me up from the ground. I wrapped my legs around his waist and my arms around his neck. I felt a bit of pain as Adam stepped in behind and joined along with Damian, their bodies working in alternating movements, pleasuring one another at the same time while grinding against me. Adam switched sides and came up behind Damian, pushing himself into him. It took very few strokes before Damian groaned and shuddered. He lay me down on the ground and buried his face between my legs as Adam continued behind him. I could feel each thrust he pushed into Damian as his mouth pressed deeper into my legs. It was like lightning rolled through my body as my back arched under his mouth. I quickly positioned myself under Damian and took him in my mouth, swirling him around until once again he moaned and groaned, shuddering while his breath hitched.

Damian moved out of the way, and Adam rolled me over onto my stomach and then jerked my hips up to him. Without warning, he entered me differently, and I struggled to get away from him. "Shhhh," he cooed. "It will feel good. Just ride it out." I tried to claw away from him, but Damian held me by my hips. Adam moved fast and hard, each thrust going painfully deeper as the tears fell one by one. Damian lay beneath me with his mouth once again teasing me between my thighs. Xavier was right. This is wrong. This is completely wrong. This wasn't what I wanted. I wanted to be back in control, even though my body did as it was told. Adam groaned and pushed hard into me as he finished. His lips lightly traced my back as the overbearing desire that had infiltrated my every sense faded and was displaced with disgust, contempt, and shame. Both of them stood up while I sat on the ground, pulling my legs up tight to my chest. I no longer felt safe. The initial fear of this place trickled back in along with an overwhelming anxiety that pressed down against my chest. I didn't want to be touched anymore. I didn't want either of them touching me ever again. I felt.... Dirty, as if I had been the one who had done something wrong. The freedom I had felt earlier had disappeared, and all I could feel was powerless and hopeless.

A light appeared across the cave. "There's our exit." He pointed over at it, and I couldn't believe what I was seeing.

"That simple?" I mumbled in disbelief, still clinging to my knees drawn to my chest.

"It took all three of us to open it," Adam replied, pulling his pants back up.

"Where does it lead?" Damian asked as he got dressed.

"To freedom," Adam answered. "You ready?" He reached his hand out to me, but I hesitated. Of course, I wanted to get the hell out of here, but I no longer felt safe at all in Adam's presence. My skin crawled just thinking about taking his hand. Xavier's warning about him was right and I felt completely disgusted with myself for what had happened between us. Nausea along with bile rose in the back of my throat and I swallowed it down, hoping my hesitation wasn't obvious.

"How do I know this isn't a trick? That this isn't an illusion?" I asked as I covered myself as best as I could while I slipped my clothes on.

Adam cracked his neck in irritation. "You never trust me. Even when I brought you the one person in the world you wanted most here."

"How do I know he's real?" I looked between Adam and Damian, searching for a lie. "How do I know this isn't some grand illusion and you are the master of the deception?"

"How do you know?" Adam laughed. "How do you know!?"

With one swift move, brought out a dagger and shoved it into Damian's chest. The blood trickled forth around the hilt as it also poured from his mouth. Small gasps and gulps escaped Damian's lips as he looked at Adam, confused and betrayed, before hitting the cave floor on his knees, then slumping dead to the ground. Panic tore through me as I watched him die in front of my eyes.

"Real enough for you?" Adam sneered, pulling the knife free from his chest.

I shook my head, my eyes growing wide with fright, and I stepped back from him. "No, no," I whispered, looking from Adam to Damian, dead on the ground. "No, no, no, no."

My feet were moving before my brain could comprehend what I was doing. Instinct had kicked in, and I was running as fast as I could to the portal that was open on the other side. The fear that I had been suppressing the entire time finally skimmed the surface of my awareness, and I was petrified about what Adam would do to me now. I glanced over my shoulder.

"You're mine, Luxina," Adam called out, slowly walking in the direction I was running. "There's no use in fighting it anymore."

"You're a monster!" I screamed back at him, pushing as hard and fast as I could to get to the portal. I ran through it, and within seconds, I was free-falling through the air in total, inky black darkness. The shadows began to part, breaking away into light I was falling toward, and I landed with a thud in a soft patch of grass. The breath was knocked from my lungs, and I lay there, momentarily gasping for air. A sharp pain ran up my leg and into my back, and I knew I had to have fractured something in the fall. I had no time to tend to my wounds or to figure out where I was. I painfully peeled myself from the ground, limping, then full-on sprinting and pushing through the agony just so I could put as much distance between Adam and me. My lungs felt as if they were going to implode as the air burned with each gulp I took in. I had no idea where I was running to or where I was running from since I free-fell from the sky into this place. Nothing looked familiar to me, so I knew I had never been here before. It had to be some sort of illusory place or trap set by Adam.

"This looks like the Garden," Xavier offered, as I ran past trees, animals, and landmarks.

"Great," I rasped through ragged breaths. "How do I get out of here?" I asked, stopping for a moment and looking in all directions.

"There should be a door to the real world or a door to the Summit," Xavier explained. *"You will have to find* the *river. It will lead you to either place."*

My lungs were now on fire as I pushed myself harder, trying to find the River of Eden, but every single turn I took felt like I was going in circles. As I paid closer attention to my surroundings, it looked odd, almost as if places had been spliced together or copy-pasted in. I stopped to catch my breath, bending over and holding my sides like the gym teacher taught us in the human world, my lungs aching for rest.

"Are you sure this is the Garden?" I asked, standing up straight with my hands on my head to get more air in my lungs.

"I'm not sure," Xavier replied. *"It looks different, but exactly the same at the same time. But I know from lore that the Garden of Eden sits on the other side of Purgatory. You HAVE to be in the Garden. Maybe your surroundings are an illusion to keep you running in circles. Look for a force field like at Starfire's place. Maybe Alpha has the exit of the Garden hidden as well."*

"Luxina!" Adam screamed out in rage in the distance.

"He's coming, Xavier!" I whimpered, nausea and bile once again rising to the back of my throat. "I don't have time to look for an invisible force field."

"Hide until he leaves," Xavier urged. *"Over there to your right. It looks like there is a foxhole you can climb into."*

I scanned the area to my right and saw what he was talking about. It was a little cave burrowed into the side of a small hill. I quickly darted for the hole as my muscles screamed for oxygen and reprieve, and my fractured bones pleaded for me to stop. I slid to a stop and climbed inside. I tried to steady my breathing, but the warm air in the hole made me feel even more starved for oxygen. Cramming myself into the tiny entrance made my body hurt three times as badly, and it took every ounce of willpower I had not to groan in pain as the electrical implosions began to race through my muscles. I couldn't breathe. I couldn't move without excruciating agony. I was fucked, even more so if he found me hiding in here.

"Luxina!" Adam called out.

He was closer. Too close. I clamped my hand over my mouth to stifle the sound of my ragged breaths. I saw his feet appear in front of my hiding hole and held my breath. My heart thudded in my chest, and my insides began screaming for fresh oxygen as I squeezed my eyes shut.

"Come out, come out, wherever you are," he cooed loudly. "I'm not going to hurt you, Luxina. I want to set you free. I want to be yours, and you mine."

I felt something wriggle beside me and glanced over to see a snake writhing up through the hole. I stayed as still as I could as it stopped and looked me in the eye before proceeding out of the hole. Adam began moving his feet, nearly stepping on the snake, when it launched itself at him, biting down and wrapping itself around his legs. The more he struggled, the tighter the snake constricted while also growing in size. By the time it had wrapped itself completely around him, it had changed from a six-foot snake to at least a twenty-foot snake. It made eye contact with me. "Run," it hissed before biting down on him again.

I climbed out of the hole, wincing in tears as my bones ground against one another and ran again, this time running through the trees off to the right. Branches whipped my face and tore at my clothes. At this point, I couldn't feel anything except the burning in my chest and the radiating lightning from whatever bones I had fractured in the fall. Flashes of Damian ran through my mind just as fast as I was going. Damian. My sweet Damian. My heart stuttered, and my steps faltered. Damian was dead. It was all my fault. If I hadn't tried to prove to him how much of a badass I could be on my own, he would be here. I wouldn't be stuck here if I hadn't gone off to fight Alpha alone before I was even powerful enough to do so. I was to blame for so much. I was such a naïve little girl who thought she was grown. This was my punishment. I deserved everything happening to me. Why did it have to be me who absorbed Xavier? Why couldn't he have absorbed me? Life would be so much easier had that been the case.

"Don't think like that," Xavier interrupted.

"It's true," I replied in my head, near tears. I was too breathless to speak out loud, and it used more oxygen to try. *"I screwed everything up. This is all my fault. If you had been the one to absorb me, then we wouldn't be in this mess. We would be free from all the extra drama, the extra pain."*

"I was the one who wasn't supposed to exist," Xavier protested. *"I was a part of* ***you****, not the other way around."*

"We don't know that for sure," I muttered. *"You can't sit there and tell me if the roles were reversed, you would have found yourself in the predicament I am in. I got Damian killed! He is dead because of me! Because I wanted to show him how much I loved him. Because I was selfish and was tired of him running away from love all the time."*

"That wasn't Damian, and deep down, you ***know*** *that!"* Xavier exclaimed. *"Can't you still feel him?"*

"No, I can't," I replied. *"All I feel is the numbing darkness threatening to swallow me whole. I was so stupid to believe Adam. I should have known he was going to hurt Damian. I should have known it was just a game, another trick. I was too blinded to see what was really happening, that he got into Damian's head because of me. That he killed Damian because he wants me. Everyone wants me as a possession, as a carnal need. A power grab. A sadistic plan to win some fucking war I shouldn't even be in."*

I broke through the trees and toppled over a cliffside, landing in water as cold as Adam's heart. I sank to the bottom of the river, my toes gracing the bedrock before springing back up to the top. I choked and sputtered, hacking up the water I had inhaled, toppling in.

"I should give up right now," I told Xavier as the crashing waves sucked me under again. *"I should let this river swallow me whole, eat me alive."*

"No, they want you to give up. They want to break you. They want you to feel hopeless because it makes you vulnerable. I am telling you right now that was **not** *Damian. That was a fake, a clone. It was too easy. Too simple. All of it. He just appeared out of nowhere and didn't immediately try to pull you out of there? How did he get there to begin with? Where is everyone else? There would be an army with him to drag you out of there. Now stop being a damsel stuck in woe-is-me, and fight like the fighter you are! You can get out of here! We just have to find the exit."*

I struggled to swim against the choppy water. Every breaststroke I took, it felt like the life was slowly draining out of me. My will to live, my will to fight, leeched into the water around me as despair filled me.

"You have to get out of the water, now!" Xavier urged.

"I'm trying," I cried, dragging my arms through the water. *"My arms feel so heavy in here, Xavier. My legs feel like dead weight."*

"Push with all of your might!" Xavier ordered. *"Fight it off. You can do it. You're strong enough to do it."*

I did as ordered and swam as hard as I could muster with my fractured leg over to the bankside, where a root from a tall tree jutted. I grabbed the root and pulled myself up as hard as I could. I collapsed on the bank and took in deep breaths while coughing out whatever water was left in my lungs. I sat up and looked around, puzzled.

"Where am I?" I asked as I gazed up at the tree beside me. A rope dangled from one of its limbs, and bodies piled up dead all around it. *"Are those dead dark fey?"* I peered closer at the bodies and then averted my eyes away from them, choking back tears and vomit as a lump rose in my throat.

"Don't look at them," Xavier soothed. "Somehow, you are in the Shadows and Nightmares part of the Otherworld," he explained. *"I have seen this tree in Damian's memories from when he escaped Alpha. This is the suicide river where the sorrowful end up."*

"How did I get here?" I cried, pushing my face into my hands. I didn't understand. I was in the Garden, and now I was in the Otherworld?

"Maybe that portal took you there?" Xavier offered as an answer. *"Trust me, I don't understand it either. Nothing about this place makes sense, especially how it all looked like rendered images spliced together."*

"How did Damian escape here?" I asked, wincing as I stood up and glanced around my surroundings.

"He found a door, and that door led him to you," Xavier answered. *"He had a map that guided him to the door because it moved quite frequently."*

I looked back at the river and shuddered. It was like icy cold tendrils of death snaked through my veins while I was in the water. I could feel it calling me, trying to get me to jump back in. It was like a siren's lullaby.

"Don't look at it!" Xavier hissed. *"Act like it's not there."*

"What happened to Damian when he was here?" I asked as I limped up the pathway next to the bank, each step feeling like glass burrowing deeper into my skin.

"It kept drawing him in, beckoning him to kill himself. It used you to lure him in, used his own trauma and feelings. This entire place tried to eat him alive. It's not safe to stay in this place."

"Why didn't he ever tell me?" I asked, making sure to keep my eyes on the path and not let them wander around my surroundings so something else could snag me.

"Come on," Xavier laughed. *"It's Damian. He's not much of a sharer or talker. He keeps everything bottled up inside until it's ready to explode and usually does explode as violence."*

I nodded reluctantly. *"Yeah, that's Damian, alright. He thinks he can take on the whole world by himself and protect everyone else."*

"Sounds familiar, don't it?" Xavier teased. *"This whole damn family has something to prove, and we usually fuck ourselves by trying to prove it."*

"I just wanted to release the mountain nestled on his shoulders. I didn't want to prove myself to anyone, really. I just wanted to ease his soul. He's been through so much, and I just add to that stress and frustration."

"You give us all gray hair," Xavier chortled. *"But that's what love does. Love makes you drive everyone around you crazy. It drives you crazy. Wanting to make sure the person knows just how much you love them and need them and want them. Wanting to make sure they're safe and nothing can ever harm them again. Damian would die for you, and up until Adam, he knew you would die for him too."*

I stopped in my tracks. "What do you mean by up until Adam?"

"Adam got in his head… bad and deep. Alpha made sure he was just broken enough still to be able to torment him, still using you. One of Adam's main purposes is to drive a wedge between you and Damian just as he did with Lucifer and Mom. The same wedge he was planning to drive between you and me with Damian, and Damian refused. But he wants it to go deeper. He wants to really peel Damian's heart out of his chest cavity and eat it. He knew exactly what he was doing when he used Damian's blood to make Adam. He wasn't sure if he could tempt you into actual love, but he knew he could tempt you enough to break Damian's heart and make him think you loved Adam."

"We have to get out of here," I replied, alarmed. *"I have to get to Damian. He has to know I love him most of all, and no one could ever replace him. He has to know that!"*

"But do you, little bunny?" Adam sneered.

I whipped around, but he was nowhere to be seen.

"Oh, I am not there, sweetheart. I am in your head," Adam explained. *"Your exit is coming up on your left, and it will tell your heart the truth. It will tell you who you desire most when you walk through it. Will you return to Damian? Or will you return to me?"*

"I watched you kill Damian," I seethed.

"You should have known better than to believe that was the real Damian," Adam laughed. *"Seriously, that Damian didn't even have any spunk in him."*

"He's alive?" I whispered out loud.

"Very much so," Adam teased. *"Now you have to decide between him and me."*

"I love Damian!" I hissed. *"I don't love you! You make me sick! You are Alpha's real little monster!"*

"Are you sure?"

I went to answer when I stumbled on my words. Am I sure? Thinking of Adam excited me in a way it shouldn't, just like when I think of Damian. I *know* I love Damian, but… no. No, Adam did things to me. Adam made me feel those things through force. He preyed on me while I was alone. He knew I couldn't resist the temptation of the terrace. He relished every single thing that happened to me there. He wants me to choose him, but I will never willingly ever choose him. I chose Damian. I will choose Damian until the day I die. Damian is my world, my other half, out of choice, not because of some bond.

"Well, what are you waiting for then? Prove it to me and prove it to yourself. Walk through that door and find out," Adam jeered.

A door appeared off to the left of me, and I walked over to it, hesitant to twist the knob. I know who I want. I know who I love. I know who I choose. Even if Adam… has some sort of hold on me. I know deep down that walking through that door will take me to Damian, just as it brought Damian to me. My heart fluttered, remembering when he appeared to me that night in the middle of the woods. I knew I didn't have to fear him. I knew he wouldn't hurt me. I knew he was there to stop Alpha and never let Alpha hurt any of us again. I knew I loved him right then and there, even though I didn't want to admit it to myself. I loved him through the injection haze when he tried desperately to help Xavier escape with me. I loved him even when we thought he had killed Sophia. I loved him when the Queen Mab threatened his life. I have always loved him. I choose him! I have to choose him! I couldn't love a monster like Adam. Could I?

"I will see you soon, Luxina," Adam whispered as I twisted the knob and stepped through the door.

"No, you fucking won't!"

CHAPTER TEN: DAMIAN

MY HEAD THUMPED as I slowly opened my eyes to the rays of light filtering into the room I was in. Panic scoured my body, and I bolted upright, terrified that Adam had been right, and Incaendiel locked me in some form of dungeon. I knew deep down he would never do me the same way Alpha had, but the fear in the moment overtook my trust and belief in him for a moment.

"Whoa, whoa, easy there, killer." Incaendiel sat in a chair across the room, coaxing me down.

I gave the room a once-over before sighing in relief. It was just a regular room. It wasn't a dungeon. Of course, Adam had gotten into my head and divulged one of my deepest fears. He was so much like Alpha it wasn't even amusing.

"Of course, it's not a dungeon," Incaendiel quipped. I narrowed my eyes at him. "Yeah, I know. Privacy." He rolled his eyes and went back to reading over the papers sprawled across the desk. "How's your head?" he asked without looking up from what he was reading.

"It's pounding, but I will live," I replied as I eased myself up in the bed.

"If it's any consolation, you look as bad as you feel," he joked while turning the page over he was reading.

"Where are we?" I asked as I teetered on the bedside as the room spun around me.

"Reikal's place," he replied, frowning. "Starfire talked me out of leaving and sent us here instead."

"And the others?" I asked as I stood up and stretched, releasing the tension in my muscles. I wavered a bit as dizziness took over my senses and then grabbed hold of the dresser next to me to steady myself.

"Around," he muttered. "Most likely holding a meeting saying how I am unfit to lead us into war against Alpha, and they should put someone else in charge."

"I'm sorry."

He looked up from the papers he was reading and stared at me. "You have nothing to be sorry for. You have uncontrolled powers and emotional instability. I have been waiting for you to have your own meltdowns apart from mine. This isn't new territory for me. Well, except I am usually the one losing control of myself, but that's beside the point." He motioned with his hand toward the outside of the cabin. "They don't understand that and never will."

"They're your family. You have to forgive them at some point for being afraid of us," I offered, looking out the window at everyone training.

"That doesn't excuse their behavior toward you," he muttered. "After everything I have put them through and the secrets they kept about it all, they have no business judging you for losing control of your powers when you were literally in and out of consciousness. They need to apologize. The only three people who were on our side were

Rafe, Asmodeus, and Metatron. Everyone else who was in that room can fuck off for all I care."

"It's not worth it to lose everyone over me," I protested. "I'm not worth—"

"One, you are worth losing everyone over." Incaendiel stood up, set the papers on the desk, and walked over to me. "Two, if they were to lock you up, what can stop them from trying to lock me up as well? What's their endgame? It's hard to trust people when around every bend there's someone who wants you locked away for their safety. I get it. We are terrifying, and we have powers that are dangerous, but locking the powers away and subduing them just makes it harder for us to learn how to control them. One day, they will bubble up, and we will level the universe because they were too afraid of us. And then they have no one to blame but themselves."

"So, what now?" I asked, walking over to the desk and picking up one of the papers to see what he was looking over.

"You and I are going to go to Purgatory and get Luxina back safe and sound," he replied, returning to his seat and rubbing his forehead. "It's just I have never been to hell nor Purgatory, and it would have been great to have someone guide us through like Uriel."

"Uriel is a no-go?" I asked, picking up the map showing hell.

He shook his head. "Uriel is team Samael."

"You know who we need?" I offered, setting the papers back on the desk.

"Who?" he asked, shifting in his seat.

"Lucifer," I said, watching his face. "I bet he knows the ins and outs of hell *and* Purgatory. He could guide us."

"Yeah, well, we have to find him too," Incaendiel sighed, pushing the papers away. "He's somewhere in hell, chained up."

I picked the map up again and pinned it to the wall so I could study it. On the map, it showed the Vestibule of Hell, but I also recognized a river name I was all too familiar with.

"It can't be," I mumbled.

"What?" Incaendiel asked, standing up to look at the map as well.

"The Vestibule of Hell is right there where we were while taking the river Acheron to the river Styx for Sheol," I explained, pointing at the map. "If we ride the river Acheron further than what we did before we departed for Styx, it takes us where we need to go. It's just on a different part of the map than what Sheol was."

"Wait, what?" he asked, now studying the map closer.

"Charon ferried us on Acheron, and then we took Styx. There were separate rivers that led to the human world, to Sheol, and such. He never did tell us what was on the river Acheron if we stayed on it. According to this map, the river leads us directly to the inner circles of hell."

Incaendiel crossed his arms and rested his chin on his hand while he thought in silence. His eyes darted back and forth across the map as he contemplated what I had explained to him.

"And you know how to get there, right?" he asked, while running plans over in his head.

"Yes and no," I replied, sighing. "We came in through the way that would lead to Sheol. The part of the Acheron we need to be on is further up the way through this heavily wooded area," I said, pointing at the area on the map that was on the opposite side of where we had gone to get to Sheol. "It shows the forest, then we enter through the gate, and past the gate is the part of the river we need to be on. I don't believe it can be accessed anywhere but there."

"Seems easy enough," Incaendiel said, raising his eyebrows. "Do we need coins for Charon again?"

"I'm not sure, but we can ask Starfire. She should know," I answered, slipping my boots on. "Who would go with us? I know it was rather dangerous going to Sheol, and I couldn't use my powers because of the risk of killing the human souls there. Plus, they said our powers wouldn't work because of the pocket outside of time it sat in. Mine could work since I am a time god, but yours wouldn't."

He shook his head, scrunching his face into a glare. "We can do it alone. We don't need the others for this."

"Fine," I sighed, opening the door of the cabin. "Let's go talk to Starfire."

Incaendiel followed me out from the cabin, and all eyes were on us as we walked past the groups sparring and training. I felt my cheeks redden with embarrassment, knowing they were whispering about me amongst themselves and how I was unstable. I pushed their thoughts from my mind, but it was hard to tune out how loud they were being with their opinions. Were we unfit to lead them against Alpha?

"Eyes ahead and ignore everyone else," Incaendiel ordered. "You're a god. Their opinions of you no longer matter. They lost that right when they demanded to put you in a dungeon."

We arrived at Starfire's cottage, and she appeared on the porch holding two coins in her hand. "Indeed," she stated, handing the coins over to us. "You *do* need these for Charon again."

"Charon?" Samael asked, walking up behind us flanked by Azazel, Raphael, and a few others. "Going somewhere?"

Incaendiel stepped in front of me, closing the gap between the group and me. "Yeah, we found where the gate of hell is, and we are doing a recon mission to get Lucifer so he can lead us through Purgatory," he answered.

"Who is we?" Samael huffed, looking around. "No one trusts you anymore."

"That's why we are going alone," Incaendiel muttered. "Don't worry, Samael. You're still in charge, as usual." Incaendiel dramatically waved his hand around and bowed in front of Samael. "Let's go, Damian," he ordered and began to walk away.

"I will go with you," Asmodeus called, running up to us. "I will go. You know I will."

"I will go as well," Raphael said, stepping forward and brushing past Samael. "You all are angry when I was the one who, how did you put it, again? Oh, right, I was the one he almost killed."

"I can help if you need me to as well, Brother," Beelzebub offered, walking from around the side of Starfire's cottage.

"I will come," Metatron assured, also pushing past Samael.

"And me," Zadkiel offered, walking up from the sparring rings. "Honestly, Sam. Why are you being this way?

"You all don't have to come," Incaendiel began, but was interrupted.

"No, we don't have to. We want to," Raphael explained and then looked at Samael. "We are family, and family looks after one another even if that means they might accidentally burn the world to the ground or—" He stopped, glanced over at me, and winked. "Or if they accidentally freeze it."

"Don't come crying to me when you're dead," Samael huffed and stalked off.

Azazel glanced between Incaendiel and me, her eyes lingering on mine for a lot longer than I think she intended them to.

"Azazel!" Samael called, spinning around to wait for her. "Let's go!"

She glanced in his direction and then back at us. She ran up to Incaendiel and hugged him, whispering, "I will talk to him, Brother. We all let our emotions control us at times."

"Ask him one thing for me," Incaendiel whispered back. "Does he ever plan to lock me away or put me in a cage or dungeon if he can no longer control me?"

Azazel stepped back, looking up with remorseful eyes at Incaendiel. She nodded. "I understand." She took off across the yard to catch up with Samael, and they disappeared behind the row of cabins.

"Here's everyone's coins," Starfire interrupted, breaking the awkward goodbye that had taken place.

They each took their coin, and she waved her hand, opening a portal to the Dark Woods. "You begin there, but be warned. This is not like the trip to Sheol, and you mustn't travel into the second level, where Purgatory is. You *must* portal out of there before entering, or else you will get stuck."

"Understood," Incaendiel acknowledged with a nod. "Let's go get Lucifer."

Incaendiel stepped through the portal, followed by Zadkiel, Beelzebub, Metatron, Raphael, and Asmodeus. I gave one quick glance back at Starfire for reassurance. Her eyes were solemn.

"It's the only way and whatever happens… it was supposed to happen."

"What does *that* mean?" I urged, walking over to her.

She offered no explanation and instead turned around and walked into her cottage, closing the door behind her. A gnawing doom filled the pit of my stomach as I turned back around and stepped through the portal. The portal closed behind us, and before us stood what could only be described as what they were called: Dark Woods. Shadows seemed to have a life of their own as they clawed their way through the remaining light before darkness engulfed the forest in front of us.

"Everyone, stay close together. No need in getting lost," Incaendiel murmured as he stepped out of the light and into the casting shadows of the trees.

We all walked single file into the woods with Asmodeus flanking the rest of us. A dark heaviness blanketed me, and shivers ran down my spine. Nothing hardly ever frightened me, but there was an unsettling tension in the air within this abysmal forest. The trees grew in such ways that they were gnarled and twisted as they fought one another for sunlight. It was a fitting metaphor compared to Alpha's creations, always fighting to be the apple of his eye. There were no paths, no landmarks, no life whatsoever within the dense copse. It felt like we were walking into the belly of some beast, totally unaware of the danger, but its warnings lingering on our skin like a wool blanket in the summertime. The further in we walked, the denser the foliage became, as if their main point was to choke the life out of us as we clambered in between the tree trunks and tripped over the roots. Everywhere I turned, it felt like eyes were on me, hungry eyes that hadn't eaten in millennia, and I was the main course.

The hair on the nape of my neck prickled, and I couldn't shake the feeling that something bad was going to happen. We wandered aimlessly for what seemed like hours, if not days, lost inside a labyrinth that wasn't a maze at all. The only sounds that broke the silence that flirted with our hearing were our footsteps crunching through dead leaves and snapping twigs. Dread clung to my skin like a clammy sweat you couldn't shake. I wasn't sure how much more of this feeling I could take before I turned around and ran in the opposite direction just to escape the threat of being swallowed whole.

"I see a light!" Incaendiel called from the front of the group.

He was a ways ahead, and as we closed in on him, a ray of sun peeked through the leaves of the trees ahead. I sighed in relief, knowing we were at the end of the woods.

"Headcount!" he shouted.

"Here," Raphael said. "Here," Beelzebub said. "Here," Zadkiel said. "Here," Metatron said. "Here," I replied. I waited before turning around.

"Asmodeus?" I called out in a panic. I looked around, but he was nowhere to be seen. "Asmodeus!" I called, cupping my hands around my mouth. Silence answered. We all began to call out his name, pivoting in all directions to see if he had strayed. No answer came to us.

"Where is he?!" I yelled, turning to Incaendiel. "He was *right* behind me the whole time! How did he just disappear?" I went to walk off when Incaendiel grabbed me by my shirt.

"Where are you going?" he demanded, narrowing his eyes at me.

"Asmodeus!" Zadkiel called from off to the left.

"To look for Asmodeus," I answered, wrenching from his grasp. "He's lost. He needs our help!"

"You're not going to find him alone," Incaendiel refuted. "Next thing you know, you're going to be the one lost. Then what?"

"I don't know!" I yelled, glaring at him. "But we need to find him!"

"Asmodeus!" Beelzebub continued calling out.

"Here," he said, walking out of the shadows to the left. I let out a sigh of relief. "It was the strangest thing. I could see you all and hear you all, but I couldn't walk to you, and you couldn't hear me, shouting your names."

"We couldn't see you at all," Zadkiel replied.

"Let's get the hell out of these woods, then," Asmodeus muttered, walking toward the light shining through the treetops.

When we emerged from the trees, everyone exhaled heavily as if releasing a breath they had been holding the entire time.

"That was insane and intense," Zadkiel mumbled, rubbing the back of his neck. "Did anyone else feel as if something was pressing down on you the entire time?"

"Yeah, it was unnerving," Beelzebub responded, rubbing his arms as if he were cold. "The entire time, it felt like something bad was going to happen. I was waiting for something to jump out and try to eat us or some shit."

"Glad to know it wasn't just me," I mumbled. "I just have this horrible, gnawing feeling that something terrible is going to happen to us while here."

"Not if we stick together," Incaendiel interjected. "Everyone, stay close to one another. Use the buddy system if you have to. Obviously, this place is full of tricks. It's designed to trap you. I mean, we are literally walking toward hell."

"Where to next?" Metatron asked Incaendiel, and everyone turned to him.

He pulled out the map we had studied and opened it to make sure he was right.

"We could climb to the top of the mountain and go over it to get to the river, or there is a path to the left here. The path looks longer than going over the mountain, though. It's up to you all," he replied.

"If the mountain is shorter, let's take it," Raphael chimed in.

We began the trek up the mountain, and what seemed like a brisk climb turned into an arduous time. The terrain was steep and grew steeper with every step we took upward. We could hardly keep our footing as we ascended. Several times, I slipped and was caught by Asmodeus. About a third of the way up, a throaty growl cut through the air, and we all looked up to see a monstrous-sized leopard ahead of us. It had to be the size of a hippopotamus. When it bared its teeth at us, there were several rows visible that could easily slice through flesh. Just as Incaendiel drew the flaming sword to take on the leopard, a lion appeared a bit further up behind it. It was twice the size of the leopard, and its claws dug into the terrain with each step it took. To the right of us, a massive but gaunt wolf appeared, larger than the leopard but smaller than the lion. It was emaciated and licked its lips, preparing to devour its next meal. Incaendiel sheathed his sword slowly.

"Get down the hill as quickly as you can," he urged.

We all turned around and began to dismount the mountain as quickly as we could, as the beasts snapped and snarled, holding their place on the mountain. The first to lunge was the wolf as we slipped and slid on the terrain as nimbly as the ground allowed. Incaendiel tossed fireballs over his head, striking her every so often when she was close to him. The other two beasts, enraged by the attack on their comrade, began to pound down the side of the mountain, their claws digging deep into the bedrock to keep them steady without slipping. My foot hit loose rocks, and I fell, rolling and tumbling down the mountainside until I could right myself and slide the rest of the way down. I thudded at the bottom as the others scurried down the side of the mountain. Incaendiel didn't have time to stop and throw any fire at the beasts, and they were nearly caught up to the group.

I raised my hands, and shards of ice began to pelt down and smash into the mountain. I tried my best to keep them grouped solely over the beasts, but they had spread out across the hillside and were coming in different directions to attack. Every piercing point seemed to miss the beasts as they zigzagged along the terrain, gaining ground on the group still descending.

"Get down!" I yelled, and they did, foregoing running and sliding down the side as I had.

I pushed with all of my might, and ice rained down on the beasts, momentarily halting them until the group had all made it to the bottom and out of the threat of danger. The beasts stopped as soon as Incaendiel brought up the rear and stepped off the mountain. I lowered my hands, and the ice assault halted.

"I gave them everything I had, and it was like the ice just bounced off of them," I mumbled, looking at Incaendiel.

"You didn't give it your all, and you know it," he replied, watching the beasts climb back up the hill. "If you had, they all would be dead." He motioned around to the group, dusting the dirt off themselves. "I didn't even have time to fight them off myself, so you did well holding them back, what little you did. The ice slowed them down, and we are alive because of it."

"So I guess this means we are taking the path?" Beelzebub asked, interrupting Incaendiel and me.

"Looks that way," Incaendiel replied, as he continued to brush the dust off himself. "Let's get a move on, and no one is to stray off the path. Who knows what else lurks off of it?"

The group went to the left of the mountain and down a hardly discernible path. The beasts walked around the top of the mountain, making sure we didn't try to climb it from another angle until we lost sight of the mountain completely. On either side of the path were more dense trees, and every so often, we would hear someone call for help from them. As Incaendiel ordered, we all ignored them and stayed on the path. It wasn't long before we arrived at an arched structure that was just in the middle of nowhere. There wasn't a mountain or any kind of apparatus it was attached to; there was no wall, nothing. It simply stood there. You could walk freely around either side of it, but in the front center, behind a closed, iron gate, was a passageway that led into darkness.

"Is this the gate?" Metatron asked, inspecting it closely.

"It appears to be," Incaendiel replied, backing up to read what was written across the top of the stone gateway. "All hope abandon ye who enter here," he read.

"There's nothing behind it, either!" I shouted as I walked behind it, only to find it was bricked in all the way to the top, serving as a boundary when there should have been open space. "It's walled in and leads absolutely nowhere."

"Maybe the gate is a type of portal?" Beelzebub offered, lifting his hand and motioning. "Maybe once we walk in, it transports us to somewhere."

We all gathered in front of the gate, exchanging nervous glances.

"It could be a trap," Asmodeus offered, lifting an eyebrow.

"It very well could be," Incaendiel sighed, inclining his head.

"Then what are we waiting for?" I asked as I walked up to the gate and pushed it open. "Let's get trapped."

I stepped through the opening and began to walk toward the back of the structure, surprised I hadn't met the brick wall yet. The light from outside slowly dissipated the farther in we walked, and soon darkness enveloped us, choking out what little sense of sight we had left. Moans began to grow in crescendo, followed by cries and shrieks. The hum of the voices was loud and, apart from the occasional wail, almost sounded like a beehive buzzing with activity. Light crept back in, allowing our eyes to adjust to the lighting, even though the air still felt dismal and inky, like decay clinging to the walls of a casket. As the passageway grew larger and opened up into a vestibule, I stopped dead in my tracks. Souls roamed around the entrance, looking half-dead, half-alive. It was a scene out of a zombie movie. They were all naked and frantically darted around for more than the eye could see.

"How many people do you think are here right now?" I whispered, my eyes trailing the masses that shambled around.

"I have no idea," Incaendiel mumbled, eyes wide, taking in the grotesque displacement of human souls.

Flies and wasps flew in hordes, stinging souls as they desperately tried to escape. Bits of flesh, blood, and nastiness dripped to the ground, where they writhed with worms and maggots feasting on the rotting remnants of life. The smell hit my nose, and I ran off to the side, retching.

"How could Alpha be so cruel to the humans?" Zadkiel breathed, gazing around at the sheer horror Alpha had hidden away for two thousand years. "This is worse than the draugrs."

"Because he's a monster," I hissed, wiping my mouth and rejoining them.

Blood, pus, and ooze covered every inch of the floor we had to walk across to get to the river. Each step was like wading through the dumpster of a morgue that didn't follow the proper protocols of disposal. We covered our noses and mouths with cloth to keep the putrid stench from stopping us every few feet to vomit. The cloth barely helped as we tiptoed through the sludge. As I gazed out into the sea of faces, I saw one I recognized. *No, it can't be! Nautila? How could it be? She was a dark fey.* That's when it dawned on me what this was. This was a place between heaven and hell. It was for people who were neither good nor evil, and they would rot here, never ascending to heaven nor going further into hell. They had been rejected by both for a special kind of endless torment. I caught Nautila's eyes, hoping for a spark of recognition, but it was like she was staring into nothing.

"I don't think they're aware of us down here," Incaendiel whispered into my ear, patting my shoulder.

"How do we help them?" I asked, swallowing back the lump in the back of my throat. Nautila was here because she was half human, so Alpha trapped her soul when she was killed by Zephar while helping me escape. This was her punishment and mine as well. How many others were trapped in here because of me?

"The only way, I guess, is by defeating Alpha and releasing them back to the giving tree," Incaendiel answered sympathetically. "Let's keep going. We are almost through the room."

He pulled me into his side as I fought the wave of despair threatening to cripple me, and I buried my face in him as the tears threatened to spill. No sooner had we left the vestibule than we arrived at the river Acheron, where souls huddled along the riverbank. They looked nothing like the festering sores of the vestibule, and as terrified as they appeared, they must have been new arrivals who were walked through the gates like we were to see what happened to people who were neither remarkable nor villainous. Whatever torture awaited them across the river most likely enticed them more than the rotting gorefest of those who sat in putrid rot.

"What happens to them?" I wondered out loud.

"They wait until their name is called, of course," Charon shouted as he pushed his ferryboat up to the dock. "Sometimes, they wait forever, simmering in their fear, panic, and chaos of not knowing what's to become of them. A punishment of its own until they arrive across the ways."

"You're a busy man, Charon," Asmodeus remarked, glaring at the ferryman.

He held his hands up in defense. "I do what I am told to do," he explained, wiping his brow with his sleeve.

"Do they pay coins as well?" Metatron asked, looking around at all the wayward souls.

"No," Charon huffed. "Alpha thought it best they sit and languish here until he felt it fit to cross."

"Sounds like Alpha," Beelzebub sneered. "Even in death, you can't escape his wickedness."

"What can I do for you all?" Charon asked as he tied his ferry to the dock and stepped off.

"We request a ride to the other side," I replied, stepping forward and offering my coin to him.

"You… you want to go to hell?" Charon shook his head in disbelief.

"We need to find Lucifer," Incaendiel explained, also producing his coin. "And we brought tokens."

"My, aren't you a big fella," Charon laughed nervously. "I thought that fella over there was big," he continued, pointing at Metatron, "but you sure do have him beat."

"Enough with the chit chat," Incaendiel growled, thrusting the coin in Charon's face. "We need to go, now."

"Look, boys, as much as I would love to take your coins and give you a ride over there, it's just not the same as the Underworld crossing. They don't pay to ferry here, and until a name is called, I am docked. It's against orders to cross without permission," Charon informed, glancing between their faces.

Incaendiel grabbed him by his collar and dragged him in close. Charon shook as he looked into his eyes. "Fuck what Alpha says," Incaendiel sneered. "Take us."

"...Vahr-Zuhl," Charon whispered, his eyes widening in fear.

Incaendiel let go of Charon, and he fell backward, scrambling to get to his boat. "Get on! Get on!" he yelled as he untied his boat from the dock.

Everyone loaded on and took a seat as he pushed off from the bank. He maneuvered the boat to point directly across from the dock where he was sitting and started pushing it toward the other bank across the Acheron. Incaendiel sat facing Charon, his arms crossed, staring him down as he pushed the boat onward. The ride this time with Charon was quiet, more intense considering he pissed Incaendiel off. I ducked my head and smiled, thinking about it. Charon was such a dick the first time we met him until he realized who I was, and then it was smooth sailing. Maybe this will finally teach him manners.

"Look, I don't mean to cause any trouble," Charon began, nervously wiping his brow as Incaendiel stared him down. "Many things have changed in the universe since you were in charge and Alpha, well..." He paused. "Let's just say Alpha pretty much rules everyone these days."

"He doesn't rule me," Incaendiel muttered without flinching.

"Well, the rest of us are still terrified of him," Charon shot back.

"And I plan to fix that," Incaendiel retorted.

"By fear and intimidation, just like him?" Charon huffed. "You're no better than he is!"

Incaendiel gritted his teeth, glaring at Charon before speaking. "I am nothing like him," he sneered. "You refused to help us, essentially siding with Alpha. Just like last time, when you claimed you didn't deal with Alpha's *boys* and refused my men passage until Damian here showed you who he really was. You play as if you don't take sides, and even when they presented tokens, you told them no. But you sure let Alpha's men across with their tokens. So, really, who is more like Alpha? The person standing against him or the person licking his boots?"

Charon was silent for a moment. "What do you need with Lucifer?" he asked, changing the subject.

"He can be our guide getting through Purgatory," Incaendiel replied, looking off into the water as we slowly rowed to the other side.

"What's in Purgatory?" Charon prodded.

"My daughter," Incaendiel answered, bringing his gaze back to Charon.

The boat began to turn sideways as Charon docked. "Lucifer is in the ninth circle of hell. You will go through Limbo, Lust, Gluttony, Greed,

Wrath, Heresy, Violence, and Fraud before you reach where he is in Treachery. Unlike Purgatory, these circles won't trap you. So once you get to the ninth circle, you can leave freely without going on into Purgatory. Once you have a game plan, you can return for your trip to Purgatory, and I will ferry you."

"Thank you," Incaendiel replied, gratefully. "That's all I want, help and support. Not sarcasm and hostility."

We disembarked the boat, and Charon pushed off, heading back across the water. I expected to hear screams of anguish and torment, but it was silent, with the occasional sigh emitted from the inhabitants. Occasionally, you would hear a baby cry, and as quickly as it would ramp up, it hushed. As we walked through, the souls that languished there appeared to be just bored. No activities. No punishment. Nothing. Just sitting around and waiting, as if someone is supposed to come call their name or number to meet their therapist.

"The map says that Limbo is where people go who weren't baptized into Christianity," Incaendiel said as he rolled the map back up and put it away.

"Alpha really took the whole follow me or be punished shit literally with the humans, didn't he?" Zadkiel asked, as we walked past all of the lost souls.

"It's not fair, but expected," I sneered. "He treats us the same way. Why not the humans, too?"

"Let's keep moving," Incaendiel spoke softly as we moved through Limbo. Before long, we came to a meadow that seemed to stretch on for a ways. We passed by a castle with a stream that I was sure housed the wealthiest atheists who could have existed. There was nothing extraordinary about this place other than the type of punishment the souls experienced. These souls belonged in Sheol because they belonged to other gods. Alpha had become a greedy miser with souls, and it was looking more and more like he had planned on farming them for power this whole time. Once we broke Luxina and Lucifer free, we would have to come back and gather these souls before Alpha could sink his teeth into them.

The wind picked up the further we walked through the meadow, and by the time we reached the second level, it was a gale. It was darker in here than it had been in Limbo, but we could still see our surroundings. We heard the cries and screams of the souls before we could even see what was going on. Human souls were tossed around in the air, carried up by a whirlwind, where they received no peace or rest. We dropped to our knees, digging our hands into anything we could find to make it through the circle and not be picked up by the wind. As we neared the point of descent, the wind caught me in the torso and picked me up. I began to flail as I tried to steady myself and get back low to the ground. My feet started to lift when a hand wrapped around my ankle. Metatron struggled to keep himself from being lifted up and to keep me from being carried off. Another hand grabbed my other ankle as Raphael helped him pull me back down.

"You're not supposed to learn to fly like that!" Metatron jokingly shouted over the howl of the wind as he tucked me under his body.

"I will try better next time," I joked back, shouting over the raging winds.

We crawled across the floor for what seemed like forever when the wind began to ease up, and we could once again stand without the threat of being sucked into oblivion. That's when the rain began. At first, it was just a mist of sprinkles here and there, but the further we descended, the heavier the rain became until it was pouring.

"What is that smell?" Zadkiel asked, covering his nose.

"It's the mud," Incaendiel answered, looking down at his sinking feet.

"It smells like shit and death," Beelzebub gagged, putting his arm over his mouth and nose.

"That's because that's what it is," I groaned as I looked onward.

Bodies on bodies lay naked in the mud, bloated from the constant onslaught of rain. I had a feeling that the rain was literal shit, but cold and bitter, mixed with snow and hail. The souls lay in the filth of the putrid mud, some writhing and others ripping open while their insides fell out onto the wet ground below. Our feet began to sink as we pushed on through this revolting circle. We had to rip our feet free with each step we took, fearing we would eventually get stuck in this nasty pit.

A low growl cut through the cold, dead air, and I jerked my head up to see what we were in for.

"There wasn't a monster listed on that paper," I yelled, panicked as I tried to rip my feet from the mud faster.

The more we struggled against the mud, the deeper it sank up our legs. It was like a bog of putrid quicksand threatening to swallow us whole. The growl grew louder as whatever protected this place or haunted this place came closer. A loud, snarling bark erupted as Cerberus emerged from the shadows, and I let out a sigh of relief.

"Come here, boy," I called and whistled, patting my legs with my hands to get his attention. His ears perked up, and he came bounding over to me, wagging his tail. "Yeah, you remember me," I said, reaching out and petting his wet fur. "What are you doing here? Hades is going to be mad you aren't doing your job." One by one, we got Cerberus to pull us free from the mud and carry us over to the drier land where we could walk without sinking into the pit of rot. "Alright, boy,"

I cooed as I pet him. "Get on home!" Cerberus wagged his butt, shot off through the mud, picking up one of the bodies deteriorating on the ground, and took off into the dark.

"Let's get out of here," Asmodeus muttered, kicking the stinking mud off his boots and pants.

We continued on our way to the next circle, Greed. It was very different than the others we had been through, reminding us more of Limbo, but with a weird punishment. Souls were split into two groups, and they pushed a large boulder around in front of them like a marble run. They would get to a certain point and roll back to the center, colliding with another soul's stone just to have to push the heavy boulder back up the path. Shouting would ensue, and they would argue over who was in their way to get to the point they needed to be. It repeated endlessly with them pushing their stones in opposite directions just to collide in the center again, argue, and repeat. Most of them had on formal wear of the Catholic and Protestant churches.

"These are church officials," Incaendiel concluded, inspecting them closely and pondering. "Their greed through donations and then living lavish lives as opposed to using the money to help the poor people is what landed them here. Honestly, it's pretty fitting for them, considering it was their social power that helped Alpha become so well known and worshipped among the humans and left honest people to suffer."

We moved beyond the edge of the circle and came upon a dark marsh. The stagnant waters looked like a thickened slurry. Souls floated in the water, violent and chaotic. They would hit one another, claw at their flesh, ripping it from the bone, and even bite each other, taking chunks of tissue and muscle as they went. Bubbles rose to the surface of the water, and I peered down beneath the murk and gunk to see barely visible people who were submerged with their mouths moving. The bubbles that gurgled to the top were bubbles of air as they tried to speak. Atop the water, they were wrathful, and below the water, they were sullen, equally stuck in turmoil.

As we walked further up the bank, a boat appeared, docked on the bank just as Charon always docks.

"Man, he is the busiest person in the dead scene," I mumbled as we grew closer to the boat through the mist.

The person inside the boat was not Charon. When we arrived at the boat, the cloaked figure didn't utter a word and just pointed to the seats for us to climb in and sit down. Once we were all boarded, he removed his hood and pushed off from the dock. Incaendiel studied his face carefully before speaking as it dawned on him who the mysterious ferryman was.

"Abel?"

CHAPTER ELEVEN: DAMIAN

ABEL STOOD MOTIONLESS with his punt pole, staring at us. He quietly sat down on a stool at the back of the skiff.

"You are not dead souls," he said finally after what seemed like an eternity. "No one knows my name here. How do you know who I am?"

"The better question is, why are *you* here?" Metatron asked, furrowing his brows. "Why weren't you recycled into the giving tree?"

"I was never born," Abel explained. "I do not belong to the giving tree, as I was plucked out but never used. I don't belong to Sheol or hell because I never lived nor died. I am stuck in a perpetual state of half-existence."

"Because Anniel took your birth spot, right?" Incaendiel asked, raising an eyebrow. "You were chosen and ready to be conceived for Eve, but at the last minute, Alpha switched her soul out with yours and couldn't put you back in the giving tree because you had already been pulled from it and had not gone through the purification of Sheol to be reborn again."

"Not everyone returns to the giving tree," Abel explained. "Even ones who are born and go to Sheol or this," he motioned around, "place of constant torment. Only certain souls are chosen to be reincarnated."

"How long have you been here?" I asked, watching his face.

He turned to me to answer. "Since Alpha created it. He needed someone to ferry souls, but

Charon was already worn thin with his task. He agreed to the initial ferry from the vestibule but could not take on the task of being here while also ferrying to Sheol."

"And you agreed?" Zadkiel huffed, shaking his head in disapproval.

"Do you know what it's like to exist without existing?" Abel cried, glaring at Zadkiel. "I was never born. I never lived, and I am never allowed to rest. It is a hell in itself. So yes, I agreed to move the souls deeper into the circles to give myself some form of purpose since my initial purpose was thwarted with Alpha's game with Omega. If that b— if she hadn't done what she did with my father, I would have been born. I would have lived and died. I could be at rest, but instead, I am punished like the rest of the first humans. At least these souls have some sort of afterlife, even if it's torment and pain. They say there's no rest for the wicked. This is paradise compared to my lack of existence. So innocence was weaponized, and I became the face associated with wrath and heresy. Now, are you ready to go to the other side or not? If not, then get off my damn boat."

"Let's go," Incaendiel answered, settling back in his seat. I could see the wheels turning in his brain, probably wondering what would happen to Abel once we set the souls free. What *would* happen to him? If he couldn't return to the tree, couldn't go to Sheol, then he really was stuck in a limbo-type state of existence, being neither alive nor dead. Had he been alive, he would have been the first person to die. I know they said his blood cried out from the ground when Cain slew him, but since that was Anniel and not him… I suppose his blood still does call out, just from the pits of hell, since he was never allowed to live.

Abel pushed the boat across the waters, and sludge dripped from the punt pole every time he lifted it from the water. It was like slime or scum buildup, and the smell made me gag as he stirred it up with every stroke of his oar.

"What are you guys doing here anyway?" he asked, breaking the awkward silence of the ride. "Aren't you angels supposed to be out doing other things rather than playing around in hell?"

"You haven't heard?" Raphael asked in disbelief. "The war started several years ago. We are here to get Lucifer so we can take down Alpha."

Abel snorted. "You really think you can take down Alpha?" he asked. "And then what? New world order of angels running the scene."

"Something like that," Incaendiel answered, pursing his lips.

"You're different than the others," Abel mentioned, looking Incaendiel up and down. He turned his gaze to me. "You too. You aren't angels."

"We are a long story," Incaendiel replied, as the boat landed on the shore. "A story for another time."

"Another time?" Abel asked. "What, you're coming back?"

"When we have a plan on how to collapse this place, yes," Incaendiel answered, stepping off the boat. "We will be coming back."

We all followed Incaendiel off the boat and stepped onto the shore of the next circle, Heresy. Tall iron walls surrounded the place, and a single closed gate stood as an entrance.

"What about me?" Abel asked. "What's going to happen to me?"

"That's what we have to figure out," Incaendiel replied, frowning. "We will see you soon, Abel."

"I won't hold my breath," Abel sneered, steering his boat back across the water.

"What's this place called?" I asked, scanning the gated area.

Incaendiel pulled his map out and scanned it, trying to find the sixth circle of hell. "This is the City of Dis."

"Well, well, well. Look what we have here," a voice called out from the top of the wall. "We have been expecting you."

We looked up to see who was talking.

"Mephistopheles?" Metatron asked, stepping forward.

"Hello, Brother," Mephistopheles sneered. "Long way from home, aren't we?"

"What are you doing here?" Metatron asked, furrowing his brow.

"We are doing our job," another voice answered.

Two other figures walked from opposite sides of the wall and joined Mephistopheles.

"Babylon? Belphegor?" Zadkiel muttered, narrowing his eyes.

"Oh, what a lovely family reunion this is," Babylon smirked, crossing her arms.

"Let us pass, and we won't hurt you," Incaendiel offered, extending his hand. "We are still family."

"Family!" Belphegor shrieked, throwing his head back in a laugh. "We are *not* your family." They all laughed and began flying overhead.

"You are Lilith's little pet," Mephistopheles sneered. "You were put on a pedestal while the rest of us fought tooth and nail just to earn a nod from Alpha."

"You are a parasite," Babylon added as they circled the group from above.

"You don't deserve to call us family," Belphegor spat. "We were never your family."

"I am trying to right all the wrongs Alpha has created," Incaendiel defended, narrowing his eyes. "It's not my fault our parents chose favorites. It's not my fault that they created me to be more powerful than all of you."

"Spoiled brat," Mephistopheles hissed. "Especially that one over there," he sneered, pointing at me. "Alpha's little monster, that one."

"Eat me, twinkle toes!" I shot back.

"You better scurry on back to Alpha before he gives you a spanking," Babylon teased. A sinister smile spread across her face. "Or do you like the whip? I bet you do, you little freak!"

"We are going to get Lucifer whether you like it or not," Asmodeus chimed in. "So either let us pass or experience wrath."

"Asmodeus, as I live and breathe. When did you start sucking cock other than Alpha's?" Belphegor chastised. "You were so far up Alpha's ass, we didn't know where he stopped, and you began. Do you really think he's on your side, Incaendiel? You thought Michael was a sneaky little punk, but Asmodeus here," he paused. "Asmodeus here has special orders."

"Lies!" Asmodeus hissed, jumping and trying to grab Belphegor by the foot.

"Infiltrate. Gain their trust. Then drag the boy back to Alpha. Wasn't that the game plan?" Mephistopheles added. "How you doing on your little quest? I see you've checked off two of the bullet points. What's stopping you from carrying out the last?"

"And Zadkiel," Babylon continued, playfully flying around just out of reach of Zadkiel's head. "Didn't you and Alpha orchestrate that little fall scenario? Pretend to be cast out and plead your loyalty to Incaendiel so you can gain some extra power from him so Alpha could secretly syphon it?"

"You shut your filthy lying mouths," Beelzebub interrupted, scowling at them as they flew in circles overhead.

"Ah, Beelzebub. You're right where you're supposed to be, as usual," Belphegor teased. "Did you take a knee and yell, 'Hail to the King,' as Alpha instructed?"

I stared at Asmodeus, and Metatron, Raphael, and Incaendiel all turned to stare at the remainder of the party.

"Is it true?" I demanded, walking over to Asmodeus, grabbing him by his shirt, and pushing him backward.

"Of course, it's true," Mephistopheles laughed. "He was supposed to drag you back when you were in Sheol. He didn't get the chance, though, as you went psycho and took out the ones who were guarding Lailah. Alpha told him to wait, and the opportunity would rise again when he got you alone outside of Lightshade."

The world felt like it was tilting. "It's *not* true!" Asmodeus shouted, his eyes pleading with mine as he grabbed my shoulders. "I went through hell getting you free from Alpha."

"Also, part of the plan," Babylon cooed. "Help Damian fake escape. Help Incaendiel fake escape. Lead them both right into Alpha's trap. Tell them, Asmodeus. Don't lie to save face now."

My heart pounded in my chest, and everything began to spin. It all made sense. Asmodeus was always the one closest to me. He made sure to gain my trust. Alpha's cold shoulder to me was all part of the plan to keep me loyal to someone in his ranks, so he put Asmodeus in charge of it all. He was the only father figure I had. The one who fed me and took care of me when beatings happened, feigning fear of Alpha as the reason he never intervened. He could have interceded. He could have told Alpha it was too much for me, and Alpha would have listened. He was high-ranking enough to be the one in Alpha's ear. I took a step back from him.

"Damian, no!" Asmodeus pleaded, grasping at me as I shook his hands off. "You have to believe *me!* They're lying!"

"It's not true! None of it!" Zadkiel added as we all backed away from them.

Even though we had our powers, we didn't know how stable it was in here to use them to fight, and we were outnumbered. Plus, using them would put the others in danger because of their proximity.

Panicked, Beelzebub broke forward, running over. "I can touch the sword!" Beelzebub defended, kneeling before Incaendiel. "I can touch the sword! You know my allegiance lies with you! Starfire and Maveth spoke on my behalf as well! Please! I am *not* Alpha's spy."

"Poor, poor, Incaendiel," Mephistopheles teased, tutting his teeth. "Who are you going to believe?"

Shrieks erupted over the wall, and three furies emerged at the top, flying in tandem with the fallen angels. They began to swoop and dive at us as we ducked, drawing our swords to parry their attacks. With the addition of the furies, if they really were part of Alpha's plan, we couldn't take them all at once without using our powers and risking Metatron and Raphael.

"While this has been fun," Babylon began, pulling her sword from its sheath, "we have a job to do." She gave a whistle, and a figure began to emerge from the top of the wall. "Medusa, darling. See to it they all turn to stone."

"Avert your eyes!" Raphael shouted, rapidly turning his back to the wall.

We all followed suit, knowing that if she caught us in the eye, we would be petrified into stone. Without being able to look behind us, the six of them pummeled attacks from behind. We were absolutely defenseless. The claws of the furies gnashed and gnawed at my back, shoulders, and head as I whipped my sword around, trying to catch one of them without turning around.

"Grab the boy!" Mephistopheles ordered. "Alpha would be delighted to have him back."

"Don't fucking touch me!" I seethed, as one of the furies dug their talons into my shoulders and began to lift me. I reached up to its legs and grabbed onto them, releasing a freeze. The fury screeched in pain and dropped me down to the ground, where I landed with a thud. "I will kill you all!" I warned as thunder rolled in the distance.

"At, at," Babylon warned, wagging her finger. "You will kill your friends, too. You wouldn't want that."

Another fury swooped down and dug its claws into my back to pick me up where I couldn't reach it. They were right. I couldn't risk hurting the group, taking them out.

"Let me go!" I hollered, trying to wriggle free from the fury's feet.

"Get him out of distance from here, and we will take care of the rest of them," Belphegor ordered.

A flame was tossed in the air, hitting the fury, and I careened back to the ground, landing on my chest and stomach. The air was knocked from my lungs for a moment, and I struggled to breathe.

"Over my dead body," Incaendiel growled. "We might not be able to bring ourselves to full power in here, but we know how to wield it and still fight."

"Keep him busy!" Mephistopheles order. "I will grab the boy!"

"No!" I screamed, about to roll over and face him.

"Damian, don't! Medusa's gaze will freeze you in place!" Asmodeus warned.

A net was tossed down on me, trapping me inside as I squirmed to get myself out of it.

"Say your goodbyes," Babylon cooed with a sadistic laugh.

Across the distance, two winged beings emerged, most likely to join ranks and fight against us. They were fast, shooting through the air like missiles. They went up and over us, and we prepared for the onslaught attack from behind us. A piercing shriek erupted through the chaos, and a head rolled in front of our feet. Upon closer inspection, the snakes that writhed around as hair indicated it was Medusa's head.

"No!" Mephistopheles hissed, turning his attention to the wall.

"Back off!" a voice growled.

We turned around to see Samael and Azazel as they kicked the leftover body of Medusa off the top of the wall to the ground before us. We now had the upper hand. Incaendiel lifted his hands and pummeled the furies with fireballs as Mephistopheles, Babylon, and Belphegor fled the area. The furies burned in the air, their violent screams turning to total ash that floated quietly to the ground.

"We need to get them before they go back to Alpha!" I shouted, taking off on foot.

Incaendiel grabbed me by my shirt, stopping me. "That's a fight for another day. We need to finish what we came here to do."

Samael and Azazel jumped down from the wall, landing with a thunderous thud. "It seems you were getting your asses kicked by some furies," Samael stated, his face hard, staring at Incaendiel.

"That's what happens when you try to reason with family," Incaendiel replied, stepping up to him and looking down to stare into his eyes.

"That's no family of mine," Samael shot back, looking Incaendiel up and down. "In fact, I had to come and save my family's ass because they're stubborn dicks who don't like to listen." They stared one another down until Samael reached out and hugged Incaendiel. "I'm sorry, Brother."

Incaendiel hugged him back. "So am I."

"You guys showed up just in time," Metatron sighed in relief.

"We've been tailing you the entire time," Samael said, rubbing the back of his head. "We didn't know if you would need us or not, or if you even wanted us here."

"I'm glad you followed us," Incaendiel offered with a nod. "We always need and want more help."

Azazel pushed a lever on the wall, and the gate began to lower. "Have you figured out where Lucifer is?" she asked as she walked back to join us.

"Charon said he was in the ninth circle," I answered, my back turned to everyone, still going over the accusations the three had thrown at Zadkiel, Beelzebub, and Asmodeus.

"Well, what are we waiting for?" Samael asked, looking around at everyone. "Let's get it done."

"We have a problem," Metatron interjected, glancing back at Beelzebub, Zadkiel, and Asmodeus.

"What's the problem?" Azazel asked, eyeing the three of them suspiciously.

"According to our nasty brothers and sister," Raphael began, glancing at the trio and then back at Azazel and Samael, "these three are working for Alpha and using trickery."

Beelzebub hit the ground on his knees again, pleading with his hands. "I have proven my loyalty over and over. I swear I am not in league with Alpha! Give me the sword! I will touch the sword and prove it! Just let me touch it!"

Incaendiel exchanged glances with Samael, and Samael nodded his head. "It was one of the reasons you had Reikal work on it. We know it works."

"Can it wait?" I asked, panic rising in my chest as I looked at Asmodeus, not ready to face the impending possibility of who he really was. "Can we do it when we return to Lightshade?"

"Do you really want to be working with the enemy?" Azazel asked, narrowing her eyes at me.

Incaendiel put his hand on my shoulder. "It has to be done now." He unsheathed the flaming sword, and the fire leapt to life. He held it up before the three of them and explained, "If the sword remains burning, then I know you are loyal. If it snuffs out, well…"

Beelzebub rose to his feet eagerly, running up to Incaendiel with an open hand. "Hand it to me."

Incaendiel handed the sword over to Beelzebub, and the flame continued burning. "He speaks the truth," Incaendiel remarked, clapping Beelzebub on the back. "Didn't doubt you for a second, bud."

Beelzebub nodded anxiously and walked over to stand with Metatron and Raphael, relief washing over him like warm water.

"Which one of you wants to go next?" Incaendiel asked, looking between Zadkiel and Asmodeus while holding the sword up.

"I will," Zadkiel answered, walking forward and grabbing the sword. He held it up as it remained lit. He handed it back to Incaendiel and joined the others as Beelzebub had.

Incaendiel stood motionless, staring down at the sword. "That leaves you," Incaendiel breathed, motioning the sword at Asmodeus as his hand slightly shook.

"You know me!" Asmodeus hissed, glaring at Incaendiel, then the rest of the gathered group. "I saved you. I saved him," he spat, pointing at me. "If it weren't for me, he would be dead and you," he continued, pointing at Incaendiel, "would still be locked away in that dungeon, if not here in hell."

I walked over to Incaendiel and snatched the sword from his hand. I thrust it out at Asmodeus, nearly putting it through his chest. "Take it," I ordered.

"Damian," he pleaded, shaking his head. "It's me!"

"Take it, or I cut your fucking head off!" I screamed, thrusting it once more at his chest, my voice echoing in the valley.

Asmodeus's eyes scanned the group standing behind me, waiting for someone to speak on his behalf. I once again bounced the sword at him, motioning for him to take it. He swallowed and grabbed the sword from my hand. The flame burned for a few seconds before it slowly snuffed out. He dropped the sword to the ground, and it clattered loudly, the last sound I heard before my hearing went mute. His mouth moved, and his eyes pleaded, but I heard nothing. He was the only person in the world I had ever trusted my whole life. Everything with him had been a lie. He didn't protect me. He didn't save me. He hadn't done a single thing for me except spy for Alpha.

Hands grabbed at me as I fought against them. I fought to free myself so I could tear his eyes from his sockets. I wanted to rip the skin from his body and roast him over a pit of fire. Everything I had been through while locked up by Alpha bubbled to the surface, and my anger turned to a violent fury. The beatings. The whippings. The starvation. All of the abuse… even what happened at night when they would—he had his hand in it all. Zadkiel and Beelzebub grabbed either side of Asmodeus and wrestled him into submission as his face contorted. The innocence he once displayed turned to malice. I struggled against the arms that bound me so I could pry his head from his body and leave his carcass to rot in this place, fitting for his betrayal. Eternally damned to hellfire and punishment. A portal to Lightshade rose behind him while Beelzebub and Zadkiel dragged him through it.

"Have Samyaza lock him up!" I heard through the ringing in my ears. The portal snapped shut as they disappeared with him, and Incaendiel stood before me, his hands on my face.

"Damian!" he shouted, shaking me.

The rage and fury that coursed through my veins were displaced, and anguish consumed me. I fell to the ground in heaves, crying and pounding my fists into the ground.

"I trusted him!" I screamed as each punch left ice in its wake in the dirt. "He… he…" I sobbed hard as the air grew cold and snow began to fall. "It was all a sham!"

Incaendiel bent down low to the ground to get eye level with me. "I know. I know!" He gathered me into his arms and squeezed me tightly against his chest. I fought against him, punching and kicking, trying to wriggle free. I didn't want his arms around me. They were suffocating, and reminded me of the nights as hands flashed through my mind.

"My whole life with him was a lie," I whispered, gasping for breath. "He didn't love me. He fed me to the wolves along with Alpha."

Incaendiel rocked me back and forth as I surrendered to his bear hug, shushing as he rubbed my hair. "I know," he croaked.

"I thought he loved me as his son, as his family," I croaked, burying my face deeper into his chest.

"I thought that too," Incaendiel murmured, shaking his head. "He had us all fooled."

"Why does everyone I end up calling family end up betraying me? What is so wrong with me that no one sees me for more? I'm just a fucking monster to most, a plaything for others, or a weapon to the rest," I cried, punching the ground again.

I felt a hand on my shoulder and looked back as Samael knelt behind me. "We see you. We are your family, now," he assured, his eyes soft but serious.

An awkward silence fell over us all. Asmodeus was one of the last people we expected to be allied with Alpha, even if Michael warned us equally about it when we let him into Lightshade.

"Let's get going," Incaendiel spoke quietly. "We are almost done with this place."

He peeled me from the ground, and we quickly made our way through the gate. On the other side was the City of Dis, littered with tombs with souls burning from the waist down, moaning, screaming, and writhing in the flames. We moved fast without words, moving from the sixth circle to the seventh when a monstrous minotaur blocked our entrance into Violence, rearing to fight to the death. The group worked effortlessly, taking down the creature, maneuvering around its carcass, and entering the seventh circle. A nauseating coppery-sweet smell hit us in the face with hints of sulphur as we came upon a river of boiling blood. People were either fully submerged or standing up to their knees in the boiling blood while they shrieked, unable to pull themselves from the river. The flesh melted into hot liquid, and the pungent smell nearly made me retch again. Souls who tried to escape were pushed back inside by centaurs patrolling the banks. They rolled down the bank and plopped into the blood, sizzling as they submerged and screaming as they re-emerged from the depths. Their faces blistered and oozed while the skin slowly slipped from their bones.

Stepping stones emerged from the shallow end of the river, and we all hopped across them, watching our balance to keep from falling in until we were all on the other side of the river. Before us stood a dark forest like the one we had originally walked through to find the gate of hell. Once again, there was no path to lead us through the woods, so we walked closely with one another through the twisted woods.

"What is this place?" Samael whispered, walking cautiously through the knitted and thorny trees grouped tightly together. "It's... unnerving. I can't put my finger on it,"

"The map said violence against self was past the river of boiling blood," Incaendiel replied, his foot catching a root and breaking it in half. Blood oozed from it, and wails rang on the wind. Each of us, startled, bumped into trees, breaking branches and snapping twigs off as blood dripped from them and screams and cries echoed through the forest. Shrieks from above caught our attention as harpies that were nested in the trees began feeding on the leaves.

A sickening realization hit me, and I wanted to vomit. "The trees are the souls," I mumbled, looking around in horror. "Violence against self. They're people who committed suicide."

A soul burst through the trees ahead of us, terrified and crying as hellhounds snapped and snarled, chasing her down. She was pale and had needle marks on her arms. The hellhounds leapt and took her down, ripping her to shreds just for her to respawn, and the pursuit started all over. We moved through the trees as carefully and quickly as possible, as more and more souls ran past us and were chased down by the hellhounds. Addicts, gamblers, alcoholics, and many others. Each twig or branch we accidentally snapped or broke called out in pain and torment, bleeding as if still alive. Dread settled in the air, and despair wrapped around me like snakeskin. We emerged from the woods straight into a vast desert. It was barren, and heat rose from its burning sand, crystallizing into shards of glass and remelting over and over. Flames rained continuously from the sky, covering the souls trapped there in an endless torture of fire.

"How are we supposed to get through that?" Azazel demanded, her eyes wide, looking around the molten land of lava.

"One of two ways," I answered, facing the group. "I can throw a shield up in the air and try to block the falling fire, or I can freeze time for us to go through."

"We can't freeze time," Incaendiel pondered. "We don't know if they will freeze with it," motioning around to everyone standing there, "or if it will freeze at all, considering this place is a pocket that also works outside of space and time."

"It worked fine in Sheol," I argued.

"That was Sheol. This place is different," Incaendiel retorted. "We can't even portal into this place, just out."

"Well, then we have to try my ice shield," I offered. "It withstood your powers and the explosion at Chernobyl."

Incaendiel furrowed his brows and pursed his lips. "You're not going to let me forget that, are you?"

I shrugged and held up my hand, and a large umbrella-shaped shield sprouted over everyone. "Stick close together and do not go outside of the umbrella," I warned.

They all huddled together, and I led the way down the only path through the burning wasteland. We passed bodies lying flat on their backs, motionless, skin sizzling like an egg in a skillet as it melted off, exposing bone just for the skin to grow back and start over again. Others walked nimbly across the coals of the sand to beat the heat. Those who stopped caught fire and burned to ashes, only to respawn and do it all over again. The remainder of souls there crouched on the sand, tiny fires lighting their feet as they clutched their purses. Their skin clung to the molten glass the flames created, stretching from their skeleton with any slight movement they made. The souls here were being punished for crimes against work, nature, and god. Alpha was a sick and twisted bastard.

We followed a riverbank that flowed with pure molten lava coursing downstream until we reached a path that led us to the next circle, Fraud. When we entered the circle, it funneled downward toward a central well in the middle of the terrace. Along the walls were ditches, and each ditch contained different souls. The first one had souls marching in two opposing lines as they were whipped relentlessly by horned demons who stripped their backs bare of flesh. They had to represent the sins of the flesh as they moaned out both in pleasure and torment. The next ditch, the people were submerged in shit and piss, disallowed to stand cleanly. They must be the ones who were, more or less, people who were full of shit and willing to kiss anyone's ass to get what they wanted. The third ditch had them buried headfirst in holes with their feet sticking out from the dirt. A flaming torch passed over their feet, melting them down to bone. This had to be the ones who sold fake promises of spirituality or made people pay for "salvation."

The fourth ditch had souls whose heads were twisted backward, while they were only allowed to walk forward. They had to be the diviners and fortune tellers. If they could see the future, then they should be able to walk without seeing what's in front of them. The fifth ditch souls were being boiled in a tarry substance while it clung to their skin, melting it and stretching it off as the tar pulled away from their bodies. They were more corrupt people in power. Some of these people truly did deserve this torment. In the sixth ditch we passed, souls walked slowly under heavy, gilded lead cloaks that crushed them from within. These were the hypocrites who swore to one thing while believing something entirely different. In the seventh ditch, souls were bitten by serpents while their bodies transformed, merged, burned, and reformed repeatedly. They must be thieves, which made all of the punishments make more and more sense. The punishments often metaphorically fit the crimes they committed. The eighth ditch had multiple singular flames that burned one soul in each. This ditch represented people who led others astray on purpose, most often for selfish reasons. In the ninth ditch, souls are split in half or mutilated while the wounds heal and reopen repeatedly. These people, while alive, often caused division whenever they got a chance and deliberately fractured communities. The last ditch hit us in the face with a god-awful stench. They suffered from disease, madness, and decay. These people counterfeited reality. They made fake gold, stole identities, forged things, and bore false witness to destroy others.

We made it to the center well, and through it we could see an icy terrain below. I was the first to jump from the top of the well down to the ice, nearly slipping when I landed. It was a frozen lake, and the air was beyond freezing. Even as someone who had power over ice, this place made my lungs feel like they would seize, and I would instantly freeze over. Ice started to form slowly on my clothes that I had to constantly shake off. One by one, they all dropped down the well. They didn't fare too well in the cold like me, except for Incaendiel, who seemed to somewhat tolerate the cold winds that could break your skin off in frozen chunks if given the chance. As everyone huddled together to stay warm, Incaendiel lit up a fire shield to keep the cold wind off of us as we walked. It didn't completely warm us, but it kept us from freezing to death. I now understand the saying "cold as hell," because, indeed, the very bottom pit of hell was a frozen tundra that could fuck right off. The first zone of the final circle we came across had people buried up to their necks in ice. You could hear their teeth chattering, but that was about all the noise you would get from them. The next zone had them buried to the tops of their shoulders. They could move their head and neck some, and a few would reach over and bite one another. The third zone had souls lying flat on their backs. Their faces were turned upward to the sky, and whatever tears they tried to produce would freeze in their eye sockets. They were frozen alive, essentially. The last zone had souls completely encased in ice, sealed away. They couldn't move, speak, or do anything.

"Why ice?" Raphael asked, his teeth chattering.

"Because Alpha is a cold-hearted bastard and ice shows no love. It's controlling. It suppresses. It contains. It denies agency. You can't move. You're stuck as if time itself has stopped. It's the perfect punishment for those who betray others. It's sealed silence and isolation," Incaendiel answered, shivering in the cold.

"Did he really pervert your guardian powers and turn them into torturous pain instead of the cleansing powers they represent?" Azazel asked, bewildered.

"It seems so," Incaendiel agreed.

"Where the hell is Lucifer?" Metatron shouted above the roar of the bitter wind. "How much further in could he have possibly been hidden?"

"Alpha made sure if anyone tried to rescue him, they would certainly freeze while being treacherous," Azazel added, her teeth chattering as ice built up on her clothes.

"We can't take much more of this cold," Raphael stated, rubbing the ice building up on his arms. "We are going to freeze in place and be stuck here just like Lucifer."

"What's that moving in the distance over there?" Zadkiel asked, pointing a ways off to the right.

"Let's go check it out," Incaendiel said, and we all walked nimbly over.

If we went too fast, we began to freeze faster because the air was so frigid. If we trekked too slowly, the ice piled on. We were damned either way. Off in the distance, Lucifer stood frozen from the waist down, trapped in a boulder of ice. His wings beat, and with each stroke down, he sent winds that ripped through our skin like icy shards of glass and howled through the atmosphere. He was the one moving the cold winds in this place.

"Lucifer!" I shouted over the noise of the wind. "You have to stop moving your wings!"

"I can't!" he cried, completely exhausted. "I will completely freeze over! It's pushing the cold away from me!"

"You have to trust us!" Incaendiel yelled, bending at the waist to keep his footing against the wind. "We are going to get you out of here!"

"How do I know you aren't going to kill me when you get me free?!" he hollered, pumping his wings faster to push us further away. "How do I know I can trust you?!"

"Well, we can just leave you here if you like!" Samael responded as our feet began sliding backward on the ice. "I'm sure you can beat those wings all day for the rest of eternity like you yap your jaw!"

"Do you think we would have come all of this way just to kill you?!" Zadkiel called out, hand over his face so the wind didn't freeze his eyes closed. "Come on, Brother! Let us help you!"

Defeated, Lucifer stopped beating his wings, and we all ran over as fast as we could as the ice began to build further up his body. Incaendiel raised his hand as he ran and shot a stream of fire at the base of the ice block, and it exploded upon impact. Lucifer fell to the ground with ice still threatening to cover his body. We reached him, and Incaendiel threw up a circle of fire around us to melt the growing ice off him.

"We have to move fast. The fire is no good against the cold here," Incaendiel urged as the fire began to fade around us within seconds. He waved his hand, and a portal appeared to Lightshade as Samael and Metatron scooped Lucifer up from the ice. The ground began to shake, and ice that clung to the tops of the cavern began to crash down on the frozen lake. Cracks began to form, threatening to break open to the freezing water below.

"Get through the portal!" Incaendiel demanded, and we all ran through it, barely escaping the crashing of the ice and torrential waters that lay below it.

The portal closed, and Metatron and Samael laid Lucifer down on the ground, ice still clinging to his body. Incaendiel threw up a force field around us so no one could see what was going on. "He's not breathing, Incaendiel!" Samael shouted, laying his head on his chest to listen for his heartbeat.

Incaendiel ran over and placed his hand on his chest. The ice rolled off in rivulets of water and steam. Completely unthawed, he didn't wake up. "He's still not breathing!" Metatron shouted, sitting back on the ground and running his hands through his hair.

I waved my hand in the air, and everything around us stood still as I froze time. "What are you doing?" Incaendiel shouted, panicking over Lucifer.

"I had to freeze time to give us time to get him breathing," I explained as I walked over to Lucifer's body. I vigorously rubbed my hands together to generate friction and static electricity. "Before you ask what I am doing, if I have the power over ice and ice storms, then I should also have some form of power over water particles. That means I should be able to produce electricity too." I continued rubbing my hands together until I felt a steady charge between them and then touched them to Lucifer's chest. His body bucked under the current flowing through him. No response.

"Do it again," Incaendiel urged.

I rubbed my hands together as fast as I could and then once again laid them on his body. His body responded, jumping off the ground, then lying flat again. No response.

"One more time," Incaendiel pleaded, his eyes darkening and worry creeping across his face.

I rubbed my hands together one last time and placed them on his chest. His body arched, and he gasped to life mid-air. As he hit the ground, I unfroze time.

"I was dead," he croaked, staring up at Incaendiel and me.

"No one stays dead long around us unless we want them to be," I replied, holding my hand out to him to help him to his feet.

"You all kept your word," Lucifer stated, sounding surprised.

"We also don't lie when we make promises," Incaendiel answered, patting Lucifer on the back. "We have a lot to talk about, but first, you need to warm up more."

Starfire appeared as if on cue. "Come with me, Lucifer. I have a tea that will warm you right up," she said, taking his arm and guiding him into her cottage.

"What the hell did you two do?" Raphael asked, confused. "One minute he was dead, and the next he was awake and talking."

"Froze time to save him, then shocked him back to life," I answered with a shrug of my shoulder. I turned to Zadkiel as he came running up to us. "Where's Asmodeus?"

"Chained up, not speaking to anyone," he replied, glancing around. "We need to call a meeting about him. We don't know when the last time was that he checked in with Alpha, or even how, considering he never leaves here."

"Well, it had to have been since we began talking about infiltrating Hell and Purgatory," I guessed, shaking my head. "They said, 'We were expecting you.' How he was communicating to him, I have no idea."

"Maybe Lucifer knows," Azazel suggested with a shrug. "He was deep in the trenches right beside Asmodeus. I am sure they all had some sort of system for checking in."

"He's here?" Zadkiel asked, looking around.

Incaendiel raised a finger to his lips. "This stays between us. No one is to know Lucifer is here except on a need-to-know basis."

Zadkiel nodded. "How is he?" he whispered.

"He was barely alive when we found him," Metatron replied. "I'm sure whatever we ask him, he will freely give us the answer with that kind of betrayal from Alpha."

"And if he doesn't, I can get it out of him," I offered with a sweet smile.

Incaendiel narrowed his eyes at me and pursed his lips. "There will be no torture of Lucifer."

"You know, the older you get, the less fun you become," I muttered. "You're getting soft, old man."

He made a mocking face at me, and we turned toward Starfire's cottage to go talk to Lucifer. Starfire had him sitting on the couch with his feet in a steaming, hot bucket of water, wrapped in a blanket, and drinking a cup of freshly made tea. We walked in and took a seat across from him on the other couch and just watched him drink his tea.

"I don't know where Alpha is or what his next plan is, if that's what you want to know," he said before we could ask him anything.

"That's not what we were wanting to know," Incaendiel replied, shifting in his seat. "How long have you been locked up down there?"

"Aw, if I didn't know any better, I'd say you really cared," Lucifer sneered, taking a drink of his tea. Silence fell in the room as we waited for him to answer. He sighed and leaned backward into the cushions of the couch. "Since the day you two escaped. Asmodeus told him I was the one who helped him, or so that's what I was told."

"Who told you that?" I asked, leaning forward and picking an apple up off the table to nibble at.

"Astaroth. That was the buzz, she said," he answered, shrugging. "She went on saying it caused an uprising or something and divided us into factions of those loyal to Alpha and those loyal to Damian since I chose sides."

"Was there really an uprising?" Incaendiel asked, grabbing some grapes off the table and popping one in his mouth.

"I honestly couldn't tell you," Lucifer responded. "Michael hadn't spoken about any when he came to visit before Alpha moved me to the ninth circle."

"Yeah, that's what he told us too," Incaendiel said, lost in thought. "Do you know who the loyalists are to Alpha and who really turned their back on him?"

"Astaroth is good. She was already planning to jump ship whenever you made it out of Chernobyl," he replied, thinking. "Mammon too."

"What about Asmodeus?" I asked, gritting my teeth.

Lucifer stared at me a while before answering. "I honestly have no fucking idea. Some have told me he is loyal to Alpha. Others told me he was the one who orchestrated your escape, then pinned it on me. If I had to really guess at it, I would say he's loyal to Alpha." A twinge of guilt washed over him. "He was the one who gave the order from

Alpha for them to beat you with that whip the time they almost killed you."

I closed my eyes as I let the words roll around in my head.

"I'm not telling you that just to upset you," Lucifer stated, sitting forward on the couch. "I know you two were close, and no one ever got as close to you as Asmodeus did. I'm not trying to shake that bond or whatever. But every single time you were ever tortured, Alpha handed that order off to Asmodeus, and he had it carried out. He watched through the window the last time they strung you up just so he could swoop in and be, I don't know, your knight in shining armor like some damsel shit."

I rubbed my forehead anxiously. "So everyone knew that, then. Everyone knew that Asmodeus... was just doing whatever Alpha told him to, and he never cared about me."

"I wouldn't say everyone knew," Lucifer responded, setting his cup of tea on the table. "The loyalists definitely knew. Those who were planning the uprising thought that he was on your side, and he most likely played right into that hand."

I jumped up and started pacing the room, chewing on my nail as I walked back and forth.

"Why all the questions about Asmodeus?" Lucifer asked, keeping his eyes on me. "What happened?"

"He played us all for fools," Incaendiel answered, watching me and then looking at Lucifer. "He was with us when we went through the circles of hell. When we stumbled upon Mephistopheles, Babylon, and Belphegor, they played the game two truths and one lie with us to expose the traitor among us."

"Who else was with you that they accused?" Lucifer asked, intrigued.

"Zadkiel and Beelzebub," Incaendiel replied, still keeping his eye on me as I stared out the window.

Lucifer waved his hand. "Those two are not Alpha loyalists. Alpha *barely* had his claws in Beelzebub, and you fucked him up in the head when you ripped his wings off. Zadkiel was never among the group. He's completely harmless. A dick but harmless."

"Yeah, we figured that all out," Incaendiel said, standing to his feet and drawing out the flaming sword.

"Is that..." Lucifer began.

"It is. I have a little warlock friend here who enchanted it," Incaendiel explained, turning the sword over in his hand. "It will only leap to life for those who are loyal to me and not Alpha." The sword sprang to life on command. "We handed it to all three of them. Guess who failed."

Lucifer nodded his head. "Asmodeus."

Incaendiel pointed the tip of the sword toward Lucifer. "Correct."

"So where's the prick at now?" Lucifer grumbled, pulling his feet out of the bucket of water and drying them off on the towel Starfire left for him.

"He's here. Locked up. Waiting for you to torture information out of him," Incaendiel replied with a smirk.

Lucifer smiled wickedly. "I like the way you think, Brother."

"Just one thing before we go do this," Incaendiel said. "And it's ok if..."

"Give me the damned sword," Lucifer huffed, snatching it out of his hand. It stayed lit, and he handed it back over by the hilt. "Hail to the king."

"Well, isn't this just...chummy," I groaned, swallowing back the nausea the two of them were causing.

"Want to come with me to interrogate and torture him?" Lucifer offered Damian.

Incaendiel went to protest, but I beat him to his and replied, "Of course, I do, Uncle Lucifer."

"Ah, so you all know about that, too," Lucifer asked, averting his eyes in shame.

"Water under the bridge," Incaendiel answered, holding his hand out to shake. "I know Alpha made you do it. Like literally, made you do it."

Lucifer grasped Incaendiel's open hand and shook it. "Let's go get Asmodeus to squeal on dear old Daddy, shall we?"

CHAPTER TWELVE: DAMIAN

ZADKIEL LED LUCIFER, Incaendiel, and me to where Samyaza held Asmodeus prisoner. Screams grew louder as we got closer to where they were hiding him.

"He hasn't quit screaming like a banshee since we put him in there," Samyaza explained, as the scream grew in pitch and frequency.

"Is he being tortured?" Incaendiel asked, covering his ears.

"No, I do believe he is trying to torture us instead," Samyaza replied, glaring through the window at Asmodeus, chained up.

"Who should go in there first?" Lucifer asked as he cracked his knuckles.

"Me," I replied as I stepped forward to turn the doorknob.

"No," Incaendiel refuted, putting his arm in front of me. "Let Lucifer go first."

"Why?" I demanded, glaring at him with a clenched jaw.

"You know why," Incaendiel muttered. "The next thing I know, we will be resurrecting him because you lost your cool and killed him."

"I would not!" I hissed defensively.

He cocked an eyebrow at me. "Really? You tried to rip his head off in hell. I can only imagine what you would have done had you gotten your hands on him. Probably something that would have put the torture down there to shame, honestly."

"That's not fair. I was caught off guard!" I protested, bucking up to him.

"And what do you think will happen now? Anything he says to you about you being raised by him will catch you off guard. Let Lucifer break him first," Incaendiel declared firmly. "And then you can have your time with him."

"Fine," I muttered through gritted teeth and narrowed eyes. "What would you like me to do in the meantime?"

"Go find Uriel, but don't let her know why we need her or that Lucifer is here," Incaendiel said, glancing around to see if anyone was watching. "Make sure no one else finds out we have him back. We are going to use him to flush out people who are reporting back to Alpha."

"I want to go in with Lucifer," I said, changing my mind about helping in other ways.

"He can stand in the back," Lucifer offered, patting Incaendiel on the shoulder. "I will make sure he doesn't lose his cool."

Incaendiel rubbed his forehead in frustration. "Fine. He can come in with us. All three of us." He turned to Zadkiel. "Find Uriel, please. And—"

"I know. I heard what you told Damian," he replied, taking off on foot to hunt down Uriel.

Lucifer twisted the doorknob and turned to us. "Let's do this."

We walked in and closed the door behind us. The incessant screaming immediately ceased, and Asmodeus sat chained in his chair, breathing hard.

"I see they let just anyone walk out of hell," he hissed, his eyes dark and wild. "Alpha should have buried you under the ice there."

Lucifer walked over to him and pulled a chair up to sit directly in front of him. "Oh, do tell me how you feel, Asmodeus."

"Why is he in here?" Asmodeus growled, motioning his head over at me.

"He wanted to be in here," Lucifer replied, sitting up straight in his chair. "Does his presence bother you?"

"I don't want him in here," Asmodeus seethed, trying to rip himself free of the chair. "Get him out of here."

"He can go if he wants or stay if he wants," Lucifer countered. "We don't control him."

"Incaendiel, make him leave!" Asmodeus hissed, glaring in our direction.

"Why does he make you uncomfortable, Asmodeus?" Lucifer asked, leaning into his face. "Is it because you can no longer play pretend daddy to him? Or are you afraid he's going to rip your intestines out through your asshole when he hears you spill everything you've done for Alpha?"

"I had to follow orders. Alpha would have—"

"No one here believes that bullshit. We all know you crawl on the ground for daddy's approval," Lucifer interrupted, grabbing Asmodeus by the jowls. "Now, you're going to tell me every single little thing Alpha has planned out up until your capture. How you've been communicating with him, and who here in Lightshade is a loyalist to him. Everything. Or I am going to filet you open and syphon your grace out through a straw."

"You don't scare me, Lucifer," Asmodeus laughed. "You think you're the top dog among us all. Daddy's little favorite, but you aren't worth the shit from hell still stuck on the bottom of my boots."

I ran up to Asmodeus and got in his face. "You didn't get to see the circle of hell we found Lucifer in, but oh my, it gave me some ideas about what to do to you. Nothing but subzero ice as far as the eyes could see. Souls encased in tombs so cold, their eyeballs were frozen open, and they couldn't move, or speak, or do anything except lie there in agony of being frozen to death. I will freeze your body in ways that would make hell look like paradise in comparison, you treacherous bastard! And when you stop breathing, and you think your torture is over and you can float peacefully off to Potter's Field, Incaendiel here is going to warm that ice off your body, and I will shock you back to life just for me to repeat every single little thing over and over until you break so hard, you beg me to fucking kill you."

Lucifer's eyes were on me. "I would listen to the kid. Hell seems to have taught him a trick or two."

“Or better yet,” I continued, “we will put you through every single circle of hell on a repeat cycle. Boiled then flambeed in a pit of shit and piss while tar is poured over your head and kept alive long enough for us to heal your wounds and then freeze you to death just to do it over and over and over until you cry out for help to me. Beg me for forgiveness, crawling on your knees through worms and maggots, sludgy rot and decay, and your own melted skin.”

Asmodeus stared at me wide-eyed, lips trembling. “Hell is just a taste of what our powers can do, and Alpha tried to copy it. Imagine being frozen in time with relentless and endless torture, dying and respawning. The difference between hell and me, those souls are already dead. It might feel like death to them, but they've already died. They're just stuck in the pattern of hell, but everything they feel isn't real. What I will do to you is very real. Hell is just a place to Alpha, but I am hell incarnate. So start fucking talking.” I popped him across the cheek with my hand and stepped back, and he gritted his teeth.

"Uriel is the one reporting to Alpha and relaying my tasks for me to complete," Asmodeus confessed, tight-lipped and bitter.

"Throwing Uriel under the bus the same way you did me, are we?" Lucifer asked, reaching over and popping him in the back of the head. "Spill!"

"Alright!" Asmodeus hissed, glaring daggers at Lucifer. "Ever since the battle where Incaendiel ripped Beelzebub's wings off, Alpha had me as commander. Most of the big names had fallen already or were playing recon from the other side, so he couldn't use them, and Beelzebub was useless after Incaendiel traumatized him. So I became his right-hand man. It was my job to snatch the babies when the portal opened, but only one was there. He didn't bank on that. So I grabbed Damian and hauled ass before I was caught. He made me a wet nurse, tending to the baby. Making sure the baby didn't cry. Feeding the baby. Making sure nothing happened to the baby. Keeping the baby happy. Keeping the baby healthy. The baby, the baby, the baby! I hated that little shit. I had finally moved up the rank just to be somebody's God damn babysitter. I was a Forsaken. I was feared. I was powerful. I was dark. He turned me into a joke. I was humiliated!"

I swallowed the lump forming in the back of my throat and pinched back the tears threatening to fall.

"Alpha knew about the one left behind at the Summit when the portal closed and was elated to know it was a brother. Like you and Michael. He had his perfect twins that he could shape into monstrous killers and take over the universe. That was until he found out they had dreams, so he spied on Damian and learned about the girl. He had to have her. I figured he would lure her here or some shit. Instead, I was tasked with torturing Damian to ensure he remained in submission to

Alpha. I enjoyed it too," Asmodeus proclaimed, staring at me wild-eyed. "I got my licks in when he was unconscious, and then I would play nightingale and swoop in to be the loving and doting uncle, the father he didn't have and wished he did. He preferred me to Lucifer when he thought that he was his father, and it was so easy to manipulate him. Without that manipulation, the plan would have never worked. He was broken and eager for someone to see him for more than Alpha's little toy. And I broke him *so good.*" Asmodeus shivered in delight. "I wasn't wiping noses anymore. I was breaking them. And I relished every single second of it. Even now, I am still breaking him. Slowly diffusing him from the inside."

"What plan?" Lucifer demanded.

"Do you really believe they escaped Alpha because I helped them? No. No, no, no. Alpha needed them to trust me even more. So he let them escape. He let them believe I saved them, so when I came knocking on the door, they'd have no reason not to believe I was on their side and would let me in." Asmodeus grinned wickedly, craning his neck back and forth between Incaendiel and me. "They all but escaped themselves. Either could leave at any time, but wouldn't leave without saving someone like a suicidal, love-sick muppet. Incaendiel and poor, poor Anniel. And Damian, he wouldn't leave without Incaendiel or else little Miss Luxina wouldn't crawl into his lap so he could raw dog her into the next millennium."

"Why was it important for you to be in the inner circle?" Incaendiel muttered, pacing the room. "Why did you need our trust?"

"Hail to the king, of course," Asmodeus sneered. "Through every single one of us who joined your ranks but were secretly loyalists to Alpha, we were slowly siphoning off your power. It's why you were soooo exhausted that day. Not because you used it too much, but because there was a tap on the vein of it. And each time you used your power, it dripped into his collection jar until he had all he needed."

"Why did he need my power? I don't understand," Incaendiel asked, confused. "He's powerful enough on his own."

"He's not a Guardian," I answered, the pieces clicking into place. "He needed Guardian energy to activate Adam."

"Bravo, young master!" Asmodeus chided. "One hundred points go to Damian for being correct and so fucking pathetic. No one loves me. Everyone hates me. I'm ugly. I'm an outcast. I'm a spoiled brat who can't control my temper like my egotistical father. Someone has to wipe my ass because I can't, and oh my God, the love of my life is fucking another man!"

I lunged for him, and Incaendiel grabbed me, holding me back. "I'm going to fucking end you!"

"You can't even end your own morose life. What makes you think you can end mine?" Asmodeus laughed. "You're weak. A little fucking lapdog that needs a security blanket and to suck its thumb when shit gets real. Alpha's little monster, please. Try Alpha's little whiny ass brat who cries at every little thing that happens to him. I'm surprised you didn't cry when you fucked all those women the other day. You're a waste of space who should never have existed and will soon cease to exist. Because I'm the one who trained Adam using your clones. I'm the one who fed him the list of all of your flaws and weaknesses, and he knows where to hit you where it hurts, starting with your obsession with Luxina! It was my idea to take her to the Lust Terrace just so he could fuck her four ways to Sunday, and you would feel it each time she came, sitting in his lap. I wanted you to shatter into a million little pieces."

I tried to wrestle free from Incaendiel's grip on me, but it was no use. He held me firmly in place.

"You judged your mother so hard for something she didn't even do, thinking she and Lucifer were pounding one another behind the scenes, and that's how you were created. That she tore apart your happy little family and abandoned your precious siblings, in a pursuit to find you. Tell me, how does it feel to become your mother? Not only knowing that the love of your life is taking it hard from behind, being ravaged by another man. Tempted away into his arms with every thrust. And the cherry on top… You fucking every single pretty face with legs in this place as that lust bug crawls deep into your loins. They tell you it's not your fault, but deep down, you know you wanted it with those two. You wanted to bury your bone so deep in something that you didn't care who or what. You didn't even think about her as you pounded away."

"Why do people think I'm the one who set everyone free? Why was I sent to hell?!" Lucifer demanded, grabbing Asmodeus by the collar of his shirt and shifting the questioning back to the information we needed.

"Because you really did care about the boy!" Asmodeus laughed. "Your job was to play daddy, not try to be his daddy. You were so cute trying to convince Alpha to give him to you so you could run off with him to live some happy fucked up fantasy. What happened to you?" Asmodeus hissed. "In the beginning, you were so eager to fuck Incaendiel over. You hated him. You were jealous of him. You wanted his powers and were so angry that Alpha gave them to him, but you bent over backward to prove to Alpha you were better than him. What happened?"

"I got to know the real Incaendiel and not the image Alpha fed us to keep us pissed at him," Lucifer answered. "Alpha made us hate him so much just so he could keep us in line. Alpha fed us lies about him. He made him out to be the unworthy monster when it was Alpha who was the real monster. Incaendiel was just a victim. A literal victim whose entire family was slaughtered just so Alpha could farm more power for himself. And when he couldn't control that power, he tried breaking it instead. Through lies. Through betrayal. Through heartbreak. Anyone who follows Alpha is no friend of mine."

"And that's why Alpha got rid of you and tossed you into the deepest pit of hell so far away from the light and from him that you froze in place. Alpha couldn't have you spoiling his plans any more than you were, especially trying to show dominance to Incaendiel while he was chained up. And to think that at some point, you really began to think you were Damian's father. The way you got so angry and jealous when Damian showed a morsel of infatuation with his real father after being told all of his life that you were his father. It pissed you off, and I got such a kick out of it because everyone, and I mean everyone, has always hated you. And you got put in your place by a fucking baby."

"You shut your fucking mouth!" Lucifer seethed, clapping his hand across his jaw.

Asmodeus howled in laughter. "You went against every order and expected to remain Alpha's favorite? Alpha knew you weren't his little lap dog anymore. So he got rid of you and blamed their escape on you so he could control the rest of the people who were loyal to you. It's hard to believe people actually like you, but sadly, they do. They look up to you, and you just walk over them because you think you're better than everyone. Maybe hell knocked you down a peg or two." Asmodeus grinned wickedly at us. "Your time is coming, Guardians. And when it does, I will happily slurp the blood from the ground where your carcasses lie. Especially you, you insignificant pain in my ass! When I get the chance, I'm going to wrap my hands around your scrawny little neck and wring it until your head pops like a pimple! I should have drowned you when you were a baby! Ripped your grace straight from your body and fed it to a hellhound. You are nothing! You are that putrid mud in hell that's good for nothing except sucking people off! And we both know you're good at that. I saw you through that window every night. I saw the things they did to you and the things you did for them to stop the abuse. You on your knees. You tied down while they—" I ran up to him and punched him in the mouth to stop him from speaking anymore on the matter.

My heart thudded in my chest, and I nervously looked around the room at Lucifer and then Incaendiel. I didn't have to read their thoughts to know what they were asking in their heads. They wanted to know what he meant by that and if he meant what they assumed. And he did mean what they assumed. A pit of nausea formed in my stomach as my heart raced. No one but those who were in the room with me when those things happened knew exactly what went down. I didn't know Asmodeus watched them—he let them— the thought made my skin crawl, and I wanted to crawl in a hole and fucking die right in that moment. Bile rose in the back of my throat that I tried to choke down, but it was an exercise in futility. I ran over to the wastebasket against the wall and vomited into it. It wasn't Asmodeus's right to say that in front of anyone, as if I liked what happened or had any choice.

In an instant, Incaendiel was on Asmodeus, landing his first punch square in Asmodeus's jaw. Another to his eye socket. He had punched him several times before Lucifer pulled him off.

"Do you know what it's like to boil from the inside and not die?" Incaendiel sneered as steam began to rise from Asmodeus's skin. Trails of charring veins rose as Incaendiel stared him down. Asmodeus screamed in pain as every vein on his body lit up on fire from the inside.

"Fuck you!" Asmodeus shrieked, blisters bubbling to the surface of his arms and face.

"No, no," Incaendiel cooed, craning his neck around while his eyes burned like fireballs. "You can go fuck yourself."

Asmodeus's body arched as the trails of fire from his boiling blood raced through his chest and up the sides of his neck. Flecks of embers breaking free from his skin began to float upwards as his body turned beet red. Just when he was about to explode from the pressure and about to catch fire, Incaendiel yelled, "Now, Damian!"

I raised my hand and blanketed him with ice, dousing the flames burning deep within him.

"Now we can do this all day," Incaendiel sneered, inches away from Asmodeus's face. "I certainly would enjoy seeing you writhe in agony over and over as a personal punishment for you disrespecting *my* son the way you did, for you allowing what happened to him to transpire while you stood outside the door watching eagerly like some sick twisted pervert, but I need names. And you can either give them to me willingly, or you will bleed them from your asshole because Damian here is going to freeze time, but keep you conscious just enough for you to feel me run my hands through your organs and then heal you up and do it again while you roast on a spitfire. And just when you think you can't bear any more agony, Damian will send jolts of his electricity through that tiny dick Alpha gave you until your testicles explode. Do you feel me, Asmodeus? Are you going to answer Lucifer's questions without any additional lip, or would you rather I painfully take a trip through your mind and, while in there, leave some worms and maggots to fester until you're a drooling, bag of shit with no purpose left in life except to have your ass wiped with wool glass."

Asmodeus swallowed hard, breathing heavily as the blisters on his face popped and oozed down his burned flesh. His face was hard as stone, and his eyes stared straight through Incaendiel. "Fine," he spat through gritted teeth, not breaking eye contact. "What do you want to know?"

Lucifer sat wide-eyed and shocked when Incaendiel stood up straight and walked away from Asmodeus. Flickers of fear and admiration trailed across his face before he turned his attention back to Asmodeus to question him more. "Why is Uriel here?"

"Isn't it obvious?" Asmodeus sneered, spitting out a mouthful of blood. "Divide and conquer. Luxina is trapped in Purgatory. Anniel is literally conditioned to jump when Alpha says so. Damian was the next target to extract, leaving you alone and defenseless."

"I am hardly defenseless," Incaendiel snorted. "I can take anyone out with a flick of the wrist."

"Uriel is here to turn the renegades against you. Anyone loyal to you, she plans to talk back over to Alpha's side. An army. A horde. Here in Lightshade," Asmodeus cooed. "And you are making it all too easy for her, too. Samael doesn't know just how much he helped with that little spat you two had over Damian. And now, that horde we have been growing has numbers."

"You won't fight against them and put everyone else in danger, including the inhabitants here," Lucifer explained, glancing over at Incaendiel. "It's not in your nature."

"Just like in hell when Mephistopheles and everyone attacked us. You refused to use your powers because we were there, and you didn't want to hurt the souls there or us," Asmodeus continued. "It's your flaw, Incaendiel. You're too nice."

"And when I surrendered?" Incaendiel asked, pacing the room and chewing on his thumbnail.

"Chain you up and lock you in the abyss," Asmodeus answered, grinning widely. "Lucifer locked in hell. Damian locked Alpha knows where. No one to save you. No one to care. Those who oppose Alpha would have to crawl back on their hands and knees and possibly receive forgiveness for their transgressions. The original fallen ones he would take pity on, but those who stayed back in the Summit with him, they would be in a world of shit."

"How many has she swayed to her side? Who?" I hissed, walking up to him inches away from his face.

"What's the fun in telling you that?" Asmodeus cackled, throwing his head back.

We all turned to leave the room, and he shouted, "Have fun playing *the game!*" Lucifer slammed the door shut behind us to drown out his laughter.

"We have a problem," Lucifer announced, glancing around Lightshade at everyone there. There were an infinite number of people who seemed to double each day as more and more joined us.

"We are fucked," I muttered, unsure of who we could trust.

"We know the core people that are loyalists," Incaendiel added, a glint of hope lingering around his words. "Samael, Azazel, Raphael, Zadkiel, Beelzebub, Michael, and Metatron. They are all safe areas."

"Are they?" Lucifer asked, turning to face him. "Metatron and Sandolphon or Jophiel would be a problem, and I *know* those two are loyalists to Alpha. Even Michael could now be problematic with the hope of getting back in Alpha's good graces."

"I can't test every single person with the sword," Incaendiel griped, throwing a hand in the air. "That would literally take forever."

"And Lucifer can't help us either to see if they are lying or not," I added. "He's supposed to be lying low so no one knows he's here with us."

"Follow me," Incaendiel ordered the two of us.

We followed him behind all of the cabins and entered through the back of Reikal's cabin. He checked to make sure no one was paying us any attention out the front door before he closed it. "This is where we meet and talk. I will grab Samael and Azazel, and we need to come up with a gameplan. Asmodeus didn't want to touch that sword, knowing it would show he was a traitor, so it's going to be some trial and error getting key players to prove their loyalty once again. Suspicion is not on our side.

"Shouldn't you test those two first?" Lucifer asked, plopping down on the couch in the den area.

"I already have, and plus, they literally saved our asses from Alpha's minions when they were trying to snatch Damian," Incaendiel replied. "I trust those two with everything in me."

"Alright, if you trust them, I trust them," Lucifer sighed. "Who are we testing first? Michael or Metatron."

"Michael," I answered.

"Why Michael?" Incaendiel asked, puzzled.

"He needs to know we have Lucifer, and it will be easier to take on Metatron with more people in case he has turned sides," I replied. "Michael can easily be subdued by us before he tries to flee back to Alpha. Metatron will most certainly give us a hell of a fight and draw a lot of attention if not contained."

"Good point," Lucifer remarked, pointing at me and nodding his head. "Go get my twin and let's interrogate his ass. He knows a lot more than what he has told you, I am sure."

"Yeah, like the fact that Uriel works for Alpha," Incaendiel sneered. He looked over at me and walked closer to Lucifer and leaned into his ear, whispering. "What you heard in there..." he looked Lucifer deep in his eyes. "That stays between us. Don't bring it up and don't tell anyone else what Asmodeus said about Damian."

Lucifer nodded, glancing over at me and then back at Incaendiel. "You have my word, Brother."

Incaendiel gave a quick, approving nod. "You go grab Samael and Azazel," he said, motioning at me, "and I will grab Michael."

"On it," I acknowledged and took off out the back of the cabin to go look for them. I didn't look long before I found them lounging on Starfire's porch with everybody else in our close-knit group.

"Sam. Azazel," I called and waved them over while everyone watched quietly as they stood up and walked over.

"What is it?" Samael asked, glancing around to see who all was listening.

"I will explain on the way," I whispered before speaking louder and saying, "I'm ready for the birds and the bees talk you both agreed to give me."

"Oh, mmm mmm. Not getting into that," Raphael said, slipping inside Starfire's cottage.

"Yeah, uh, one of the Nephilim asked for some extra training. So I'm just gonna," Zadkiel mumbled, pointing over at the sparring rings and walking that way.

Azazel threw her arm around my neck and chuckled. "Let's go, Damian. We have a lot to discuss, and we are the experts."

Once I knew no one was following us, I breathed a sigh of relief. "God, that was embarrassing," I murmured.

"Which means this must be important if you didn't want everyone else involved. What's up?" Samael pestered, eyeing me while walking.

"We got some intel out of Asmodeus when we questioned him," I spoke quietly. "Uriel isn't here as an ally. She's working for Alpha and turning those who pledged to follow Incaendiel against us. When we get to Reikal's cabin, I can fill you in more. I don't want anyone overhearing us, so they would warn her we know."

"I'm curious to know how you all got Asmodeus to talk. I know he never breaks with anything and would pose a hard interrogation," Samael replied, surprised. "He was built for war."

"Well, Incaendiel…" I began. "My dad has his ways of influencing people to speak." Samael and Azazel exchanged glances. "What?" I asked, defensively.

"You never really call him dad," Azazel answered, cocking a grin.

"Well, he earned it that time," I responded with a shrug. *He has earned a lot.*

"Must have been a helluva interrogation," Samael teased with a wide smile.

"Let's just say I pity the fool that ever tries to cross his dark side," I mumbled with wide eyes and raised eyebrows.

I led them into Reikal's cabin, and Lucifer gave the rundown on what was going on and who we were starting with.

"You mean you trust us?" Samael asked, surprised.

"Not a chance in hell," Lucifer replied with a grunt. "But Incaendiel does, and I trust him."

Incaendiel opened the back door and walked in with Michael.

"Lucifer?" Michael asked, shocked and confused. "How did you get here?" He looked around at all of us standing there. "What the hell is this?"

"We have a problem," Samael started off.

"There are traitors among our midst," Azazel continued.

"And we are weeding them out," Lucifer finished, standing up and walking over to Michael.

"Whatever he has told you is a lie!" Michael hissed, pointing at Lucifer.

"He hasn't told us anything," Incaendiel replied, closing the back door and joining us. "Let's just get this out of the way," he continued, pulling the flaming sword from its sheath and thrusting it toward Michael.

Michael rolled his eyes with a "pft," and took the sword. It burned brightly in his hand. "Now, care to tell me what the hell is going on?" he asked, handing it back to Incaendiel.

Lucifer explained to Michael what was said during Asmodeus's interrogation. Michael's face turned white, and he sat down. "So, Uriel and Asmodeus and god knows who else are here as spies for Alpha and to turn everyone against us to throw Incaendiel in the pit so Alpha can reclaim his throne and punish everyone who sided with Incaendiel? I summed that up right… right?"

"Pretty much," I answered, walking around the room and fidgeting with Reikal's knick-knacks.

"So, who are you questioning next? Who all has already proven their allegiance?" Michael asked, looking around at us. "And how the hell is Lucifer here?! No one answered that!"

"Well, we did a quiet recon mission to get Lucifer out of hell after Sam, and I had a falling out," Incaendiel explained, rubbing the back of his head nervously. "We needed someone who we thought would be able to navigate us through Purgatory since we assumed that Samael would get Uriel to not help us, which we were wrong about. Obviously. Everything smoothed out between us over the misunderstanding…" Samael frowned and rolled his eyes. "Anyway, while in hell, and after some accusations thrown from some of Alpha's minions, we tested Zadkiel, Beelzebub, and Asmodeus. Asmodeus failed."

My anger bubbled to the surface, and I cracked my neck trying to calm myself down as I huffed. Just the mere mention of his name urged me to go back to that room and filet his skin from his body.

"So who is next to test?" Michael prodded more. "Raphael? Metatron? God damn Uriel herself?"

"Metatron," I answered. "We needed to make sure we had enough manpower in here to subdue him in case…"

"In case what? In case he went psycho and tried to escape and let Uriel know we were on to her?" Michael hissed, pacing the room. "Have you even thought this through? Do you really think we four can subdue him?!"

"Well, I would help also," Incaendiel claimed, raising his hand as if he were forgotten. "But yes, pretty much that scenario exactly."

Michael flopped down on the couch and rubbed his forehead. "It's not like I have a choice, is it?" He looked up at us all. "Who's going to get him? It will look odd for Incaendiel since he just got me. Everyone thinks that Damian, Samael, and Azazel are having a sex talk. Lucifer isn't supposed to be seen by anyone. You guys didn't really think this through much, did you?"

"He has a valid point," Lucifer responded, nodding his head along while thinking.

A knock came to the door, and we all jumped, startled out of the conversation. "Can I come in, guys?" Metatron asked through the door. "I saw Incaendiel and Michael duck in here. I also watched Damian, Samael, and Azazel enter earlier, too."

I sighed and pinched the bridge of my nose. "Yeah, Reikal's was the *perfect* place to do this," I huffed, rolling my eyes and opening the door. "Get in here, you big dummy."

Metatron walked in and looked around at all of us, walking toward the center of the room to stand with everyone. "What's with the serious faces?" he asked.

I walked over and snatched the flaming sword from Incaendiel, perturbed by how long this was already taking. "Here," I said, holding the sword out to Metatron. "Take it."

"Why?" he asked, scrunching his face and smiling.

"We will explain why after you take it!" I shouted, annoyed. "Just take it!"

"Do you guys not trust me or something?" he asked, his smile slowly fading as he dodged taking the sword.

"We all did it," Lucifer huffed. "Just ease Incaendiel's worries and take the sword."

"I want to know why first," Metatron insisted, irritation slipping out.

Samael quietly slipped in front of the front door while Azazel moved in front of the back door unnoticed by Metatron.

"Do I need to threaten you the way I threatened Asmodeus?" I snapped through gritted teeth. "Just take the damned sword, and we will fill you in on the rest."

"I don't have time for this," Metatron hissed, turning around to walk out the front door.

"Take the sword, Metatron. That's an order!" Samael barked, crossing his arms.

"You are not my boss," Metatron laughed. "No one in here is the boss of me! I outrank you all!"

"You don't outrank me," Incaendiel huffed, exasperated. "Just take the sword, Metatron."

"Look, just because you have trust issues doesn't mean I have to walk around all the time proving my allegiance to you!" Metatron shouted, getting in Incaendiel's face.

"Take the god damn sword, or I will shove it down your throat," Incaendiel growled. "I am not playing games, and I am not in a joking mood."

"Then shove it down my throat," Metatron seethed, turning his back to Incaendiel. "I am leaving this cabin."

"No, you're not," Incaendiel spat, grabbing him from behind.

Metatron wrestled with Incaendiel from behind while kicking at anyone who tried to tackle him from the front. "Let me go, Incaendiel!" he bellowed using his god voice.

"You don't outrank me, so that voice does nothing to me!" Incaendiel growled in his ear. "Now be a good little angel and take the fucking sword and prove to me that you're not working with Uriel because right now, *Brother*, you look guilty as fuck!"

Metatron stopped struggling against Incaendiel, and Incaendiel let him go. Metatron raised his hands to his head and ran his fingers through his hair. "Let me explain," he began.

"You fucking traitor!" Lucifer hollered. "I knew it! I knew you would be the one to cave."

"Alpha has Sandolphon and Jophiel!" Metatron cried defensively. "What was I supposed to do?!"

"Sandolphon and Jophiel lick Alpha's boots willingly," Lucifer groaned. "They're not prisoners. They are his puppets."

"Lies!" Metatron seethed, lunging at Lucifer. "They would never side with that monster."

"Lucifer has no reason to lie!" I exclaimed, stepping in between the two of them. "Uriel told us herself that they 'fled' into Purgatory as Alpha chased Uriel with smites. If Alpha was never smiting Uriel, then Uriel also lied about them fleeing for their lives, too."

"Uriel wouldn't lie to me," Metatron continued, shaking his head in disbelief.

"Why would we?" I asked, knitting my brows and pleading with my eyes. "We are your family and have been for a while."

"They might be my family," Metatron hissed, pointing around the room. "But you aren't my family."

It was like the air was punched out of my lungs. "But… you saved me from the whirlwinds in hell. You took Incaendiel's side and spoke up for me when the incident with Rafe happened. You have—"

"I couldn't let the only card I had to play get hurt, could I?" he asked, glaring at me. "I was trading you for Sandolphon and Jophiel. He had made promises." He whipped his head in Samael and Azazel's direction. "But you two ruined it! You just had to follow us! You couldn't stay mad at Incaendiel for long. I should have known better than to think that. Now we have to come up with some other plan."

I turned away from the group and just stared out the window. I couldn't take hearing another word from some other person who feigned loyalty or care for me when it was just to get something fruitful from it. Kindness and love were supposed to be gifts without strings attached, and every single fucking person who faked it had motives. Asmodeus was right. He is still breaking me from the sidelines through every single person who acted like they cared while siding with him and Uriel. I am nothing and mean nothing to everyone. I am worthless.

"Hey!" Incaendiel shouted. "Enough of that, Damian!"

"Get out of my head," I mumbled, swiping away a stray tear that betrayed me.

There was a commotion behind me, and I turned around to see Incaendiel pick Metatron up by the throat and slide him up the wall. His face began to turn red, and he pounded against Incaendiel's arm, trying to loosen his grip that refused to budge as Incaendiel's eyes burned with rage. "You are the second person today to make my kid feel like he is worthless, and honestly, I am so fucking tired of it. So here's the deal, and you can take it or leave it. You can sit with Asmodeus after receiving the same burning punishment I gave him and wait for whatever hell I unleash on those of you who meant to really do my family wrong, or you can beg me for forgiveness, and we can all figure a way out to save, convince, whatever, Sandolphon and Jophiel back to your side. I gave safe haven to those I knew weren't loyal to me, and I expected them to have some sort of rebellion against me planned, but I am sick and tired of being lied to my face by those claiming to be loyal but are really snakes in the grass, ready to bite my damn ankle. I should really just burn you to a crisp right now and toss your dying carcass in hell where nobody can find you, and nobody can take your soul to Potter's Field, but unlike Alpha, I *do* have mercy for my enemies. Especially the enemies I called B*rother*!"

He dropped Metatron to the ground as he coughed and sputtered, gasping for air.

"I'm beginning to like this new version of Incaendiel," Lucifer joked, patting Incaendiel on the shoulder. "He gets shit done."

Incaendiel ignored him and knelt in front of Metatron. "What's it going to be?" he growled, clenching his jaw.

Metatron stared back at Incaendiel. "What do I need to do?"

"You're going to infiltrate Uriel's little group, big group, whatever it is, and you're going to report back to me and be a double spy. I will let you know what you can tell her, and we will set a trap. The whole backstabbing shit ends today! I am so sick and tired of you all making me watch my back because I don't know who I can and can't trust."

"It will be easy to do since I hang with you all anyway to report to her," Metatron offered, getting to his feet and Incaendiel standing with him. "I'm sorry, Brother. I shouldn't have… I just should have told you what was happening and not left you to be blind sided by Asmodeus."

"You knew about Asmodeus?" I barked, anger tearing through me. "You knew what he thought about me and still let me walk around like he was one of the most important people in the world to me, knowing he hated me emphatically just because Alpha made him take care of me."

"I didn't know everything," Metatron spoke softly. "All I knew was he was playing recon for Alpha along with Uriel, and he led me to believe you were also playing sides as well. That you would fake your capture. I didn't expect you to fight back as hard as you did against the furies, and knew then that must have been a lie. They're in cahoots together. Don't let him make you think she is the mastermind. Honestly, he is the mastermind, and she follows his orders. She reports to Alpha for him since he can't get away without looking suspicious since he's 'reunited' with you."

"I figured that much," Lucifer chimed in. "The way he so callously threw her under the bus when we started questioning him made it obvious."

"So what does Uriel know as of right now?" Michael asked, changing the subject back to the issue at hand. "Does she know Lucifer is back?"

"No, she doesn't," Metatron replied. "But Mephistopheles, Babylon, and Belphegor all knew we were there to rescue him."

"They don't know if we succeeded or not," I interjected. "We could barely make it through that last circle of hell because it was so cold. Even In—dad had problems making it through that frozen tundra without freezing. The only person who could possibly check and see is Alpha, and he probably thinks we high-tailed it out before finding him, fearing we would freeze ourselves."

"Damian has a point," Samael agreed, glancing around at everyone. "Lucifer, who carried you into the ninth circle of hell?"

"No one," he answered. "They tossed me down the well, and I flew as fast as I could across that cavern, trying to find the exit to Ante-Purgatory. I was almost there before the ice started weighing me down, and then as soon as it touched the frozen ground, I was stuck."

"So even Alpha hasn't been in there," Azazel asked, nodding. "This could work. Metatron can tell Uriel, *if* or *when* she asks, that we couldn't make it to Lucifer because of the cold. That even Incaendiel couldn't beat it."

"That could work," Metatron acknowledged with a nod. "We are supposed to meet here in a little bit and go over what exactly went wrong in hell and why Damian wasn't taken captive. She knew that Samael and Incaendiel had their falling out, so he and Azazel showing up really foiled our plans."

"We are also going to eventually have to either convince her that Alpha is inherently evil or lock her away with Asmodeus to get that key for Purgatory," Lucifer added, picking at his nails. "She's the only one who has the key. There are no copies or duplicates, and it's the only way to get into Purgatory. She wears that damn key like a trophy."

The front door popped open, followed by the question, "Why do you need to go to Purgatory?" as Luxina walked through and closed it behind her.

CHAPTER THIRTEEN: DAMIAN

I COULDN'T BELIEVE my eyes. She was here. She had escaped. She was safe. I ran to her, pulling her into my arms. "You," I breathed, gripping my arms tighter around her. She lightly hugged me back, and I released her. "How did you…" I began.

"Adam helped me escape," Luxina explained, looking around the room. "I really thought he was going to play games with me more, but here I am."

"Did he hurt you?" I asked as I began to look over her body for bruises or scars.

"No, but he does have a message for everyone," she answered, taking a deep breath. "When he can get away from Alpha, he plans to join us in our war against Alpha."

Silence filled the room, and I tried to process what she said. "Join us?"

"He said he spoke with Dad before, and he was right," she continued, looking over at Incaendiel. "You told him Alpha just uses you for whatever you can give to him, and when you're no longer useful, he gets rid of you. Like how he was with Damian." She glanced at me and quickly averted her eyes back to Incaendiel. "Alpha has already begun treating him differently. He doesn't know what changed with him, but he knows he's on the chopping block now."

"When does he plan to arrive?" Incaendiel asked, walking over and wrapping her in a hug. "It's good to have you here."

She smiled up at him. "I missed you, Daddy." He released her from his arms. "He said he would follow me soon after I escaped. He had some loose ends to tie up, but would pop in."

"Alright, well, we will be waiting for him, and if it's a trap..." I paused. I don't know why, but something just felt off with her.

"You have to give him a chance," Luxina urged. "He's not the evil, vile creature you think he is. He's not another monster Alpha tamed." She grabbed my hands and held them in hers. "Do you trust me?" she asked, peering into my eyes.

"I trust you," I began, "it's just him I don't trust. So many people I have trusted have turned out to be just as cruel as Alpha."

"I would never lie to you, Damian," she cooed, brushing her hand against my cheek. "Now, where is Reikal?" she beamed, changing the subject. "I need some new weapons."

"Follow me, and we will look for him together," Incaendiel offered with a smile, wrapping his arm around her shoulders and squeezing her to his side.

They exited the cabin, followed by everyone else except Lucifer and me. I watched them walk off from the cabin before closing the door. She didn't even want to spend personal time together. I had waited all this time to get her back and have her in my arms, and the moment she is back, she goes off with everyone else as if the last time we saw one another didn't need to be discussed. I know I screwed that up. I wasn't ready to accept the fact that someone truly loved me and cared for me. I wasn't ready for *her*. I needed time to sort out my damage because no matter how much people say I am not, I *am* damaged goods. I have trauma. I have skeletons. I have emotional baggage. Mommy issues. Daddy issues. I was a psychiatrist's wet dream, all wrapped up in a pretty bow, ready to be torn open and displayed on a wall of enlightenment. It wasn't the time to open those wounds and spill myself to her. It was something only time could manage for the right moment.

I didn't know why, but on the edge of my senses it screamed that this wasn't right. That something was wrong, but I couldn't quite grasp what it was. Was this jealousy? Had her time with Adam meant something to her? The way she spoke about giving him a chance was the same thing she did with me when everyone had universally decided I needed to be eliminated. Was he being manipulated by Alpha, as I had been? The last time we spoke, she was afraid of him, afraid of what he would do to her or what would happen with him if she stayed any longer in that place. What happened during that gap? Was everything that happened to her a manipulation of reality and all in her head? Did she know that, and that's why she is so nonchalant about it now? So many questions ran through my head that had no answers. At least no answers, because if I asked the questions, I would seem distrusting to her, and that's the last thing she needed right now, considering she just escaped the abuse Alpha and Asmodeus had schemed together and came up with.

"I know what you're thinking," Lucifer spoke, breaking the silence. "And you're not wrong."

"Wrong?" I asked, casting him a confused glance before returning my attention out the window.

"She *does* seem odd," he answered, sitting down on the couch. "I haven't been around her that long, but I have been around your mother when she was split. Whenever Alpha would bring Anniel out of sleep, she was the same but... different. I couldn't explain it. She had both Sophie and Anniel's memories together, but she just seemed... wrong. The way she spoke. The way she acted. It was like she was a different person even when she wasn't."

"She just escaped Purgatory and whatever abuse Alpha and Adam put her through," I countered, making excuses for her when I myself had doubts. "She just needs time to process what happened to her. She will be back to herself." It took time for me to be somewhat normal after what happened to me during those nights. She could be masking it all.

"Just..." he began and stopped.

"Just what?" I asked, spinning around to face him.

"Before you get lost and wrapped up in her," he continued, running his hand through his hair, "make sure she's the person you love and trust."

I glared at him even though I knew he was right. He was asking the right questions out loud when I was too much of a pussy to.

"Pay attention to all of the details," Lucifer added. "If something is amiss with her, it will pop out least expected." He eyed me curiously. "I already know you have your doubts just because you are here with me instead of out there with her. And she hasn't questioned it yet. She didn't ask you if you were coming along. Everyone knows she's a daddy's girl, but everyone also knows how crazy she was about you, too."

"They do?" I walked over and sat down beside him.

"Yes, we do," Lucifer emphasized, raising his eyebrows. "Talk gets around, and even before she spent any time with you outside of you taking her prisoner for Alpha, she was crazy about you. Wanted to make sure you were safe and okay and away from Alpha. The same things she is saying about Adam now."

I was quiet, mulling over everything he had said, a sinking feeling moving through my chest. "She loves him, too," I whispered.

"I don't know if love is the right word, but it seems she does care deeply for him," Lucifer replied. "Probably cares enough for him to fight anyone who would try to hurt him, just like your mom is conditioned to do for Alpha."

"I hadn't thought of that. She very well could be conditioned to protect Adam," I said, rolling it around in my head. "It would make a lot of sense, too."

"Yeah, so be careful," Lucifer urged, poking me in the arm. "And remember, your mom still loved Incaendiel, even when conditioned to follow Alpha's orders."

I didn't want to say it out loud, but I was terrified. Alpha or Adam could have manipulated her in so many ways that she may not even love me anymore. Another person down the drain I cared about. "If anyone comes looking for me, just tell them I am in my room," I said, standing up and walking toward the back door.

"Not a problem," Lucifer responded, sitting on the couch, looking bored.

I walked out of Reikal's cabin and looked around to see if anyone was near to see me. The coast was clear, so I walked behind the row of cabins until I hit the tree line. I broke off into a sprint. I didn't want to be found just yet. I didn't want to have to deal with the next item on the list of things to prepare for battling Alpha. I was so tired of spending each and every minute plotting and planning. I never had a moment to myself to just breathe. I never had a moment to absolutely lose my shit in peace. My sprint turned into a full-blown run, and I tore through the thicket like a streak of lightning. The air whipping past my face felt hot and humid, and the tree branches ripped at my clothes, but I didn't care. I needed to run. I had been cooped up for so long, whenever the chance arose, running was the next best thing to sex. Sex… another thing I had to talk to Luxina about. I knew about her and Adam, but she didn't know about me and my escapades because of the lust bug from the terrace.

It's not like I haven't had sex before. Alpha would grant me time away from world domination here and there. I would hit up the pubs in the Otherworld and dance around with the fey and dark fey. The dark fey girls are little nymphomaniacs, and they are absolutely wild. They adored having orgies, and I partook in quite a few of them before Alpha put me under strict lock and key, before all of the things... Sex was just sex. Intimacy was something I was not familiar with. Taking my time undressing someone and marveling at their body while they ran their hands across my chest. I didn't like being touched, but with the right person, I knew it could drive me wild. Being able to put enough belief of safety into someone was hard for me. I never felt safe around anyone because no one had ever shown me how to feel safe. It was still a learning curve, even with Incaendiel acting the way a parent was supposed to act when it came to their child. I never knew what any of that felt like, just the hard end of the whip when I disappointed.

I shot down a path I had yet to explore, and it led me down the side of the mountain to the bottom of the waterfall that spilled into a massive lake. Birds flew over the water while butterflies zipped from flower to flower. Fish popped to the top of the water to grab bugs and would dart back beneath into its depths for protection. Deer stood on the banks and drank from the water without a care in the world or fear for safety. The lake stretched on for as far as the eye could see. It was magnificent. Lightshade was my safe haven and showed me the beauty I had missed out on while locked away in solitude. I didn't feel vulnerable here. I didn't have to sleep with one eye open, waiting for someone to drag me from my room, fighting for my life.

I sat down at the water's edge and just zoned. I could sit here forever, honestly. I could stay here and never go back. They would never find me, and there wouldn't be all of this drama in my life. I wouldn't have to worry about anyone planning nefarious plots against me. I could build a cabin down here and just stay out of the way, and let all of the others deal with Alpha and his loyalists. Luxina was now safe, so I didn't have to worry about her. I didn't have to come to terms with the fact that she may love someone else now, either. I could just sit in a bubble of pure naivety and live out my days in ignorant oblivion, but I knew that would never happen. Even if we defeated Alpha, he would still have those who were loyal to him to worry about. People just don't switch sides because someone is no longer in power. That's how revolts happen. That's what was definitely going to happen, and every step of the way, Incaendiel and I would be compared to him. We would be just as vicious and cruel, or labeled uncaring and sadistic, just like Charon had told Incaendiel when he threatened him.

The way he tortured the information out of Asmodeus… I wanted to do that not because I enjoy inflicting pain, but Incaendiel doesn't need blood on his hands when he starts the new world order. He doesn't need to stoop to the depths that I have been or even be known as the next Alpha. People were already making comments about him, and it would just get worse when they found out he did what he did to Asmodeus, all because he said hurtful things to me. It's half true. He lost his shit because of what he said to me, but he also needed the information about who was a traitor among his ranks. We needed to know the whys on stuff, especially for Lucifer's sake. He was put in hell, and we needed to know exactly why and who had done it. But if everyone knew how he used his powers on Asmodeus, burned and boiled him from the inside out to get what information he needed, there would be riots.

Never in a million years would I have thought the man who raised me, trained me, and treated my wounds absolutely despised me. No one knows what that truly feels like. The only reason

Alpha and Incaendiel butt heads is because Alpha couldn't control him or his power. To know, to your face, a person is one way, but behind your back, something completely different is defeating. I pulled my knees to my chest, staring out at the water, thinking about all the years Asmodeus never once cracked under his guise of false love. He really put on a show. I wondered how many of the Forsaken actually knew it was fake and how many of them would be just as surprised as I was when I learned he was a traitor.

I picked up a rock and tossed it across the water, and it skipped nearly to the other side of the lake. I stared into the water and thought of Metatron. That was one of the last people I thought would have turned against Incaendiel. He had been an ally with him since the war began. But love does make you do crazy things. He thinks Jophiel and Sandolphon were being held captive by Alpha because of Uriel. I was willing to do whatever it took to get Luxina back, even if it came down to having to sacrifice others to get what I wanted. I guess that's why Incaendiel went easier on him than Asmodeus. Incaendiel had been in that position so many times, and people were there for him to help him burn down the world. Had Metatron just come to us, we would have helped him. Who knows what Uriel put in his head about why he couldn't ask Incaendiel for help and had to choose sides, unless it was her withholding the key. If she's not on our side, then

Metatron would never have the chance to save them.

A twig snapped behind me, breaking me from my thoughts, and I twisted my body to see who was spying on me. It was Metatron. I clambered to my feet.

"Don't take this the wrong way," I began, dusting off my pants, "but I don't exactly trust you."

"What are you doing?" he asked, looking around at the scenery.

"Just sitting here," I replied. "It's quiet here and no one to spy on my thoughts."

"Yeah, but it's not safe for you to be alone either," he insisted, waving his hand for me to follow him. "Let's get back with everyone else."

"How did you know where to find me?" I asked cautiously, staying put and not moving.

"Starfire said you might be here," he explained. "We are getting ready to move on Uriel, and Incaendiel wants you there."

"You go on ahead," I informed him, shooing him away. "I will be there in a bit."

He sighed. "I'm sorry for saying the things I said," he relented, his face apologetic. "I didn't really mean them. Heat of the moment."

"I understand why you did what you did because I have done the same, but I don't trust easy, especially when the trust has been broken." I watched his face, and he nodded.

"I get it, too," he replied, running his hand through his hair. "I heard about Asmodeus after some additional questions to your dad. I didn't know everything, just that he was working with Uriel. I didn't know… I just didn't know it was all fake for him."

"That makes two of us," I agreed.

"To find out that the person who raised you also hated having to raise you and carried a secret grudge because of it… I can't imagine," he spoke softly and turned to walk away before stopping. "I didn't save you in hell because I needed you for Alpha. I saved you to save you. I just wanted to hurt you is why I said what I did. Everyone—they blame you for this war. The sides that were chosen. Some really did choose to side with you, and you're resented for it. But I don't hate you or blame you for anything." He continued walking and shouted, "Oh, and Luxina is also looking for you."

I took one last look at the lake and started back toward the village. I walked, taking my time and enjoying the scenery. I still wanted to sit and process everything that had happened recently, but of course, war doesn't offer you personal moments even if you sneak away and try to hide. Someone will always find you. Another twig snapped, and I knew I wasn't alone. My head whipped from side to side as I came to a halt to see who was spying on me in the woods.

"You mean daddy left you all alone?" a voice rasped from the shadows of the copse.

Asmodeus emerged from the darkness of the trees to my right. His face was still blistered and oozing from Incaendiel setting him on fire from within.

"How did you get free?" I huffed, narrowing my eyes at him.

He walked through the clearing and stood twenty feet away from me, and we circled one another.

"I have friends in high places," he mused, a maniacal grin spreading across his face. He looked around in all directions and then back at me as we continued to circle one another slowly. "Didn't think you would be stupid enough to come out here alone until I followed Metatron. Even after finding out people were actively trying to send you back to Alpha, you came out here to be by yourself. Were your feelings hurt?" He made a pouting face at me. "Did wittle Damian need to come out here and cwy away his big boy emotions?" He cackled as I glared at him.

"What's your game plan, Asmodeus?" I sneered, reaching inside my pocket for my sword. "Plan to steal me by yourself?"

"First, I'm going to beat your ass," he muttered, gritting his teeth and pulling his own sword out. "And then once you have been incapacitated, my friends are going to tote you away to Alpha for me."

People emerged from behind the trees. Eisleth and Metatron appeared along with a third, Elisha. I should have known he was out here for someone else and not to bring me back for a meeting. He used Luxina as bait, knowing I would follow to go talk to her. But Elisha, that took me by surprise, but it also made sense. The way she played and toyed with me and threw herself on me for sex. Of course, she was working for Alpha. They all drew out a sword, prepared to fight me along with Asmodeus.

"Aw, you didn't know that Metatron was one of Uriel's minions, did you?" Asmodeus mocked, feigning sadness. "Or your little fuck buddy!" Elisha wiggled her fingers at me, winked, and blew me a kiss.

"Four against one is hardly fair," I claimed, clicking the button on my sword. I twirled it around in my hand as I had grown so accustomed to doing. Fighting was the one thing I was good at, and Asmodeus had another thing coming if he thought he could beat me. He may have trained me, but he didn't teach me everything. The hilt of my sword turned blue, and electricity ran through the blade like a lightning bolt.

The air began to grow hotter, and sweat dripped from my brow. "Hardly fair," Luxina shouted, emerging from the shadows of the trees. Flames wrapped her whole body as she glided over toward us, taking a place at my side.

"How did *she* get here?" Asmodeus hissed, nostrils flared. "You know what? It doesn't matter. Alpha will be glad to have both of you back."

The four of them began walking toward us as Luxina, and I readied our weapons. As they drew closer, Metatron stepped in front of Eisleth and pushed her back.

"What are you doing?!" Eisleth seethed.

"My job," Metatron replied, raising his sword.

He brought his sword down, and she blocked it with hers. "Double agent, are we? Uriel is going to be pissed when she finds out."

"She's not going to find out because you're not leaving these woods alive," Metatron snarled, swinging his sword around twice as hard.

Luxina squared off with Elisha as I took on Asmodeus. "How cute. Both your girlfriends fighting one another," Asmodeus chided. "Does Luxina know you slept with Elisha yet?"

As Luxina held her dueling swords up in the air, she glanced over my way, a pained look spreading across her face. Her face contorted, and rage brimmed to the surface as she swung one of her arms down, striking Elisha's sword and nearly knocking it from her hands.

"I'm going to enjoy skinning you from head to toe," Luxina sneered, glaring hatefully at Elisha.

Asmodeus struck first with his sword, and I blocked it. We danced back and forth, delivering blows, parrying, and blocking. The sound of clattering metal echoed through the trees.

"I find it hilarious Luxina is fighting Elisha," Asmodeus jived, striking my sword from the left and trying to jab with his right fist. "Do you want to know what the funniest thing about it is?"

I ignored him as I delivered blow after blow to his sword. He kicked me away with his foot. "I lied to you," he grinned. "When I told you the lust bug hit you because of her being on the terrace, that wasn't true." He brought his sword down on mine, and I pushed him off. "I gave you the lust bug so you would be preoccupied with finding your next lay." My blood boiled with fury. "Like mother, like son," he laughed. "How do you like being a whore?" I began pelting him with more sword blows as he blocked them, kicking me out of the way again. "Of course, you always were a whore. I know about all the little fey you slept with. The orgies you were a part of. A little nymph yourself. And then of course, all of those nights in that dungeon. But once you had your sights on Luxina, you became a little prude. Nautila knew all about your cock blocking."

"You leave her name out of your filthy mouth!" I hissed.

"You know, it's your fault that bitch is dead," he continued, circling me while spinning his sword. "It's your fault she's stuck in the vestibule, wandering around like a rotting meat suit. Had you just fucked her, she would have never left that room."

My face must have betrayed my silence. "Oh, I was there." He grinned at me, wild-eyed. "I scouted ahead of the others, or so that's what I told them, and I watched everything." He caught me off guard and tripped me with his foot. "It's such a shame she ended up in hell. That's what happens to people who get too close to you. Bad shit," he seethed, as he brought his sword down over me. I braced for the strike when Metatron stepped in front of the blade and blocked it.

"You know, Asmodeus," Metatron sneered. "You always have been a whiny ass dickhead."

Elisha barrel-rolled away from Luxina and threw a dagger, striking Metatron in his shoulder blade. I scrambled to my feet as Metatron reached around to try and grab the blade and tackled Asmodeus to the ground as he went to swing his sword at Metatron. Simultaneously, Luxina swung her sword, catching Elisha in the neck and taking her head off. Eisleth lay on the ground in the opposite direction with her own sword jabbed through her midsection. The three of us surrounded Asmodeus.

"You can't kill me," he laughed. "You *need* me. I have all of the information you need! I am the one in charge!"

Luxina grabbed him by the back of the neck and lifted him into the air. Fire erupted from her hands as she squeezed, and his entire neck began to glow red and catch fire.

"Incaendiel needs me!" he garbled, as his legs and arms flailed while trying to escape her grip. He burst into flames, howling until nothing escaped his lips anymore. She dropped him to the ground in a flaming pile of burning embers.

"He's not here," she muttered, glaring down at his roasting body. Her eyes met mine, balls of burning embers. "We need to talk," she snarled.

***

We broke through the thicket into the village, and Luxina was still yelling at me. "When were you going to tell me you were running around sleeping with everyone here?!" she demanded, punching me in my arm.

"It wasn't my fault!" I shrieked, rubbing my arm and walking away from her faster.

"Oh, no!" she seethed, grabbing me by the arm and spinning me around. "You don't get to go and hide this time. You are going to explain yourself!"

"What the hell is going on?" Samael asked as he and others ran up to us.

"A long story," Metatron groaned. "Can you pull this knife out of my back, please? They've been too preoccupied to help."

"Why is there a knife in your back?!" Azazel asked, alarmed.

"Talk about it in private," Metatron replied, looking around at those gathering where Luxina and I stood arguing.

"I should have known you were like all other men," Luxina cried. "The moment another woman falls into your lap, you're yanking clothes off with her. A fucking man whore."

"It's not like that!" I protested. "It's no different than what happened with you on the terrace!"

"It's way different!" Luxina grunted, getting in my face. "I didn't have a choice."

"Oh, you had a choice," I muttered. "You gave in to temptation just like I did."

"Against my will!" she cried, tears brimming.

"It was against mine too!" I yelled, unable to control my anger. "Did you not hear Asmodeus?!"

"Guys! Guys!" Incaendiel shouted, interrupting us.

"What!?" we both hollered, looking at him.

"There's a crowd," he spoke low, glancing around at everyone gathered. "Let's talk about this inside, quietly."

"So you're going to side with him?" Luxina demanded, glaring at him.

"I am not siding with anyone, but all of this needs to be taken away from the public and into the private. Now go," he growled, pointing his finger toward Reikal's cabin.

Luxina huffed and stomped off, steam rising with each step she took. Incaendiel walked beside me with everyone else flanking us. "What the hell happened?" he snarled.

Once inside, he shut the door behind him. Lucifer sat quietly on the couch, and Samael and Azazel were tending to Metatron's knife wound while Luxina stood over in the corner quietly fuming. "Don't make me ask again!" Incaendiel yelled, staring between us.

"I went to find Damian like I was told," Metatron began. "He was off by the lake just like Starfire said. On the way back, I ran into Asmodeus, who was still under the impression I was part of the renegades against you. He had Eisleth and Elisha with him."

"Elisha is that Nephilim, right?" Azazel asked, then glanced at me when it dawned on her why Luxina was irate.

"Yeah," Metatron answered. "Asmodeus knew somehow Damian was in the woods and had me wait with them until he followed me out so he could attack."

"Where's Asmodeus now?" Incaendiel asked, pinching the bridge of his nose.

"Dead," Metatron replied. "Along with Elisha and Eisleth. We didn't have a choice."

"I told you not to engage with Asmodeus!" Incaendiel yelled at me.

"So I was supposed to just stand there and let him kill me?" I shouted back. "Why are you mad at me for him escaping to kill me?!"

"You shouldn't have killed him and instead, brought him back here to lock him back up!"

Incaendiel snapped. "And which one of you stabbed Metatron!"

"You automatically assume it was me who killed him!" I huffed, punching a hole in the wall. "Typical. Damian's the murderer in the room. Damian's the one with an unhinged emotional regulation. Of course, he's the only one who could have and did kill Asmodeus." I glared at him. "And Elisha is the one who stabbed Metatron in the back when he stepped in front of Asmodeus's blade before it hacked my head off."

"If you didn't kill Asmodeus and Metatron was too injured, then who killed him?" Incaendiel demanded, pounding his fist on the table beside him.

"I did," Luxina replied, breaking her silence. "I burned him to a crisp. You can check if you like."

Incaendiel rubbed his forehead. "Sam, will you get Michael and Rafe and go clean up the mess before someone comes along and finds it, please?"

"Sure," Samael replied, easing out of his seat and leaving through the back door.

"How bad is your wound, Metatron?" Incaendiel asked, walking over and looking at his shoulder blade.

"I will live," he answered, glancing at me, then back at Incaendiel.

"Unbelievable," I snorted, clapping my hands against my legs.

"What?" Incaendiel snapped, jerking his head in my direction.

"You lose your shit on me for defending myself from an attack that at the time looked like four on one until Metatron turned out to be on my side and Luxina arrived. You blame me, fuming over it, that Asmodeus was killed, and when it turns out to be Luxina who killed him, everything changes. Is it because she's not a homicidal maniac like me? Is it because she knows how to regulate her emotional outbursts, and I don't? Or is it because she's your darling little girl who does no wrong in your eyes, and I'm still the new brat you only tolerate?" I was heated. Incaendiel went to speak. "Just fucking save it, *dad.* I will always be held to a different standard than anyone else, even though I was the one literally tortured my entire life. Not just emotional abuse but actual whips, chains, knives, swords, punches, gags, starvation, sleep deprivation, and on and on and on, so excuse me if I have a god damn problem controlling my emotions."

I yanked the front door open to walk out. "Where are you going now?" Incaendiel demanded. "We aren't through here."

"Wherever the hell you aren't, *daddy,*" I snarled, glancing over my shoulder at him. "Bond with your real fucking kid because it ain't me." I slammed the door shut behind me and stalked off toward Starfire's cottage. I made it to my room and slammed the door behind me, locking it in place.

No sooner had I locked it than the doorknob jiggled.

"Leave me the fuck alone!" I shouted as I crashed onto my bed.

"Damian, open the damn door!" Incaendiel shouted at me.

I didn't answer. I just let him bang on the door and jiggle the handle. He could break it down if he really wanted to, but he wanted me to let him and not force his way in. At least he respected some form of boundaries. Who was he to be pissed at me for defending myself and not even being the one who actually killed Asmodeus? I brought my hand down on my bed, punching it in frustration. Why am I always the one in the wrong, even when I am innocent? And Luxina! God damn! Blaming me for what Asmodeus did to me?! Saying it's not the same as what she went through?! How's it not the fucking same? It's exactly the same. He hit me with the lust bug. He did that to me like some pervert getting his jollies off of my erection, forcing me against my will once more just so he could watch like he always had through the window.

A softer knock came to the door.

"Go away. I don't want to talk to anyone," I cried, a tear slipping from my eye. I quickly wiped it away. *You cry about everything.* Asmodeus's words echoed in my head. *You're weak!* Alpha shouted at me. *You're pathetic,* Asmodeus laughs. *Poor, poor, Damian.*

"Damian, please open the door," Luxina asked quietly.

I squeezed my eyes shut, fighting off all of the emotions swirling around in my head.

"I don't want to talk." My voice broke. I swallowed the lump forming in my throat.

"Come on, Damian," Luxina pleaded, knocking again.

"Go talk to your fucking daddy," I snarled, clenching my jaw. "He's got his precious little girl back. No one else matters now. Go have your little family reunion and leave me out of it!"

"Damian," Incaendiel whispered. "Open the door."

I bolted out of the bed, walked over to the door, and ripped it open. "You're not my family. I don't have a family. I never had a family. And I don't want one!" I slammed the door back in their faces before they could say anything. I heard their footsteps retreat from the door, and I grabbed a bag. I started packing all of my shit that I had in the room and threw the bag over my shoulder. I opened the door, bounded down the stairs, and out the front door before anyone could see. Starfire stood there in front of me.

"Don't you dare spy on me, old lady!" I hissed as I moved past her and down the stairs.

And then I ran. I cut across the yard and started down the backside of the cabins. I ran through the woods, down the mountain past the waterfall, and kept running up the banks of the lake. I ran for what felt like forever before I stopped near a cave on the other side of the valley. I tossed my bag inside it and crawled in. I drew my knees to my chest and wrapped my arms around my legs. No one would find me here. No one could hurt me here. I was safe here away from everyone. Here is I was just Damian, not a problem. Screw the war. Screw family. And screw being some sort of god who was supposed to inherit the universe. Most of all, screw love. I didn't want any of it. I curled up on my side inside the cave as everything ran through my head, and I couldn't stop it. It was in that silence, when everything slowed down, that I was able to mourn the loss of the person who was once my mentor and friend. Asmodeus would never have a chance to apologize or change his story to say anything different than what we knew. In the recesses of my mind, I had still clung to the hope that what he was saying was just out of spite and not really what he meant. I will never know now if that hope was all in my head or real. He was gone, and with his death, my sanity was taken as well. At some point, mental and emotional exhaustion overtook me, and I drifted off to sleep.

CHAPTER FOURTEEN: DAMIAN

I AWOKE TO the sound of voices calling my name in the distance. I had no idea how long I had been there or even how long I had slept since the sun never sets in this place. Their desperate shouts indicated it must have been a while since Starfire told them I had run off. Quietly, I pulled myself into the far recesses of the cave I could so that no one could look in and see me.

"Damian!" Incaendiel shouted. Don't think anything. Don't think anything. Don't think anything. "Damian!"

"Come on, Damian!" Luxina shouted, sounding annoyed. "We know you're out here somewhere!"

I kept calm, keeping my breath steady and even, focusing on it rather than them.

I'm sorry, Incaendiel thought. *I didn't mean to lash out as I did. I just don't want you to have to be the monster. It should be my burden to beat. Not yours.*

I stared across the lake to the other side and closed my eyes. I opened them, and I was on the other side of the lake in the shadows of the trees, far away from them. I didn't want to go back. Shit was too complicated on the other side of the lake. I could peacefully live over here. Turn into a hermit if need be. I didn't need them. They needed me. They needed my powers. That's all I would ever be to them is a weapon. It's all I am to anyone these days. Everybody was always making a grab for me to win points with Alpha or use me to end the universe or to end Alpha. I was tired of it all. I was a stupid teenager with an attitude problem. I wasn't the answer to ending the apocalypse. They could achieve that on their own. Hell, it might be best if the apocalypse did happen and we couldn't fix or save anything. Just let cosmic law take over from there.

I walked deeper into the woods and further away from the shouting voices. When things de-escalated, I could leave Lightshade and hideaway in the world where no one would ever find me again. Hell, I could go off-world. Live somewhere else in the galaxy. I wasn't restricted to Earth. It's just Alpha's favorite place in the world. Life could be simpler, better for me.

A voice cut through the quiet. "I was like you once."

I stopped and looked around on alert. "Who's there?" I called out, drawing my weapon out and holding it up.

"I just wanted to disappear from the world. Everything was put on my shoulders. Power. Envy. People wanted to use and abuse me for what I could give them."

I spun around in a circle trying to find where the voice was coming from.

"Me disappearing didn't solve anything. It just paused everything around me until I returned."

"Show yourself!" I demanded, continuing to spin to find who I was talking to.

"You have so much potential, Damian." An old man stepped out from under the shadow of a tree. He was old with a long white beard and a colossal giant.

"Who are you?" I demanded, pointing the sword at him.

He held up his hands to show me he wasn't armed. "Someone just like you who had so much piled on me at once, I caved under pressure. A short temper. Emotional dysregulation. And, in the end, hunted by the same person who is hunting you."

"What did Alpha want with you?" I demanded, unwavering with my sword pointed at him.

"The same thing he wants with you. My power." The old man crossed his hands in front of his body.

"And that's supposed to tell me who you are?" I asked, quickly glancing around the area in case I had to run.

"You don't have to run from me, Damian. I'm not going to hurt you." He smiled at me. It was warm and genuine and instantly calmed me.

"How do I know you aren't going to hurt me?" I asked, my sword wavering in the air.

He snickered and shook his head. "I would never hurt my great-grandson!" he exclaimed.

"Great-grandson?" I asked, shaking my head in confusion. "How are you my great-grandfather?" I was thinking about the creation story we were told by Maveth, and it never mentioned anything older than Kharuun.

He laughed. "Not that old, my son."

"You can read my thoughts?" I looked around nervously, waiting to be ambushed by others.

"Yes," he answered with a smile. "I am Yahweh, Alpha's father."

I sheathed my sword. For some reason, I believed him. "That makes sense. You seemed familiar, but at the same time… nicer. I don't know how to explain it."

"Alpha tries to be like me. They say imitation is the best form of flattery, but in this case, it's just how he hides from who he actually is. He lulls people into a false illusion of who he is at his core," Yahweh grunted, knitting his eyebrows together in contemplation.

"What are you doing here?" I asked, looking around at the empty woods. "Shouldn't you be back in Lightshade, I don't know, meeting everyone?"

"Why, looking for you, my boy!" he replied jolly. "Why are you hiding away from your father? He's really worried about you, by the way."

"He shouldn't have been a dick and yelled at me for something that wasn't in my control," I snarled, flaring my nostrils. "Everyone treats me like I am a ticking time bomb. I get it. I lose my cool every once in a while. But what happened with Asmodeus was not my fault."

"Ah, Asmodeus." He pursed his lips and nodded his head. "My understanding was Luxina was the one who took care of him."

"Yes, and it was immediately blamed on me. Why did I engage him? Why did I fight him? Why did I kill him? And when it came out that Luxina was the one who killed him, crickets. Not a single word was said to her or any bitching at her. If I killed him in self-defense, I was in trouble. She killed him, and she's golden!"

"Sometimes, fathers lash out because they're scared more than they are angry," he explained, placing his hand on my shoulder. "It looks the same in both cases, but when it's a circumstance they weren't there to help or intervene, it's taken personally. He's probably more upset with himself for not taking Asmodeus off the table before he could present a problem trying to hurt you. And then for not being the one to come and get you and sending Metatron in his place."

"How do you know all of that?"

He winked at me. "I know a lot for an old man. Like, for instance, I know you want to just disappear and not have to deal with all of the stress put on your shoulders." He looked around the woods, rubbing his beard. "Yes, you're right. This would be a nice spot for a cabin to hide in until the apocalypse blew over."

"There's absolutely no privacy in this damn family," I muttered, scrunching my face.

He laughed heartily. "Unfortunately, no. No privacy in this family. I have been watching you all from the sidelines for some time now, biding my time to pop in for a visit. I figured it was time, so here I am."

"And what do you have to offer to us?" I asked, scrunching my face. "No offense, but you're pretty old, so fighting is out of the question."

He raised his fists and ducked and jabbed. "I still have some moves." We shared a laugh at the joke. "I am here to bequeath my power. Alpha always expected it and still does. He thinks he can replenish himself with what I have withheld and is banking on that for his plans to succeed."

"But you're not giving it to him, are you?" I asked, furrowing my brows.

"No," he replied with a warm smile. "I am giving them to you."

"Me? Why me?" I asked, bewildered. "Why not Incaendiel?"

"He and Anniel have Barbelo's powers," he replied. "My great-grandchildren need my powers too."

"So you're giving them to Luxina too?" I asked, relieved I wasn't being picked as a golden child.

"Not just yet. Hers will be set aside," he explained, thinking deeply.

"Why? Why not give them to her now?" I asked, confused. "Shouldn't we get them together?"

"In due time, you will understand why I am making this decision," Yahweh stated, clapping me on the shoulder. "Just accept this gift, will ya? You already have some of my gifts in the making. That electricity took you by surprise when you used it, didn't it?"

"That's one of your powers?"

"It sure is. Well, yours is underdeveloped. It's actually lightning. It's your father's, too. When his emotions get the best of him, storms brew. Like father, like son," he mused.

"Are you going to come back with me to the village and meet everybody?" I asked, pointing and walking toward the village.

"Not yet," he replied. "It's too soon for me to appear to so many who may be spies for Alpha."

"So, you're just going to give me my allotted powers here, then?" I asked, scratching my head.

A hush fell over the forest, and the sounds of wildlife came to a halt. He leaned down to me, eye level, and blew gently in my face. Bright sparkles floated from his mouth and surrounded me, swirling around and growing brighter until I was a beam of light.

"I will see you again, soon, my boy," he said as he faded away into nothing.

"Wait!" I shouted, but it was too late. "What powers did you give me?"

The light that surrounded me grew whiter and brighter. Pain tore through my body much like it had the day we all activated our powers. *Will I explode every single time someone gives me powers?* I could feel the stretching and tension of my muscles, and my skin tightened, threatening to rip from my skeleton. My bones popped and cracked, snapping and reforming as a howl escaped my lips. *What the hell is happening to me? That old man tricked me!* The shirt I was wearing shredded and ripped from my body as my pants tightened and threatened to split at the seams, the bottoms of the legs tearing. My feet busted through the cloth of my shoes, and I was left barefoot, half-naked, standing in the middle of the woods. And as quickly as the silence had fallen over the woods, the sounds of life returned with crickets chirping, birds squawking, and fish jumping out of the water.

A deep ache settled in my bones, and I limped back to Lightshade. I needed Starfire's help to stop whatever was happening to me before it killed me. Every step I took felt like glass in my bones. Lightning pelted down around me as I gritted my teeth and pushed through the pain. Electrical bolts sparked from my skin with each labored breath, and I collapsed just outside of the thicket in the village, crawling and pulling myself along by my arms. The sky darkened, and the sun was snuffed from view, casting everything into an eerie gloom as the wind picked up and shrieked with torrential speed.

"Damian!" Incaendiel shouted, running over to me and dropping to his knees on the ground, the wind kicking up dirt and debris. He tried to touch me, but the electrical current flowing through me shocked his hand, and he yanked it away, shaking it. "Don't touch him!" he warned as others knelt around me. "What happened? What's wrong?! Who hurt you?!" Lightning rained down all around us, barely missing those huddled around me.

"Yahweh," was all I could muster before passing out.

***

My eyes fluttered open, and I found myself staring at the ceiling in Starfire's cottage. Lightning flashed in my memory as the grandfather clock on the wall ticked, and the sound suddenly stopped. Silence fell over the room, and I sat up from my lying position. The room was filled with those who had huddled around me, but they were frozen in place, including Incaendiel. He had never frozen when I used my powers. Furthermore, why were my powers misfiring right now? Why is everything frozen? Usually, my emotions spark them by accident, and I hardly use them except for necessity. So why, now of all times, is everything standing still?

"If you don't learn to control them now while you're young, you will never master them," a voice echoed in my head.

I stood up and walked around the room, squeezing my eyes shut and opening them, trying to unfreeze everyone. Before, I could just wave my hand and freeze, then unfreeze, but for some reason, this accelerated power of mine isn't responding to my own commands.

"Unfreeze!" I shouted, looking around and waiting. Silence echoed through the room, and not a single person moved. I snapped my finger, hoping that would break the freeze. It did nothing. I didn't understand. I ran my fingers through my hair and swiped a lamp off the table beside me. I paced the room. No one had tried to learn or explain what my freezing powers were beyond the lore of the first universe when I was made. I would freeze time for Luxina to come in and cleanse the world. But what does it mean to freeze time? Can I actually stop the entire universe from spinning on its axis? Generally, that's what time is. Time is equated by the movement of space itself. Without movement, there isn't time, but the absence of movement doesn't mean time is frozen. It just means… I am outside of time. I am standing outside the movement. I am not freezing time. I am stepping back and looking in on it. But how do

I step back inside the movement? How do I escape the pocket I have created?

"You wanted to be alone, isolated. A hermit. Now that you have that isolation, it's your chance to run away from your problems. Stay outside the movement of time. Leave everything behind, just like you said."

"I want to do that on my own terms!" I seethed, stomping my foot.

"These ***are*** *your terms, Damian. No one did this to you. You have to learn how to undo it yourself."*

"I barely know how to use my powers as it is!" I yelled, throwing my hands up in the air and shaking my fists angrily.

"You let your emotions control you so easily. Learn to control your emotions, and controlling your powers will come second nature."

"Incaendiel was usually right there with me whenever my powers would spill over to bring me back down emotionally, even if it was forceful. I don't know how to do this on my own. I can't wrap myself in strong arms and force myself into submission with safety."

"Is that what he makes you feel? Safe?"

"Yeah. Even when he's dangerous, something tells me he would never hurt me, and I believe that feeling. In those moments… I love him as my dad."

"Why don't you call him dad instead of using his name?"

"It feels like it cheapens everything. That title is reserved for someone who deserves it, and so many have walked through trying to claim it and failed me miserably. What if he does the same? He already takes sides most of the time with Luxina, and I couldn't bear it if I put my whole faith into him just to be pushed aside."

"Of those people, who made you feel like he did when wrapped in their arms?"

"None of them. I have never felt safe with anyone but him."

"Then stop fighting it."

I breathed in deeply. Every whip lashing from Alpha. I felt my back as the sting landed. Every hug from Asmodeus. My chest tightened, making my heart pump faster. Every single word they had ever said to me and took back rushed through my head. Alpha cheering me on then having me beaten nearly to death. The labored breathing from my collapsed lung sent me to the floor. The gladiator ring. Those secret nights when the chain gang slipped into my room, with or without Alpha's say so to… Fear gripped me at the throat because I knew I wouldn't make it out of there alive. Nightmares and Shadows. Asmodeus showing up again and again. *Alpha's little monster. The perfect weapon.* It all swirled around and around, dizzying me, choking the breath from me.

And then I thought of Incaendiel. *"Now, did you really think we were going to let you die in there?"* Before he even knew he was my father, he saved me. *"Kid, what part of no one cares about themselves as much as they care about you three do you just not get?" "You were never a monster, Damian." "You're the second person today to upset my son." "I certainly would enjoy seeing you writhe in agony over and over as a personal punishment for you disrespecting my son the way you did." "Don't tell anyone else what was said about Damian." "You son! He kept you!"*

Alpha not only kept me away from Incaendiel as a punishment to him, but he also kept me away as a punishment to me. He kept me from my dad. He kept me away from safety because Incaendiel would burn the world down for me just like he would for Luxina. He kept me away from pure unconditional love, the only love a parent can give their child, and not care if their kid hates them, wishes they weren't their real parent, or anything I have said and done to him since finding out. I hadn't realized it through all of the repressed emotions, but he was an anchor for me, whether I wanted him to be or not. My anger had been present for so long that I couldn't separate it from the grief, the loss, and the forced abandonment. Alpha had stolen away everything memorable, everything I could cherish. He stole away my autonomy, my identity. He stole my childhood, my expression. He forced me to grow up faster than I needed to. He stole me away, and even though I am free, I am still his prisoner unless…

"Dad?"

CHAPTER FIFTEEN: DAMIAN

THE SOUND OF the grandfather clock ticking was the first thing I heard before the commotion of the room came rushing at me all at once. Dad was on his feet, running to me and then throwing his arms around my shoulders. He squeezed me tightly into his chest, and for once, I didn't fight or try to push him away. Instead, I wrapped my arms around him as well and squeezed him back.

"You're taller," he croaked with a laugh, putting his hand on the back of my head.

"I hit a growth spurt," I replied, for once, really feeling what it felt like to be hugged by him. He went to pull back, but I squeezed him tighter. I didn't want to let this feeling go away. Relief. Security. Wholeness. Love. It was all rolled up into one in his arms.

"What happened to you out there?" he asked, responding to my deepened hug by clutching me tighter. "We thought… Alpha…"

"I was lost, and then I was found by Father Time," I whispered, burying my face into his chest. "I've been lost for so long and didn't realize it. I was here, with you, but I wasn't completely here. I was still wandering forgotten in my own head. Trapped inside a prison that I escaped physically, only to learn a part of me was left behind in there. That part of me was a scared little child who thought he was abandoned by choice. I just didn't know who held the key to freedom."

"You found him lost in the wilderness, wandering out of choice, not necessity. You surrendered yourself, your powers, and he appeared, didn't he?" Azrael asked, entering the room.

I let go of Dad, and she walked up to me, peering up deeply into my eyes.

"Who?" Samael asked, breaking the silence.

"Yahweh," Azrael answered with a smirk.

I nodded, looking down at her. "Yes. He said he had been watching us and waiting for the right moment to appear," I replied. "He said he would be back again to give Luxina the rest of the inheritance of his powers. She wasn't ready for them yet." Her eyes peered up at me seductively, and she gave me a wink.

"Well, that's hardly fair," Luxina snarled, scowling at Azrael and me. "How are you ready for your inheritance, but I'm not. At least I know how to control myself. When is he coming back to give me mine?"

"Asmodeus would beg to differ," Dad answered in disapproval, ignoring her question of Yahweh's return.

"He deserved what he got," she hissed, narrowing her eyes at him.

"No, he didn't," I countered, turning to face her. "He was just another pawn like all of us in Alpha's little game. He had time for growth. Everyone has time for growth."

"I'd say someone did some growing up out in those woods," Azazel murmured with a smirk.

"Who are you and what have you done with Damian?" she laughed.

The room filled with the buzz of everyone talking at once to one another, while Azrael still gazed up at me. "Walk with me?" she asked, pulling me along with her hand.

I followed her outside of Starfire's, and we began to walk around, quiet at first. "Yahweh giving you his powers was very significant," she said, looking around at the flowers we passed by.

"Why is it significant?"

"Just like certain angels were reaper angels," she began, "certain gods born are also given the responsibility of handling death and souls. Before Alpha took you from your universe, you had matured enough into the role, and Maveth was about to crown you in her place so she could retire. Yahweh imparting his powers on you accelerated your own maturing powers, and you're ready now to accept the crown." We stopped walking, and she turned to face me. "This has always been your destiny. It's one reason you have the power over time. That's just one of the powers yet to show itself to you. Your ice and storms come from your inheritance as the lineage of Incaendiel through Kharuun. More powers and intuition are going to start blossoming since Yahweh sped up their maturity."

"So I will be in charge of all of the reaper angels and other death deities?" I asked, pondering everything she had told me.

She nodded and then bit her lip. "I've been wanting to talk to you about the library."

I rubbed the back of my head nervously. "Same," I replied as guilt wrapped through my insides. We started speaking at the same time.

"We should give this thing a go."

"I didn't mean to take advantage of you."

She laughed. "You didn't take advantage of me, Damian."

"Asmodeus hit me with the lust bug, and I oozed lust to everyone I was around," I replied sheepishly. "You weren't feeling your own desires. You were feeling mine, and I'm sorry about that."

"Don't be sorry," she whispered, stepping closer to me and peering up at me with her beautiful purple eyes. In the sunlight, they looked even more beautiful as the light bounced off, showing the multiple shades of purple that made up her irises. "For me, it wasn't just your desire I felt." Her eyes danced along my chest, and it dawned on me I was shirtless.

"Azrael," I began, trying to be as gentle as possible. "You're sexy, gorgeous, and perfect in all the right ways."

"But?" she asked, her eyes searching mine and her hand giving mine a gentle squeeze.

"But I love Luxina," I answered. "Had Asmodeus not manipulated me, I would have never... I wouldn't have been out of my mind with... I'm sorry. I don't even know how to phrase this without making you feel less desirable because don't get me wrong, you…" I chuckled nervously. "You are a firecracker."

"Well, the offer stands," Azrael teased. "If things go sideways with Luxina, you still have me. You have always had me, since time began, Caelvryn."

"I may be Caelvryn on a soul level, but I am not him as a person," I explained cautiously. "I am Damian with my own memories and my own experiences. Whatever happened between us then is in the past, and I don't remember it."

She stood to her tippy toes to whisper in my ear. "I can remind you anytime you like." She smirked salaciously at me, her hand lingering on my bicep and chest. A flicker of a memory bounced forth. She was breathless, wrapped up naked in sheets as Caelvryn lay on top of her, kissing the back of her neck.

"What's going on here?" Luxina demanded, walking up to us. She glared at Azrael and narrowed her eyes at me, crossing her arms.

"Azrael was telling me about my next 'ascension' planned since my powers are maturing," I explained, pushing Azrael's hands off of me and turning to Luxina.

"You fucked her too, didn't you?!" she snapped, clenching her jaw.

"See you around, Damian," Azrael mumbled, brushing past Luxina and quickly making an exit.

"Don't lie to me about it!" Luxina ordered, walking up to me and scowling.

I stared quietly into her eyes, trying to find my footing with her. Ever since her return from Purgatory, she had been acting so weird. Jealous. Angry. Being bratty. I know what she went through in the Lust Terrace was a lot, and I have no idea what Adam told her to manipulate her in any way, but it felt like a constant barrage of attacks against me since she returned, and I didn't like it. She was always in my face, accusing me, and if she wasn't in my face, she was off being by herself.

I licked my lips and pursed them. "Yes," I answered. "While infected with Asmodeus's lust bug, I had sex with her. Meaningless sex."

"Unbelievable," she huffed with a sarcastic laugh and shaking her head. She began to walk away.

"So, it's ok for you to have sex with Adam under the influence of the Lust Terrace that Asmodeus created for Alpha, but it's not ok for me that I was also under the same influence and couldn't control myself?" I asked heatedly, walking up to her.

"That was different, and you know it!" she hissed, bucking into my chest, angry.

"You don't see me running around asking you questions about what happened or what it was like or anything of the sort, acting like a selfish and jealous bitch like you," I countered, glowering at her. "I don't know what your deal is. I know you were traumatized, and I know everything that happened there was forced, but you do not get to stand here and judge me for having the same thing happen to me that made me feel terrible afterward. Do you feel terrible for sleeping with Adam?" My question caught her off guard, and she stuttered trying to find the words to say. "That's what I thought, Miss he's just misunderstood. Now get off my back!" Lightning struck at the same time I yelled at her.

"You were supposed to love me and only me," she whispered, tears brimming on her waterline.

"And I do only love you," I cried, raising my hands and shaking them in frustration. She reached her hand toward my chest, and I snatched it mid-air and stared down at her. At one point in time, I had let her run her hands all over my scars, but now, she hadn't earned that sense of trust and safety back. I didn't know why, but my instincts screamed at me all the time to not let her touch me. That she was going to hurt me.

"You let all the others touch you and still won't let me," she muttered, her face falling.

"They're not going to hurt me," I whispered.

"Elisha tried to kill you," she mumbled, swiping a tear away.

"After the fact, yes. But she also didn't get to touch me either," I growled. "I didn't trust her."

"So you don't trust me?" she asked, her eyes peering up at me in huge pools of confusion.

"Not yet, I don't," I breathed, anxiety welling. "I don't know that if I give you my trust, and instill a sense of safety in you, that you're not going to rip it from under my feet by running to Adam and choosing him over me."

"I wouldn't—" she began.

"You don't know that," I interrupted softly. "You're acting out of character, not even in your own head right now. Who knows what you will say and feel after decompressing from that place?"

"I love you, Damian," she pleaded, searching my face for answers.

"But a part of you also loves him, too," I whispered, choking back the lump in my throat. "I can feel it, Luxina. I can feel everything, remember."

She averted her eyes shamefully. "I'm sorry," she croaked.

I lifted her chin up so her eyes would meet mine. "I know. And I am too." I gently kissed her lips. I wanted to get lost in her arms, to deepen the kiss, but I knew it wasn't the right time. "We just both need a little time."

I walked away from her and made my way back inside Starfire's cottage and up to my room. I gently closed the door behind me and walked to my bed, sitting down on it. I ran my hands through my hair as I rocked, quelling the mounting feeling of fear bubbling beneath the surface. *Had I lost her forever? Will she choose me, or will she choose Adam?* I didn't know the answer when, at one point in time, she tried to prove to me how much she loved me by trying to take on Alpha alone. Was I pushing the same love she tried to show me then away now? Was I getting in the way of my own happiness? Self-sabotage was one of my weaknesses. Was that what I was doing right now? Sabotaging my relationship? The door opened and closed, and I looked up to see Luxina standing there.

"No," she said, shaking her head. "No, I don't need time. I need you." She ran over to me and took my head in her hands. "I need *you*."

She straddled her legs over my lap and wrapped her arms around my neck, pressing her mouth into mine as her hands played with my hair. It was our first kiss since she had returned, and a range of emotions tore through my chest, from elation to anger to grief. I stifled them and responded to her. I wrapped my arms around her and pulled her as close as I could to my body while I returned her kiss. Something felt off. It tugged at the back of my mind like a scratch I couldn't reach, but I pushed everything out of my mind to be in the moment with her. My hands roamed through her hair, grasping it lightly as her mouth moved across my neck. She leaned back and yanked her shirt over the top of her head, and came back in hungrily and fervent with her mouth.

"I've craved you," she whispered in my ear while grinding against my pelvis. "I've craved you towering over me and running your hands all over my body. I need you, Damian." She moaned lightly in my ear with a soft gasp. "Take me. Please," she whimpered. Her hand slipped down between us and began rubbing me through my pants.

I stood up, picking her up with me to turn her around and lay her down on the bed. I lingered over her, completely mesmerized by the soft glow she emitted before placing my mouth on her neck and kissing her body down to the top of her pants. Kneeling on the floor, I grasped the sides of her pants and slid them down gently, pulling each leg out of its pant leg and then tossing them to the side on the floor. I buried my face in her, and she arched her back as she gasped. My hands grasped her hips and pulled her tightly to my face. Steam rose to her skin as she flushed with ecstasy. I stood up to remove my pants, and as I did, she sat up to take control and unbuttoned them for me, peering up at me seductively. She undid my zipper and yanked the pants down off my hips. I stepped out of each of the pants' legs, stepping on them and pulling until I was free, then kicking them aside. Her eyes trailed from mine down my body as she bit her bottom lip.

I climbed on top of her as she lay back on the bed, her skin hot as fire against my coolness. Her hips matched my every movement as she panted. "Faster," she cooed, and we picked up the speed. "Faster," she urged, her nails digging into my back and clawing down toward my sides. She moaned and groaned, and it took every ounce of willpower I had to stay in the moment and not lose it. "Harder!" she cried as her legs wrapped around my waist. Sweat dripped from my body and pooled on her chest just to steam away as she pulled me harder into her with her legs and hands. I faltered momentarily as something on the edge of my brain teased at me. *Something's not right.* I brushed it off as I picked her up, leaning on the back of my legs as she sprawled her body against me, gasping and panting as we finished.

We fell sideways on the bed, breathless and exhausted. All you could hear were soft pants in the quiet of the room as we dared not move. I pushed my arm under her and draped my other one across her, pulling her close to me. Without warning, she pushed away and sat up on the side of the bed. I tried to tug her back down to lie with me, but she stood up and walked around the bed to find her clothes.

"What's wrong?" I asked, propping myself up on my elbows.

She was quiet as she got dressed. She slid her pants on and turned her shirt inside right then pulled it over her head. "Where are my shoes?" she asked, looking around the edges of the bed before finding them pushed under it.

"Luxina?" I asked, sitting up in the bed, unsure of what I had done.

"What?" she answered, sounding exasperated.

"Is something wrong? Did I do something…" I trailed off.

She chewed her lip, contemplating what to say, and immediately, I felt exposed. I reached over and grabbed the edge of my blanket to cover myself. My cheeks flushed with the mounting insecurity my brain was manifesting as I ran everything over in my head of what I had done wrong. Did I finish too soon? Did she not like it? Did she not want it anymore at some point? Did she not want… me?

"I just…" she began and stopped.

"You just what?"

"I thought choosing you… making that decision for myself would quiet everything… but it didn't," she whispered solemnly.

"Quiet everything?" I asked, confused. "What do you mean?"

"Quiet the urges. The feelings. Quiet… Adam," she mumbled.

My heart felt like it had been ripped from my chest, and the room began to spin a bit.

"Maybe I do need time," she offered, staring down at the ground, ashamed. "You know I need you."

"Yeah, it's always you need me and never you want me," I replied, standing up and pulling my pants back on.

"That's the same thing," she defended, shaking her head irritated.

"It's not the same thing," I replied, buttoning my pants and meeting her eyes. "You didn't choose. You experimented. You used me to fulfill your bubbling desire, and you didn't have Adam around to do it for you."

She walked over to me and went to put her hand on my chest when I snatched it mid-air. "You haven't earned that yet," I muttered, dropping her hand away from me.

She cast her eyes to the floor. "I'm sorry," she whimpered, sniffling.

"Do you love me, or do you love him?" I hissed, eyes narrowed. My chest rose and fell with ragged, aching breaths as my heart pounded away inside. I felt like the wind had been knocked out of me, and tiny little needles were pricking my veins.

"I don't know," she mumbled. "He's not that bad of a guy," she added. "He just needs to be saved from Alpha."

I pushed by her and opened my door. "Get out," I growled, pointing out of the room.

Her eyebrows knitted together while she looked at me pitifully. Damian…"

"Get out of my room!" I yelled, glaring at her, my jaw clenched tight.

She walked to the threshold and spun around. "I can't help that I was forced into the feelings I have."

I shook my head in disbelief. "You don't get to use that as an excuse," I huffed. "Not after what you just did."

I slammed the door in her face. I knew I shouldn't blame her for what Alpha did, but her treating me like a toy and nothing more hurts. *"Do you think she loves you as much as you do her?"* Alpha's words haunted me. Maybe that's why it was so easy for Adam to gain her trust and affection in Purgatory. I shouldn't have let this continue just now. I should have stopped her. She wasn't ready for this next step of intimacy. I let my own wants and needs outweigh the voice of reason, the intuition that this wasn't right. It wasn't. The timing was wrong. The mood was wrong beforehand. This was more like conditioned sex because she had done something wrong and needed to make up for it. I had taken advantage of her emotional vulnerability and was no better than Adam. Maybe that's why she was so confused about how she felt. Maybe some part of me reminded her of Adam.

Again, something about her had left me unsettled since her return, and I couldn't quite place my finger on it. Her behavior was so strange. Jealousy felt new to me regarding her. I had never seen her jealous before. She was wrathful as well with the way she handled Asmodeus. Prideful and greedy over her deserving powers over me. Apparently, she was still lustful as well. It wasn't like her personality at all, and it bugged me something fierce. I didn't understand this version of Luxina. I mean, I get that she was now a god with improved powers, that she most likely has a problem controlling, just as I do. It's new territory with this version of her, and I had yet to be around her since our ascension until now. But she felt different in a way that was inexplicable. What else was different about her? Or maybe Purgatory affected her more than we believed. Had she been there so long that every terrace had seeped through to affect her, absorbing it all like a sponge?

Someone knocked on my door. "What?" I asked, rummaging through my drawers to find clothes that actually fit. "Doors open."

The door opened, and Samael walked in. "We have Uriel in the holding cell and are about to interrogate her. You need to be there when we do."

I was grabbing shirts and pants, holding them up, then tossing them on the ground. Nothing fits. "Ok, I will be there shortly," I huffed. Samael went to leave when I stopped him. "Hey, do you have anything I could wear that would fit me?"

Samael turned to face me with a smirk on his face and snorted. "I am a string bean compared to you. Ask Metatron for some clothes."

"I'm not *that* big," I defended, offended.

"Have you looked in the mirror?" Samael joked, a toothy grin plastered across his face. "You look like a titan."

I pursed my lips and narrowed my eyes at him. "Fine," I relented. "I will be down as soon as I get some clothes."

Samael bounded down the steps and out of the cottage while I walked down the hall to Metatron's room and knocked on his door. He yanked it open and was surprised to see me standing there. He looked up and down the hall before saying anything. "What do you need, Damian?"

"Clothes," I huffed, while rubbing the back of my head anxiously. "Got anything that might fit me?"

He laughed. "Maybe. You're bigger than me now. Might be a tight fit."

"Anything is better than these busting pants and going shirtless," I muttered, looking down at my ruined pants and then crossing my arms across my chest. "It feels wrong not having a shirt on."

He disappeared for a minute before returning with some clothes in hand, thrusting them over at me. He held up a finger. "Oh, also," he said, disappearing and reappearing with a pair of boots. "Your feet *do* look the same size as mine now."

"Thanks," I replied as I began walking back to my room.

"No problem, squirt," he laughed, shutting his door.

I scowled. Squirt my ass. I laid the clothes out on my bed. He gave me a few all-black outfits I could change into. I took off my pants and tossed them in the wastebasket before putting on the new ones. They were tighter fitting just like Metatron warned, but they did fit, and when I bent my knees or kicked my leg up, they didn't rip. Hopefully, the lust bug Asmodeus had hit me with was completely worn off, or else all the women in the vicinity would rip them off with their teeth. There wasn't much left to the imagination with how tightly they fit my body, but at least they had some stretch to them. I yanked one of the short-sleeved shirts on, and like the pants, it was tight as well. I could see my pecs through the shirt. It was better than going bare-chested. I mean, I'm glad other guys have the confidence to walk around without a shirt on, but I still feel every scar that was ever on my body, even though they healed when I ascended. I still felt exposed and ugly. Luckily, the boots were just the right fit when I slid them on and laced them up. I clipped a sword to my side and left my room. I bounded down the steps and ducked out the door to meet up with everyone waiting for me to arrive.

Outside the building where they were holding Uriel, Samyaza stood guard. "How long have they had her here?" I asked, walking up to him.

"When you ran off into the woods, they thought she had grabbed you for Alpha," he replied curtly. "Incaendiel tied her up and was trying to get information out of her about where you were. We didn't know if Asmodeus spoke to her before trying to find you in the woods, and since Asmodeus had said another kidnapping was the plan, he assumed the worst. Starfire stopped him before he did unspeakable things to Uriel and said you were somewhere out there, but she wasn't spying on you for them since it was personal reasons for your departure."

I rubbed the back of my head shamefully. "Has anyone gotten anything useful out of her about Alpha's plans?"

"Not yet," he muttered. "It's wrong what you all are doing to get ahead of Alpha. Torturing one another. It's not right."

I nodded. "You're right. It's not." I opened the door and stepped into the room where Uriel was chained to a chair.

Dad had done a number on her during his interrogations. I wasn't sure if how she looked was him questioning her about Alpha or questioning her about my whereabouts, but Samyaza was right. This was overboard. Her face was bloodied and burned. Scorch marks ran up her arms, and most of her hair had been singed off. One of her eyes was purple and swollen shut, while the other one was blood red from all of the veins bursting in it. Asmodeus was personal. Very personal. Uriel hadn't done anything out of the way to say she wasn't on our side to illicit such a vindictive punishment. Uriel's bloodshot eye met mine, and she let out a wicked laugh.

"Bringing in the kid to help do your dirty work?" she huffed, blowing a strand of her hair out of her bloodied face.

Dad turned around, unaware I had walked through the door. "He's just here to observe," Dad remarked coolly. Without hesitation or warning, he brought his fist around, striking Uriel in the face. "Talk!" he ordered.

I stood quietly in the back. All of this felt wrong. It was an unusual feeling because I had never shied away from torture before. I relished torture. I knew exactly how to get into someone's head to figure out just what they feared the most. I loved inflicting pain on others because I knew exactly what it felt like. I knew how it was to be waterboarded because I was waterboarded. Face up on a table with water poured over my face, covered with a towel. I knew what drowning torture was. Hands tied behind your back and your face forced into ice-cold water until you're sucking it down into your lungs and pulled back before you could die. I was burned with red-hot pokers. I was strung up upside down and bound for days. There wasn't a single implement of torture I hadn't experienced, including being sexually violated. Now, standing here watching this unfold, I couldn't help but feel sympathetic to Uriel. I couldn't help but want to stop it all and fight for her.

"Dad, maybe we should try a different approach," I suggested, walking over to them.

Dad stopped and turned to me. A look of confusion spread across his face. "What would you like to try?" he asked, unsure of what I was doing.

I pulled a chair up and sat down in front of Uriel. I reached out to her, and she flinched away. "I'm not going to hurt you," I said, as I reached for her face again. I touched her face and healed her wounds.

"Good guy bad guy routine doesn't work," Uriel snarled, spitting in my face.

I calmly wiped her spit away. "Torture isn't who we are and shouldn't become who we are identified as either," I replied, sitting up straight in my chair. "We should be making alliances by merely our word than forcing people into compliance because, seriously, that's Alpha's method, and we want nothing to do with the way he handles those who are to be his loyalists."

She laughed, and not a short chuckle, but a deep guttural laugh. "I'm sorry," she shrieked in between gasps of air as she cleared her throat. "You can't honestly believe that would have worked on me?" she snapped, glowering at me. "I watched you cut someone open and freeze their insides and then sew them back up as they struggled for each breath they took in their iced-over lungs. You are a *monster* when it comes to torturing people." She looked around the room at everyone standing in here. Samael and Azazel were leaning against the wall in a corner. Raphael stood in the back of the room. Michael stood near a table with his leg perched up on it. Dad stood behind me with his arms crossed. "Can't help but notice Asmodeus isn't with you when he is *always* stuck up your *ass*," she grunted through gritted teeth. She leaned forward, narrowing her eyes at me. "Bet he's lying somewhere dead because you couldn't handle the truth that he was working with me."

"So he *was* willingly working with you," I boasted as her lips became loose. "We weren't completely confident with that accusation until now. So thank you for that. Who else here is working with you and Alpha?" I met her gaze with my own. Cold. Calculated. Relaxed.

"No one terribly important to you," she sneered, face placid.

"You mean Metatron isn't important?" I asked, propping my feet up on a stool beside me. "Because that's where you are wrong. Metatron is family."

She snorted. "Metatron is weak under *his* command," she snapped, motioning her head at Dad. "He used to walk tall and exude strength and willpower. Now he's a little lap dog, pissing on your leg for praise." I watched her without interruption. "He used to move mountains for Alpha. Now he bakes cookies or some shit while *he* and *you* make all the plans. You two don't work with the others. You enslave them to do *your* bidding under the guise that you're better than Alpha. You're nothing in comparison."

"Agreed," I cooed, narrowing my eyes. "Why would we want to be a tyrannical, manipulating wannabe? We are nothing like Alpha, but we also do not claim perfection. We don't make decisions alone, and instead we put them to votes and counseling."

She cackled. "Put it to a vote? Every single major action I have seen taken place has been orders for compliance, nothing more. Like storming the Underworld—"

"Those of us who went there all volunteered after talking extensively about the place," Samael interrupted.

"Your traipse through hell—"

"Again, all voluntary," Raphael chimed in. "As a matter of fact, we had to force them to let us go with them."

"Killing Asmodeus!" she whimpered, her bottom lip quivering. "I know all about his death. I'm not an idiot, and there are ears everywhere around here." She swallowed. "You took him from me!" she hissed. Realization set in, and it couldn't have been any more transparent.

"I didn't know you two were seeing one another," I stated.

"He didn't tell you all everything, obviously!" she spat. "Especially, *you!*" She glared at me. "He *hated* you *so much!* A wet nurse is what he called himself. And then sent off to keep an eye on you during your fake escape so the leash didn't get too long." She leaned forward. "Do you really think you're protected here? That Alpha can't get to you. Or that Starfire herself hasn't been recruited by Alpha, faking your safety. Do you think those warlocks like that you are in their space? No, they're just biding time until Alpha tells them to attack like good little mutts."

I sat up. I wanted to yell at her, telling her I knew she was lying. That Starfire would never betray us like that, but what she said made complete and total sense. Prep us for Alpha and then feed us to the wolf. *Alpha can't come through these borders,* she had claimed, and put on a fake performance of protecting this place from his power. And then Lilith and Adam both slipped in, Lilith dropping the bomb that nothing can stop a god from entering anywhere because mortal magic wouldn't work on us anyway. Alpha came and took Anniel just like planned. Which means... if she was listening the other day while I spoke about Yahweh, Alpha knew I had received half of his powers, and he's due back to get them to Luxina when she's ready. So Alpha can swoop in and take them for himself.

She smiled sweetly. "I see it just clicked into place," she snickered and winked. "You know, I'm a reaper angel, if you catch my drift. So trust those instincts." *A reaper angel... Focus, Damian.*

"What do you know about Adam?" I asked, leaning back in my chair.

"He's set to inherit everything from Alpha," she replied, shrugging her shoulders.

"So you are all ready to take orders from Adam when Alpha tells you to?" I asked.

"There's going to be a hierarchy," she defended. "We are going to be part of all the plans made."

"And you really believe that?" I laughed heartily. "He's going to boss you around just like Alpha does, demanding blood sacrifices for the greater good. No, you're going to be Adam's puppet, and when you're no longer useful, they're going to cut your string. You are all sacrificial lambs to the slaughter. How do you think Asmodeus ended up dead? Alpha knew the stakes if he were caught, and he was banking on it because when people know too much, they're a liability. And Asmodeus knew a hell of a whole lot more than you did, didn't he?"

"Which one of you did it?" she asked, her eyes cold. "Which one of you killed him?"

"I did," Luxina replied, shutting the door behind her. We all looked back at her as she stood in front of the door.

"What are you doing here?" Uriel asked, visibly shaken and confused.

"Adam helped me escape," she replied, slowly walking up to Uriel. "And then I burned Asmodeus to flaming embers. He called out your name with his dying breath."

Why was she lying? That's not in her nature, especially being cruel. She's not a cruel person, like at all. And she's never lied like that to get under someone's skin.

"I see Alpha's getting better at plotting and not telling anyone about it," Uriel smirked, looking Luxina up and down. "Especially considering my key is the only way in and out of Purgatory unless you travel through the abyss and up through the garden."

"Adam is more powerful than you credit him for," Luxina glared, crossing her arms defiantly. "He has ways around the rules of Purgatory. With a flick of his wrist, I was free," she beamed, flicking her wrist to emphasize the statement.

"Is that right?" Uriel sneered with a smirk as if she knew something no one else was aware of.

"Yeah, that's right," Luxina claimed, moving up beside me. "He's going to join me here soon to help make plans to take down Alpha."

Uriel laughed deeply once more and looked around at us all. "You all are blind!" she snarled. "Do you really think thi—"

Luxina grabbed the sword from my side and, in one swift motion, cut Uriel's head off as she spoke. Blood splattered me in my face as her head rolled across the floor. I looked at Luxina, horrified, and I couldn't tell if my hands were shaking from shock or from something colder settling in my chest. Nausea floated to the back of my throat, and I swallowed it back down. What the hell did they turn her into while they had her imprisoned?

"What did you do?" I asked in shock as Uriel's blood dripped from my face and onto my shirt, which hid the stains that seeped into the fabric.

"We don't need her anymore," she replied coolly. "Can't have her escaping and running off to Alpha with our plans again."

"You didn't have to kill her!" I fumed, jumping from my seat and snatching my sword from her hand. "We could have made a deal with her! We were so close to having her switch sides! She was telling us everything we needed to know about Alpha!"

"And her be a double agent?" Luxina snorted. "Please, she would have never disobeyed Alpha."

She turned to walk away from me, and I grabbed her by her arm and whipped her around to face me. "You don't know that!" I defended, irate at her callous actions.

She wrenched from my hands and got in my face, fire burning in her eyes. "I do!" she insisted. "Who do you think locked me away in Purgatory to begin with?!" she hissed.

So that's what it was. This was revenge. This was her getting back at Uriel on a personal level. Revenge was now how she healed her trauma and wounds.

"This is not you!" I snapped, grabbing her by the shoulders and giving her a gentle shake. "You are not this person!"

Once again, she pushed my hands away from her and glared at me. "You act like it's the first person I have killed to cut a spy to Alpha," she growled. "Or did you forget Gwynevere? I killed her without flinching, too."

I narrowed my eyes and shook my head. "What did they do to you there?" I asked, unable to believe that this was the Luxina now.

"Things you can't imagine," she quipped, clenching her jaw and staring me down. "Get over it."

"You first," I shot back, looking her up and down. "You going to add anything to this?" I turned and asked Dad.

"It's going to take a while for her to come back to normal," he defended, compassion filling his face. "She's been through a lot."

"Yeah, and if she keeps killing people, those who are loyal to us won't stay loyal for long," I snapped, trying to keep my cool. "They're already pissed we are torturing people as Alpha does, and now we are killing them like him, too. Do you want to lose more people than we gain?"

He sighed. "You're right."

Luxina whipped around to face Dad. "So what then?" Luxina asked, throwing her hands up in the air. "What are you going to do? Lock me in my room? Hold me hostage?"

"You're no longer allowed to interrogate people," I answered sternly, my face set in determination.

She was in front of me like a bolt of lightning. "You're not the boss of me!" she yelled in my face.

"Damian is right. You don't need to be in here anymore until you've done the healing work," Dad agreed, hardening his face. "End of discussion."

She laughed. "The healing work? What are you, a hippy commune now?" She glared at everyone in the room. "We are at war! There are going to be casualties! There are going to be gruesome things that happen! I'm not a little girl anymore! I can fight. I can do big *boy* things just like Damian. Stop treating me like a princess in distress!"

"Then stop acting like one! We don't have to be complicit in those things," I argued, pursing my lips. "We don't have to become monsters to destroy a monster."

"When did you become such a pussy?" she stammered, her face painted in disgust. "Of all *monsters,* I figured you would be the one to understand me the most. Did daddy love the monster out of you?"

"When did you become such a spoiled brat? Better yet, when did you become such a little bitch!?" I shot back. "Newsflash, but trying the whole Daddy's princess can do no wrong act is tiring and overworked. Stop being an insolent little snot and stick to the plans we have. Stick to the rules because without them, it's just chaos."

"Whatever," she muttered and walked to the door. "If anyone needs me, I will be in my room."

She slammed the door behind her, and the room was quiet.

"What's going on between you two?" Dad asked, watching me.

"Nothing," I stammered, running my hand through my hair. "She's just been… different since she returned. Like her whole personality has done a change-up, and I feel like I am the only one aware of it."

"She's been through a lot," Azazel offered as an excuse. "Cut her some slack."

"No," I replied, shaking my head. "There's something wrong that I can't quite put my finger on, and it doesn't have anything to do with what happened to her. Something is *wrong* with her. Luxina would have never acted like that. She knew the hard limits, and she's crossing every single one of them."

"Trauma changes people," Raphael interjected. "Especially the kind of trauma and abuse she was put through."

I leaned over the table behind me and took a deep breath. "I am *telling* you," I spoke slowly. "There's something wrong with her, and it's not the abuse. She is jealous. She is wrathful. She is proud. It's like she is reflecting the seven deadly sins. I was going to ask Uriel how the energy worked there to see if Purgatory's terraces had a unilateral effect on her before she cut her fucking head off! There's something wrong, and it needs to be fixed before we burn all the bridges we have with everyone outside that door."

"I think you're paranoid," Michael said, clapping my shoulder. "Purgatory doesn't work that way. It's all in your head. Maybe this is something going on inside you that you are displacing blame for."

I shook my head. "I know what my instincts say, and I know I should trust them."

"She hasn't been back that long," Dad interrupted. "Give her time to go back to normal."

I shook my head and waved my hand at everyone. "Whatever, don't listen to me then."

"Not to change the subject," Samael interrupted, "but now, the main question is when is Adam supposed to arrive?" Samael asked, looking around at everyone. "Luxina said he was coming."

"I don't know, but we need to be on our toes," Azazel replied, crossing his arms. "That boy is trouble."

"And even more importantly," I began. "What are we going to do about Starfire?"

CHAPTER SIXTEEN: DAMIAN

I SAT AT STARFIRE'S table, tinkering with my cup of tea as she sat across from me, drinking hers silently, as I watched her. Could she really be working with Alpha? Uriel had no reason to lie, but then again, displacing trust in those who are really our allies would be a power tactic. Like how Alpha sent Dad nightmares about showing up and taking everyone, and then he did show up. And whereas I wanted to believe it was all a lie, my gut was telling me Uriel wasn't lying about Starfire prepping us for Alpha. Could she really be biding our time in false security while Alpha played on the edge of the woods, waiting to strike at just the right moment?

"Out with it," Starfire barked, interrupting my thoughts.

"Huh?" I asked as I methodically took a drink of the tea. I was tasked with getting the information out of her. Dad felt that, since I handled Uriel so diplomatically, I should be the one to ask questions. I guess along with Yahweh's powers came the ability for me to be able to persuade confessions out of people, and they tell me the truth. It's weird.

"Ask it," she demanded, setting her cup down and looking me in the eyes. I sighed. I trusted Starfire, but the tug in the pit of my stomach told me she was keeping a secret from us.

Here goes nothing. "Did Uriel lie, or are you really working on the downlow for Alpha?" I asked, setting my cup down as well.

She sighed, clasping her hands together and averting her eyes. "No, she didn't lie."

That was it? That's all she had to say. Just matter-of-factly self-incriminates herself.

"Why?" I asked, deeply hurt by her confession. I reached out and touched her hands. "I thought we were like family here."

"Before you all showed up here, I was on your side," she began, drinking her tea slowly. "Until the vision changed again, and I saw what the new future looked like. Alpha extended an olive branch with promises, and I accepted."

"What changed? How do you know Alpha didn't show you something fake?" I asked, unaware that the future had changed before Luxina absorbed Xavier.

"There are many decisions to be made between now and then. Things to discover and uncover. It's all a game of choices to be made, and the choices I witnessed led to the same outcome. Adam would be in charge of everything. He would inherit all of Alpha's conquests, and there hasn't been a single thing happen so far to change that outcome. I conferred with Gabriel about the new vision. He said he had seen it too and confirmed it was real. It wasn't a lie from Alpha. Alpha wins. It is still all going according to the vision," she explained.

"Including Yahweh giving me his powers?" I asked, sitting up straight in his chair. "Was that in your vision?"

She watched me carefully, studying my face, and I couldn't quite understand why.

"No," she replied, releasing the breath she had been holding. "That was not part of the vision. It was unexpected and not seen."

"So what does that mean?" I asked, shifting in my seat. "I was the reason that everything was going to end?"

She waited before answering. "Yes and no."

"Explain, please," I urged, waving with my hand for her to continue.

"You have been out of control with your emotions, your wants, and your actions," she continued, frowning. "However, Luxina showing up sparked something deeper within you to battle, and you forced your shadow self to the top and surrendered control of everything."

"Was Luxina supposed to show up?" I asked, thoroughly confused.

"Yes," she affirmed with a nod. "But some outside influence directed this to a different degree, and your powers began to accelerate. Then Yahweh gave you your lot of inheritance, and Alpha didn't expect that. He believed he would slay Yahweh and steal his power."

"Maybe Yahweh saw something no one else could see in me then," I replied quietly.

"I believe he did. He kept this power bequeathing to the last minute without making a definitive decision, so it wouldn't have been in anyone's thoughts or future visions. He's a master builder, so he most likely knew Alpha would be watching for this decision." She poured herself some more tea and offered me more. I obliged, and she poured more into my cup as well. "I also believe it was what you and Azrael discussed privately. You being crowned by Maveth when you're ready, and she's ready to release into the energy of the universe. That's a bigger responsibility than any other God has been given. My understanding is you were already supposed to have taken over for her, but Alpha thwarted that." She set her cup down and sighed. "I haven't seen what the new future holds, as it is still being written. So you did change something, and that changes things with mine and Alpha's covenant."

"Which is?" I prodded for more information.

"That if the real future changed from being already written to being currently written, then I would no longer be his slave," she spat. "My warlocks won't have to choose to align with a monster like him. It nullifies our agreement. So I am biding my time until the future becomes apparent again."

"And what happens if the new future you see is that we win?" I asked, curiously. "Does that nullify the covenant as well?"

She nodded. "He's so ego-driven and self-absorbent, narcissist even, that he doesn't see a future where he loses, so he didn't believe he had anything to lose striking up that deal with me. Now, I know what I did was wrong, but that covenant guaranteed a safe haven for my warlocks. That's my main concern, you know?"

"I understand," I acknowledged sympathetically. "I would do anything to protect my family, too."

She gently smiled. "You have grown a lot since your wandering in the wilderness."

"I agree," I laughed. "I feel like a different me. I feel… I feel like the noise and chatter that gnawed at me from the inside quieted, and I could finally breathe deeply. I trusted safety and love."

"Be careful trusting love, dear. It can torture you more than you ever dreamt possible at the hands of Alpha's whip," she warned, raising an eyebrow. "Nothing bleeds more than the wicked lies of love."

"Is there something you're not telling me?" I asked, leaning back in my seat and picking at my nails.

"Like Uriel told you, trust your instincts. If something feels off, wrong, or anything, look into it deeper." I stared into her eyes and knew she was telling me something important. "Yahweh gave you certain powers of discernment. You had already inherited these just by being born through Alpha and Omega's powers of creation. They were starting to bud. Yahweh made sure they began to blossom. Once they're fully blossomed, that's when you will be crowned as Maveth's heir."

"What all comes with that territory?" I had no idea what it meant to be death itself, let alone what all Maveth controlled in the universe.

"A lot. You have your original guardian powers that were gearing up to become death all those years ago. Alpha added his power, and thereby some of Yahweh's power, when he molded the bodies of your parents. Barbelo imparted her power to your parents, and you share that power as well. Alpha farms powers like these. He doesn't want you to use you for your power," she stated, worry crossing her face. "He wants to suck the power from your body to make his own kingdom with Adam. That would make Adam the heir of Death. It would throw everything into chaos since he isn't supposed to be the heir and is just a copy molded and the breath of life breathed into him."

"That doesn't exactly tell me what I look forward to with Yahweh's powers or Maveth's legacy," I chuckled. "But it does explain the seriousness of Adam. Luxina said Adam is on our side now, too. Is that why the vision has gone dark? Could it be that Adam did revolt against Alpha? Choose us?"

"I don't know," Starfire breathed, annoyed. "I want to find that out myself as well."

"As part of Alpha's olive branch, were you reporting on us to him?" It was the main question that needed to be exposed. We needed to know just how deep in shit we were around Starfire.

"I reported your ascension. That was all I was tasked with. Lilith, I am sure, reported some things as well as Adam when he was here," she replied curtly. "But Uriel and Asmodeus did most of the betrayal. They reported to Alpha every plan you made so he could be five steps ahead of everyone."

"Yeah, it always seems like he is five steps ahead on everything," I muttered, staring at my empty tea cup.

"Things are about to change," she urged, leaning forward and grabbing my hands in hers. "The playing field is about to be leveled, and Alpha isn't going to be five steps ahead much longer. You all are very close to exposing what secrets he has left up his sleeve. There will be visitors who come to you with intel. There will be expositions of more treachery. There is something huge on the horizon. I just can't see it. I can feel it, though. Pretty soon, you're going to feel exactly what I feel as well. That flower is nearly unfurled within you."

"Thank you for being honest with me," I spoke respectfully.

She smiled. "You don't like being lied to, and I don't like telling lies. No one ever asked me if I had any agreements with Alpha. I would have spoken the truth if questioned about it."

"Why did you come to me when I was locked up with Alpha?" I asked, shaking my head in confusion. "If you've had this agreement with him since my escape, why did you come to me and ask me to leave with you?"

She sighed. "Alpha told me you would never leave," she began, staring out the window. "I knew he was right. I had seen all of the possible future outcomes. My job was to let you know what you had to do. You had to become the Shining Ones in order for any of his plans to work. You never believed that you belonged here because of the fake memory slipped to Sophie about her affair with Lucifer. You hated yourself. You hated where you came from. Alpha needed to motivate you without telling you the truth. He needed you to squirm just a bit longer."

"What was he going to do to Luxina?" I asked, not daring to make eye contact with her this time.

"To rip Xavier from her and give him to Adam," she relented. "Try to manipulate her into loving Adam more than you. He wants his own kingdom with those who are loyal to him. He has your mother, even if she was conditioned into the way she is."

"Wouldn't that lessen Luxina's power by removing half of her soul?" I asked, scrunching my face. "I don't understand how that helps anyone."

"Xavier is his own person, even if he was meant to be part of Luxina," she explained. "Xavier's powers are not her powers. Her power fractured when he was born, and it mended itself over time. She doesn't need his power even though it belonged to her originally. The wound healed over, so there wasn't a fusion of power on that level. It's why she can still talk to him as if he exists."

"Then how can he fuse Xavier into Adam?" I asked, still not understanding it all.

"Adam was made uniquely." She paused. "He's a vessel for Xavier. He was made using your blood and fed Guardian power through the power exchange between Incaendiel and all of his loyalists playing behind the scenes, but he doesn't have a soul. Xavier is his destined soul."

"Why would he give that opportunity up to help us?" I questioned, processing it all. "Why would he remain soulless to stop Alpha?"

"That is the question that needs answering, isn't it?" she answered, arching her eyebrow,

"Damian?" Luxina interrupted, poking her head through the doorway of Starfire's cottage. "Want to go for a walk so we can talk?"

I returned my attention to Starfire. She smiled. "Go. If you need to know anything else, I am an open book. I won't hide anything from you if you ask me."

"Thank you." She nodded, and I got up from my seat and walked over to Luxina.

"Where do you want to go?" I asked, staring down at her beautiful face. On some fundamental level, I was still mad at her about Uriel, but right in this moment, all of that melted away when she said my name. But even as I looked at her, I couldn't help but feel some sort of way about her presence.

She smiled up at me. "Let's go to the place on the lake you found." I nodded, and she took my hand to lead me out the door.

We walked quietly through the woods. Leaves crunched under our feet and twigs snapped, offering some form of sound from our presence. She stared off into the trees as we walked, not glancing once my way. She irritated me on a level I wasn't used to from her. Before, it was easy and natural to be in her presence. Now, it felt forced and like an obligation. I didn't like the way it felt. It felt strange, aberrant. It wasn't because of what happened in the Lust Terrace to her. It wasn't jealousy over Adam or anything like that. I owned that as my fault, my mistake, my guilt. At times, it just felt like she was standing here with me, but it really wasn't her. The spark between us had fallen flat. Before, when I kissed her, it was like kissing shooting stars and wildfires burning out of control. Now, it's like those feelings are reserved, either on her part or mine. I didn't understand it.

"You were right to be angry with me," she stated, breaking the awkward silence that had fallen between us since disembarking Starfire's cottage. "You were right about a lot of things."

"Like what?" I asked, shoving my hands into my pockets.

"Everything that's happened since I have been back," she replied, looking down at the ground as we walked. "I let my anger get the best of me. Jealousy. Everything else in between," she explained quietly. "There's a rage within me, and I don't know why it's there. I just want to hurt everyone without a single care in the world about it. I wanted to hurt Asmodeus for hurting you. I killed Elisha because she had manipulated you, alongside Asmodeus, into sleeping with her while she was a traitor. I was enraged that Uriel would speak to you the way she did. Furious that she was the one who locked me away in Purgatory for Alpha to…" She fell quiet, a tear sliding down her cheek. "There is something wrong with me!" she cried angrily.

I stopped walking and pulled her into my chest, wrapping her in my arms. "You just need time," I whispered, as she cried. Maybe everyone was right about her, and it was the trauma from Purgatory making her act this way.

"I don't know who I am anymore," she croaked, squeezing her arms around me tighter. "I don't know what I feel. I don't know anything." She peered up at me with her red-rimmed eyes, and I couldn't help but fall into them as I had so many times before. I was letting my guard down around her for her this time. She needed softness from me. She needed to heal from whatever she had gone through.

"We can do this together," I offered, running my thumb down her face and brushing her hair out of her eyes.

She nodded and quickly wiped her tears away while walking away. I matched her stride and grabbed her hand in mine. I understood it now. She felt different because she was holding up a mask for everyone. She was repressing everything to protect herself. I let my paranoia get in the way of everything instead of reaching out to help heal her. Everyone else was right. She needed to heal to move forward. She needed safety and trust. Was I still that safety net, though? Did she blame me for everything that happened to her? Was there resentment toward me for her walking into Alpha's trap? Hopefully, in due time, I would be able to ask her these things, and she would tell me the truth and not run from the answers.

The lake was mesmerizing as we walked down the bank. The water lapped gently at the shore, pushing and pulling the sand. I sat down on the sand and she sat down between my legs, leaning back against me. We listened to the sounds of nature as she pulled my arms around her. She lay her head against my bicep and snuggled in deeper.

"Is this where you found yourself?" she asked quietly.

"No," I replied, kissing the side of her head. "This was where I lost myself. I loosened my grip on everything I couldn't control. I offered it up to never look back." I chuckled.

"What's so funny?" she asked with a smile.

"I was making plans in my head of building a cabin out in these woods, far away and hidden so no one could find me," I explained, staring out at the water.

"Why alone?" she mumbled, scrunching her face while running her thumb over the top of my hand.

"Because everything and everyone was a mess as a whole," I murmured. "I couldn't take the noise inside anymore. I didn't want to be the answer for anything. I was done with it all. Done with Alpha. Done with being a Guardian. Done with the stress and pressure pushing down on me all the time. I was spinning out of control, letting my emotions get the better of me. Fear. Anxiety. Loneliness. No one understood me. Nearly everyone here feared me. I was still seen as a monster, and that would be my identity forever."

"You're not a monster," she cooed, twisting in my arms to look up at me. "I didn't mean that earlier. I am sorry. I was just angry and—"

"We all are monsters," I replied, interrupting her and gazing down into her eyes. "We all hold the power to do great things and to do evil things. It's the choice of who you are in your core that sets you apart from the evil monsters. And I choose to be the best person I can be. I have to be for what's coming next."

"What's coming next?" she asked, shaking her head in confusion.

"It was always my destiny to take over Maveth's place as Death. You can't be out of control when you own that role. You have to be calm and collected. You have to be able to sit in the stillness. You have to be able to choose not to play god when you absolutely can."

She pulled my face down to hers and kissed me, twisting her body completely around in my lap to straddle me. I invited the kiss and ran my hand up her back, one roaming through her hair, the other pulling her closer into me. She began unbuttoning my pants when I stopped.

"I don't want a repeat of last time," I stated, holding her face and searching her eyes.

"I choose you, Damian," she replied, kissing my forehead. "I will always choose you."

She leaned in again, her mouth on mine, but it still didn't feel right.

"If I had the choice, I would give up Xavier to Adam. Surrender myself just like you," she breathed, kissing my neck.

I pulled her away. "Don't say that! Xavier wasn't a tool. He was a sacrifice. You're making what he gave up seem pointless by giving him away," I snapped.

"I would give up everything to be with you," she cooed in my ear. "We could run away. Not have to deal with the responsibility we've been dealt."

"Giving up Xavier is not holding on to a responsibility!" I shouted.

"I'm trying to surrender myself here the same way you did!" she sneered, narrowing her eyes at me.

"Planning a surrender into stillness is not the same thing as surrendering yourself," I muttered, pushing her off my lap and buttoning my pants. "This is just a power grab, isn't it. You're still mad Yahweh hasn't given you your powers."

"It's not fair!" she shouted, balling up her fists. "After all I have been through, I should be just as worthy as you!"

"He didn't show up because I thought I was worthy of having his powers!" I argued. "He showed up because I didn't want them anymore! I didn't want anything!"

"And that makes you a coward!" she seethed. "I keep choosing you when I am pulled to Adam, and this is why. You're not someone who can protect me anymore. You've gone soft! " It was like a knife to the heart hearing that. "You're not Damian anymore!" She stood up and began walking away.

"Stop running away!" I seethed, pleading with her to talk it out. "Stay with me!"

She turned around and narrowed her eyes at me. "No." She continued on her way and disappeared into the trees. I picked up a rock and chucked it across the lake. I didn't even see it land in the water because I threw it so far. She promised she would always stay with me. She begged me to stay with her. And now it's all about Adam. She doesn't love me anymore. She chose him, and if I love her, I will stand by the decision.

"But it's Adam!" I sneered out loud. "He's not good. I know he's not good, which means he doesn't deserve her!"

This wasn't jealousy. This was revelation. Luxina was too good for me and too good for Adam. He was literally soulless. Without a soul, he can be bent and twisted in so many different ways because there was no moral compass to point him in the right direction. She needed more than either of us could offer her. Was this it, though? Was this the end of us? Did I fail her that much? I should have put everything else on hold and saved her instead of letting everyone else dictate what we did. But I fell in line and waited too long. She had to save herself. She had to manipulate her way out of Purgatory. She was rescued by the enemy, who let her go free. He showed her lies through salvation. It was my fault she had been twisted into this new version of herself. It wasn't Purgatory. It was my inability to save her when she needed me the most. This was the cost of my lack of inaction. I lost her, and I won't ever be able to get her back now.

"She frustrates me, too," a familiar voice cut through the silence.

I breathed in deeply, exhaled, and cracked my neck. "Hello, Adam," I grunted, gritting my teeth, then breathing in deeply again. I turned around to face him. He was a scrawny string bean. I could easily take him if I wanted to.

"My, Damian. You hit a growth spurt," he smirked, walking around with his hands shoved in his pockets.

"You could say that," I replied, watching him as he ambled around me in a circle.

"Did we grow… everywhere?" he mused, looking me up and down.

"Adam… I didn't know you swing that way," I chided. "I'd show it to you, but you're not exactly my type."

"No," he laughed, smiling at me deviously. "You do have a specific type, don't you. Petite, vulnerable. Angelic. Am I close? I mean, maybe that's why you and Luxina aren't working out. She's no longer an angel. Can't handle the power?"

I clenched my jaw. "Luxina can make her own decisions. I'm not going to force her into making a choice. Get her alone and take advantage of her while she's all worked up, knowing she wants something else."

"Oh, but she did want it," he cooed. "Over and over and over. I had to pry her off of me just so I could get back to work."

A rage built within me, and I breathed through it, glaring at him. I would love nothing more than to strike him down dead right now. He used her. He abused her. He forced her into doing things. He coerced her into false feelings. He made her fall for him under duress. He was worse than the scum that floated on the top of the water behind him. Once the rose colored glasses faded, she would see everything he did to her. She would realize she didn't love him and never did, that it was survivor's emotion.

He stepped closer to me. "You want to hit me, don't you?" he poked, waiting for me to make a move.

"I would love nothing more than to rip your head off and shove it up your own ass, but there are more pressing matters at hand," I sneered, glaring at him.

I started to head back to the village.

"Where are you going?" he shouted after me.

"Follow me. According to Luxina, you're supposed to be here to share some news about Alpha. Let's get to it."

We walked in silence with Adam trailing behind me. My nerve endings were set on red alert around him. I knew deep down that he was not to be trusted at all. Convincing everyone else that he was not to be trusted would be the real test because they would just assume I am jealous. Luxina in their ears telling them how he helped her escape Alpha because she's been tricked into his lovesick puppy. Him offering whatever nonsense plans Alpha has. They would believe it all over my gut instinct that was screaming that he is evil incarnate and will destroy us all.

We emerged from the woods, and I led him to Starfire's Cottage. I nudged Reikal as we passed by him on the porch. He shook his head and bounded off. He knew whenever new visitors came, he was to round up everyone to meet them here.

"Have that one trained, do ya?" Adam asked with a snort. "Put 'em to work. It's good."

"He's not *trained,*" I replied heatedly. "This is his home. He knows when to go get people when visitors show up."

"Tomato, tomahto," Adam shot back.

I closed my eyes and balled my fists, cracking my knuckles while squeezing them tightly and then releasing my grip. It was going to be a long day with him around. Every single minute I was around him, I wanted to choke the life from him and watch his eyes turn cold as I did. But I knew I couldn't do that. That was the old Damian. I am not my emotions. *I am not my emotions! That should be my mantra.* I pointed over to the sofa when we walked through the door. "Sit," I ordered.

"Yes, sir," he replied, clicking his heels together and saluting me. "Right away, sir." He walked over to the couch and sat down. His sarcasm was beginning to really grate on my nerves.

"Tea?" Starfire asked, walking from the kitchen and out into the den. "It's chamomile." She set the tray down and handed me a cup.

"It's like you read my mind," I teased with a smile. "Thank you."

I remained standing, sipping the hot liquid as it worked its magic on the mounting stress building between my shoulder blades. Starfire knew just how to make my tea the way I liked it, without me asking. Starfire sat on the sofa across from Adam and just watched him. She poured him a cup of tea, never taking her eyes off of him, and handed it to him. "Cream and sugar, there," she spoke, pointing at the china containers that held each.

"Thank you, Starfire," Adam grinned. He took three sugar cubes and plopped them in his cup, then poured some cream in after, stirring with his teaspoon. "I bet this will taste just as divine as it smells."

"You can't go wrong making tea," she quipped, emotionless. "If your tea turns out horrible, then it's the person making it, not knowing what they're doing. Everyone likes to blame the tea instead."

Adam took a sip of his cup and smiled warmly at her.

"However," she continued, "sometimes there's spoiled herbs in the mix that ruin the whole batch of tea, and it needs to be tossed out because it's not drinkable."

His smile faded. "Well, this tea is absolutely delectable. No need in tossing it out. Perfection came with this cup."

"There's no such thing as a perfect cup of tea," she replied, pursing her lips. "Everyone has their own preference, and it's a subjective phrase. Damian likes his plain with just a touch of honey. You took yours with cream and sugar. If it were perfect, there wouldn't have been any need to add extra ingredients to it to acquire perfection."

"Sometimes those extra ingredients are just fillers for others to be able to taste the perfection without being blinded by their own judgment of how it should taste compared to what it actually tastes like. If you know something tastes horrible because you've tasted the bitter bite of an herb leaf, then you expect each cup to follow, no matter the herb, to taste the same. So you compensate by making sure it won't taste that way even when you try new flavors." He set his cup down on the table. "Like, for instance, say you were to try a cup of tea that indeed had spoiled leaves in it. It would make you not want to try it again, even though fresh new leaves were brewed, because you still have the memory of what the spoiled batch tasted like. This new batch, however, has a refreshing aura to it. With some sugar and cream, it then becomes the perfect concoction to be enjoyed."

"Enjoyed by the person who prefers the cream and sugar," she countered. "Not everyone likes cream or sugar. So you're still just making a cup of tea to your liking. No one else's."

Her face was stone cold and hard, and I glanced between the two as they stared down one another quietly.

"Why are we talking about tea?" Adam asked, picking his cup back up and drinking the rest of it down before clattering the cup back to its plate. He wiped the excess that had escaped through his lips from his chin with the sleeve of his shirt as a drop hit his chest. He glanced down at it and rubbed it in.

"Because tea has a way of spilling," she replied sweetly.

Adam slowly slumped over to the right on his side, completely passed out.

I hurriedly set my cup of tea down on the table and rushed over to Adam. "What did you do?!" I squeaked in panic. I quickly checked his pulse to see if he was still alive. There was a heartbeat, good.

"Don't worry," she reassured me. "He will be awake in just a few minutes and none the wiser of what happened. I slipped him some truth herbs in that tea."

"So all of that tea talk was metaphor!" I whispered harshly.

"He's going to be spilling the tea soon," she smirked.

"Get the tea out before anyone else comes in here and drinks it," I said, rubbing my forehead and pinching the bridge of my nose.

"You will thank me later for this," she said, picking the tray up and carrying it to the kitchen. She returned with another tray of tea, cream, and sugar, along with the cup Adam had been using, so he wouldn't know we switched them out. "No one will believe you're just acting jealous this way. He will let himself slip and falter."

I stared at her with humbling eyes. "Thank you." A thought crossed my mind, and I chuckled it off.

"What?" she asked, putting her hands on her hips.

"I was thinking we could use that tea on Luxina," I explained with a smile, then became serious. "That would be wrong and an invasion of privacy for her, though. So it's not a good idea."

She looked up at me with proud eyes. "You have come such a long way from the boy who showed up here beaten and broken, wanting to burn the world to the ground to destroy your demons." I smiled back at her. "I also know you would still burn this world to the ground to protect the people you love, no matter the stillness that the role of Death places at your feet."

"I indeed would."

"Don't ever lose that," she said with a wink. She walked over and sat Adam up on the couch, just leaving him leaning back against the cushions. She returned to her seat on the couch at just the right moment when Adam sat upright on the sofa.

"What happened?" he asked, alarmed.

"What do you mean?" Starfire asked, a look of confusion perfectly implemented.

"I… never mind," he said, shaking his head. "I thought I passed out or something."

"Oh," I offered quickly. "That's the chamomile. It can hit you when you least expect it if you're not used to it. Happened to me too the first time I tried it. Out for a few seconds and back up. Scared me a bit. We didn't even notice you had closed your eyes; it was that brief."

"Hmm," he replied with a shrug. "Good stuff. Can I have some more?"

She smiled sweetly at him and poured him another steaming cup, then added his three cubes of sugar and a splash of cream. He took a sip and smiled.

"You have no idea how good this stuff is," he mused. "Alpha doesn't allow me to have anything sweet or tasty. He says it spoils you." He stopped talking and narrowed his eyes. "Don't know why I said that."

"When we find comfort in tea, we can't help but share how wonderful it is," Starfire beamed.

He smiled, unaware that he was falling into a trap no one thought to set except for Starfire.

CHAPTER SEVENTEEN: DAMIAN

EVERYONE JOINED STARFIRE and me in the den, quietly standing around waiting for Adam to speak. It was grueling and tedious watching him drink his tea and eat crumpets as opposed to talking like he was supposed to.

"I apologize," he garbled through a mouthful of food, chewing then swallowing. "I am stuffing my face with treats and ignoring you all when I am the guest."

"A growing boy needs to eat," I muttered as I leaned against a wall. "Besides, you said yourself Alpha never lets you indulge in the sweeter things in life. By all means," I raised my hand and pointed to the food on the table, thoroughly disgusted with the food falling from his mouth, "eat."

"Why doesn't Alpha allow you to eat treats?" Dad asked, scrunching his face. "We all were allowed to indulge occasionally growing up."

"And look at you now," Adam grunted, his cheeks puffed up like a squirrel's cheeks stuffed with food as he chewed and swallowed. "You rebelled against him."

Dad leaned down, stared him in the eyes, and asked, "Do the pastries make you want to rebel now, Adam?"

Adam laughed. "No," he said before his smile slipped away. He cleared his throat and took a drink of his tea.

"It didn't make us want to rebel, either," Dad replied smugly. "In fact, the sweets were what kept us in line. We did well, and he rewarded us. We did badly, and guess what? No treat. Does he reward you? Or do you just get punished?"

For a moment, I really thought he was going to spill everything and begin crying. The emotional exchange that took place across his face was more telling than words. He was only punished and never rewarded. Like me.

"Oh, you don't have to answer that," I remarked, walking over and tussling his coiffed hair. "We know Alpha adores you to death. Treats aren't a sign of affection, am I right?" I chuckled with a wink.

"Right," Adam spoke more assured of himself. "I am hardly ever punished, too." He grinned at me, taunting me.

"You know, I can say the same for me," I replied, appearing to think and tap my finger at my chin. "It wasn't until missions started going sideways and not the way he imagined they would that he began taking it out on me."

Adam's smile twitched and slowly was displaced by a flicker of panic. He cleared his throat and looked around the room, frowning. "Where's Luxina?"

"Not sure," I replied, pulling out the table chair and sitting down. "Reikal couldn't find her. Besides, she doesn't need to be here anyway. She is working through her trauma of Purgatory before we allow her in rooms with other people."

"Oh, she wouldn't hurt me," he beamed with a smile. "She would never hurt the person who freed her from her confines. I guess I am her knight in shining armor."

"I didn't mention anything about her hurting people," I mumbled, looking surprised. "How did you know she was hurting people, Adam?"

"Just a guess," he squeaked, and gulped down another drink of tea. "You mentioned trauma, and I associate that with lashing out at people, fighting them all the time, killing them in a fit of rage. You know what I mean," he finished, motioning his hand at me.

"If you're asking if I walked around killing people when I first escaped Alpha, the answer is no. I wasn't a mindless killing machine."

The room fell silent as Adam awkwardly sat there, processing how he was speaking out of character. "Why are you here, Adam?" Dad asked, sitting down across from him and breaking his focus.

"Universal domination," he replied quickly before panic filled his face. "Er, your universal domination," he corrected, furrowing his brows.

I tried not to smile, but I knew the truth serum was working its way through him, and he had no idea why he kept blurting things out. I needed to take control of the questions again before he spooked and just up and left.

"We know one of his power grabs is going to be taking the souls from hell and Purgatory to power up," I began, crossing the room and sitting down beside Dad. "Right?" I asked to make sure he knew he needed to answer that.

"Yes," he said slowly, trying to think before speaking.

"We also know there are spies here among us that report back to Alpha. Right?" I asked again for him to answer.

"Yes," he replied with a slow nod of the head.

"He was planning to rip Xavier from Luxina to put in you. Right?" I asked, baiting him carefully.

A slow nod. "Yes."

"Did he succeed?" I asked, arching an eyebrow.

"No," he stammered quickly. Good, so for now, Xavier is safe.

"Why not?" I prodded.

"He couldn't find him inside her psyche. The little shit hid well," he spat before correcting his tone. "Luxina told him to hide well."

"And your power is sustained by the covenant made between Dad and the loyalists hiding here. Right?" I pushed.

"Dad?" he answered, scrunching his face. "Oh, you mean him," he said, pointing over at Incaendiel. "Since when did you start calling him Dad?" Adam asked, popping a crumpet in his mouth.

"Recently," I replied, and abruptly took back over questioning. "Your power..."

"Yes, my power is sustained by the covenant," he snapped, his face full of contempt.

"So if that covenant is broken, does the power just disappear?" I asked casually, staring straight into his eyes.

"Yes," he grumbled. "If the covenant is broken, I am powerless without the addition of Xavier."

"So you would be useless to Alpha. Expendable. Right?" I smirked. I had him right where I wanted him, silently squirming.

"Alpha loves me," Adam muttered, clenching his jaw. "I'm not disposable like you were."

"Apparently, I am not disposable," I chirped, raising a hand in the air. "Apparently, he still needs me alive. Why is that?" I asked curiously.

"Alpha can't kill death," he sneered, glowering at me. "Death lives outside of his power and reach. He knows Maveth chose you as her heir." He leaned in closer to me. "And he has a present for you when you are finally crowned."

"Dungeons. Torture. Oh no!" I feigned fear.

Adam smirked. "If you only knew how deep Alpha has his claws in you right now, you wouldn't be poking fun."

"Why don't you tell me how deep his claws are in me?" I asked, narrowing my eyes at him. "What does he have up his sleeve that would completely decimate me or destroy me?"

"When you get your invitation to the wedding, you will know," Adam mumbled with a devious smile. "Tell me, where is my lovely red-headed vixen at? She should be sitting beside me and telling you all about our wedding plans."

"What wedding plans?!" I demanded, pounding my fist into the table and jumping to my feet. The truth serum must be wearing off.

"Oh, you poor thing," Adam said, feigning compassion. "She hasn't told you? I bet she strung you along this whole time, didn't she? Made love to you? Told her she wasn't sure who to choose?" His smile widened into a sinister leer. "She's already chosen me."

"What's your real reason for being here?!" I demanded. Dad grabbed me before I could jump across the table.

"To tell you that Alpha will be moving soon, so be prepared. I heard the abyss is quite nice this time of year. Too bad I will be the one locking you up in there instead of Uriel," Adam jeered, tossing another sugary cake into his goofy mouth.

"Why?" Samael asked, interrupting the two of us. "Why do you still want to please Alpha, knowing you are only meant to be a weapon of division? You know Alpha, and Luxina said you were here to help us. So help us!"

"Unfortunately, it's too late to help you," Adam responded. "But," he began, pausing to stare at me. "You get rid of him so I don't have to deal with him at all, and I may just find a way to help you out. From the bottom of my heart."

"Get rid of him, how?" Azazel asked, confused. "He doesn't have to be in the room when you're here if that's what you mean."

"No," Adam replied, smiling in triumph. "He has to be totally gone. Tossed into the abyss. Moved off the world. Something. Or no deal."

"Are you fucking serious?" I asked, completely dumbfounded by his request.

"If they want me, and want me away from Alpha so he can't destroy the universe, then they have to say goodbye to you." He stood cold-faced, looking at me.

"Why so you can lie and manipulate them into believing you're the good guy to turn around and rip the rug from underneath their feet?" I spat, balling my fists. "They're *my* family. Not *yours*."

"Incaendiel is just as much my father as he is yours," he relented, motioning to Dad. "I mean I was made from the blood of his blood. And just like he accepted you as his own before even finding out you were really his son, I believe he would give me the same opportunity and chance to prove myself to him." He looked over at Dad. "Wouldn't you, Dad?" He looked around the room. "Come on. Everyone, tell the truth. You are afraid of Damian, but for some reason, you don't fear me the same way. Want to know why?" Everyone remained silent. "Because Damian is dangerous and always will be dangerous. He will always be one fuse away from ending everything in the cosmos. He holds the power to do so now. You should really be looking at him differently. He is, after all, becoming Death incarnate."

Everyone looked over at me, unsure of what to say. Even Dad remained silent, shifting his eyes away from me. My heart momentarily skipped a beat as anxiety gripped my chest. I composed myself and relented to Adam, "Fine. Do what you have to do. If you need me gone to feel safe and gain Adam's help, I will go. This won't be my lesson to learn. It would be all of yours. I know what's coming is inevitable. There's no way to stop Alpha from ensuing a final battle for power. You just have to realize which side of the battle you're truly standing before it happens, or else," I looked over at Starfire sitting quietly in the back of the room. "Everything will turn to darkness."

"Then it's settled," Adam sneered, victorious at my voluntary isolation.

"No," Dad spoke, breaking the silence. "We aren't making Damian go anywhere. If you want to help us, then help us. Don't come with conditions, especially ones where you are trying to slip in a backdoor to fill in the boots of a child of mine. If you want to be treated like my son, then earn it."

"What did he do to earn that spot before you ever found out he was your son?" Adam grumbled, glaring at Dad.

"He did nothing," Dad replied, staring softly into my eyes. "He was just a kid being hurt by a tyrant and needed to be saved, wanted to be saved, and was willing to die for everyone else to be saved instead."

Adam snorted. "A martyr? Please," he huffed.

"Not a martyr," Dad continued, staring at me and making sure I heard him. "Just someone who would go to any lengths to protect the ones he loved the most."

"And I did the same!" Adam shouted. "Just as Alpha made him take Luxina, he did it with me. And then I saved Luxina just like Damian. Why can't you see me for me? Why can't you see my actions as the same worth as his?" he demanded, fury dripping with each word spoken.

"Because he didn't stand there and dangle his good deeds in everyone's face to prove he was good," Dad countered, glaring at Adam. "He thought of himself as a monster, not a savior. That's the difference between the two of you."

Adam walked up to him and stood inches from his face, breathing angrily and glowering at Dad. "I'm glad Alpha is raising me, and not you," he spat, walked out of the room, and vanished.

"He's gone," Starfire declared from her table.

"What was *that*?!" Azazel murmured loudly, looking around at everyone, bewildered.

"That was Alpha desperate and hoping we would fall for a scheme," I huffed, shaking my head, then sitting down on the couch where Adam had been sitting.

"At first it seemed like jealousy between the two of you," Raphael said, thumping his chin with his pointer finger.

"Not jealousy," I demanded, pointing a finger at him. "I worked him with those questions into telling you his truth."

"That you did," Samael agreed, nodding along. "He even tried to pull the father card on Incaendiel. Which, I mean, *technically,* he is his father. But, you know."

"The moment he suggested we isolate Damian away from us, I knew he was full of shit," Dad spat, flopping back down in his seat from earlier. "That was more than rivalry through jealousy. That was tactic."

"We also learned something more important," Michael added, shifting against the wall he was leaning against. "If we destroy any covenant you made with Alpha's loyalists, it strips Adam of the stolen guardian power. He won't be able to use Damian's powers full throttle anymore."

"If only we could have gotten out of him just exactly who here was left as loyalists," Azazel mumbled.

I sat quietly while they spoke with one another, watching them tear apart Adam's confessions. I looked over at Starfire, who winked at me and left the room.

"Thank you," I said, interrupting them all, glancing from each of their faces to the next.

"What for?" Samael asked, confused.

"For believing in me. For not going along with the plan to kick me out." I stopped and cleared my throat. "For a moment, I—"

"You're family," Samael interrupted before I could finish. "It would take a whole lot more than someone offering to be on our side against Alpha to kick you out of the family."

"I haven't been the most level-headed person here," I continued, ashamed. "I know I always let my emotions get the better of me, but I am trying not to be that person anymore."

"And we acknowledge and see that," Azazel murmured with a smile. "You did some growing up. You put in the work. The least we can do is trust you that you will make good decisions moving forward. I mean, old Damian, Adam would have been missing an eye leaving here or worse." She laughed, and everyone joined in. "You are in control now. Everyone has a temper flare. Everyone wants to beat the snot out of someone being rude to them. But you showed restraint. We are proud of you for that."

"Speaking of Adam and going back to what he was telling us, what did he mean by you being Death incarnate?" Dad asked curiously.

"I don't know much myself. Azrael pulled me aside and was telling me Maveth had chosen me as her heir, but didn't get to elaborate because

Luxina interrupted us," I explained. "Once I get the full rundown on that, I will tell you all about it."

"Oooooh, Daddy Death?" Azazel teased, pinching my cheek, and they flushed with heat.

"Azazel," Samael reprimanded jokingly, "you're making him blush."

"Alright, alright," I said, playfully tapping her hand on my cheek. "I don't know when the crowning is going to be, but I do know it's long overdue."

"Oh, how was your talk with Starfire earlier?" Michael prodded, looking around the room to see if she was nearby.

"Long story short, I don't think she's a problem to worry about," I replied, thinking back on that conversation with her. "She has her own way out of that situation. She isn't a threat to us."

"What situation?" Luxina asked, bounding through the front door. "Why didn't anyone tell me there was a meeting?"

"Because we agreed that when we interrogate people, you won't be here to escalate anything," Dad answered, standing up.

"Who were you interrogating?" she asked, scrunching her face.

"Adam," Raphael answered. "He's gone now, though."

Luxina's smiling face disappeared and was instantly replaced with rage. "You all should have told me he was here!" she seethed, glaring at us.

Her gaze stopped at me, and she narrowed her eyes. "You're the reason no one told me. You didn't want me to see him. You didn't want us to spend any time together because you think I chose him over you because of *trauma*!"

"I was the one who gave the order for you not to be included," Dad argued, crossing his arms.

"What did he tell you?" she demanded, walking over to him and shouting. "Why wouldn't I be allowed to see Adam if Damian hadn't given you some reason to disallow me to be here?!"

"Your temper is why," Dad shot back. "You have no control over yourself at all!"

"I am *not* going to hurt Adam," she sneered, pursing her lips.

"At this point, we aren't worried about you hurting him," Dad said, annunciating his words. "We were more worried about you hurting someone else here."

"Seriously!" she shrieked. "You think I am a concern for the safety of people here in this room? That sounds like bullshit! You just didn't want me seeing Adam!"

"Luxina, just sit down," I cooed and patted the seat next to me. "I will tell you everything about what happened. Drink some tea and calm yourself."

"No," she balked, flaring her nostril at me.

"It's ok," I mumbled gently. "He will most likely be coming back. We don't know if he left to cool his head or just left. If he loves you, he will be back to see you like promised."

"We're, uh, we will be around if you need us," Dad said, furrowing his brows and motioning for everyone to follow him.

I nodded, and they all left the room while Luxina stood in the middle of it, ready to break down and cry.

"Come here," I ordered softly.

She turned around to look at me and relented, walking over and sitting down next to me on the couch.

"He didn't come to see you before he left?" I asked, pouring her a cup of tea. I added some cream and squeezed a dab of honey into it for her and handed it to her. She shook her head no as she took a drink.

"I don't understand," she whimpered. "He came through on part of his promise. He showed up."

"What was the other part of his promise?" I asked, as I brushed her hair out of her face. I tenderly turned her face to mine.

"He was going to stay with me," she cried. "He wasn't going back to Alpha."

I took her cup of tea from her and set it down on the table, then drew her into my chest while stroking her hair.

"He was angry when he left," I offered, gently rocking her. "He will probably be back for you like he promised."

"You said something to him, didn't you!" she accused, putting her hands over her eyes.

"No," I answered softly. "I didn't say anything to him. If anyone threw around hurtful things, it was him. Like a wedding invitation." My heart felt like it was going to implode just mentioning the words again.

"He said that?" she breathed, peering up into my eyes. "I'm soooo sorry, Damian. I just didn't know how to tell you. I wanted to make sure I was making the right choice by choosing him. So, I was looking to see if there was anything left for us together."

The knife in my chest twisted, and I felt my heart shatter into a million tiny pieces. He wasn't lying. She had chosen him. I swallowed the lump forming and cleared my throat.

"If he is who you want, I won't stand in your way. I'm sorry I failed you. I'm sorry for destroying us," I whispered, a tear sliding down my face.

"You're right," she replied stoically. "You did fail me. You did destroy us." Her face contorted as she continued. "You didn't save me. You left me there to rot while playing hero for everyone else. So, yeah, this is your fault."

My intuition screamed at me. *This isn't like her at all. This is wrong. This is danger wrapped in a pretty little bow that's slowly been feeding from you this whole time.* "I'm sorry," I whispered.

Her eyes softened. "It's ok, Damian. I still have a lot to work through. I'm sorry for that. Will you hand me my tea, please? I don't know what Starfire puts in it, but it always makes me feel better."

I nodded and reached down to her cup. "You hungry?" I asked as I looked around the table to see what all was there that she could munch on.

"Yes," she replied, staring up at the ceiling. "I want something sweet."

I grinned when my eyes landed on them. Macaroons. I placed a few on her teacup plate and handed it to her. "Here you go," I said, smiling softly down at her. She smiled back and looked down at the plate.

"Ew," she said, setting the plate back down.

I frowned. "What's wrong?"

"I hate macaroons. They're disgusting," she answered.

My heart began to pound as I slipped a knife from my pocket. "You hate them?" I asked, needing more. Maybe it's something new…

"Yes! Dad gave me one before when I was little. They're horrid little cookies."

I placed the knife under her chin and raised her head to look me in my eyes. "Who are you?!" I demanded, staring knives into her soul.

"It's me, Damian," she whimpered. "It's Luxina."

"You're not Luxina," I sneered, growing closer to her face. "You got the macaroon story wrong."

An insidious smile spread across her face as her eyes flashed colors. "Who would have known macaroons would have been the bomb drop for you?"

I pressed the knife harder under her chin. "Who are you?!" I shrieked, anger shredding every fiber of control I had conquered.

"I'm not lying," she replied coolly. "I *am* Luxina."

A sensation crawled across my skin as my chest warmed. I finally felt what I had been avoiding this whole time.

"You have no soul," I breathed, staring into her eyes. "You're a copy. A clone. Like Alpha made of me for Adam to train against. He used her blood to make you."

Her perfect façade vanished, and I could see her for who she really was. "And it was sooo easy to make you believe I was the real her. So easy to sink my teeth and claws into you. You were so lost about me making it out of Purgatory that putting the pieces together was taking so much time. I thought I was caught when you were questioning Uriel. It's why I had to kill her before she ruined the plan completely."

The breath caught in my throat. Everything. I was right about every single instinct I had, but I couldn't quite put my finger on what was wrong with her. It wasn't that Purgatory changed her, and she was mirroring the terraces there. She was created by Alpha for a single purpose, and it was to drive me to the brink of despair. Place distrust in me from everyone else. They would only see a lovesick puppy beaten and wounded over the love of his life, choosing Adam. They wouldn't believe anything I noticed because she had experienced so much in Purgatory, and they thought she was still going through the survivor's trauma while I was going through the guilt of not saving her. He had planned it down to every single little detail to make her the perfect Lolita Luxina.

"I see you finally worked it all out in that pretty little head of yours." She smiled at me deviously, rose up to my ear, licked it, and whispered, "They're never going to believe you about this one." Her smile was displaced, and terror filled her eyes. A piercing scream ripped through the room as she played victim. "Daddy! Daddy! Help me!" I was confused for a moment. "Let me go, Damian! Daddy!"

"What are you doing, Damian?" Dad yelled as he ran into the room, looking at Luxina pinned down with the knife to her chin and then to me, holding it.

"She's not the real Luxina," I said through gritted teeth, my knife unwavering under her chin. "She's a clone."

"Daddy, he's crazy! He's jealous! He's mad I chose Adam over him!" she cried.

"Let her go, Damian!" Dad bellowed.

"I can't do that," I whispered, my eyes not moving from her face. "You have to believe me! She's lying!"

"What have I lied about?" she whimpered. "I told you Adam would come, and he did. I haven't lied about anything! You have to believe me, Daddy. It's me! Damian's lost his fucking mind!"

"You have to trust me!" I pleaded, my eyes searching his desperately.

Dad raised his hands gently. "Let her go, and we will all talk about this. Ok?" he asked. "She will sit right there and not go anywhere, and then you can explain how you came to this conclusion."

My hand that held the blade shook, and I pressed it a little harder before releasing my grip on her and dropping the blade.

"Step away from her," he urged, and I followed orders. "Now, explain."

"I've been telling you since she arrived that something wasn't right. Something was off with her. Her jealousy. Her wrath. All of it. Her constantly interrupting important conversations and meetings as if purposefully derailing them. She walked in while we were talking to Lucifer. She interrupted with Uriel and killed her. She killed Asmodeus while he was spilling information. She came by when I was talking to Starfire. She came in after Adam left. She's always there, and whenever she leaves, there's a meltdown that follows her path. You *have* to feel it too!"

"Anything else?" Dad asked while watching her face for signs that I was telling the truth.

"She's so… fucking cruel to me. And all she does is talk about Adam. Adam this. Adam that. Adam saved me. Adam will be here to join our side. But Adam proved that's not the plan at all. And a wedding? In what fucking scenario would Luxina stop to get married?"

"See, Daddy," she whimpered, quivering her bottom lip on cue. "He's jealous of Adam. If he can't have me, then no one can have me. He's fucking psycho! He made you all believe that he had his emotions under control, and look at him now. He is out of control! Can't you see it, Daddy?"

"What triggered your realization?" Dad asked, walking closer to me and holding his hand out for the knife.

I looked at his hand and my knife. If he took the knife, I couldn't stop her before she hurt everyone here. If I didn't give it to him, he would forcefully take it, and someone would get hurt wrestling it away. I sighed and handed him the knife, shaking as I dropped it in his hand. His back was facing Luxina while she mouthed, "told you," and gave me a smirk.

"How did you know it's not her?" he asked more calmly.

"The macaroons," I said, pointing over at the table. "She loves macaroons. When we arrived here and were starving after she had spent the whole year eating rabbit and squirrel or whatever Gwynevere could hunt, she stuffed her face full of them, telling us they were her guilty pleasure."

"I just don't like them now," she refuted, crossing her arms. "They stuffed me full of them while in Purgatory."

"That's not what she told me when she said they were disgusting!" I defended, balling my fists. "She said you gave her one when she was little, and she hated it."

"He's lying!" she yelled, jumping to her feet.

"When have I ever lied to you, Dad? When do I ever lie, period? I hate when people lie to me, and I would never lie to someone else," I asked, pleading with his eyes. "When… when would I have ever purposefully put her in danger unless I was forced?"

Her eyes widened. "He's still working for Alpha," she crowed. "That's what this is. He is still Alpha's little fucking monster!"

"I am not!" I seethed, glaring at her. I lunged for her, and Dad grabbed me and pulled me away.

"It all makes sense," she laughed. "Everything was always more important than finding me. I bet he never once demanded my rescue. It's why the rivalry between Adam and him is so palpable in the air. They're both trying to prove to Daddy Alpha who's the better son!"

Dad watched my face. "Well, one way we can tell who is lying and who isn't is to put it to a test."

"How?" I demanded. "How are you going to test her when everything she says is lies?!"

"Alpha can't clone angel wings," he said, staring deeply in my eyes. "They're a right of passage for our creation. So if she were a clone, she wouldn't have her wings. Show me your wings, Luxina."

"What's that—"

"Shut up, Damian!" she yelled at me, then smiled as sweetly as she could at Dad. "Well, then," she cheered happily. "Let's finally clear this up." Her wings sprouted from her back, brilliantly white and feathered. "See!" she sneered victoriously. "I have my wings."

Dad smiled at her, walked over, and hugged her. "Yes, sweetie. You still do have your angel wings." He leaned down to whisper in her ear, and his eyes flickered with cold rage. "But we aren't angels anymore."

I saw the red drip on the carpet before I realized what was happening. She stepped back away from Dad, and the knife was buried to the hilt in her chest. She reached for the handle and slowly pulled it out of her heart. "Daddy?" she asked, her eyes full of confusion. She dropped to the floor, her heart pumping out what little blood it had left in it across Starfire's beige carpet.

I stood there unable to speak as the body of the clone lay sprawled on the floor. "It wasn't Luxina," I murmured, my mind racing with panic.

"It wasn't Luxina!" I shouted, staring at dad wide eyed.

"No," he replied solemnly. "Your instincts were right all along."

"Luxina is still in Purgatory," I mumbled. "We have to go! Now!" I ordered.

Dad grabbed me by my shirt. "We have to make a plan. We can't just run into Purgatory. Plus, we don't know what Uriel did with the key."

"We could be there now, saving her if I had come to this realization sooner!" I spat. "She's still there because of me!"

"But you did come to the realization, and that's all that matters," a voice startled us. "You passed the last test, Damian." We turned around to see Maveth standing across the room.

"You knew?" I asked, walking toward her.

"Yes, and so did you," she cooed with a smile.

"You knew and didn't warn us?!" I asked heatedly, glaring at her.

"We needed to make sure you could honestly separate a soulless being apart from real beings," she explained, her face unwavering.

"We? So Azrael knew as well?" I stammered in disbelief. "You let her… eat at me from the inside out with her cruelty and said nothing?"

"Yes," she said softly. "And I am sorry for how much it hurt. You had to figure it out on your own," Maveth declared. "You were given so many signs and pieces to fit together. We knew you would figure it out without anyone's help."

I laughed. "So when Yahweh said she wasn't ready for her bequeathed powers, he knew she was fake."

She nodded. "I'm sorry you had to find out this way, but it was the only way, Damian. You had to step into the role of Death and not be forced into it."

"Screw the role of Death!" I yelled. "You let Alpha… he knew this… I was just learning to trust people. To instill in them a sense of safety."

"Did you choose the fake Luxina to be your anchor?" she asked, raising an eyebrow.

"Anchor? What's an anchor?" Dad asked, walking over to Maveth.

"He hasn't told you about his upgraded powers?" She looked at me, surprised.

"I was stuck in a pocket, and everyone was frozen. I needed an anchor so when I stepped outside of time, I would be able to step back into time," I explained quietly.

"Well, who did you choose for your anchor if not Luxina?" he asked, turning to face me.

"I chose my dad," I confessed, looking down at the ground, embarrassed. "The one person in the world who loved me without conditions and before he ever knew who I was inside." I looked up to meet his eyes. "You listen to me. You believe me. You trust me. I had to give all of that back to someone, and you were the only person who truly deserved that much investment of myself." I glanced back at the corpse of the fake Luxina.

"What do we do with her?" I asked, motioning with my head. "She didn't have a soul, so does she even really need a burial?"

"That's up to you," Maveth answered, walking up to me and gently taking my face in her hands. "I have waited so long to bestow this on you. And when we thought Alpha had completely destroyed you, I didn't know what to do. This role chooses the next in line, and it still pointed at you, even though we knew what Alpha had done to your universe." She kissed my forehead, and a tear slipped from her eye. "Caelvryn of Zul-Tama, you are hereby crowned… as Lord Death."

Particles began swirling around in the air as Maveth's body began to disintegrate, and she dispersed into the cosmos. Icy tendrils wrapped their way through my veins, and I could feel her power infuse with my own. It was like lightning reverberated through my chest, and I could feel the energy and power of every single living being here in Lightshade. I could hear their heartbeats and feel the blood that pumped through their veins. Death was more than just the quiet, final breaths floating into the sky. It was also about recognizing life and how fragile it was. And if I could feel everyone here, that meant I could feel anyone anywhere. I quietened my mind as I searched while billions of energies swirled through my head until I found the right one. The one I was desperate to see, feel, and know was okay, and I could feel every single electrical pulse that surged around like butterflies. I smiled in relief. *Thump, thump. Thump, thump.* Her heart fluttered…

EPILOGUE: LUXINA

MY SCREAMS COULD be heard from every terrace of Purgatory. I was strapped to a table, and Alpha was once again digging through my body, trying to find Xavier. The pain was unimaginable as he ran his hands through my untapped power, stoking a flame within me. I felt like I was cooking from the inside out as if an atomic bomb was about to detonate.

"Watch where you touch," Adam urged, as Alpha carelessly touched my true inner light.

"It's the only place he can be," Alpha hissed. "I have looked everywhere in here for him. This is the only place he could be hiding."

"Yeah, and that thing is a ticking time bomb!" Adam argued. "One wrong move and it will detonate, and we turn to ash!"

Alpha carefully slipped his finger into the ball of electrical power, and strikes of lightning and flames shot down all around him.

"Father!" Adam screeched, trying to pull his hand out of me.

Alpha pushed him to the side and kept digging around as the wind began to blow around in the room, lit up with flames of retribution. "Almost," he breathed, maneuvering his fingers.

I screamed, and my body arched as flames filled the room.

"Got him!" Alpha shouted as everything began to grow hazy. "Now, Adam. You will be complete."

Alpha's face was contorted in a vindictive, victorious sneer while Adam stood to the side, watching me as everything turned black and I sank into the darkness of what I prayed were the arms of death.

Kasey Hill is a critically acclaimed, versatile writer from Franklin County, Virginia, known for her work in several genres, including urban fantasy, horror, thriller, paranormal romance, and metaphysical/New Age topics. She has authored both fiction and non-fiction, with a particular interest in Wicca, specializing in Trinitarian Wicca as a historical archivist, and has an upcoming historical account of the shift from polytheism to monotheism in Abrahamic religions, for which she has published non-fiction works exploring the subject.

Her fiction often dives into the supernatural and the macabre, blending mythological elements with modern storytelling. She has published multiple novels, poetry collections, and short stories. Notable works include her *Guardians of Light* series in the mythology fantasy genre and her poetry, which has received recognition for its depth and emotional resonance. As she grows in the horror genre, she has a particular penchant for Southern Gothic storytelling, as seen in her Adult Horror novel *Devil's Claw* and her Young Adult horror series, *The Whispering Spirits,* featuring *The Haunting at Foxwood Village* and *Dark Coven.* She has several Horror short stories circulating for anthologies and Ezines featuring her unique style of worldbuilding.

In addition to her writing, Kasey Hill has also contributed to the Wiccan and occult community through her non-fiction work, making her a multi-faceted author with a broad range of interests and expertise.

www.ingramcontent.com/pod-product-compliance
Lightning Source LLC
LaVergne TN
LVHW041058080826
845145LV00007B/1615

* 9 7 8 1 9 5 2 8 8 0 3 8 4 *